THE SHADOW HERO

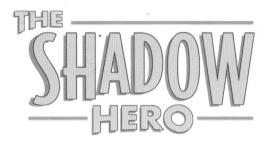

OTHER FIRST SECOND BOOKS BY GENE LUEN YANG

American Born Chinese
The Eternal Smile (with Derek Kirk Kim)
Prime Baby
Level Up (with Thien Pham)
Boxers & Saints

OTHER BOOKS BY SONNY LIEW

Malinky Robot
Wonderland (with Tommy Kovac)
My Faith in Frankie (with Mike Carey)
Sense and Sensibility (with Nancy Butler)
The Art of Charlie Chan Hock Chye

THE SHADOW HERO

Story by **Gene Luen Yang**

Art by **Sonny Liew**

Lettering by **Janice Chiang**

:01

First Second

NEW YORK

:01

Fïrst Second

Text copyright © 2014 by Gene Luen Yang
Art copyright © 2014 by Sonny Liew
Compilation copyright © by Gene Luen Yang and Sonny Liew

Published by First Second
First Second is an imprint of Roaring Brook Press, a division of Holtzbrinck
Publishing Holdings Limited Partnership
175 Fifth Avenue, New York, New York 10010
All rights reserved

Cataloging-in-Publication Data is on file at the Library of Congress.

ISBN 978-1-59643-697-8

First Second books are available for special promotions and premiums.
For details, contact: Director of Special Markets, Holtzbrinck Publishers.

FIRST EDITION

First edition 2014
Lettered by Janice Chiang
Book design by John Green

Printed in China

10 9 8 7 6 5 4 3 2 1

For my kids
—G.L.Y.

Thanks to Xueling, Clement, and Junjie for the coloring help;
and ninjagirl, for all the rest
—S.L.

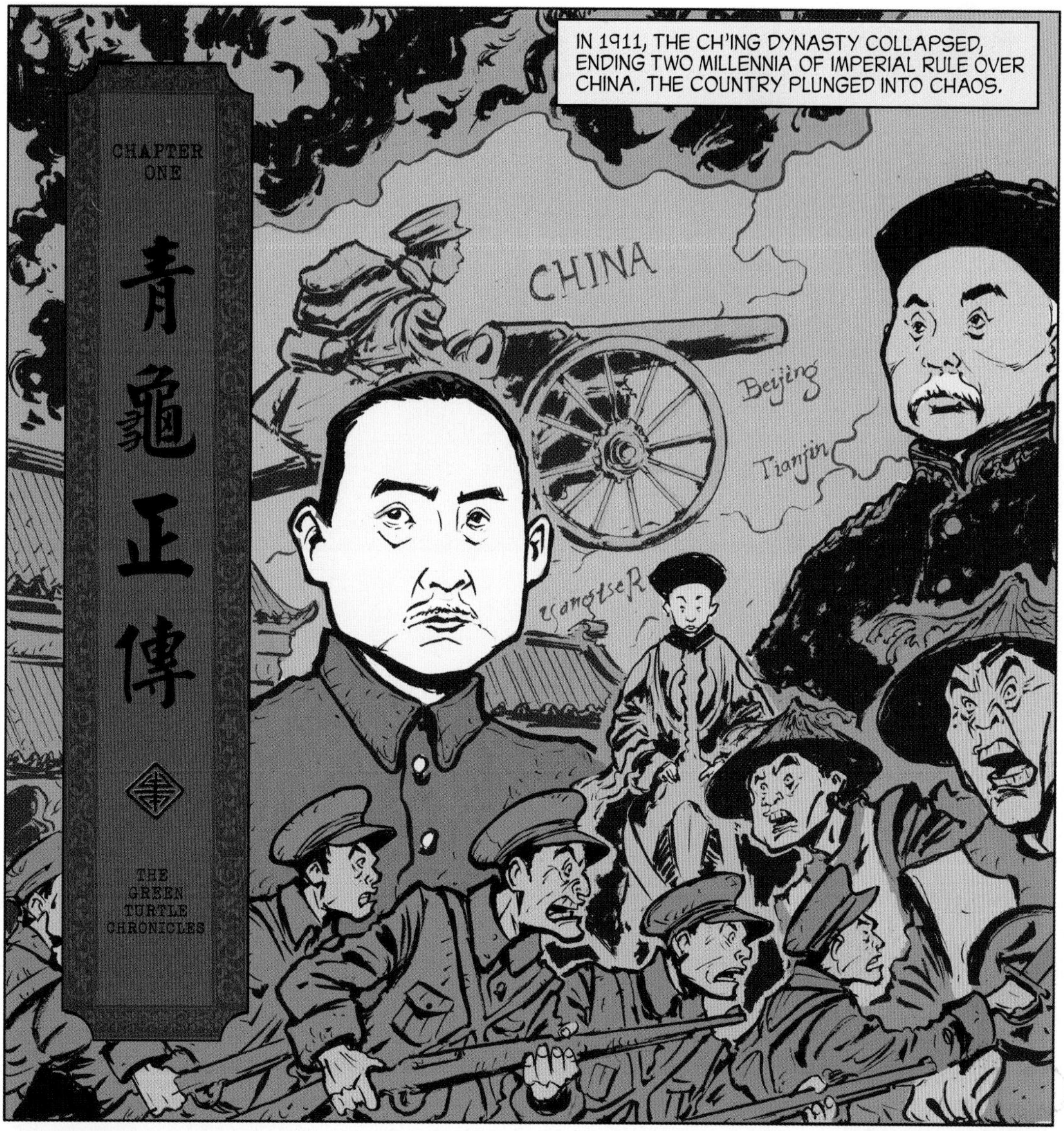
IN 1911, THE CH'ING DYNASTY COLLAPSED, ENDING TWO MILLENNIA OF IMPERIAL RULE OVER CHINA. THE COUNTRY PLUNGED INTO CHAOS.
CHAPTER ONE
青龜正傳
THE GREEN TURTLE CHRONICLES
CHINA
Beijing
Tianjin
Yangtse R.

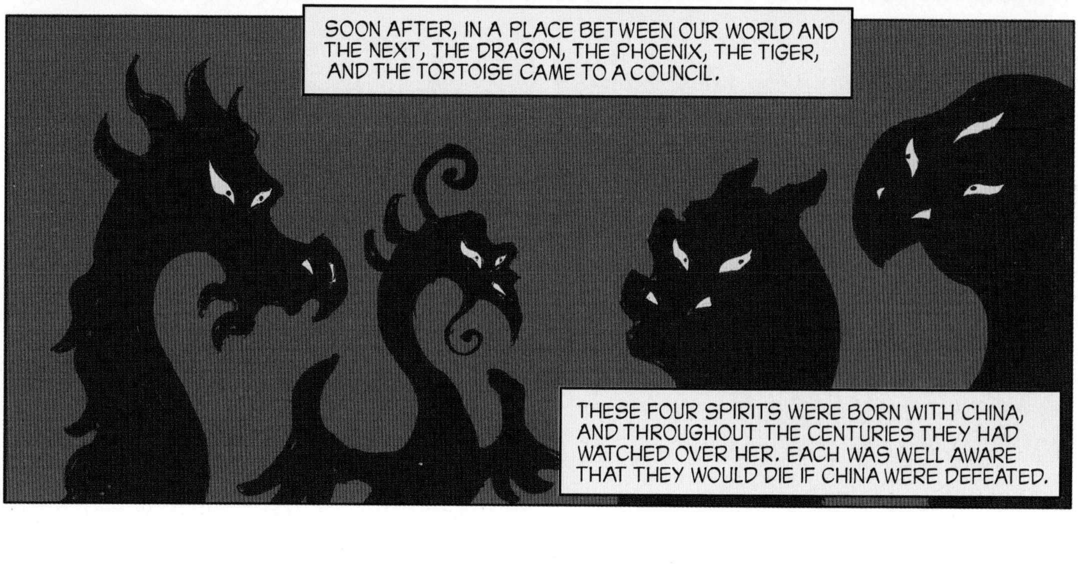
SOON AFTER, IN A PLACE BETWEEN OUR WORLD AND THE NEXT, THE DRAGON, THE PHOENIX, THE TIGER, AND THE TORTOISE CAME TO A COUNCIL.
THESE FOUR SPIRITS WERE BORN WITH CHINA, AND THROUGHOUT THE CENTURIES THEY HAD WATCHED OVER HER. EACH WAS WELL AWARE THAT THEY WOULD DIE IF CHINA WERE DEFEATED.

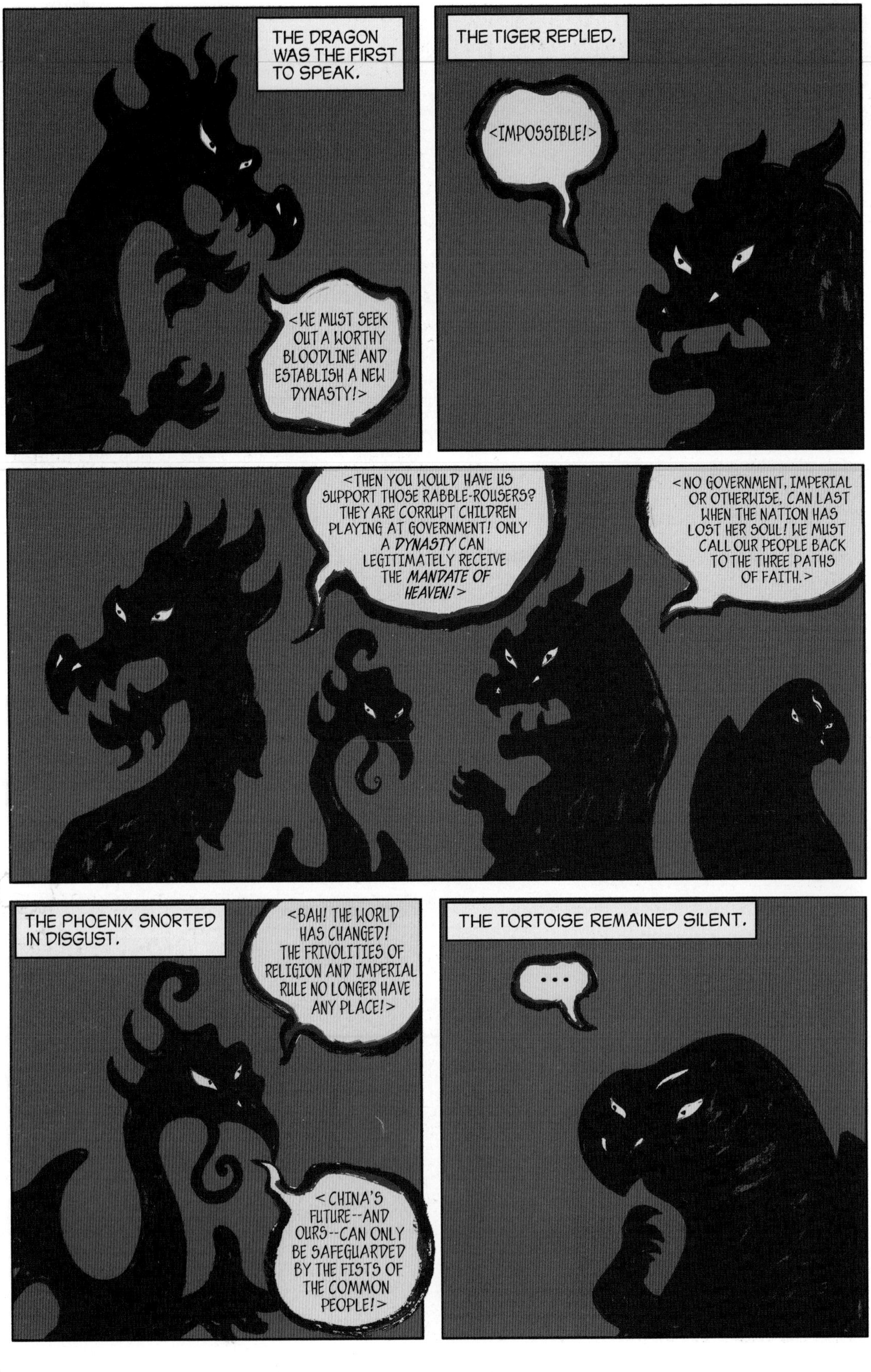
THE DRAGON WAS THE FIRST TO SPEAK.
<WE MUST SEEK OUT A WORTHY BLOODLINE AND ESTABLISH A NEW DYNASTY!>
THE TIGER REPLIED.
<IMPOSSIBLE!>
<THEN YOU WOULD HAVE US SUPPORT THOSE RABBLE-ROUSERS? THEY ARE CORRUPT CHILDREN PLAYING AT GOVERNMENT! ONLY A *DYNASTY* CAN LEGITIMATELY RECEIVE THE *MANDATE OF HEAVEN!*>
<NO GOVERNMENT, IMPERIAL OR OTHERWISE, CAN LAST WHEN THE NATION HAS LOST HER SOUL! WE MUST CALL OUR PEOPLE BACK TO THE THREE PATHS OF FAITH.>
THE PHOENIX SNORTED IN DISGUST.
<BAH! THE WORLD HAS CHANGED! THE FRIVOLITIES OF RELIGION AND IMPERIAL RULE NO LONGER HAVE ANY PLACE!>
<CHINA'S FUTURE--AND OURS--CAN ONLY BE SAFEGUARDED BY THE FISTS OF THE COMMON PEOPLE!>
THE TORTOISE REMAINED SILENT.
...

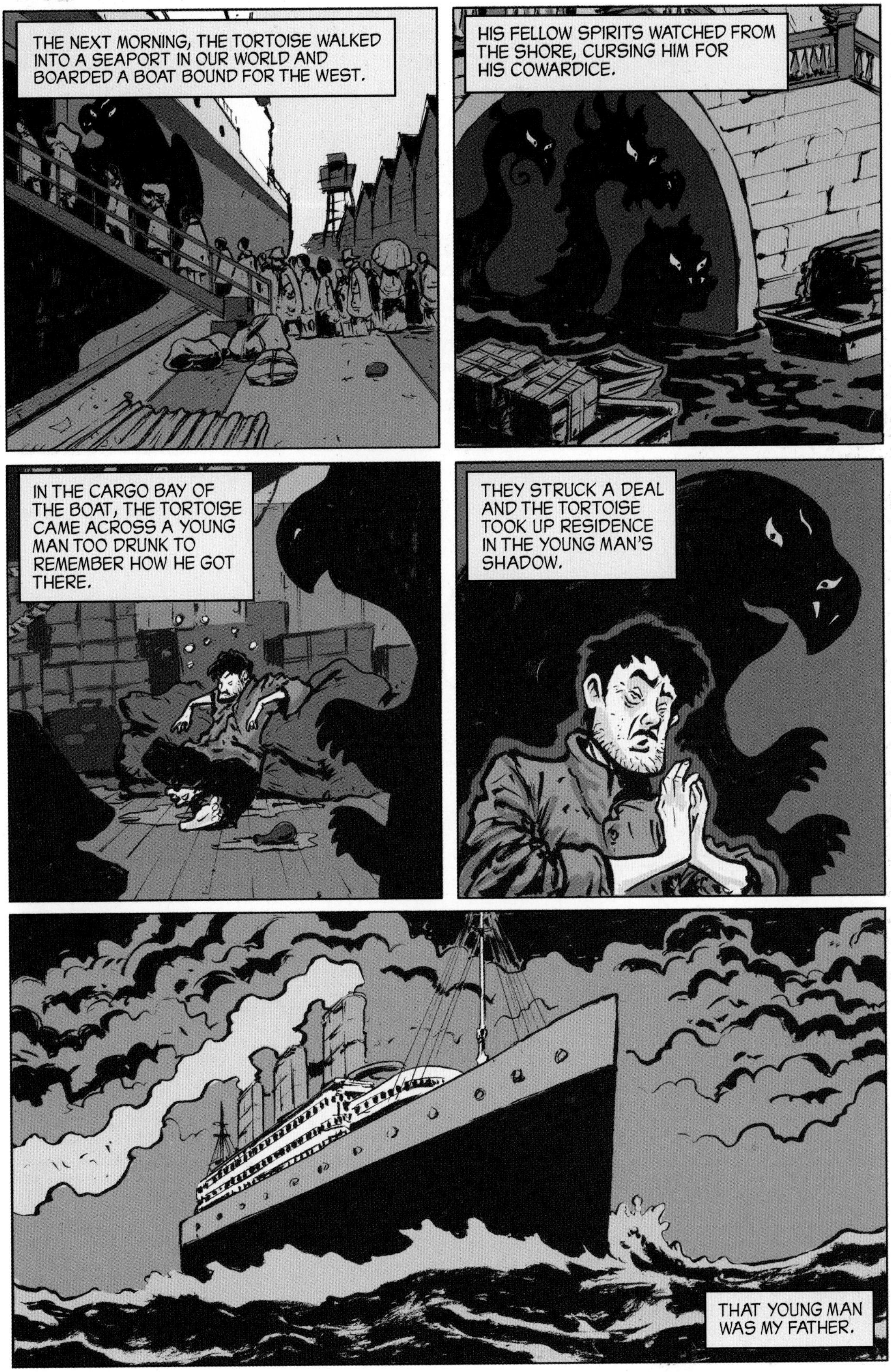
THE NEXT MORNING, THE TORTOISE WALKED INTO A SEAPORT IN OUR WORLD AND BOARDED A BOAT BOUND FOR THE WEST.
HIS FELLOW SPIRITS WATCHED FROM THE SHORE, CURSING HIM FOR HIS COWARDICE.
IN THE CARGO BAY OF THE BOAT, THE TORTOISE CAME ACROSS A YOUNG MAN TOO DRUNK TO REMEMBER HOW HE GOT THERE.
THEY STRUCK A DEAL AND THE TORTOISE TOOK UP RESIDENCE IN THE YOUNG MAN'S SHADOW.
THAT YOUNG MAN WAS MY FATHER.

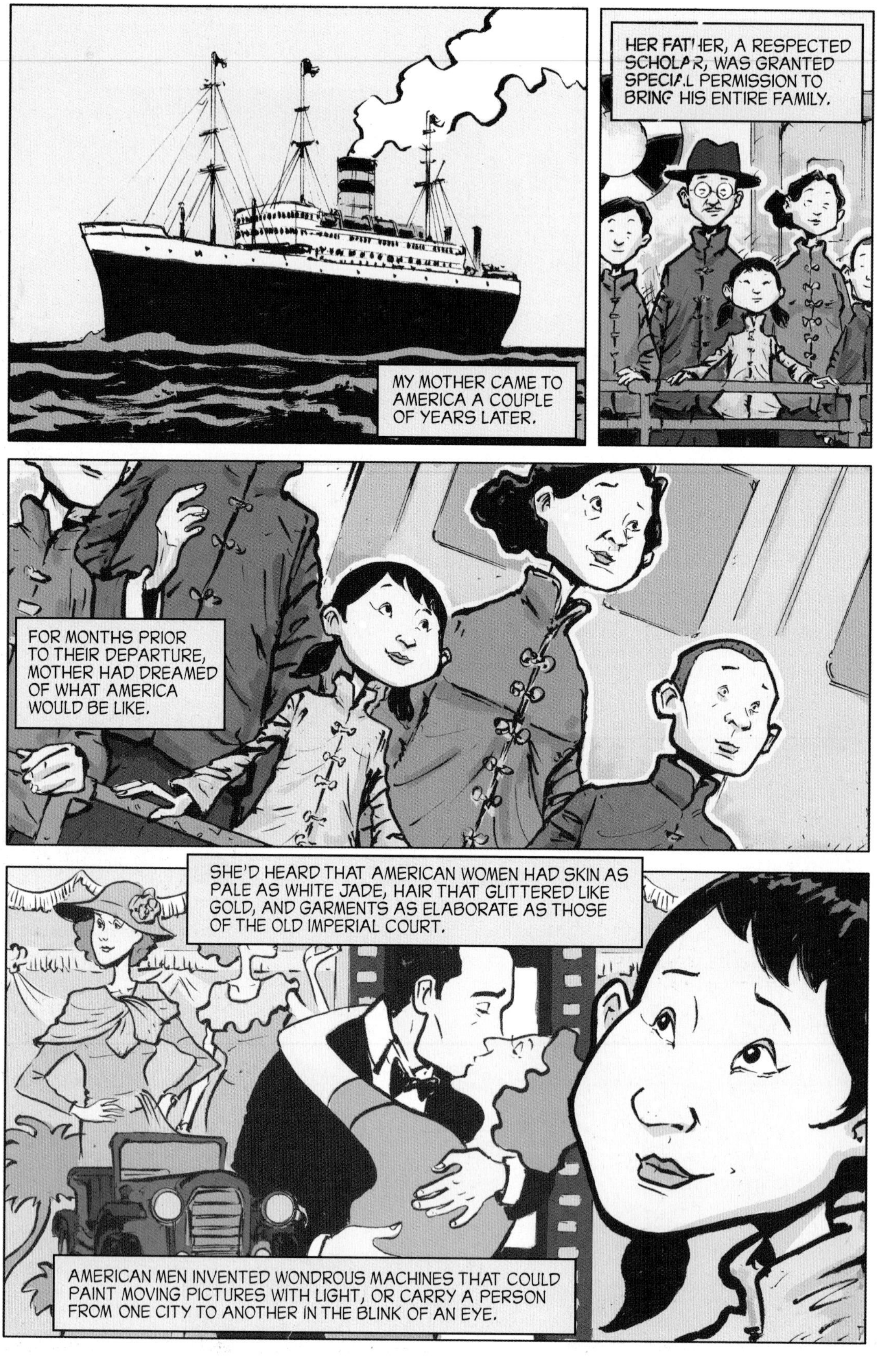
MY MOTHER CAME TO AMERICA A COUPLE OF YEARS LATER.
HER FATHER, A RESPECTED SCHOLAR, WAS GRANTED SPECIAL PERMISSION TO BRING HIS ENTIRE FAMILY.
FOR MONTHS PRIOR TO THEIR DEPARTURE, MOTHER HAD DREAMED OF WHAT AMERICA WOULD BE LIKE.
SHE'D HEARD THAT AMERICAN WOMEN HAD SKIN AS PALE AS WHITE JADE, HAIR THAT GLITTERED LIKE GOLD, AND GARMENTS AS ELABORATE AS THOSE OF THE OLD IMPERIAL COURT.
AMERICAN MEN INVENTED WONDROUS MACHINES THAT COULD PAINT MOVING PICTURES WITH LIGHT, OR CARRY A PERSON FROM ONE CITY TO ANOTHER IN THE BLINK OF AN EYE.

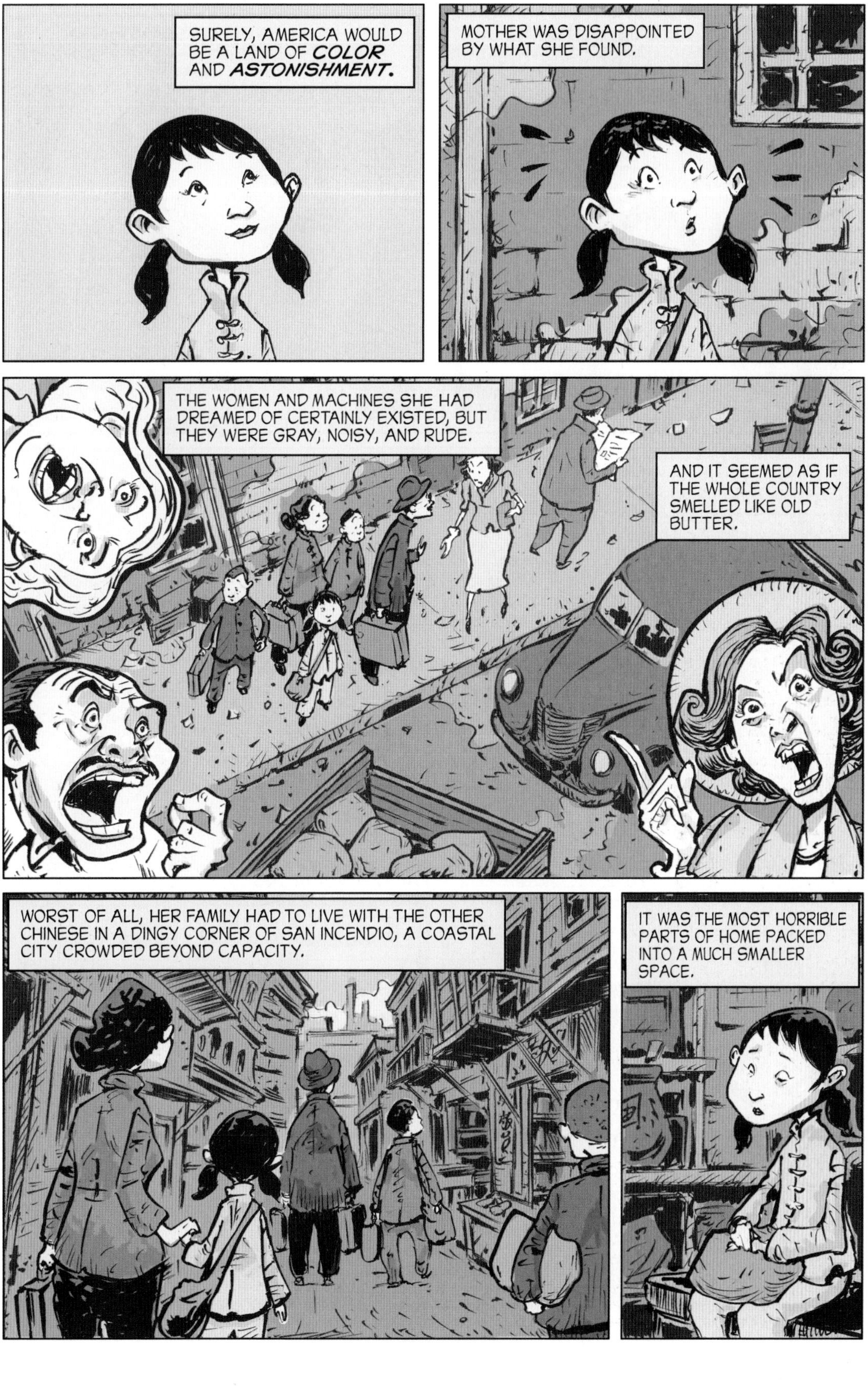
SURELY, AMERICA WOULD BE A LAND OF COLOR AND ASTONISHMENT.
MOTHER WAS DISAPPOINTED BY WHAT SHE FOUND.
THE WOMEN AND MACHINES SHE HAD DREAMED OF CERTAINLY EXISTED, BUT THEY WERE GRAY, NOISY, AND RUDE.
AND IT SEEMED AS IF THE WHOLE COUNTRY SMELLED LIKE OLD BUTTER.
WORST OF ALL, HER FAMILY HAD TO LIVE WITH THE OTHER CHINESE IN A DINGY CORNER OF SAN INCENDIO, A COASTAL CITY CROWDED BEYOND CAPACITY.
IT WAS THE MOST HORRIBLE PARTS OF HOME PACKED INTO A MUCH SMALLER SPACE.

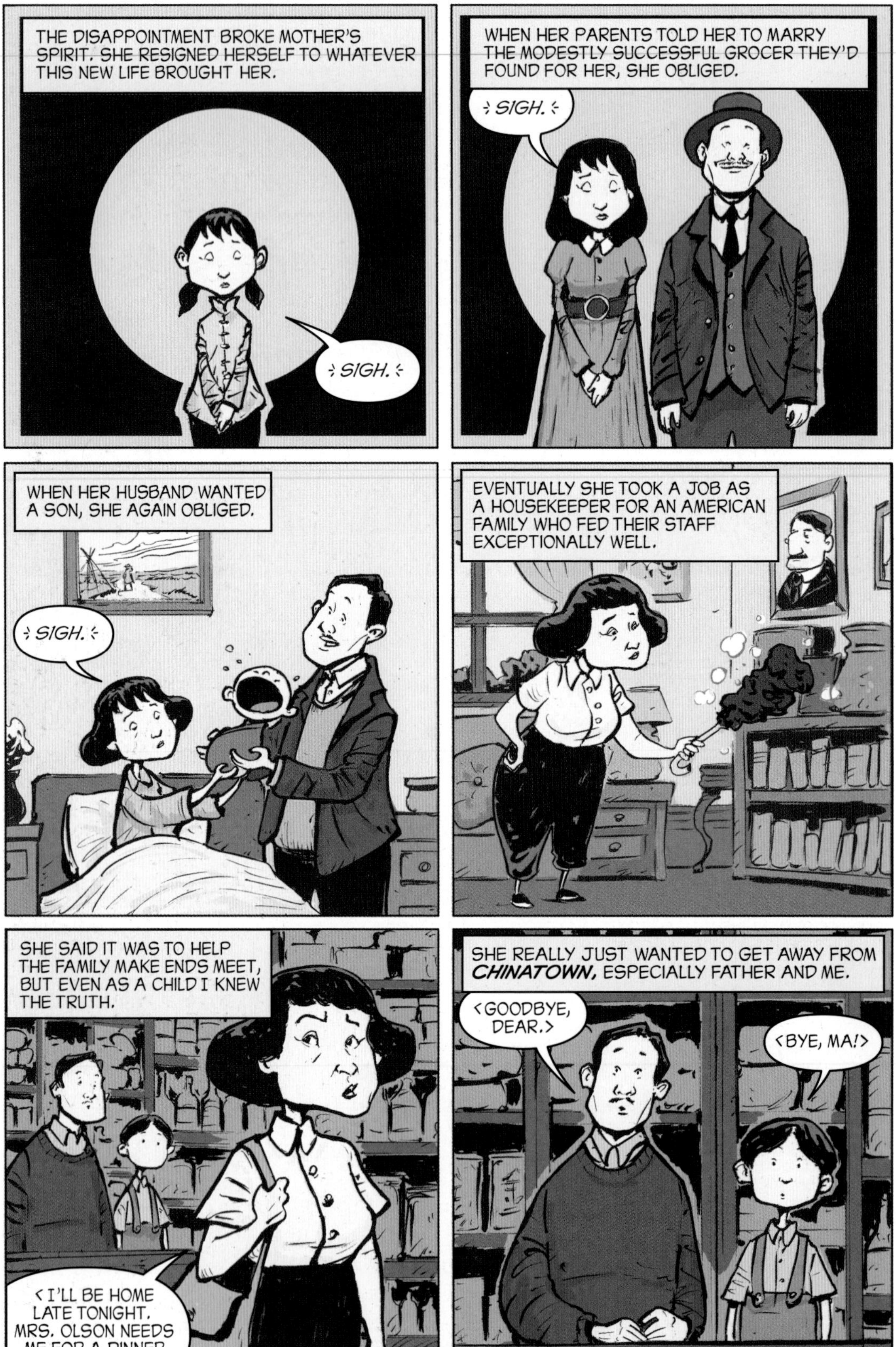
THE DISAPPOINTMENT BROKE MOTHER'S SPIRIT. SHE RESIGNED HERSELF TO WHATEVER THIS NEW LIFE BROUGHT HER.
SIGH.
WHEN HER PARENTS TOLD HER TO MARRY THE MODESTLY SUCCESSFUL GROCER THEY'D FOUND FOR HER, SHE OBLIGED.
SIGH.
WHEN HER HUSBAND WANTED A SON, SHE AGAIN OBLIGED.
SIGH.
EVENTUALLY SHE TOOK A JOB AS A HOUSEKEEPER FOR AN AMERICAN FAMILY WHO FED THEIR STAFF EXCEPTIONALLY WELL.
SHE SAID IT WAS TO HELP THE FAMILY MAKE ENDS MEET, BUT EVEN AS A CHILD I KNEW THE TRUTH.
<I'LL BE HOME LATE TONIGHT. MRS. OLSON NEEDS ME FOR A DINNER PARTY.>*
*TRANSLATED FROM CANTONESE
SHE REALLY JUST WANTED TO GET AWAY FROM CHINATOWN, ESPECIALLY FATHER AND ME.
<GOODBYE, DEAR.>
<BYE, MA!>

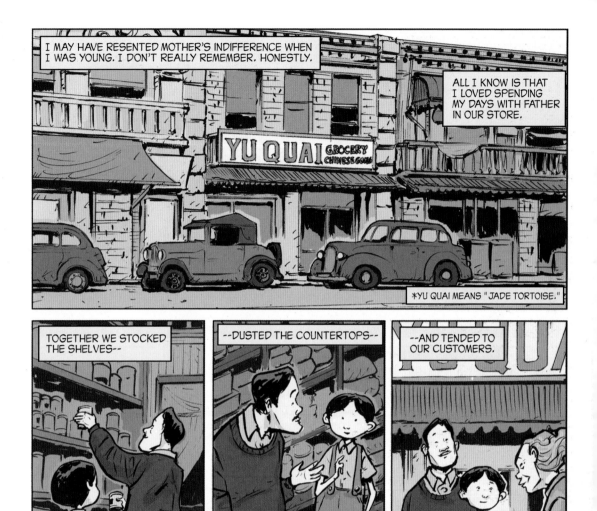

I MAY HAVE RESENTED MOTHER'S INDIFFERENCE WHEN I WAS YOUNG. I DON'T REALLY REMEMBER. HONESTLY.

ALL I KNOW IS THAT I LOVED SPENDING MY DAYS WITH FATHER IN OUR STORE.

YU QUAI GROCERY CHINESE GOODS

*YU QUAI MEANS "JADE TORTOISE."

TOGETHER WE STOCKED THE SHELVES--

--DUSTED THE COUNTERTOPS--

--AND TENDED TO OUR CUSTOMERS.

WHENEVER THE OCCASIONAL AMERICAN WANDERED IN, I WAS ALWAYS IN CHARGE.

<YOUR ENGLISH IS SO GOOD, HANK! I DON'T KNOW WHAT I'D DO WITHOUT YOU!>

7

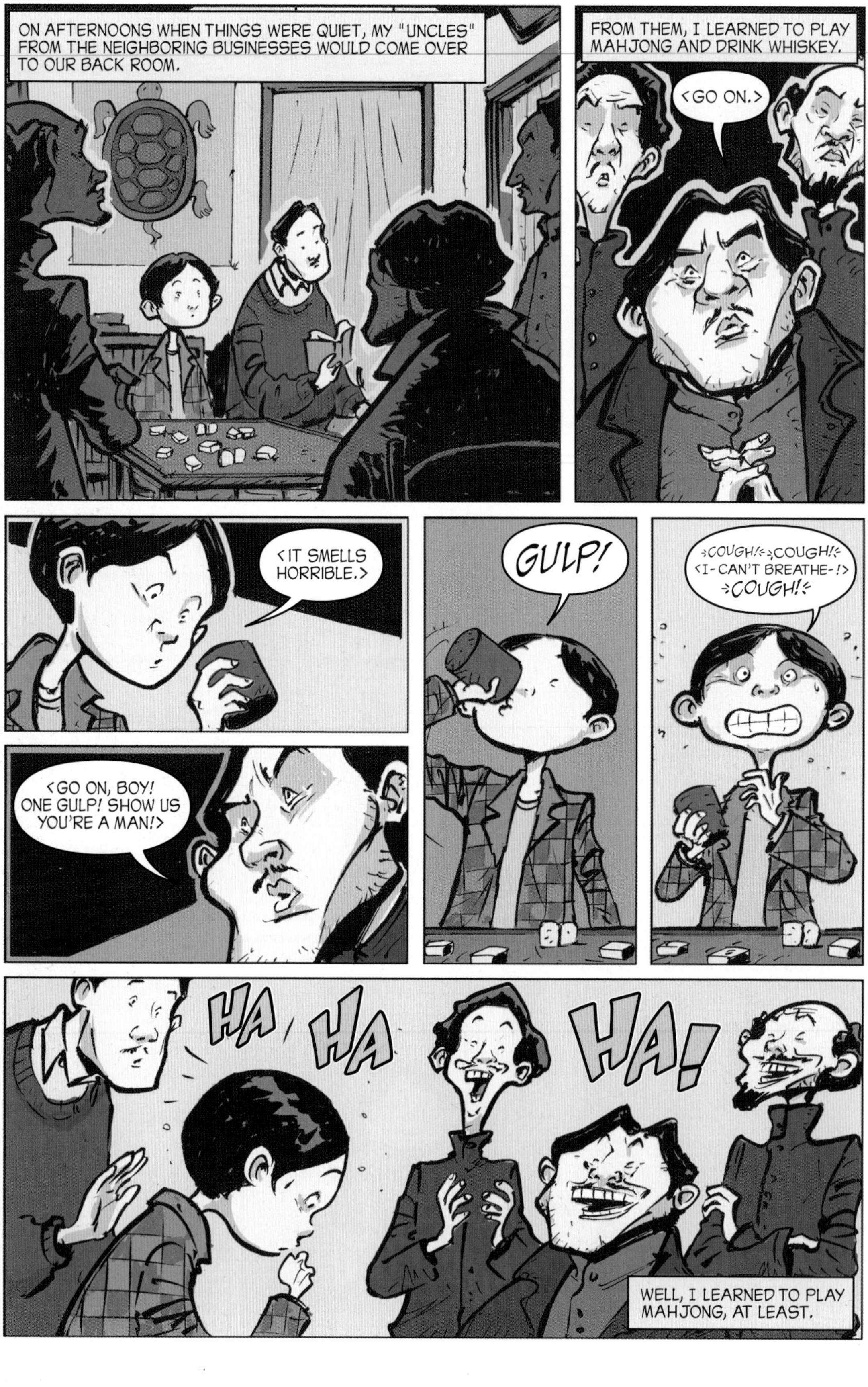
ON AFTERNOONS WHEN THINGS WERE QUIET, MY "UNCLES" FROM THE NEIGHBORING BUSINESSES WOULD COME OVER TO OUR BACK ROOM.
FROM THEM, I LEARNED TO PLAY MAHJONG AND DRINK WHISKEY.
<GO ON.>
<IT SMELLS HORRIBLE.>
<GO ON, BOY! ONE GULP! SHOW US YOU'RE A MAN!>
GULP!
COUGH! COUGH! <I-CAN'T BREATHE-!> COUGH!
HA HA HA!
WELL, I LEARNED TO PLAY MAHJONG, AT LEAST.

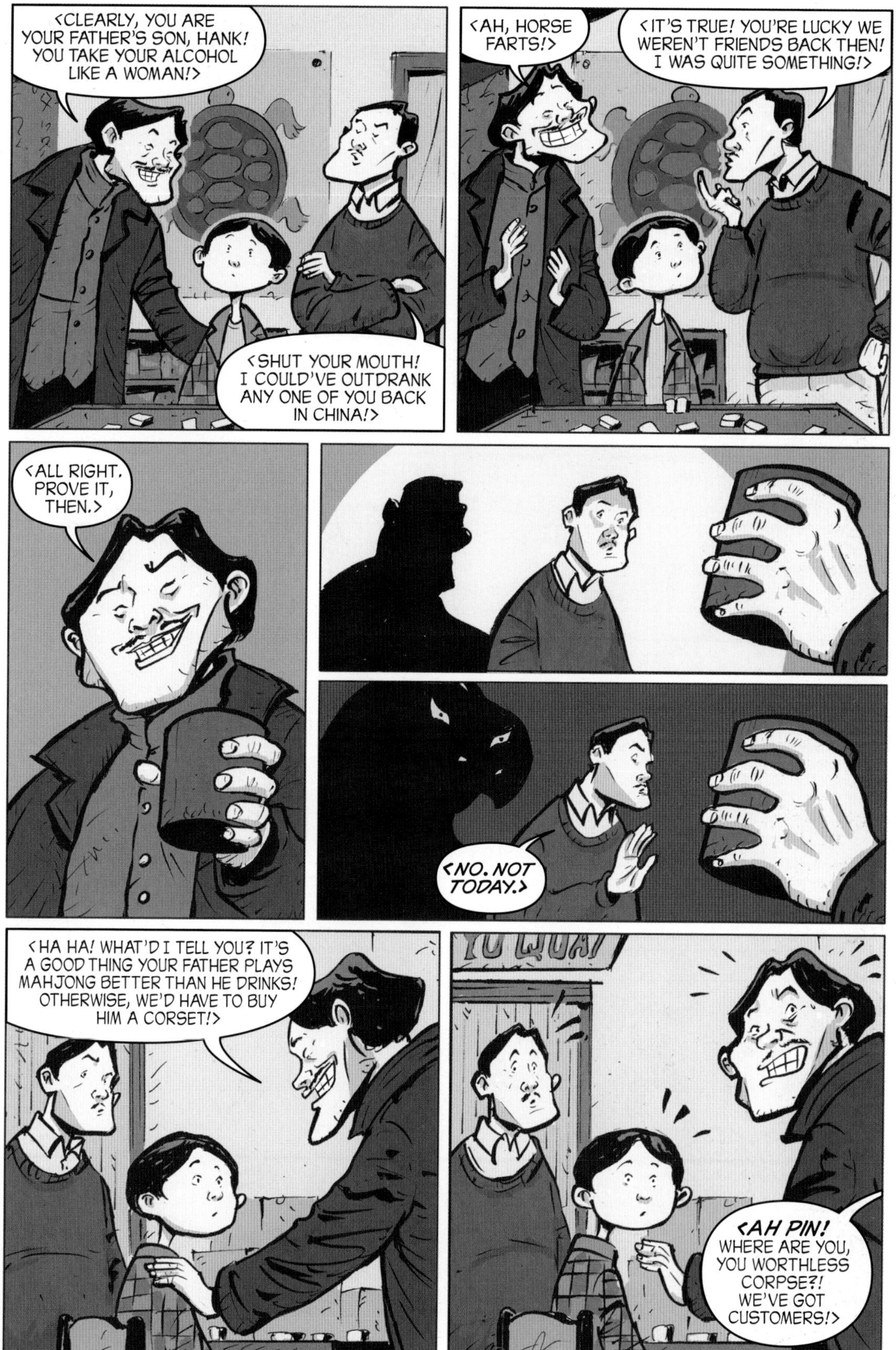
<CLEARLY, YOU ARE YOUR FATHER'S SON, HANK! YOU TAKE YOUR ALCOHOL LIKE A WOMAN!>
<SHUT YOUR MOUTH! I COULD'VE OUTDRANK ANY ONE OF YOU BACK IN CHINA!>
<AH, HORSE FARTS!>
<IT'S TRUE! YOU'RE LUCKY WE WEREN'T FRIENDS BACK THEN! I WAS QUITE SOMETHING!>
<ALL RIGHT. PROVE IT, THEN.>
<NO. NOT TODAY.>
<HA HA! WHAT'D I TELL YOU? IT'S A GOOD THING YOUR FATHER PLAYS MAHJONG BETTER THAN HE DRINKS! OTHERWISE, WE'D HAVE TO BUY HIM A CORSET!>
<AH PIN! WHERE ARE YOU, YOU WORTHLESS CORPSE?! WE'VE GOT CUSTOMERS!>

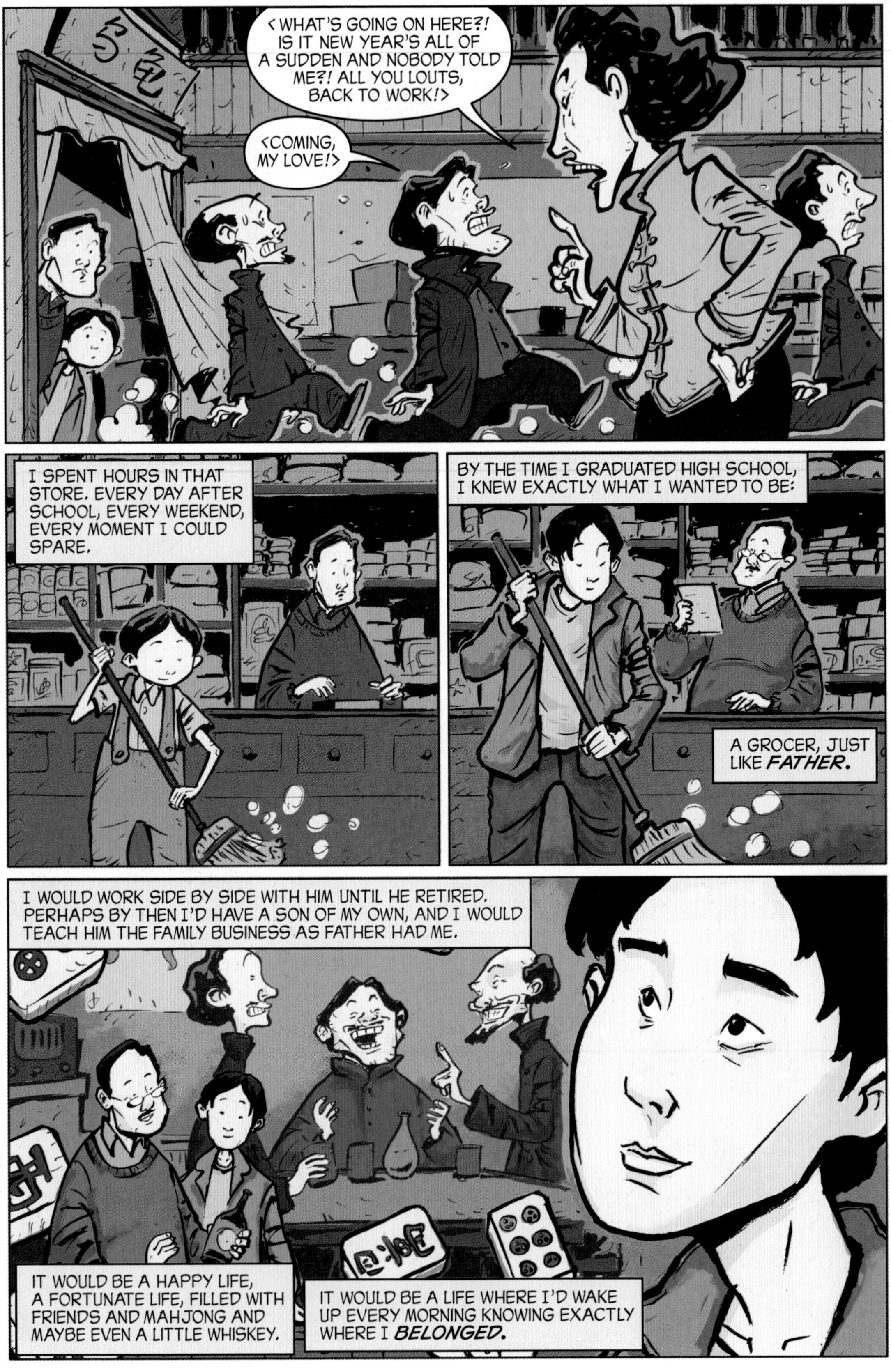
<WHAT'S GOING ON HERE?! IS IT NEW YEAR'S ALL OF A SUDDEN AND NOBODY TOLD ME?! ALL YOU LOUTS, BACK TO WORK!>
<COMING, MY LOVE!>
I SPENT HOURS IN THAT STORE. EVERY DAY AFTER SCHOOL, EVERY WEEKEND, EVERY MOMENT I COULD SPARE.
BY THE TIME I GRADUATED HIGH SCHOOL, I KNEW EXACTLY WHAT I WANTED TO BE:
A GROCER, JUST LIKE *FATHER*.
I WOULD WORK SIDE BY SIDE WITH HIM UNTIL HE RETIRED. PERHAPS BY THEN I'D HAVE A SON OF MY OWN, AND I WOULD TEACH HIM THE FAMILY BUSINESS AS FATHER HAD ME.
IT WOULD BE A HAPPY LIFE, A FORTUNATE LIFE, FILLED WITH FRIENDS AND MAHJONG AND MAYBE EVEN A LITTLE WHISKEY.
IT WOULD BE A LIFE WHERE I'D WAKE UP EVERY MORNING KNOWING EXACTLY WHERE I *BELONGED*.

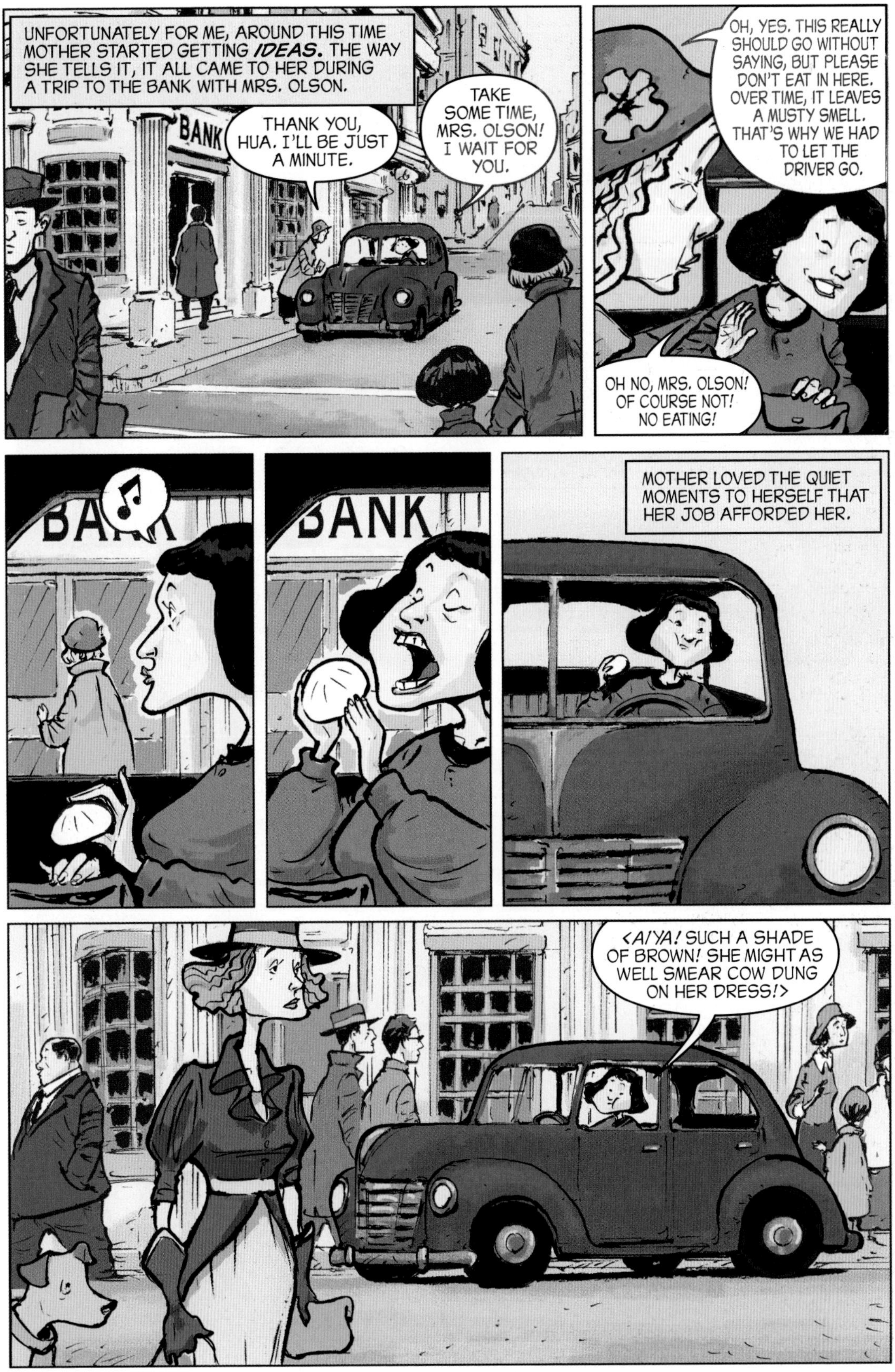
UNFORTUNATELY FOR ME, AROUND THIS TIME MOTHER STARTED GETTING *IDEAS.* THE WAY SHE TELLS IT, IT ALL CAME TO HER DURING A TRIP TO THE BANK WITH MRS. OLSON.
BANK
THANK YOU, HUA. I'LL BE JUST A MINUTE.
TAKE SOME TIME, MRS. OLSON! I WAIT FOR YOU.
OH, YES. THIS REALLY SHOULD GO WITHOUT SAYING, BUT PLEASE DON'T EAT IN HERE. OVER TIME, IT LEAVES A MUSTY SMELL. THAT'S WHY WE HAD TO LET THE DRIVER GO.
OH NO, MRS. OLSON! OF COURSE NOT! NO EATING!
BANK
MOTHER LOVED THE QUIET MOMENTS TO HERSELF THAT HER JOB AFFORDED HER.
<AIYA! SUCH A SHADE OF BROWN! SHE MIGHT AS WELL SMEAR COW DUNG ON HER DRESS!>

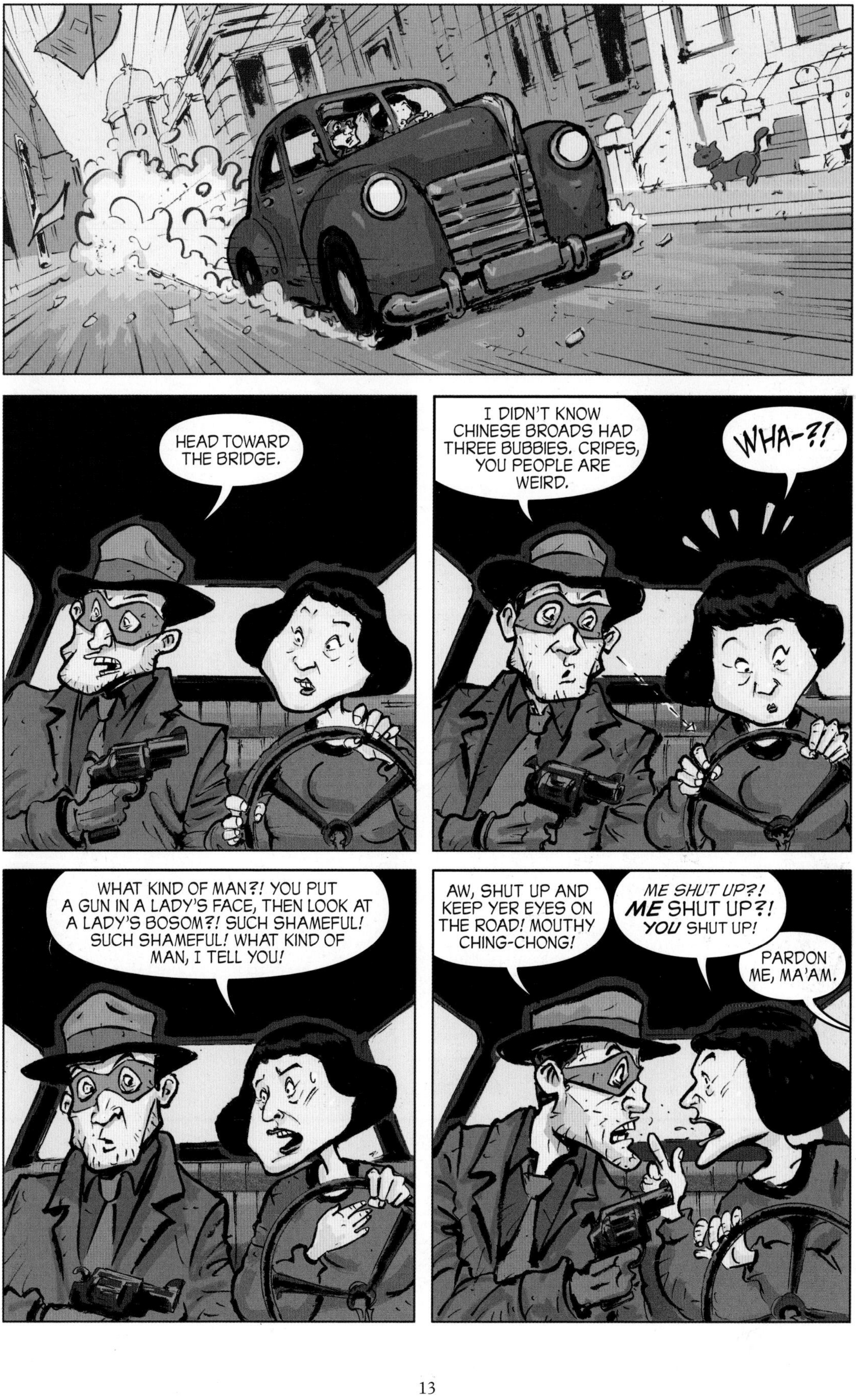
HEAD TOWARD THE BRIDGE.
I DIDN'T KNOW CHINESE BROADS HAD THREE BUBBIES. CRIPES, YOU PEOPLE ARE WEIRD.
WHA-?!
WHAT KIND OF MAN?! YOU PUT A GUN IN A LADY'S FACE, THEN LOOK AT A LADY'S BOSOM?! SUCH SHAMEFUL! SUCH SHAMEFUL! WHAT KIND OF MAN, I TELL YOU!
AW, SHUT UP AND KEEP YER EYES ON THE ROAD! MOUTHY CHING-CHONG!
ME SHUT UP?! ME SHUT UP?! YOU SHUT UP!
PARDON ME, MA'AM.

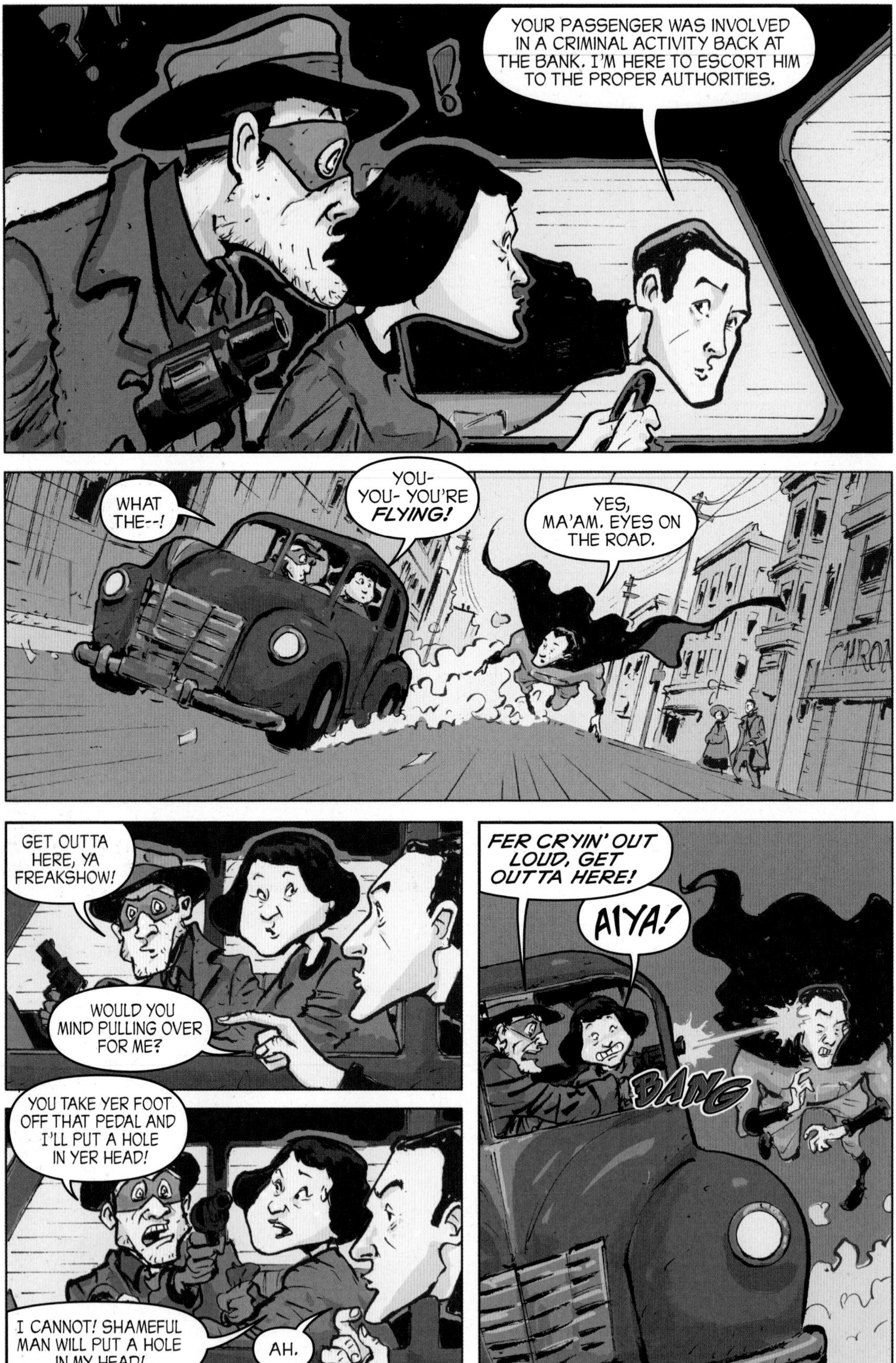
YOUR PASSENGER WAS INVOLVED IN A CRIMINAL ACTIVITY BACK AT THE BANK. I'M HERE TO ESCORT HIM TO THE PROPER AUTHORITIES.
WHAT THE--!
YOU- YOU- YOU'RE *FLYING!*
YES, MA'AM. EYES ON THE ROAD.
GET OUTTA HERE, YA FREAKSHOW!
WOULD YOU MIND PULLING OVER FOR ME?
YOU TAKE YER FOOT OFF THAT PEDAL AND I'LL PUT A HOLE IN YER HEAD!
I CANNOT! SHAMEFUL MAN WILL PUT A HOLE IN MY HEAD!
AH.
FER CRYIN' OUT LOUD, GET OUTTA HERE!
AIYA!
BANG

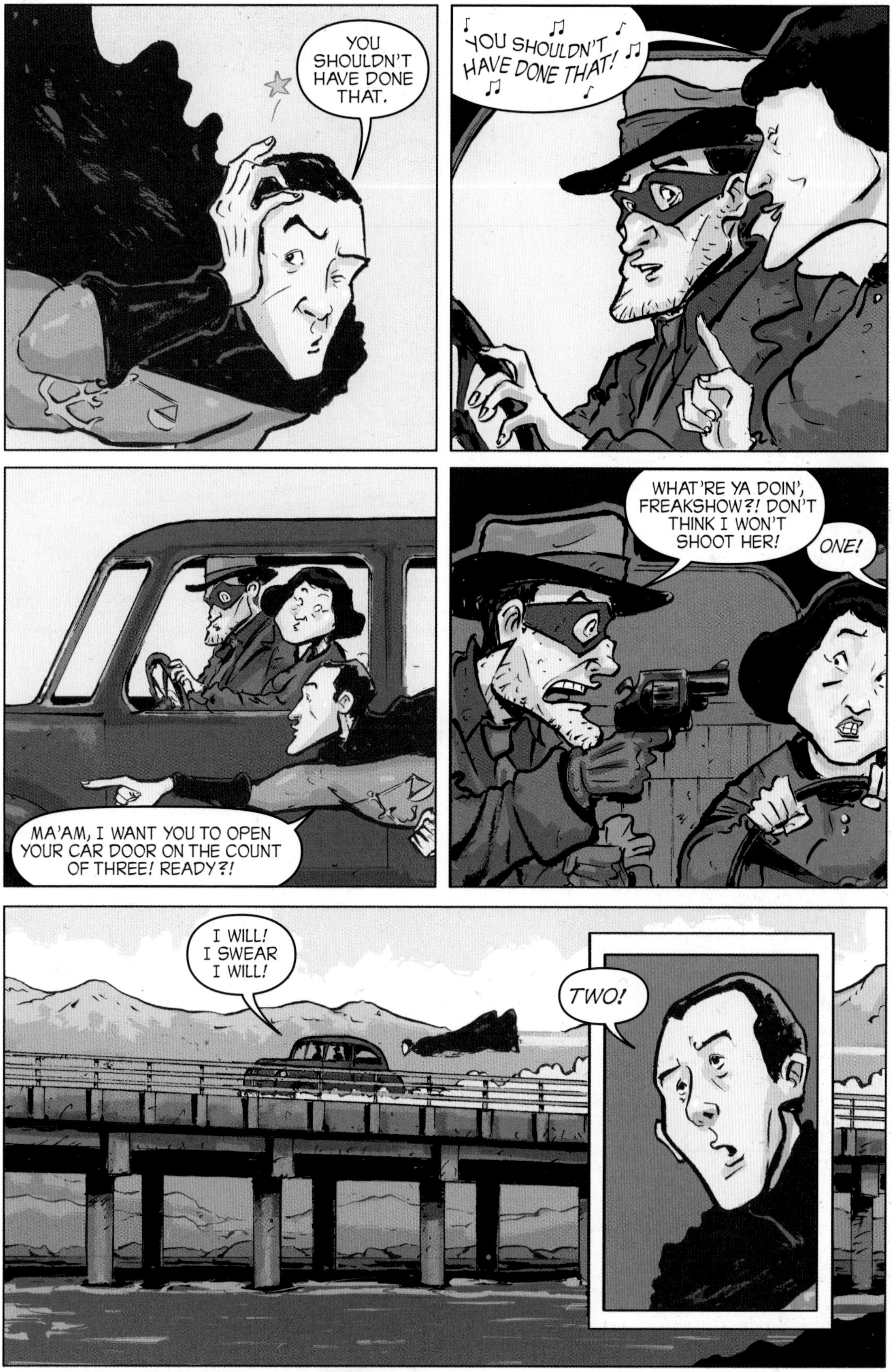
YOU SHOULDN'T HAVE DONE THAT.
YOU SHOULDN'T HAVE DONE THAT!
MA'AM, I WANT YOU TO OPEN YOUR CAR DOOR ON THE COUNT OF THREE! READY?!
WHAT'RE YA DOIN', FREAKSHOW?! DON'T THINK I WON'T SHOOT HER!
ONE!
I WILL! I SWEAR I WILL!
TWO!

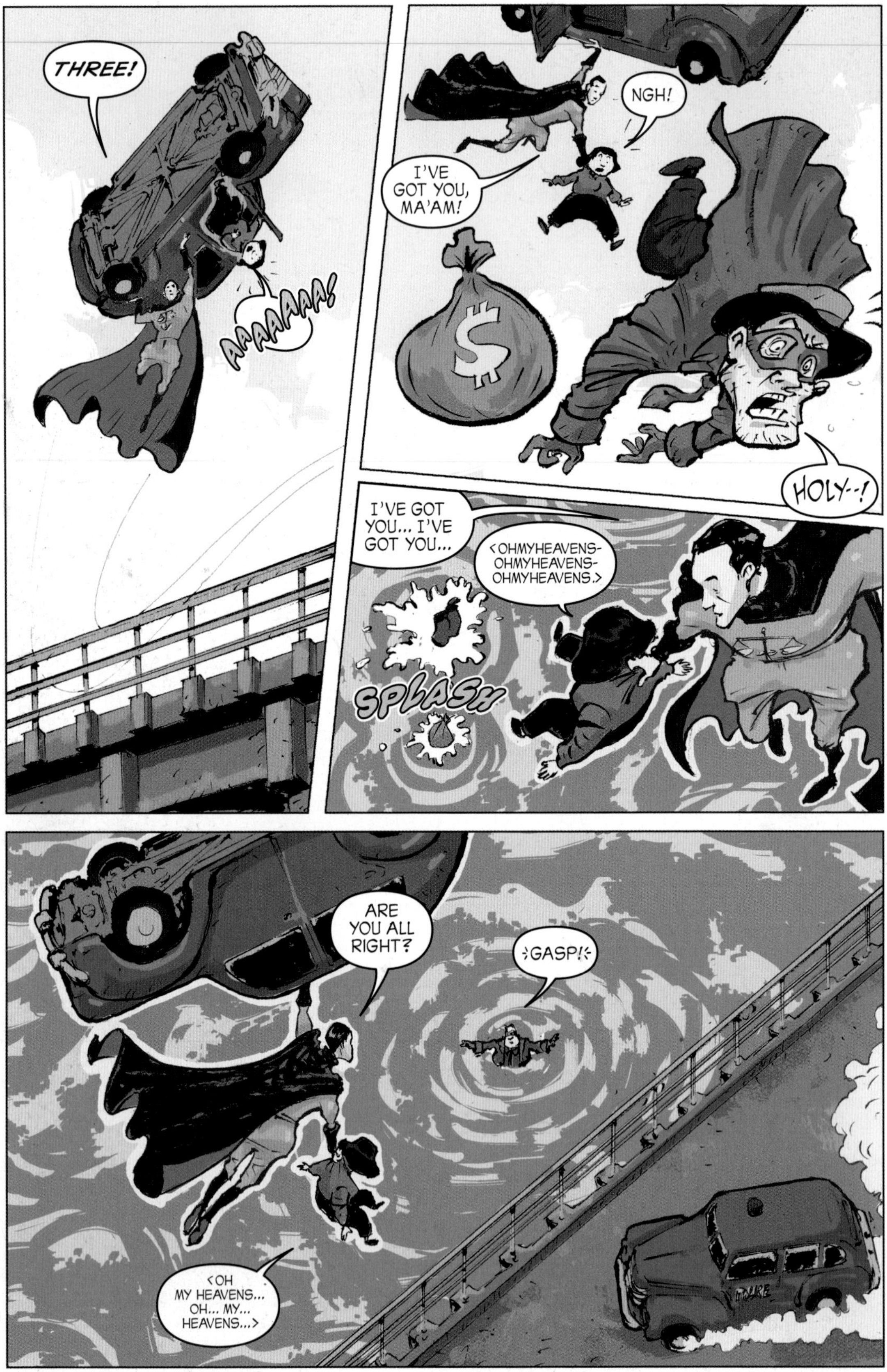
THREE!
AAAAAAA!
NGH!
I'VE GOT YOU, MA'AM!
HOLY--!
I'VE GOT YOU... I'VE GOT YOU...
<OHMYHEAVENS-OHMYHEAVENS-OHMYHEAVENS.>
SPLASH
ARE YOU ALL RIGHT?
GASP!
<OH MY HEAVENS... OH... MY... HEAVENS...>

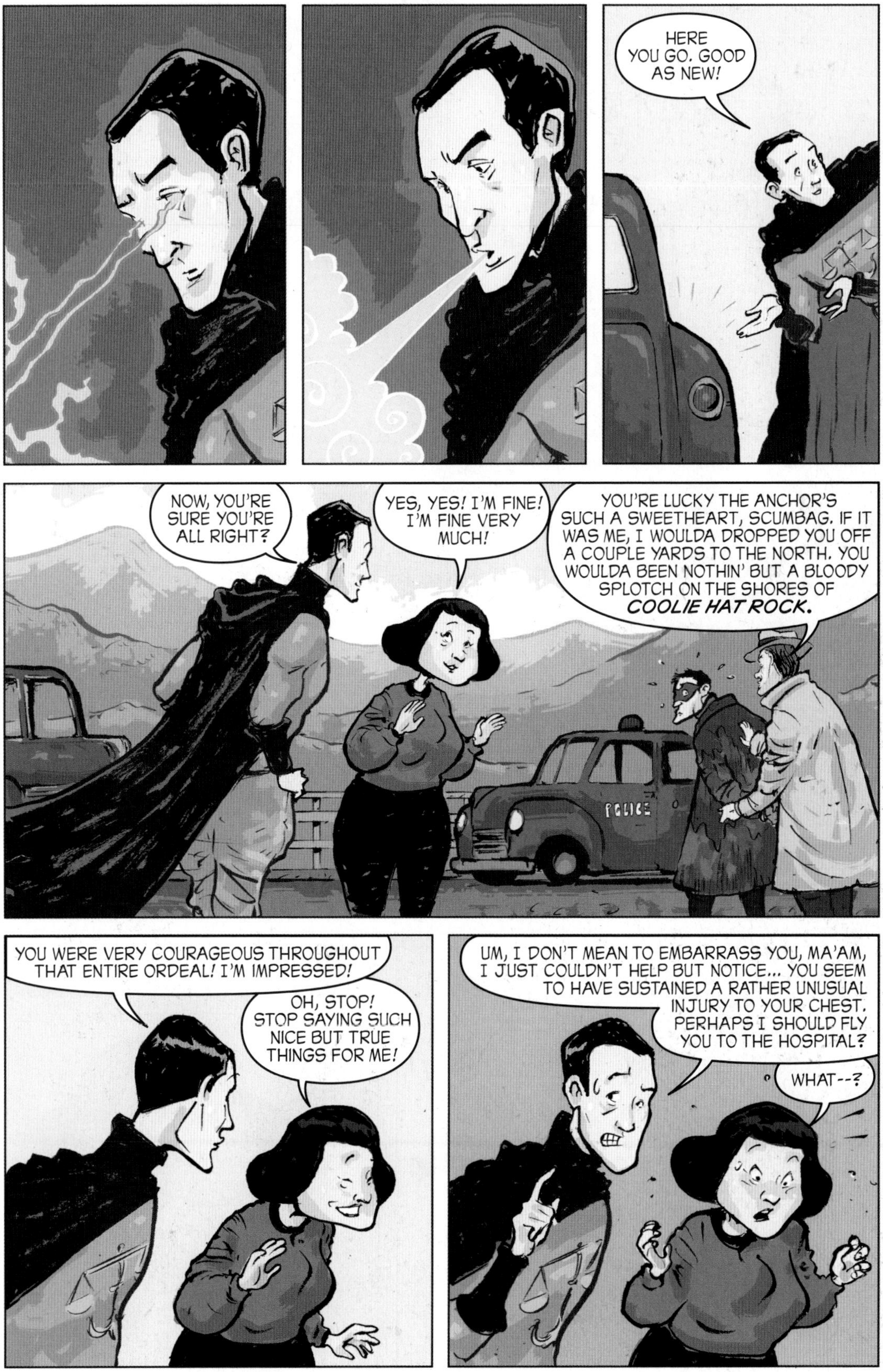
HERE YOU GO. GOOD AS NEW!
NOW, YOU'RE SURE YOU'RE ALL RIGHT?
YES, YES! I'M FINE! I'M FINE VERY MUCH!
YOU'RE LUCKY THE ANCHOR'S SUCH A SWEETHEART, SCUMBAG. IF IT WAS ME, I WOULDA DROPPED YOU OFF A COUPLE YARDS TO THE NORTH. YOU WOULDA BEEN NOTHIN' BUT A BLOODY SPLOTCH ON THE SHORES OF COOLIE HAT ROCK.
POLICE
YOU WERE VERY COURAGEOUS THROUGHOUT THAT ENTIRE ORDEAL! I'M IMPRESSED!
OH, STOP! STOP SAYING SUCH NICE BUT TRUE THINGS FOR ME!
UM, I DON'T MEAN TO EMBARRASS YOU, MA'AM, I JUST COULDN'T HELP BUT NOTICE... YOU SEEM TO HAVE SUSTAINED A RATHER UNUSUAL INJURY TO YOUR CHEST. PERHAPS I SHOULD FLY YOU TO THE HOSPITAL?
WHAT--?

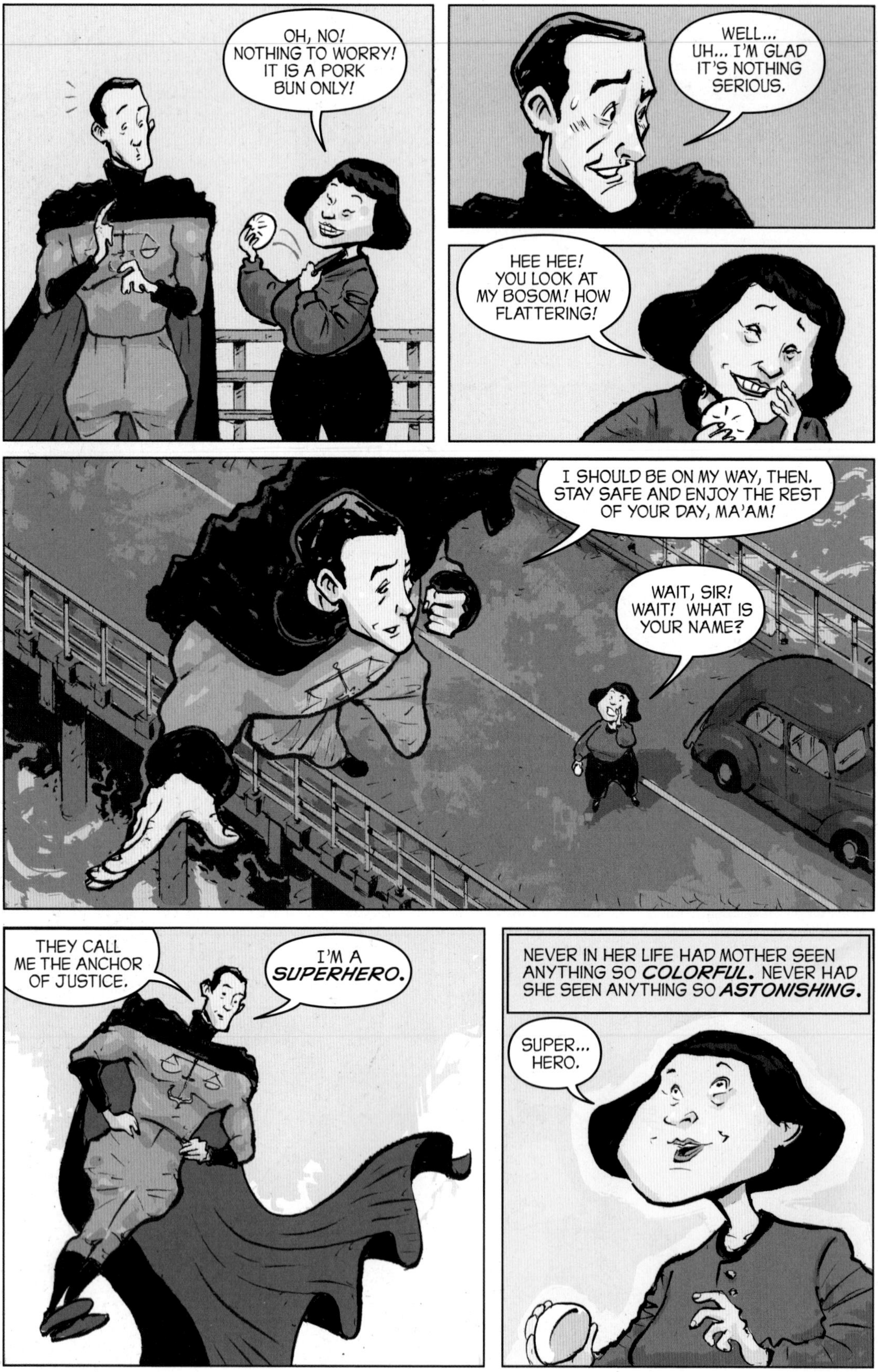
OH, NO! NOTHING TO WORRY! IT IS A PORK BUN ONLY!
WELL... UH... I'M GLAD IT'S NOTHING SERIOUS.
HEE HEE! YOU LOOK AT MY BOSOM! HOW FLATTERING!
I SHOULD BE ON MY WAY, THEN. STAY SAFE AND ENJOY THE REST OF YOUR DAY, MA'AM!
WAIT, SIR! WAIT! WHAT IS YOUR NAME?
THEY CALL ME THE ANCHOR OF JUSTICE.
I'M A SUPERHERO.
NEVER IN HER LIFE HAD MOTHER SEEN ANYTHING SO COLORFUL. NEVER HAD SHE SEEN ANYTHING SO ASTONISHING.
SUPER... HERO.

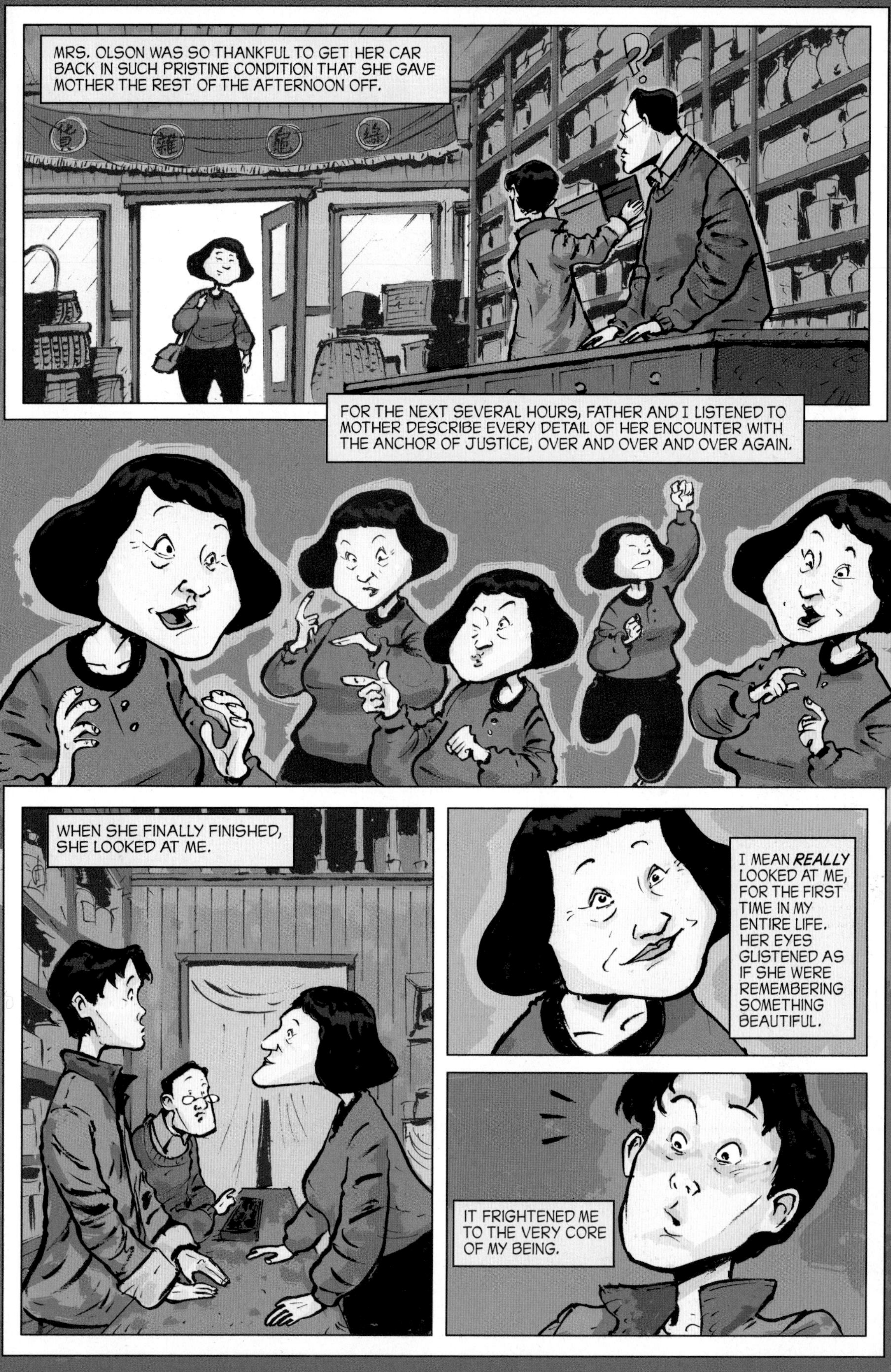
MRS. OLSON WAS SO THANKFUL TO GET HER CAR BACK IN SUCH PRISTINE CONDITION THAT SHE GAVE MOTHER THE REST OF THE AFTERNOON OFF.
?
FOR THE NEXT SEVERAL HOURS, FATHER AND I LISTENED TO MOTHER DESCRIBE EVERY DETAIL OF HER ENCOUNTER WITH THE ANCHOR OF JUSTICE, OVER AND OVER AND OVER AGAIN.
WHEN SHE FINALLY FINISHED, SHE LOOKED AT ME.
I MEAN *REALLY* LOOKED AT ME, FOR THE FIRST TIME IN MY ENTIRE LIFE. HER EYES GLISTENED AS IF SHE WERE REMEMBERING SOMETHING BEAUTIFUL.
IT FRIGHTENED ME TO THE VERY CORE OF MY BEING.

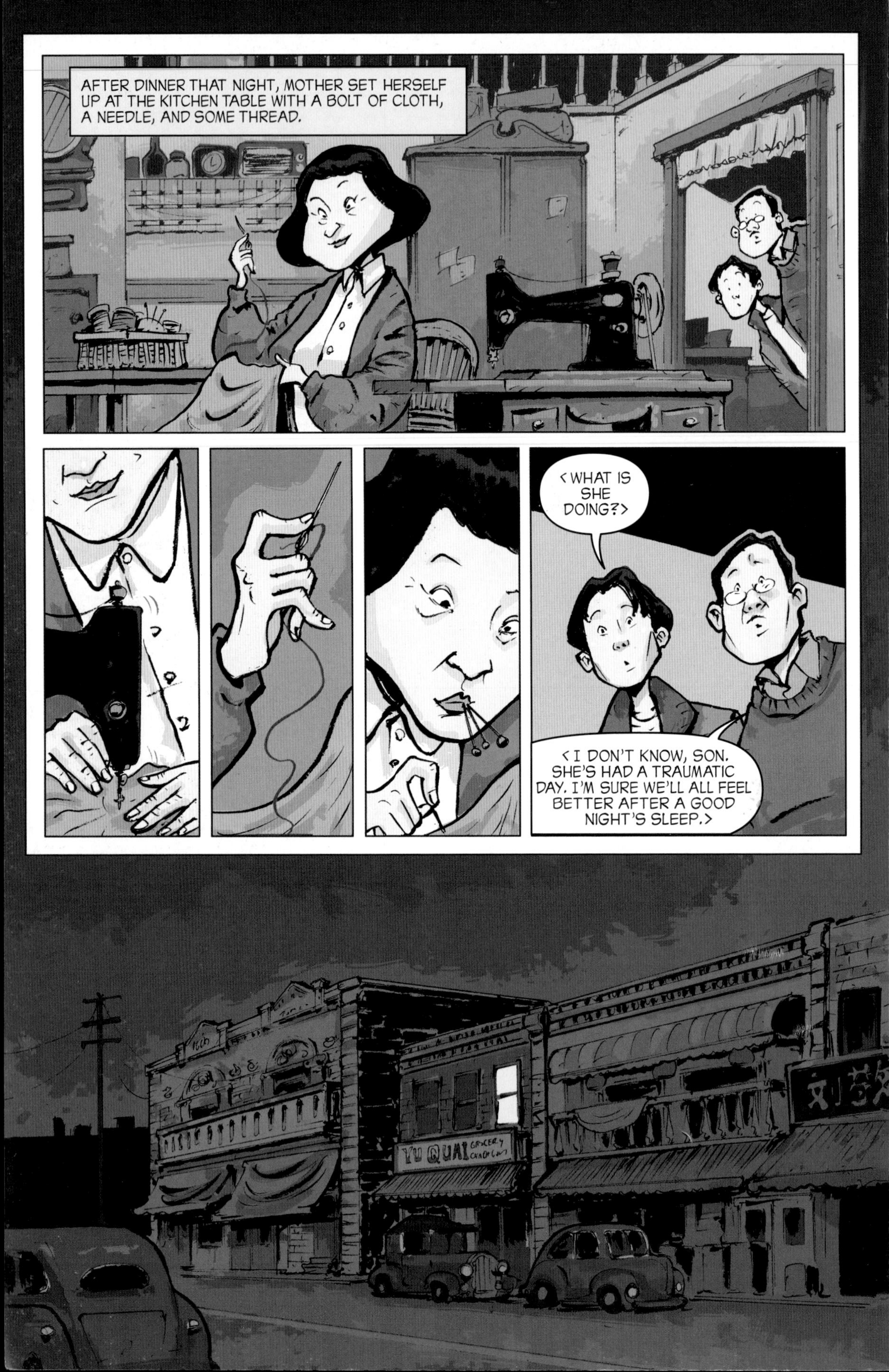
AFTER DINNER THAT NIGHT, MOTHER SET HERSELF UP AT THE KITCHEN TABLE WITH A BOLT OF CLOTH, A NEEDLE, AND SOME THREAD.
<WHAT IS SHE DOING?>
<I DON'T KNOW, SON. SHE'S HAD A TRAUMATIC DAY. I'M SURE WE'LL ALL FEEL BETTER AFTER A GOOD NIGHT'S SLEEP.>
YU QUAI

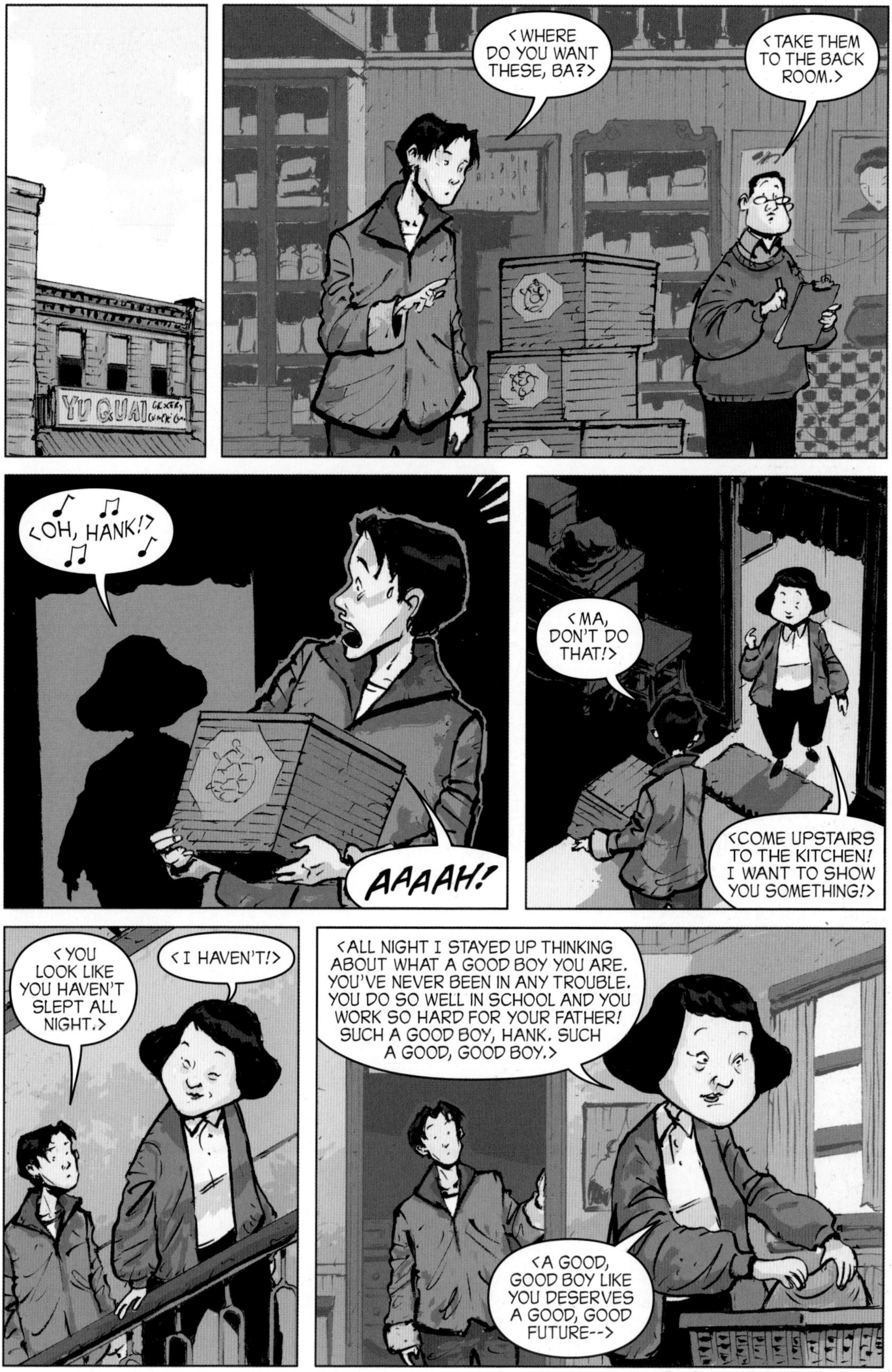
YU QUAI
<WHERE DO YOU WANT THESE, BA?>
<TAKE THEM TO THE BACK ROOM.>
<OH, HANK!>
AAAAH!
<MA, DON'T DO THAT!>
<COME UPSTAIRS TO THE KITCHEN! I WANT TO SHOW YOU SOMETHING!>
<YOU LOOK LIKE YOU HAVEN'T SLEPT ALL NIGHT.>
<I HAVEN'T!>
<ALL NIGHT I STAYED UP THINKING ABOUT WHAT A GOOD BOY YOU ARE. YOU'VE NEVER BEEN IN ANY TROUBLE. YOU DO SO WELL IN SCHOOL AND YOU WORK SO HARD FOR YOUR FATHER! SUCH A GOOD BOY, HANK. SUCH A GOOD, GOOD BOY.>
<A GOOD, GOOD BOY LIKE YOU DESERVES A GOOD, GOOD FUTURE-->

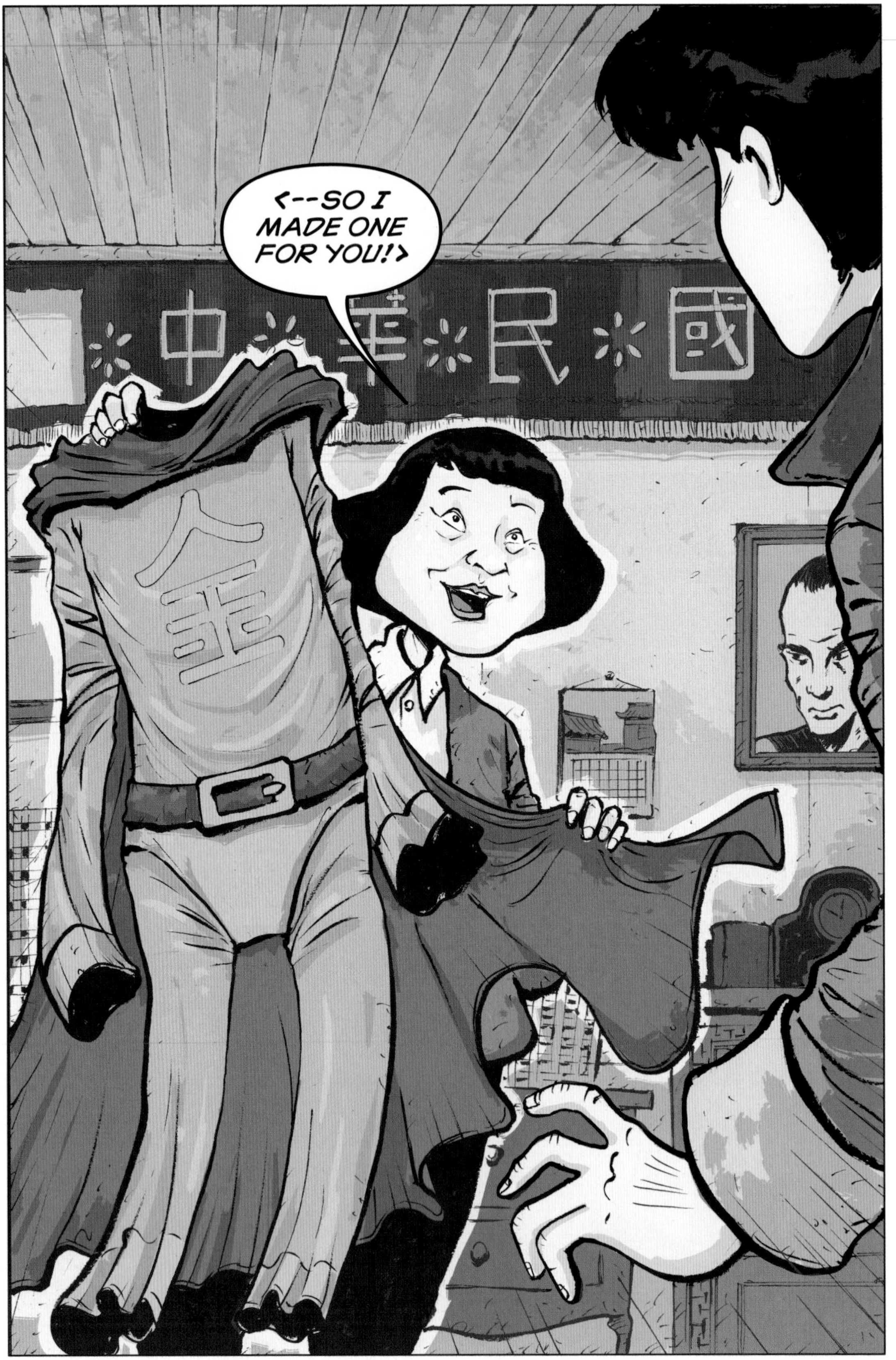
<--SO I MADE ONE FOR YOU!>
中華民國

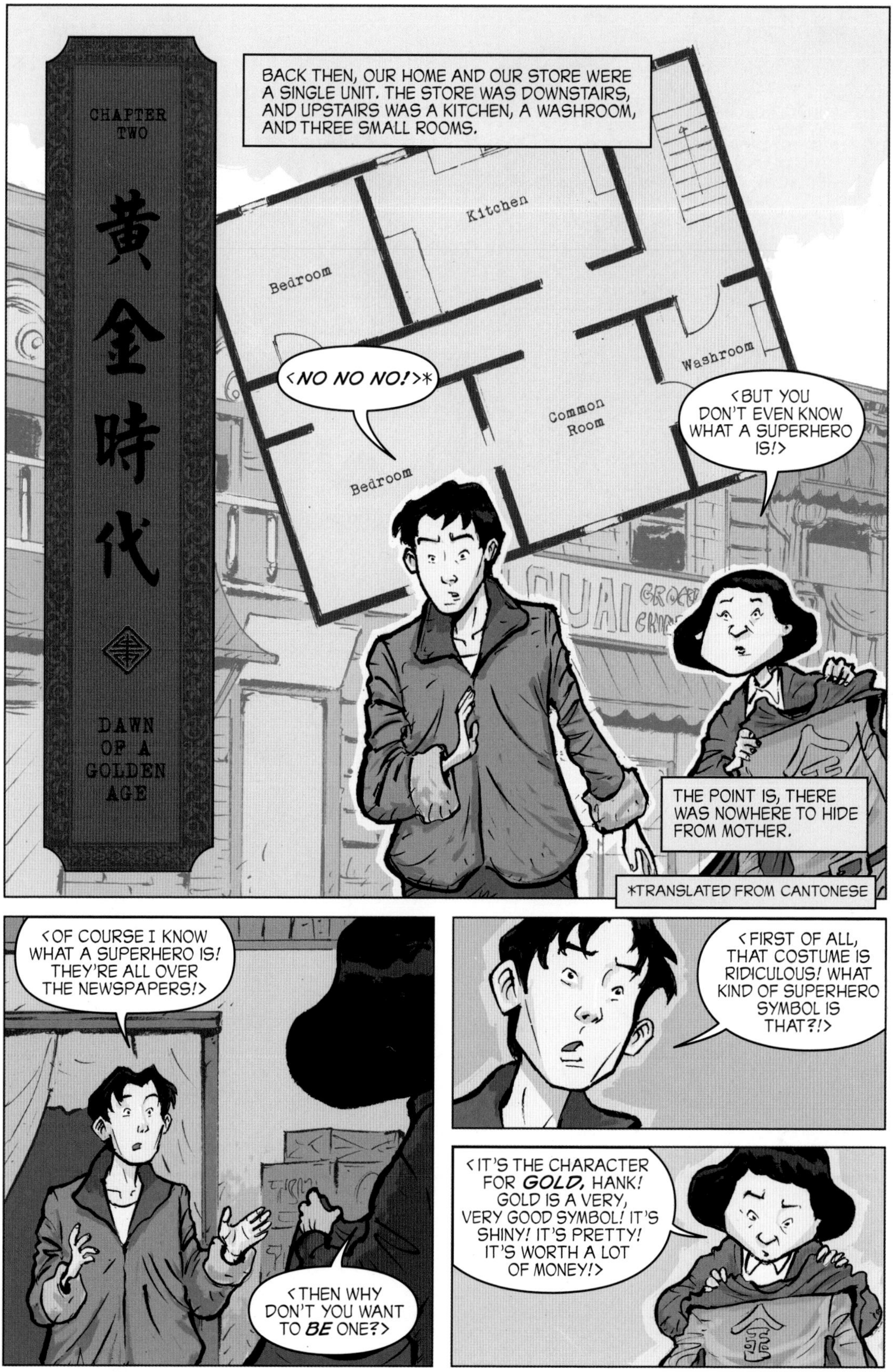

CHAPTER TWO
黄金時代
DAWN OF A GOLDEN AGE
BACK THEN, OUR HOME AND OUR STORE WERE A SINGLE UNIT. THE STORE WAS DOWNSTAIRS, AND UPSTAIRS WAS A KITCHEN, A WASHROOM, AND THREE SMALL ROOMS.
Kitchen
Bedroom
Washroom
Common Room
Bedroom
<NO NO NO!>*
<BUT YOU DON'T EVEN KNOW WHAT A SUPERHERO IS!>
THE POINT IS, THERE WAS NOWHERE TO HIDE FROM MOTHER.
*TRANSLATED FROM CANTONESE
<OF COURSE I KNOW WHAT A SUPERHERO IS! THEY'RE ALL OVER THE NEWSPAPERS!>
<THEN WHY DON'T YOU WANT TO BE ONE?>
<FIRST OF ALL, THAT COSTUME IS RIDICULOUS! WHAT KIND OF SUPERHERO SYMBOL IS THAT?!>
<IT'S THE CHARACTER FOR GOLD, HANK! GOLD IS A VERY, VERY GOOD SYMBOL! IT'S SHINY! IT'S PRETTY! IT'S WORTH A LOT OF MONEY!>

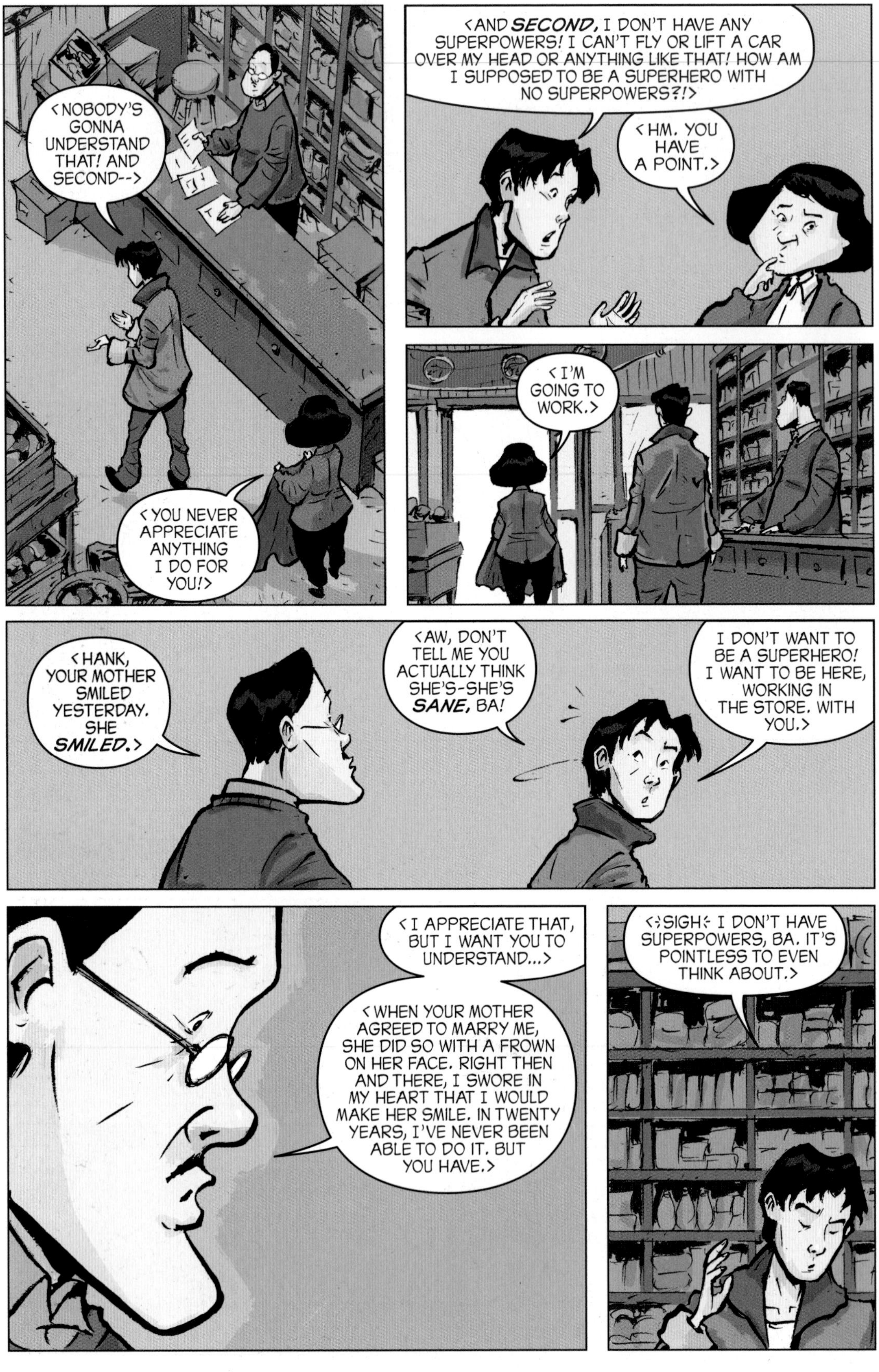
<NOBODY'S GONNA UNDERSTAND THAT! AND SECOND-->
<YOU NEVER APPRECIATE ANYTHING I DO FOR YOU!>
<AND SECOND, I DON'T HAVE ANY SUPERPOWERS! I CAN'T FLY OR LIFT A CAR OVER MY HEAD OR ANYTHING LIKE THAT! HOW AM I SUPPOSED TO BE A SUPERHERO WITH NO SUPERPOWERS?!>
<HM. YOU HAVE A POINT.>
<I'M GOING TO WORK.>
<HANK, YOUR MOTHER SMILED YESTERDAY. SHE SMILED.>
<AW, DON'T TELL ME YOU ACTUALLY THINK SHE'S-SHE'S SANE, BA!
I DON'T WANT TO BE A SUPERHERO! I WANT TO BE HERE, WORKING IN THE STORE. WITH YOU.>
<I APPRECIATE THAT, BUT I WANT YOU TO UNDERSTAND...>
<WHEN YOUR MOTHER AGREED TO MARRY ME, SHE DID SO WITH A FROWN ON HER FACE. RIGHT THEN AND THERE, I SWORE IN MY HEART THAT I WOULD MAKE HER SMILE. IN TWENTY YEARS, I'VE NEVER BEEN ABLE TO DO IT. BUT YOU HAVE.>
<:SIGH: I DON'T HAVE SUPERPOWERS, BA. IT'S POINTLESS TO EVEN THINK ABOUT.>

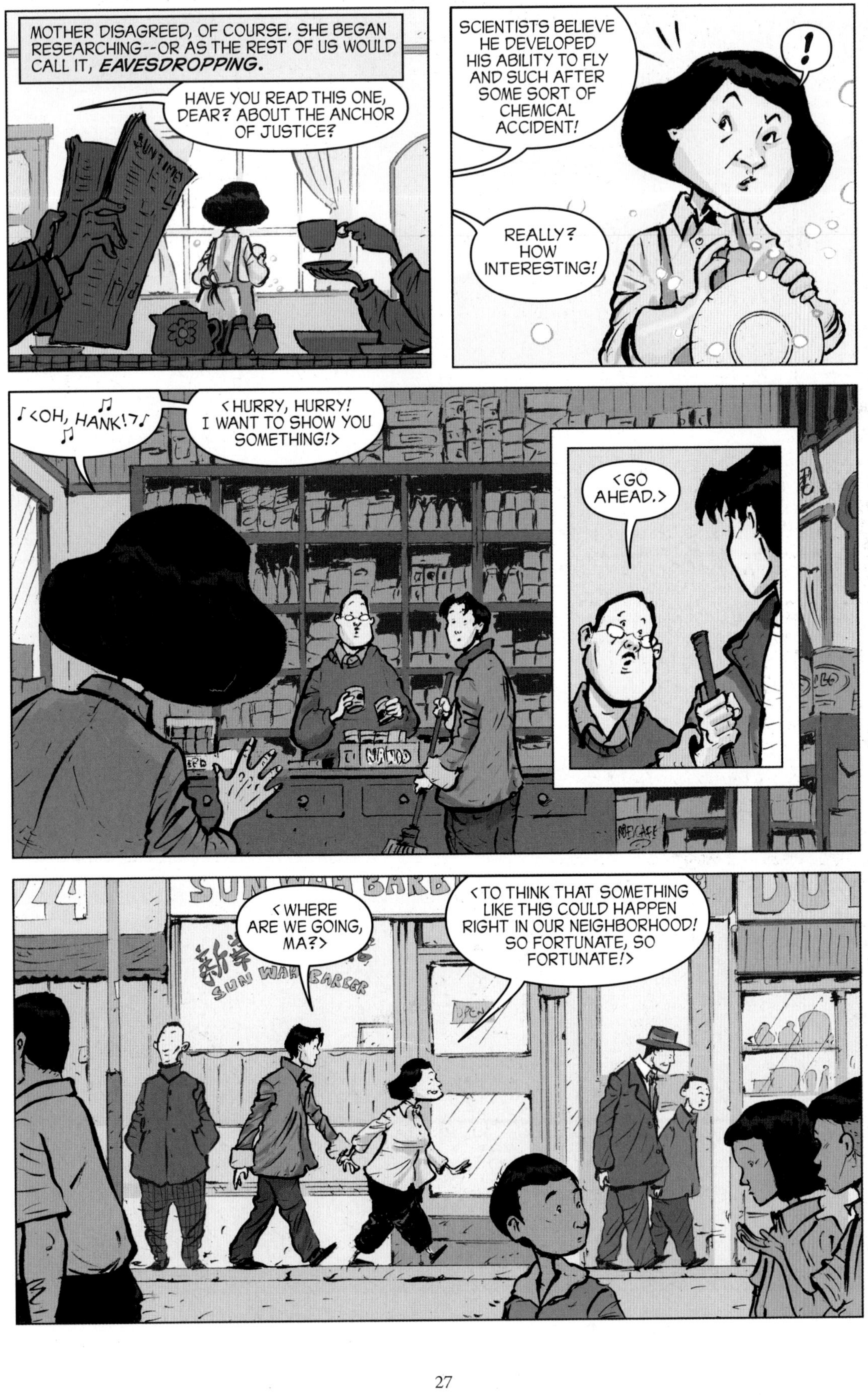
MOTHER DISAGREED, OF COURSE. SHE BEGAN RESEARCHING--OR AS THE REST OF US WOULD CALL IT, *EAVESDROPPING.*
HAVE YOU READ THIS ONE, DEAR? ABOUT THE ANCHOR OF JUSTICE?
SCIENTISTS BELIEVE HE DEVELOPED HIS ABILITY TO FLY AND SUCH AFTER SOME SORT OF CHEMICAL ACCIDENT!
!
REALLY? HOW INTERESTING!
♪ <OH, HANK!> ♪
<HURRY, HURRY! I WANT TO SHOW YOU SOMETHING!>
<GO AHEAD.>
<WHERE ARE WE GOING, MA?>
<TO THINK THAT SOMETHING LIKE THIS COULD HAPPEN RIGHT IN OUR NEIGHBORHOOD! SO FORTUNATE, SO FORTUNATE!>

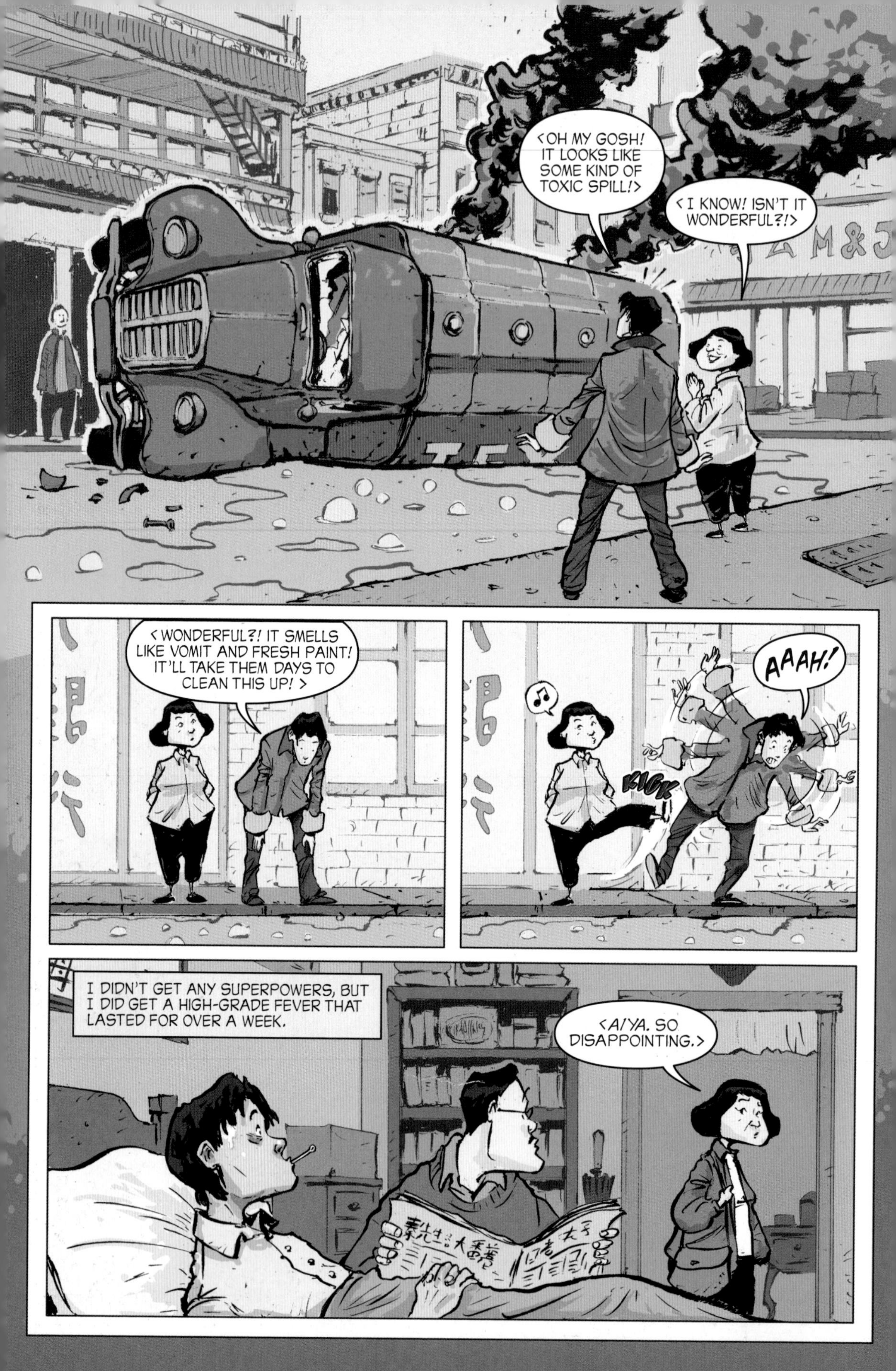
<OH MY GOSH! IT LOOKS LIKE SOME KIND OF TOXIC SPILL!>
<I KNOW! ISN'T IT WONDERFUL?!>
<WONDERFUL?! IT SMELLS LIKE VOMIT AND FRESH PAINT! IT'LL TAKE THEM DAYS TO CLEAN THIS UP!>
KICK
AAAH!
I DIDN'T GET ANY SUPERPOWERS, BUT I DID GET A HIGH-GRADE FEVER THAT LASTED FOR OVER A WEEK.
<AIYA. SO DISAPPOINTING.>

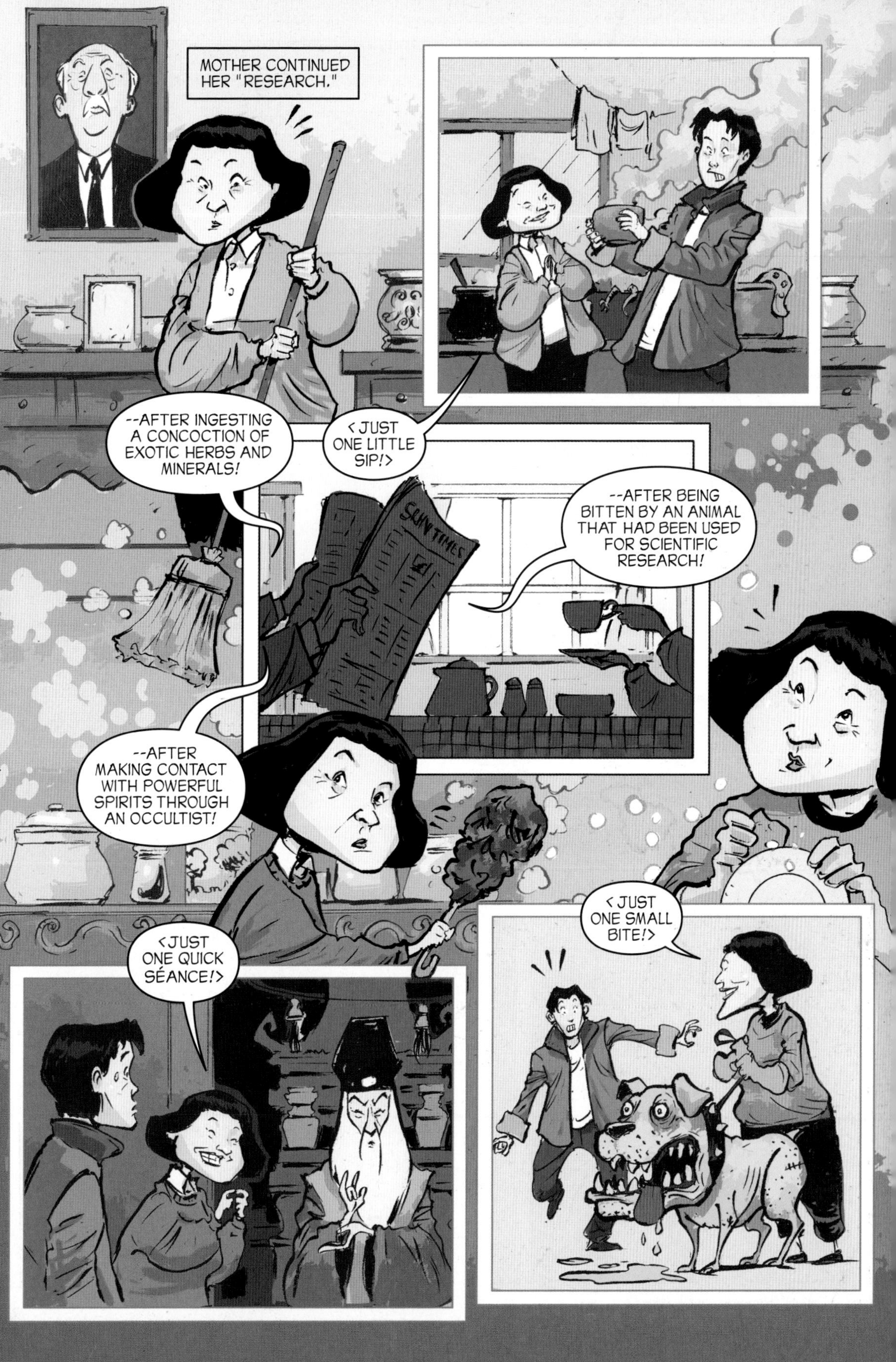

MOTHER CONTINUED HER "RESEARCH."
--AFTER INGESTING A CONCOCTION OF EXOTIC HERBS AND MINERALS!
<JUST ONE LITTLE SIP!>
--AFTER BEING BITTEN BY AN ANIMAL THAT HAD BEEN USED FOR SCIENTIFIC RESEARCH!
SUN-TIMES
--AFTER MAKING CONTACT WITH POWERFUL SPIRITS THROUGH AN OCCULTIST!
<JUST ONE QUICK SÉANCE!>
<JUST ONE SMALL BITE!>

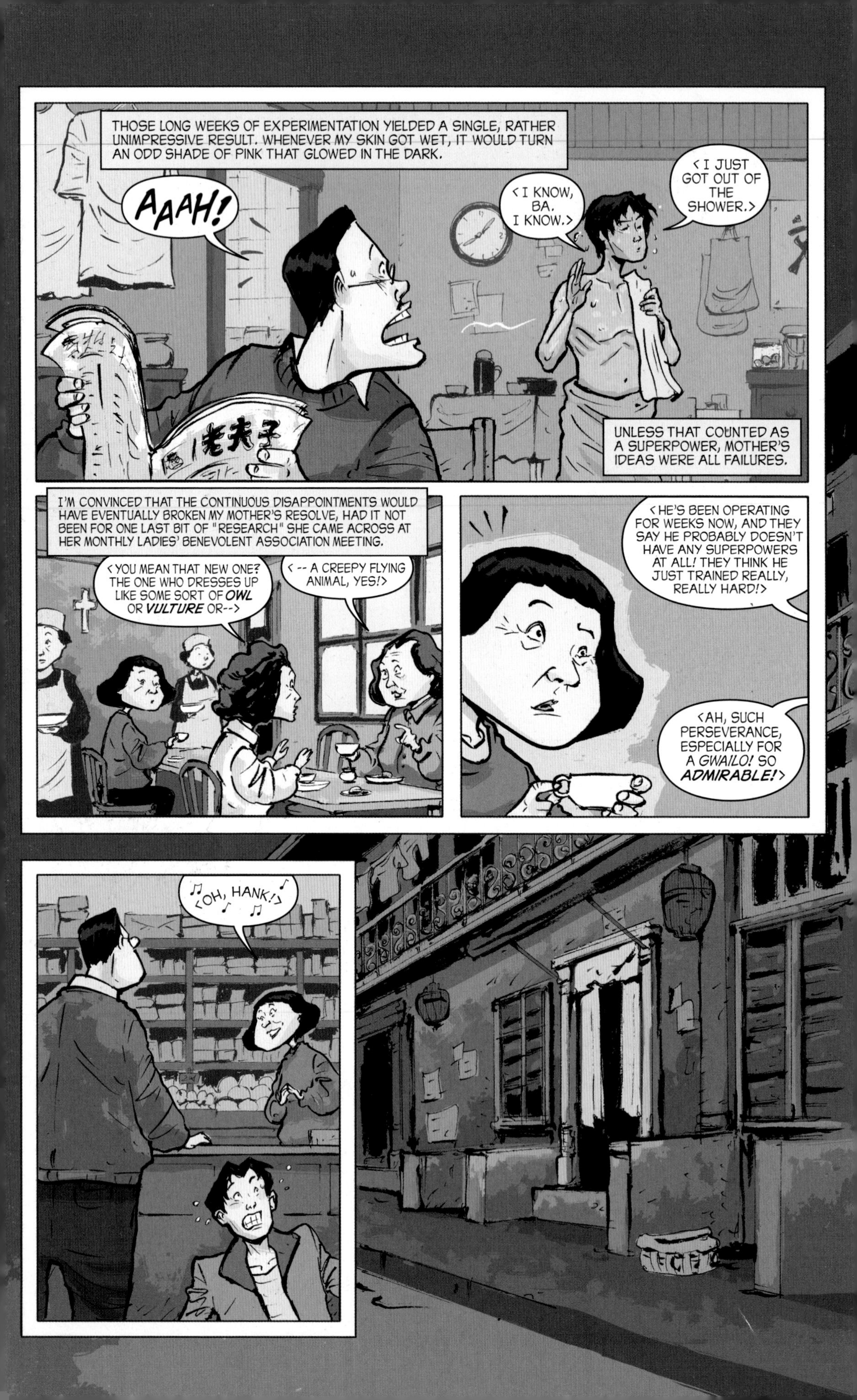
THOSE LONG WEEKS OF EXPERIMENTATION YIELDED A SINGLE, RATHER UNIMPRESSIVE RESULT. WHENEVER MY SKIN GOT WET, IT WOULD TURN AN ODD SHADE OF PINK THAT GLOWED IN THE DARK.
AAAH!
<I KNOW, BA. I KNOW.>
< I JUST GOT OUT OF THE SHOWER.>
老夫子
UNLESS THAT COUNTED AS A SUPERPOWER, MOTHER'S IDEAS WERE ALL FAILURES.
I'M CONVINCED THAT THE CONTINUOUS DISAPPOINTMENTS WOULD HAVE EVENTUALLY BROKEN MY MOTHER'S RESOLVE, HAD IT NOT BEEN FOR ONE LAST BIT OF "RESEARCH" SHE CAME ACROSS AT HER MONTHLY LADIES' BENEVOLENT ASSOCIATION MEETING.
<YOU MEAN THAT NEW ONE? THE ONE WHO DRESSES UP LIKE SOME SORT OF *OWL* OR ***VULTURE*** OR-->
< -- A CREEPY FLYING ANIMAL, YES!>
< HE'S BEEN OPERATING FOR WEEKS NOW, AND THEY SAY HE PROBABLY DOESN'T HAVE ANY SUPERPOWERS AT ALL! THEY THINK HE JUST TRAINED REALLY, REALLY HARD!>
<AH, SUCH PERSEVERANCE, ESPECIALLY FOR A *GWAILO!* SO ***ADMIRABLE!***>
<OH, HANK!>

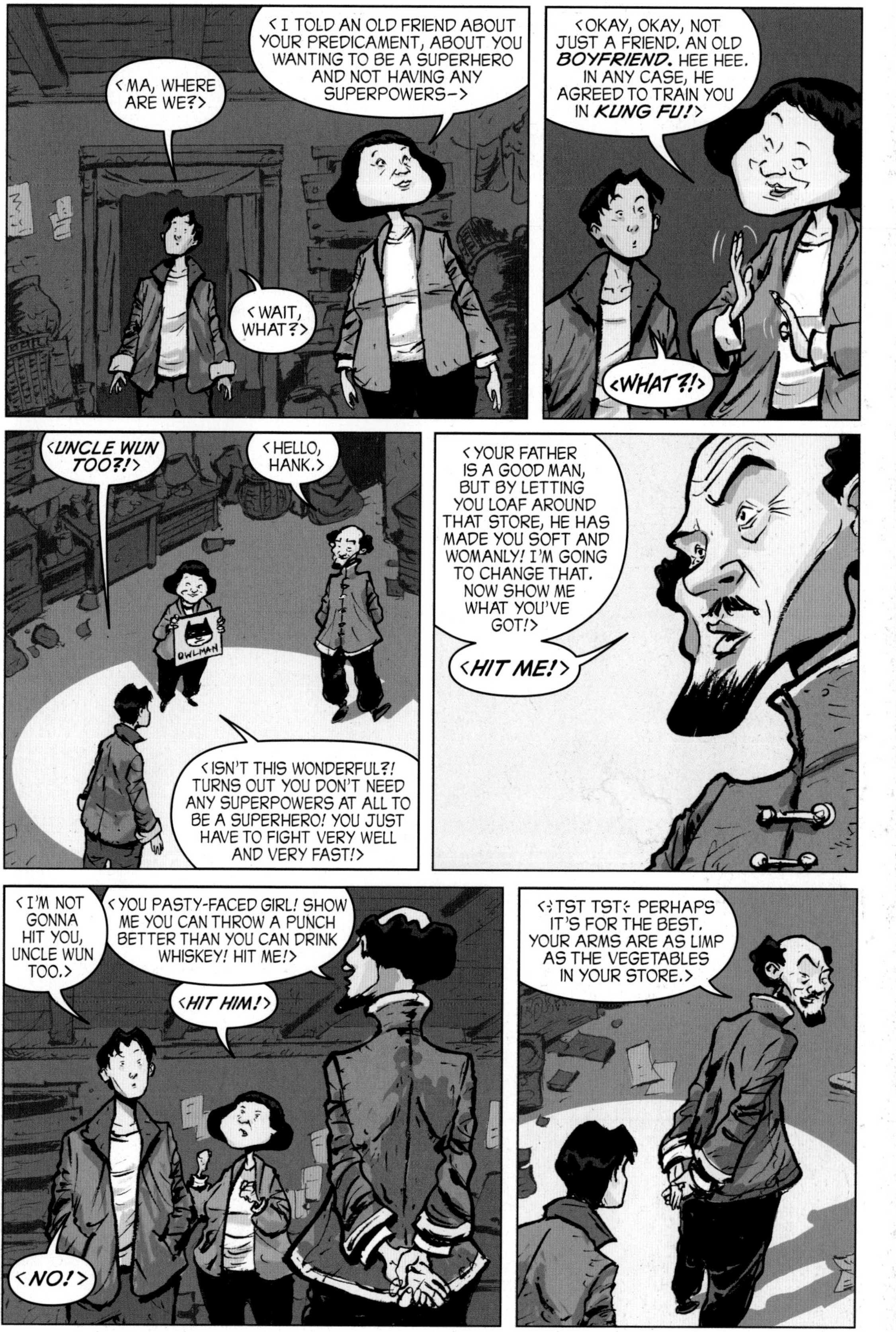
<MA, WHERE ARE WE?>
<I TOLD AN OLD FRIEND ABOUT YOUR PREDICAMENT, ABOUT YOU WANTING TO BE A SUPERHERO AND NOT HAVING ANY SUPERPOWERS–>
<WAIT, WHAT?>
<OKAY, OKAY, NOT JUST A FRIEND. AN OLD BOYFRIEND. HEE HEE. IN ANY CASE, HE AGREED TO TRAIN YOU IN KUNG FU!>
<WHAT?!>
<UNCLE WUN TOO?!>
<HELLO, HANK.>
OWLMAN
<ISN'T THIS WONDERFUL?! TURNS OUT YOU DON'T NEED ANY SUPERPOWERS AT ALL TO BE A SUPERHERO! YOU JUST HAVE TO FIGHT VERY WELL AND VERY FAST!>
<YOUR FATHER IS A GOOD MAN, BUT BY LETTING YOU LOAF AROUND THAT STORE, HE HAS MADE YOU SOFT AND WOMANLY! I'M GOING TO CHANGE THAT. NOW SHOW ME WHAT YOU'VE GOT!>
<HIT ME!>
<I'M NOT GONNA HIT YOU, UNCLE WUN TOO.>
<YOU PASTY-FACED GIRL! SHOW ME YOU CAN THROW A PUNCH BETTER THAN YOU CAN DRINK WHISKEY! HIT ME!>
<HIT HIM!>
<NO!>
<TST TST PERHAPS IT'S FOR THE BEST. YOUR ARMS ARE AS LIMP AS THE VEGETABLES IN YOUR STORE.>

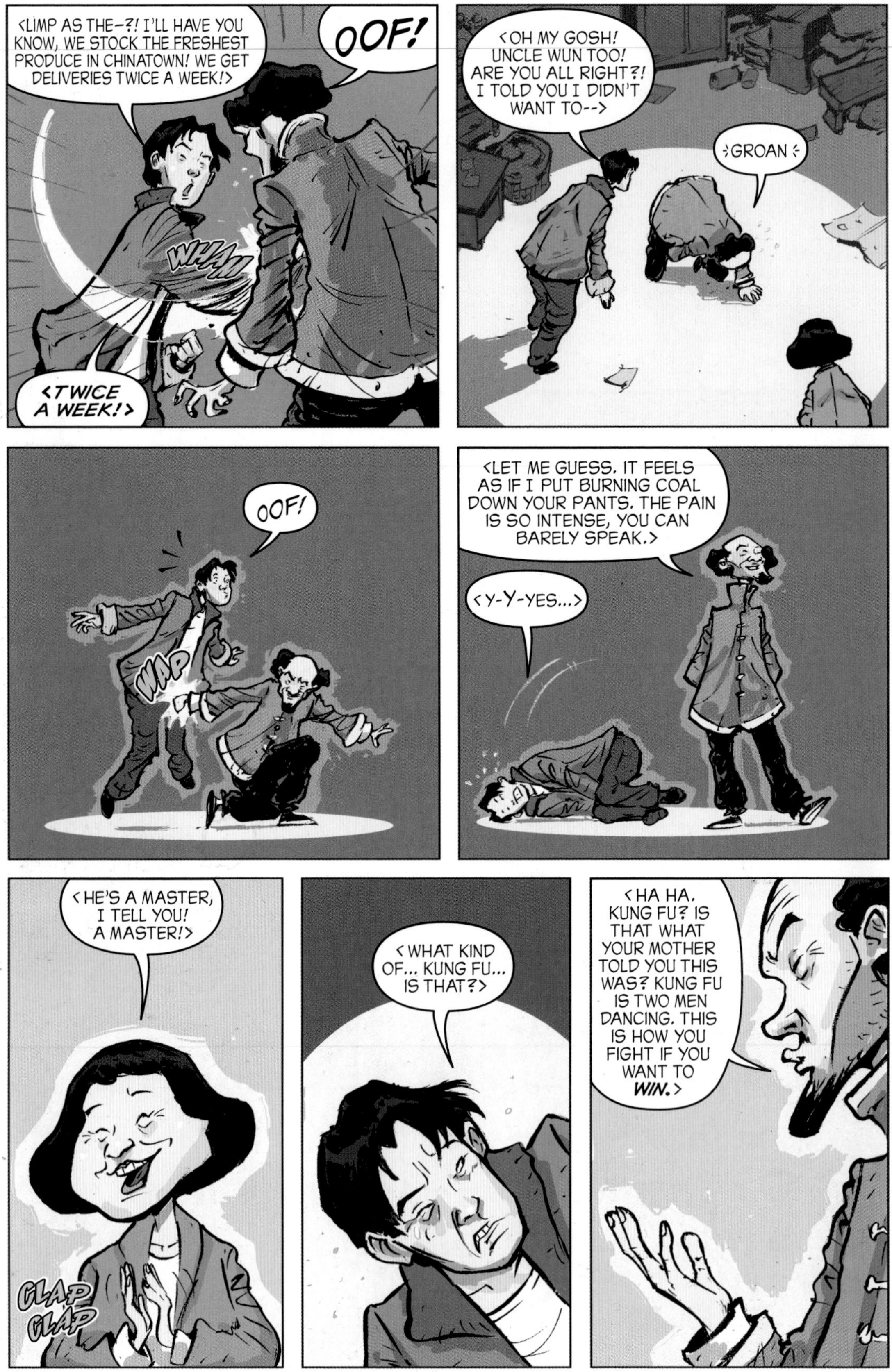

<LIMP AS THE-?! I'LL HAVE YOU KNOW, WE STOCK THE FRESHEST PRODUCE IN CHINATOWN! WE GET DELIVERIES TWICE A WEEK!>
OOF!
WHAM
<TWICE A WEEK!>
<OH MY GOSH! UNCLE WUN TOO! ARE YOU ALL RIGHT?! I TOLD YOU I DIDN'T WANT TO-->
GROAN
OOF!
WAP
<LET ME GUESS. IT FEELS AS IF I PUT BURNING COAL DOWN YOUR PANTS. THE PAIN IS SO INTENSE, YOU CAN BARELY SPEAK.>
<Y-Y-YES...>
<HE'S A MASTER, I TELL YOU! A MASTER!>
CLAP CLAP
<WHAT KIND OF... KUNG FU... IS THAT?>
<HA HA. KUNG FU? IS THAT WHAT YOUR MOTHER TOLD YOU THIS WAS? KUNG FU IS TWO MEN DANCING. THIS IS HOW YOU FIGHT IF YOU WANT TO WIN.>

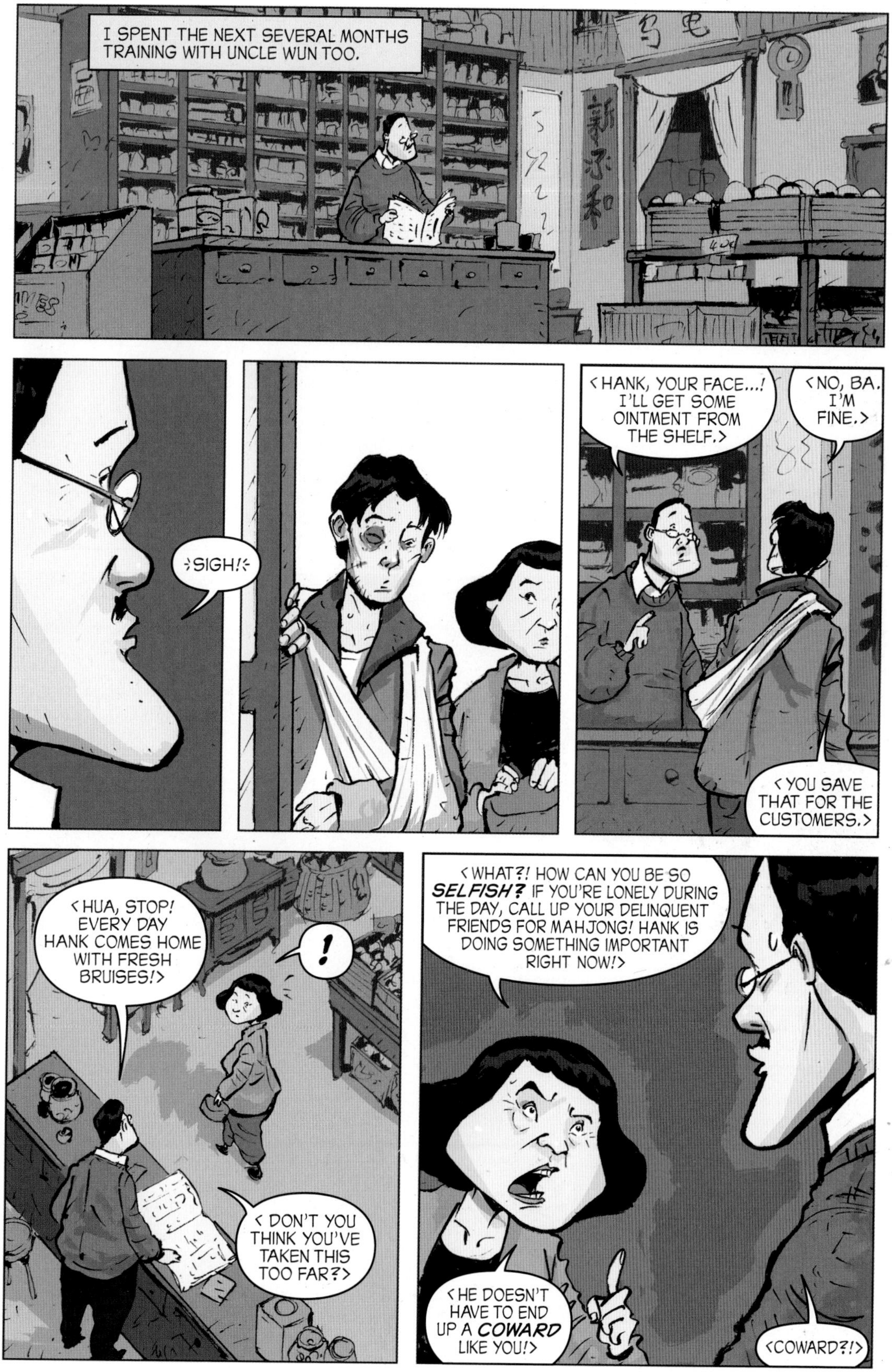
I SPENT THE NEXT SEVERAL MONTHS TRAINING WITH UNCLE WUN TOO.
SIGH!
<HANK, YOUR FACE...! I'LL GET SOME OINTMENT FROM THE SHELF.>
<NO, BA. I'M FINE.>
<YOU SAVE THAT FOR THE CUSTOMERS.>
<HUA, STOP! EVERY DAY HANK COMES HOME WITH FRESH BRUISES!>
!
<DON'T YOU THINK YOU'VE TAKEN THIS TOO FAR?>
<WHAT?! HOW CAN YOU BE SO SELFISH? IF YOU'RE LONELY DURING THE DAY, CALL UP YOUR DELINQUENT FRIENDS FOR MAHJONG! HANK IS DOING SOMETHING IMPORTANT RIGHT NOW!>
<HE DOESN'T HAVE TO END UP A COWARD LIKE YOU!>
<COWARD?!>

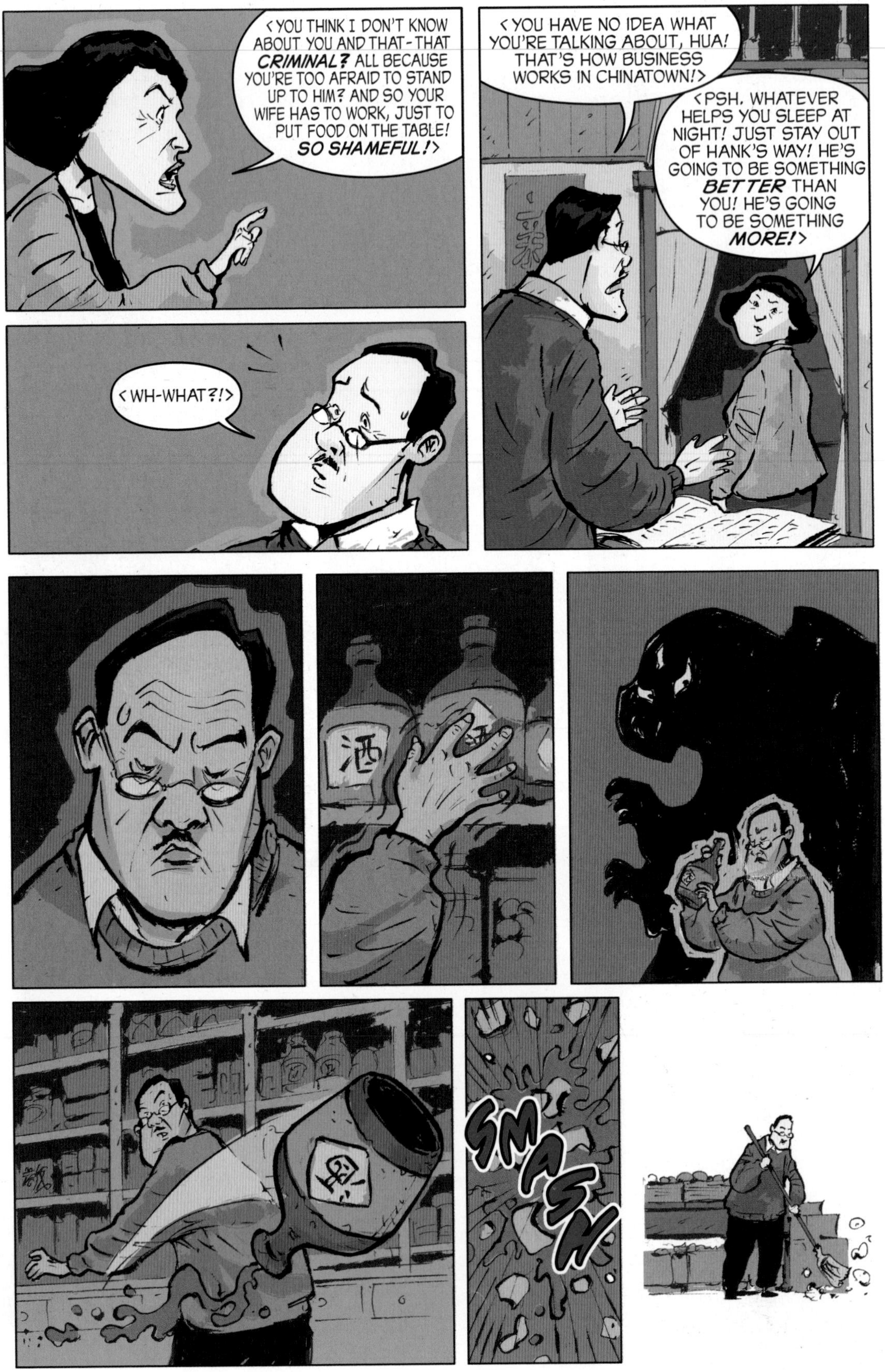
<YOU THINK I DON'T KNOW ABOUT YOU AND THAT-THAT CRIMINAL? ALL BECAUSE YOU'RE TOO AFRAID TO STAND UP TO HIM? AND SO YOUR WIFE HAS TO WORK, JUST TO PUT FOOD ON THE TABLE! SO SHAMEFUL!>
<YOU HAVE NO IDEA WHAT YOU'RE TALKING ABOUT, HUA! THAT'S HOW BUSINESS WORKS IN CHINATOWN!>
<PSH. WHATEVER HELPS YOU SLEEP AT NIGHT! JUST STAY OUT OF HANK'S WAY! HE'S GOING TO BE SOMETHING BETTER THAN YOU! HE'S GOING TO BE SOMETHING MORE!>
<WH-WHAT?!>
酒
SMASH

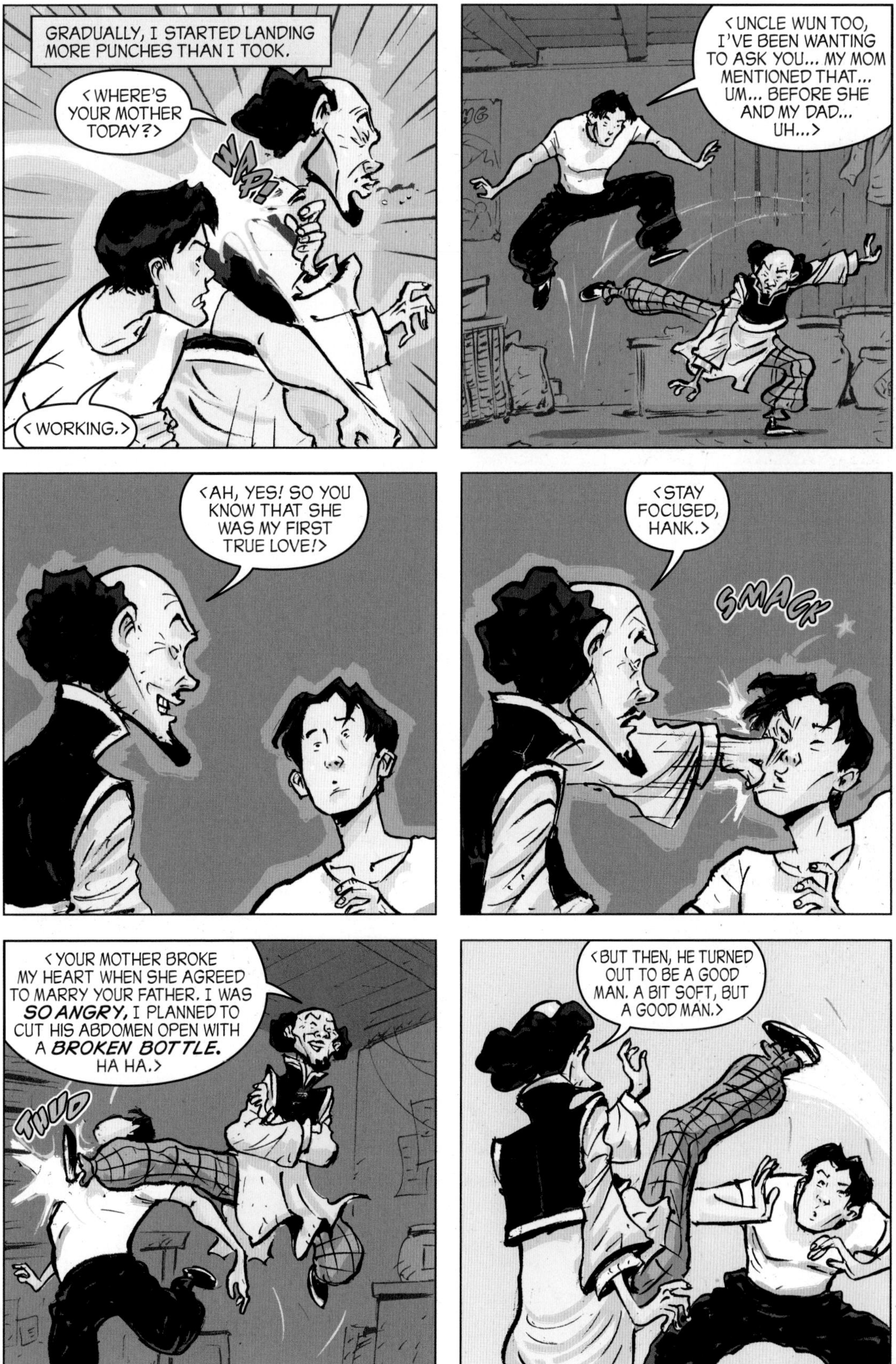
GRADUALLY, I STARTED LANDING MORE PUNCHES THAN I TOOK.
<WHERE'S YOUR MOTHER TODAY?>
WAP!
<WORKING.>
<UNCLE WUN TOO, I'VE BEEN WANTING TO ASK YOU... MY MOM MENTIONED THAT... UM... BEFORE SHE AND MY DAD... UH...>
<AH, YES! SO YOU KNOW THAT SHE WAS MY FIRST TRUE LOVE!>
<STAY FOCUSED, HANK.>
SMACK
<YOUR MOTHER BROKE MY HEART WHEN SHE AGREED TO MARRY YOUR FATHER. I WAS SO ANGRY, I PLANNED TO CUT HIS ABDOMEN OPEN WITH A BROKEN BOTTLE. HA HA.>
THUD
<BUT THEN, HE TURNED OUT TO BE A GOOD MAN. A BIT SOFT, BUT A GOOD MAN.>

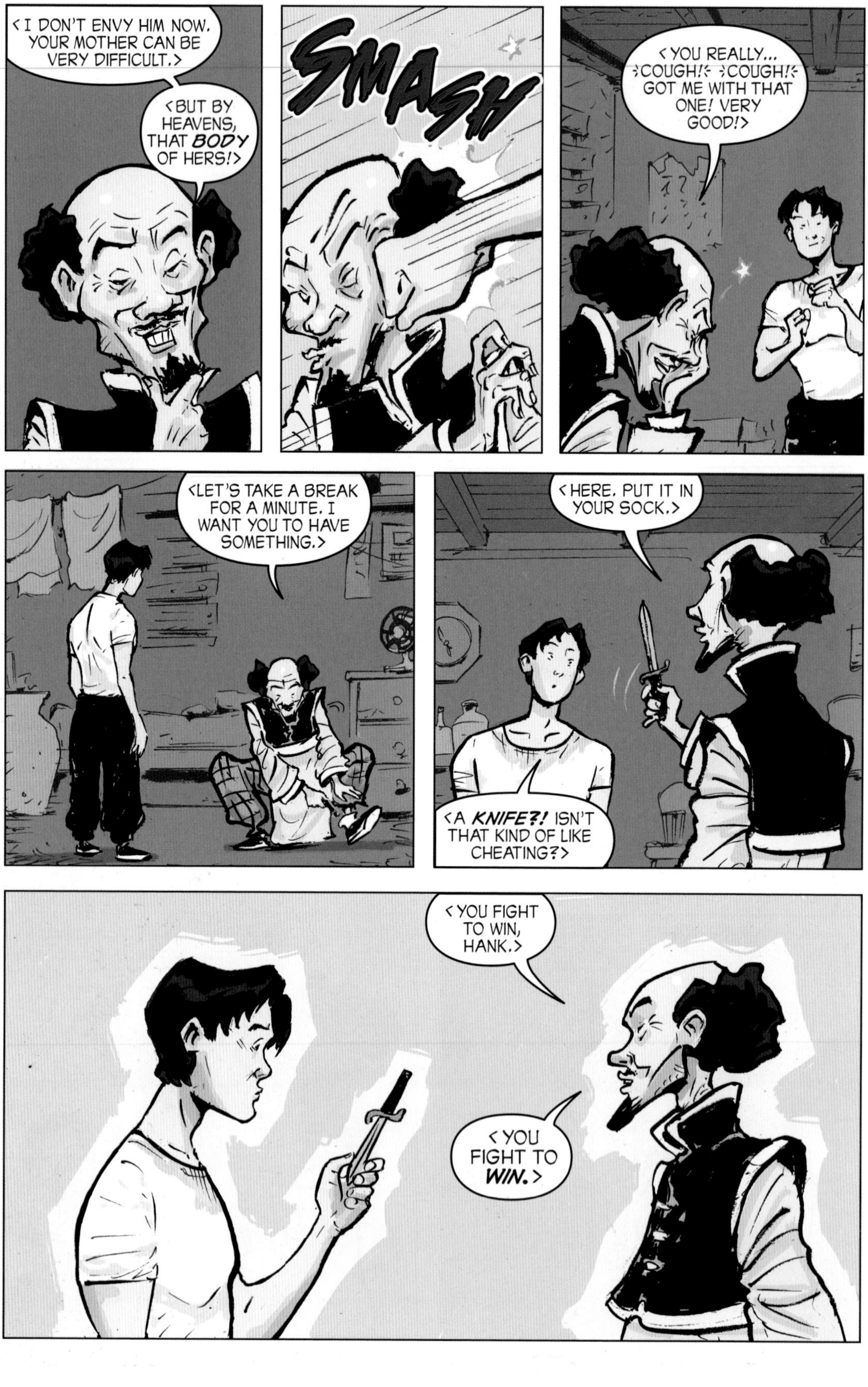

<I DON'T ENVY HIM NOW. YOUR MOTHER CAN BE VERY DIFFICULT.>
<BUT BY HEAVENS, THAT *BODY* OF HERS!>
SMASH
<YOU REALLY... COUGH! COUGH! GOT ME WITH THAT ONE! VERY GOOD!>
<LET'S TAKE A BREAK FOR A MINUTE. I WANT YOU TO HAVE SOMETHING.>
<HERE. PUT IT IN YOUR SOCK.>
<A *KNIFE?!* ISN'T THAT KIND OF LIKE CHEATING?>
<YOU FIGHT TO WIN, HANK.>
<YOU FIGHT TO *WIN.*>

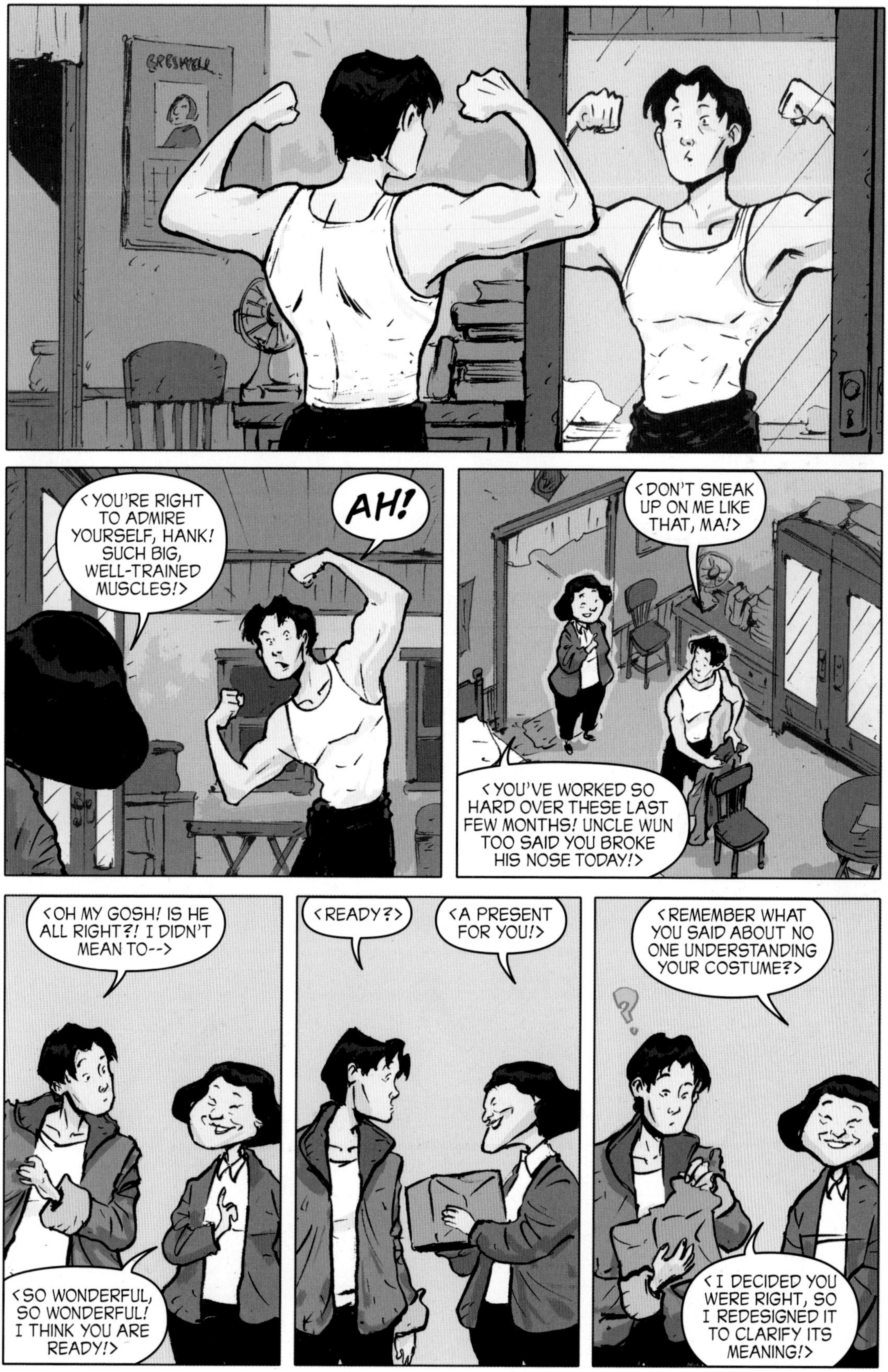

BRESWELL
<YOU'RE RIGHT TO ADMIRE YOURSELF, HANK! SUCH BIG, WELL-TRAINED MUSCLES!>
AH!
<DON'T SNEAK UP ON ME LIKE THAT, MA!>
<YOU'VE WORKED SO HARD OVER THESE LAST FEW MONTHS! UNCLE WUN TOO SAID YOU BROKE HIS NOSE TODAY!>
<OH MY GOSH! IS HE ALL RIGHT?! I DIDN'T MEAN TO-->
<SO WONDERFUL, SO WONDERFUL! I THINK YOU ARE READY!>
<READY?>
<A PRESENT FOR YOU!>
<REMEMBER WHAT YOU SAID ABOUT NO ONE UNDERSTANDING YOUR COSTUME?>
?
<I DECIDED YOU WERE RIGHT, SO I REDESIGNED IT TO CLARIFY ITS MEANING!>

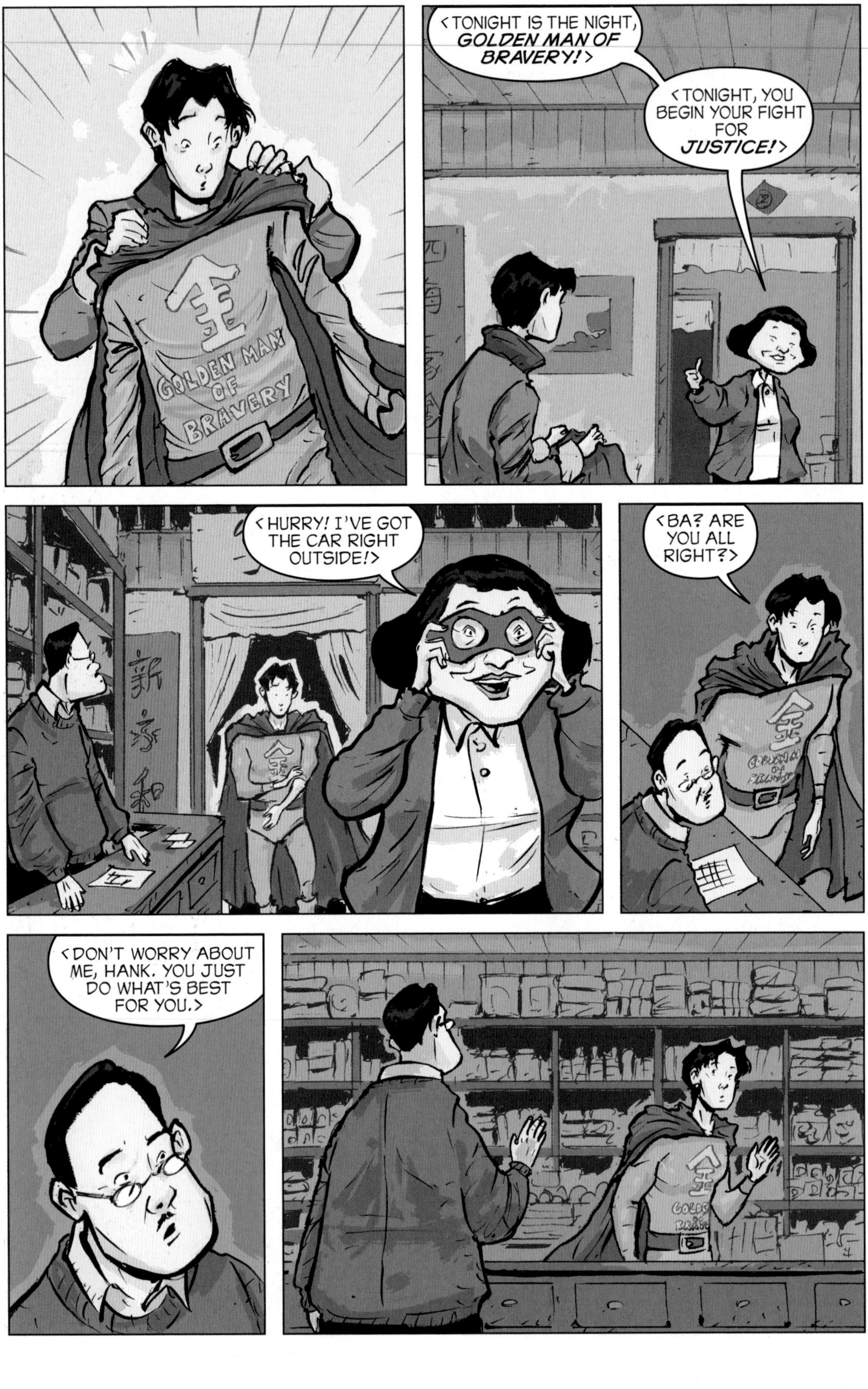
GOLDEN MAN OF BRAVERY
<TONIGHT IS THE NIGHT, GOLDEN MAN OF BRAVERY!>
<TONIGHT, YOU BEGIN YOUR FIGHT FOR JUSTICE!>
<HURRY! I'VE GOT THE CAR RIGHT OUTSIDE!>
<BA? ARE YOU ALL RIGHT?>
<DON'T WORRY ABOUT ME, HANK. YOU JUST DO WHAT'S BEST FOR YOU.>

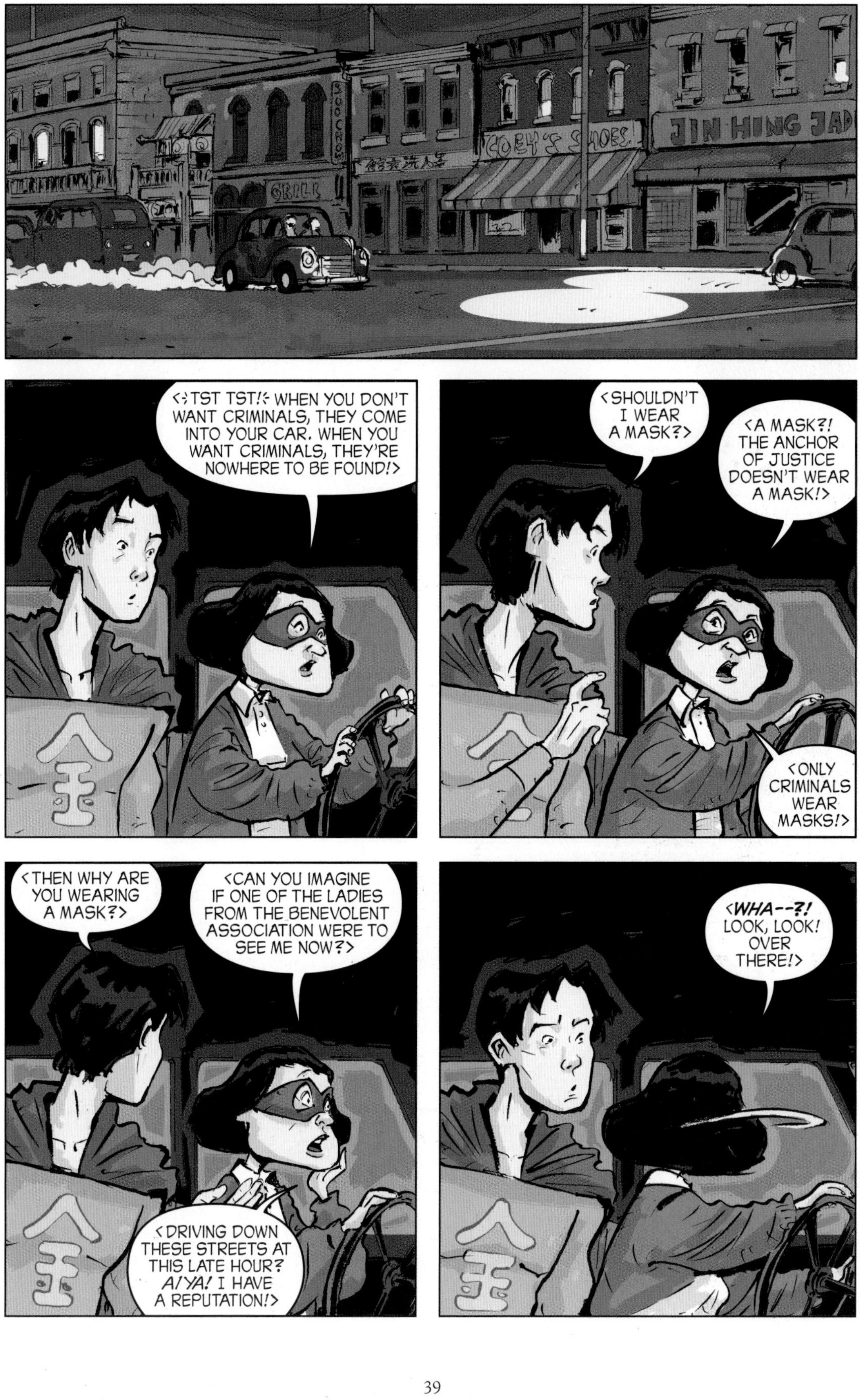
SOO CHOW
GRILL
JIN HING JAD
<TST TST! WHEN YOU DON'T WANT CRIMINALS, THEY COME INTO YOUR CAR. WHEN YOU WANT CRIMINALS, THEY'RE NOWHERE TO BE FOUND!>
<SHOULDN'T I WEAR A MASK?>
<A MASK?! THE ANCHOR OF JUSTICE DOESN'T WEAR A MASK!>
<ONLY CRIMINALS WEAR MASKS!>
<THEN WHY ARE YOU WEARING A MASK?>
<CAN YOU IMAGINE IF ONE OF THE LADIES FROM THE BENEVOLENT ASSOCIATION WERE TO SEE ME NOW?>
<DRIVING DOWN THESE STREETS AT THIS LATE HOUR? AIYA! I HAVE A REPUTATION!>
<WHA--?! LOOK, LOOK! OVER THERE!>

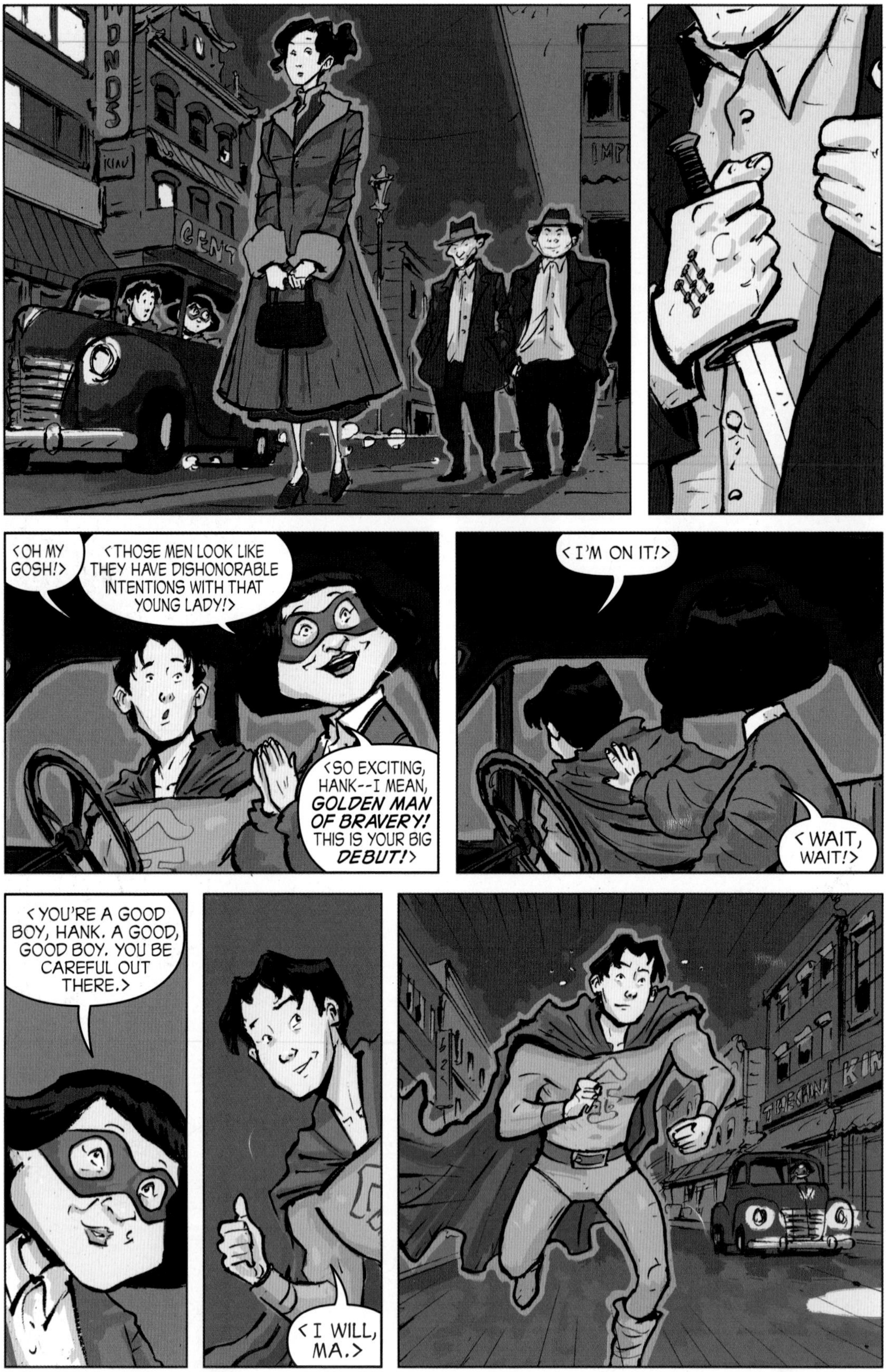
IMP
GENT
<OH MY GOSH!>
<THOSE MEN LOOK LIKE THEY HAVE DISHONORABLE INTENTIONS WITH THAT YOUNG LADY!>
<SO EXCITING, HANK--I MEAN, ***GOLDEN MAN OF BRAVERY!*** THIS IS YOUR BIG ***DEBUT!***>
<I'M ON IT!>
<WAIT, WAIT!>
<YOU'RE A GOOD BOY, HANK. A GOOD, GOOD BOY. YOU BE CAREFUL OUT THERE.>
<I WILL, MA.>

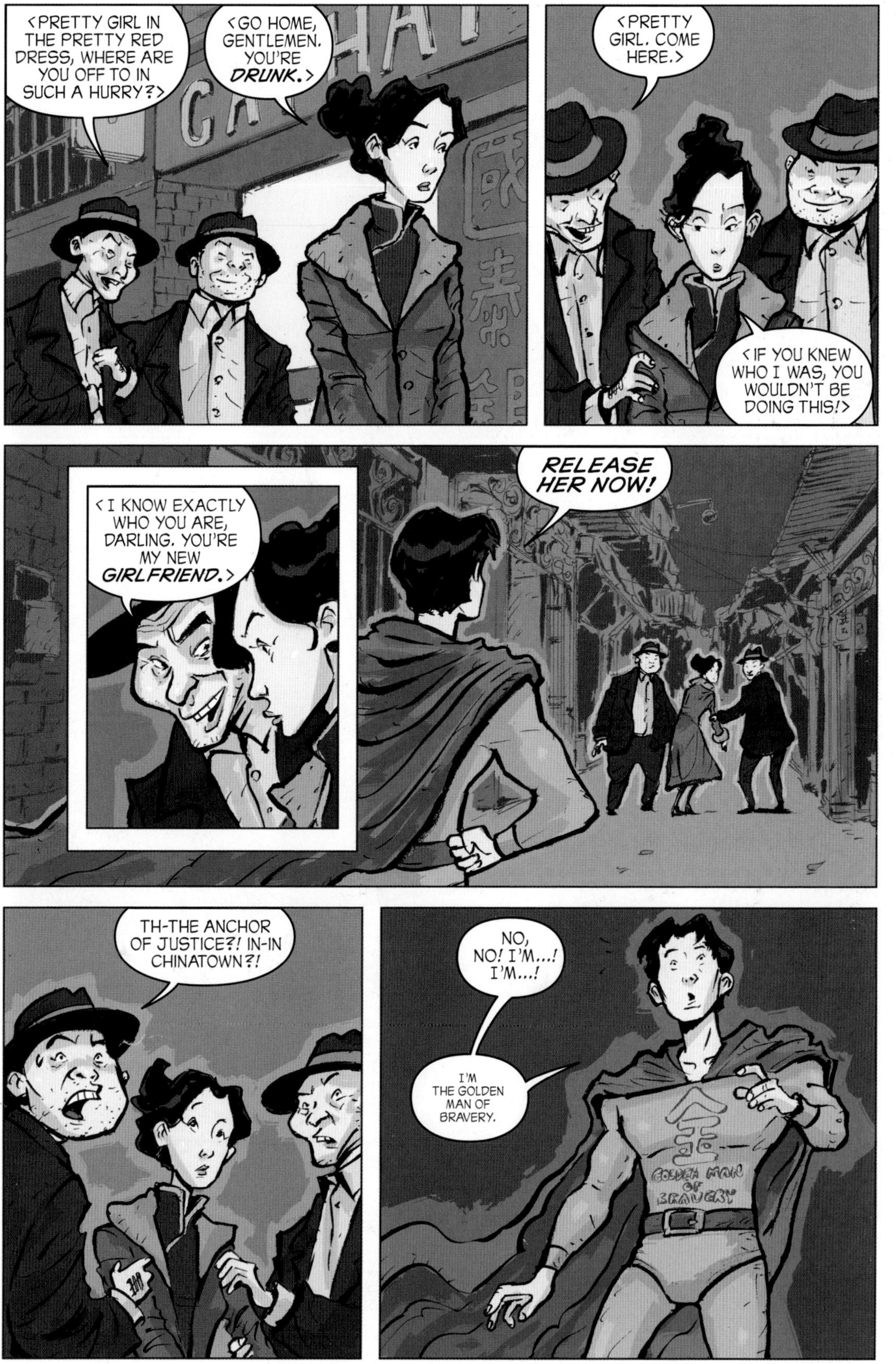

<PRETTY GIRL IN THE PRETTY RED DRESS, WHERE ARE YOU OFF TO IN SUCH A HURRY?>
<GO HOME, GENTLEMEN. YOU'RE *DRUNK*.>
<PRETTY GIRL. COME HERE.>
<IF YOU KNEW WHO I WAS, YOU WOULDN'T BE DOING THIS!>
<I KNOW EXACTLY WHO YOU ARE, DARLING. YOU'RE MY NEW *GIRLFRIEND*.>
RELEASE HER NOW!
TH-THE ANCHOR OF JUSTICE?! IN-IN CHINATOWN?!
NO, NO! I'M...! I'M...!
I'M THE GOLDEN MAN OF BRAVERY.

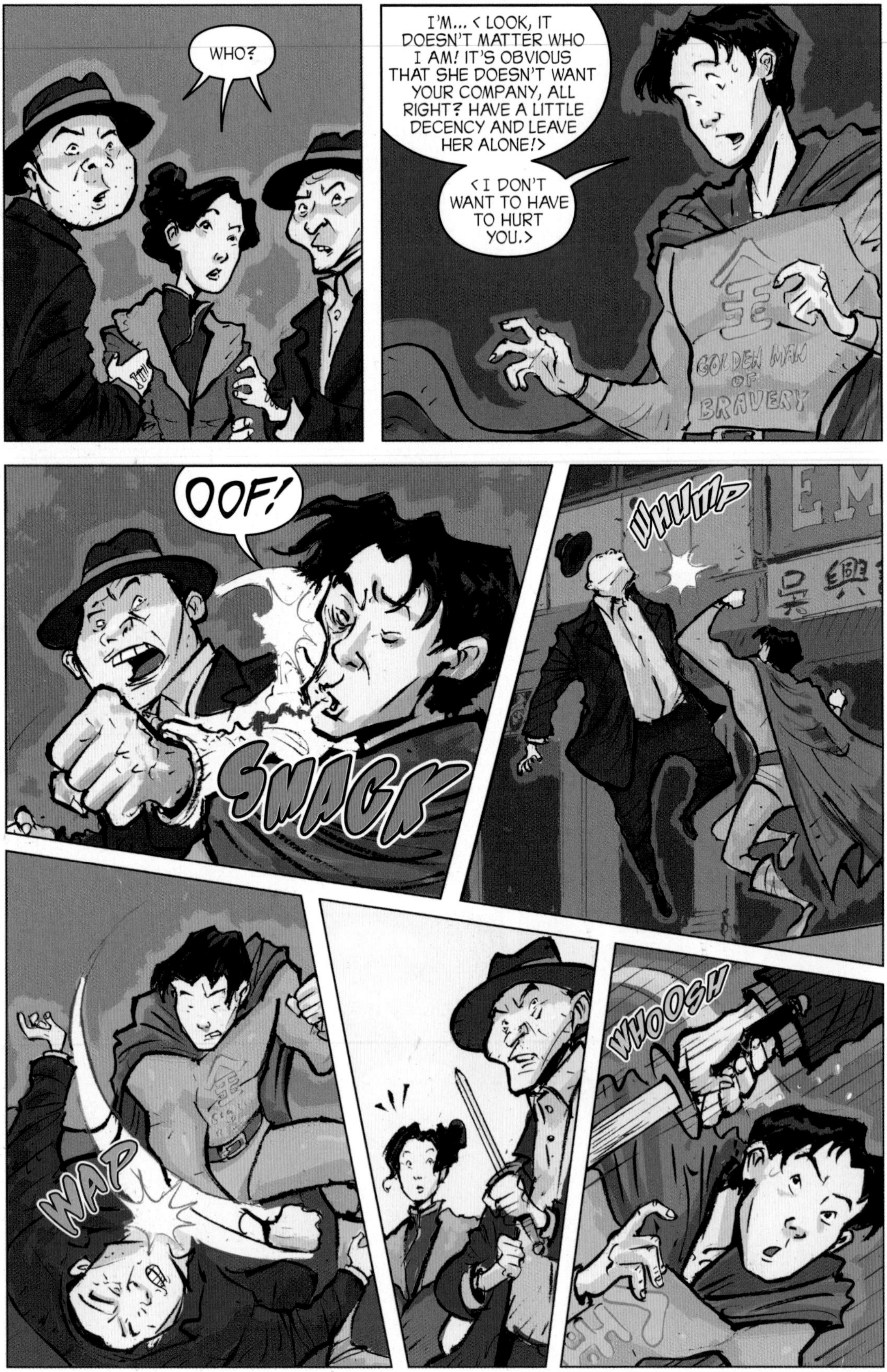
WHO?
I'M... < LOOK, IT DOESN'T MATTER WHO I AM! IT'S OBVIOUS THAT SHE DOESN'T WANT YOUR COMPANY, ALL RIGHT? HAVE A LITTLE DECENCY AND LEAVE HER ALONE!>
<I DON'T WANT TO HAVE TO HURT YOU.>
GOLDEN MAN OF BRAVERY
OOF!
SMACK
WHUMP
WAP
WHOOSH

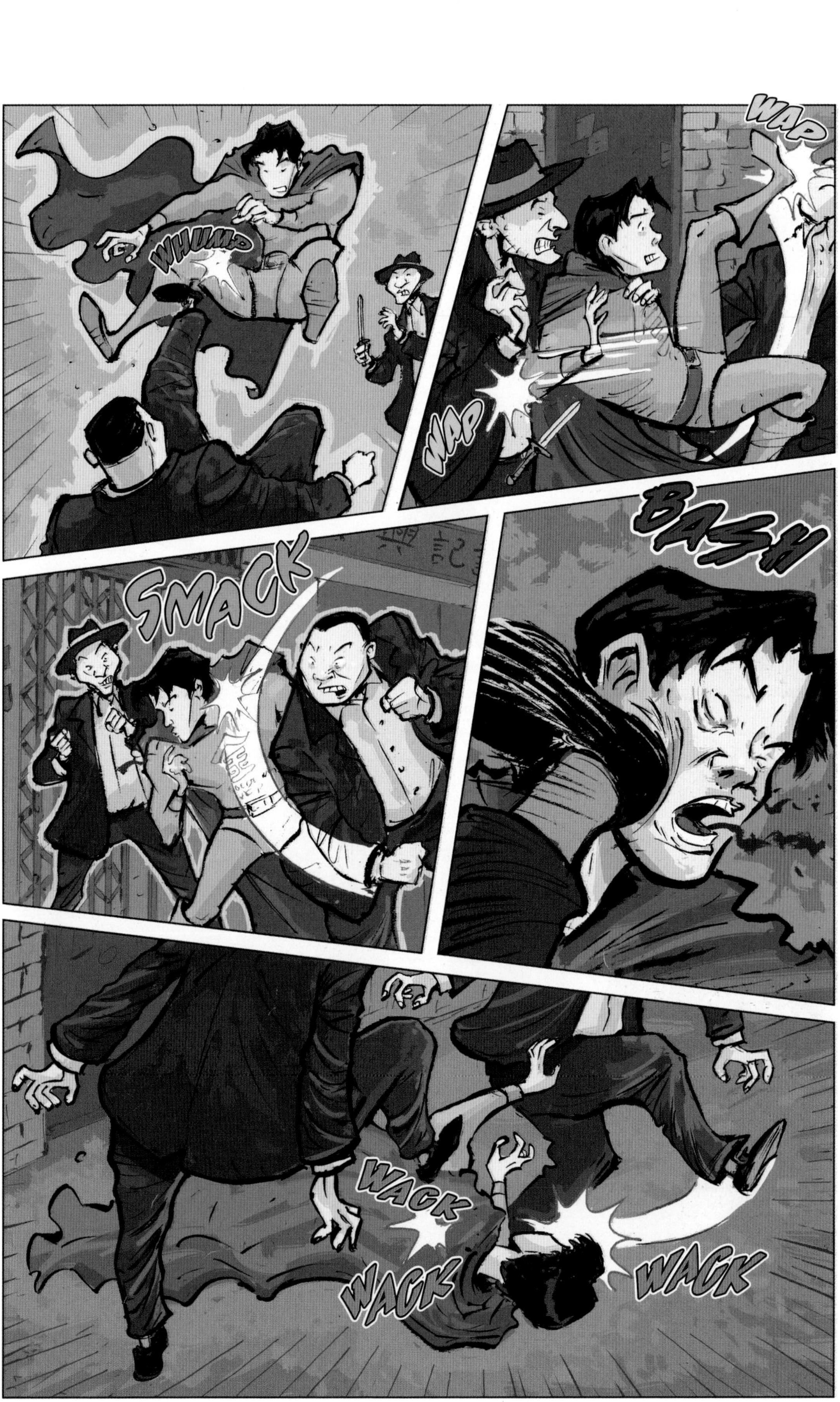
WHUMP
WAP
WAP
SMACK
BASH
WACK
WACK
WACK

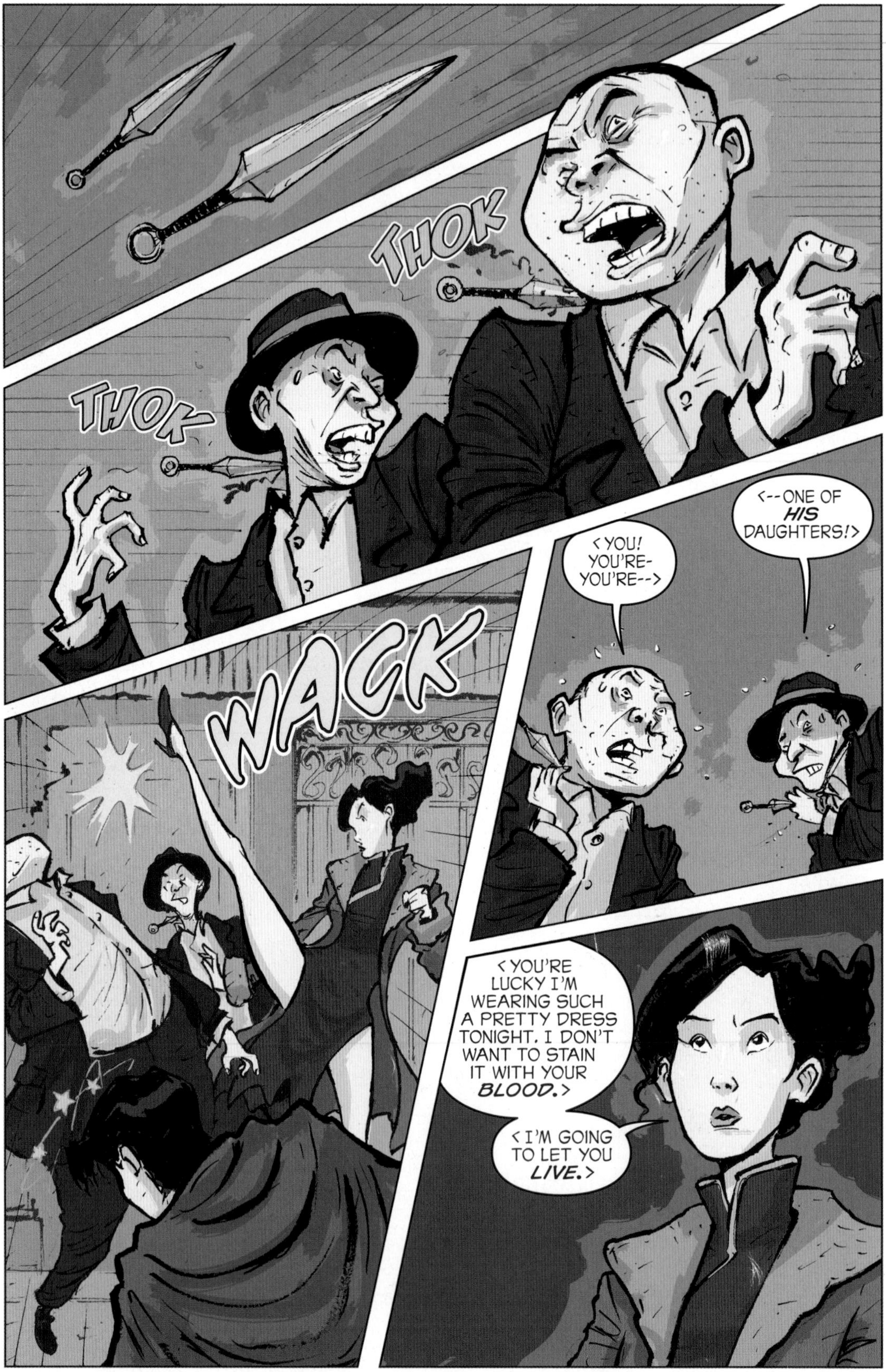
THOK
THOK
WACK
<YOU! YOU'RE- YOU'RE-->
<--ONE OF HIS DAUGHTERS!>
<YOU'RE LUCKY I'M WEARING SUCH A PRETTY DRESS TONIGHT. I DON'T WANT TO STAIN IT WITH YOUR BLOOD.>
<I'M GOING TO LET YOU LIVE.>

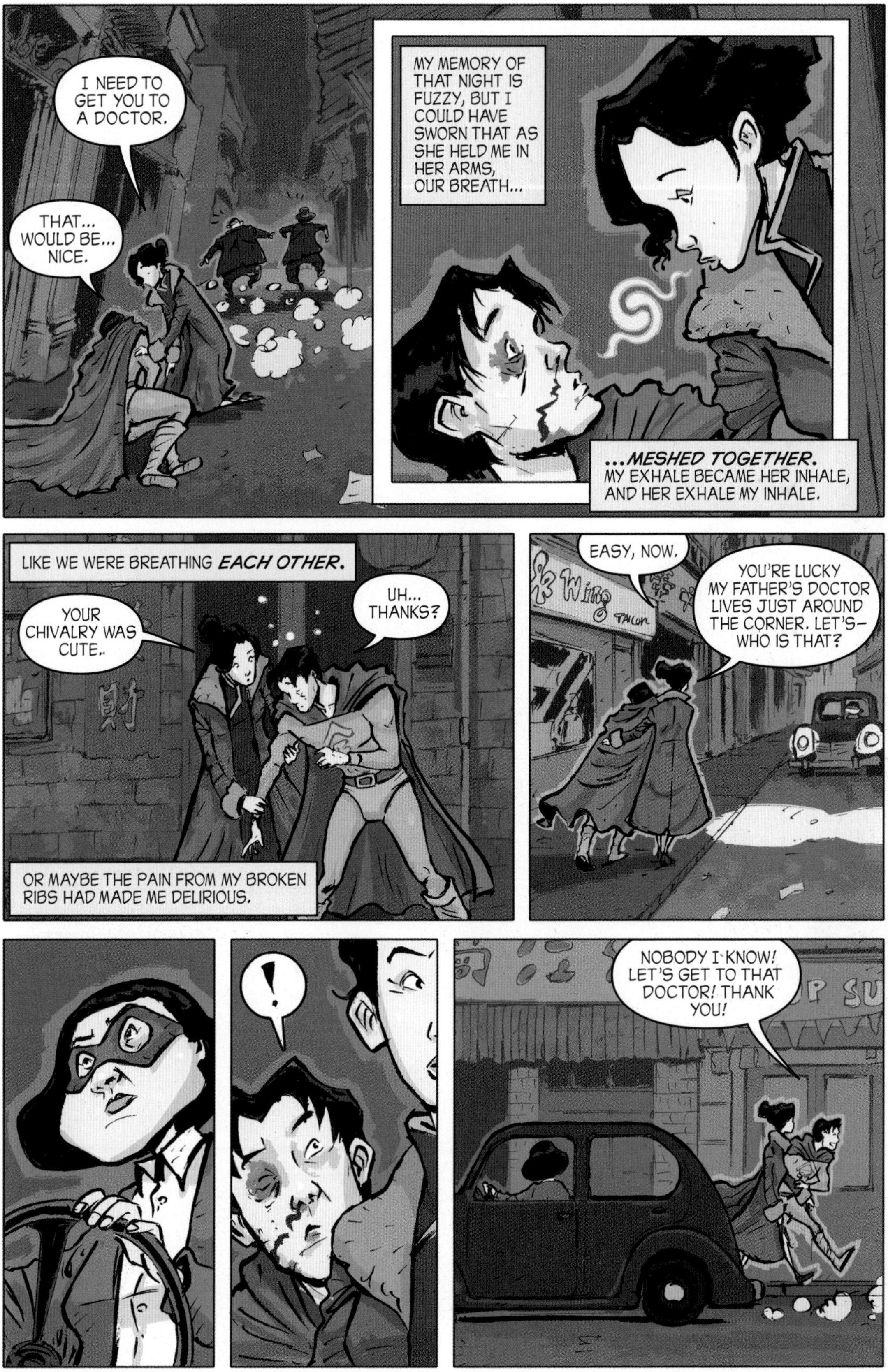
I NEED TO GET YOU TO A DOCTOR.
THAT... WOULD BE... NICE.
MY MEMORY OF THAT NIGHT IS FUZZY, BUT I COULD HAVE SWORN THAT AS SHE HELD ME IN HER ARMS, OUR BREATH...
...MESHED TOGETHER. MY EXHALE BECAME HER INHALE, AND HER EXHALE MY INHALE.
LIKE WE WERE BREATHING EACH OTHER.
YOUR CHIVALRY WAS CUTE..
UH... THANKS?
OR MAYBE THE PAIN FROM MY BROKEN RIBS HAD MADE ME DELIRIOUS.
EASY, NOW.
YOU'RE LUCKY MY FATHER'S DOCTOR LIVES JUST AROUND THE CORNER. LET'S— WHO IS THAT?
!
NOBODY I KNOW! LET'S GET TO THAT DOCTOR! THANK YOU!

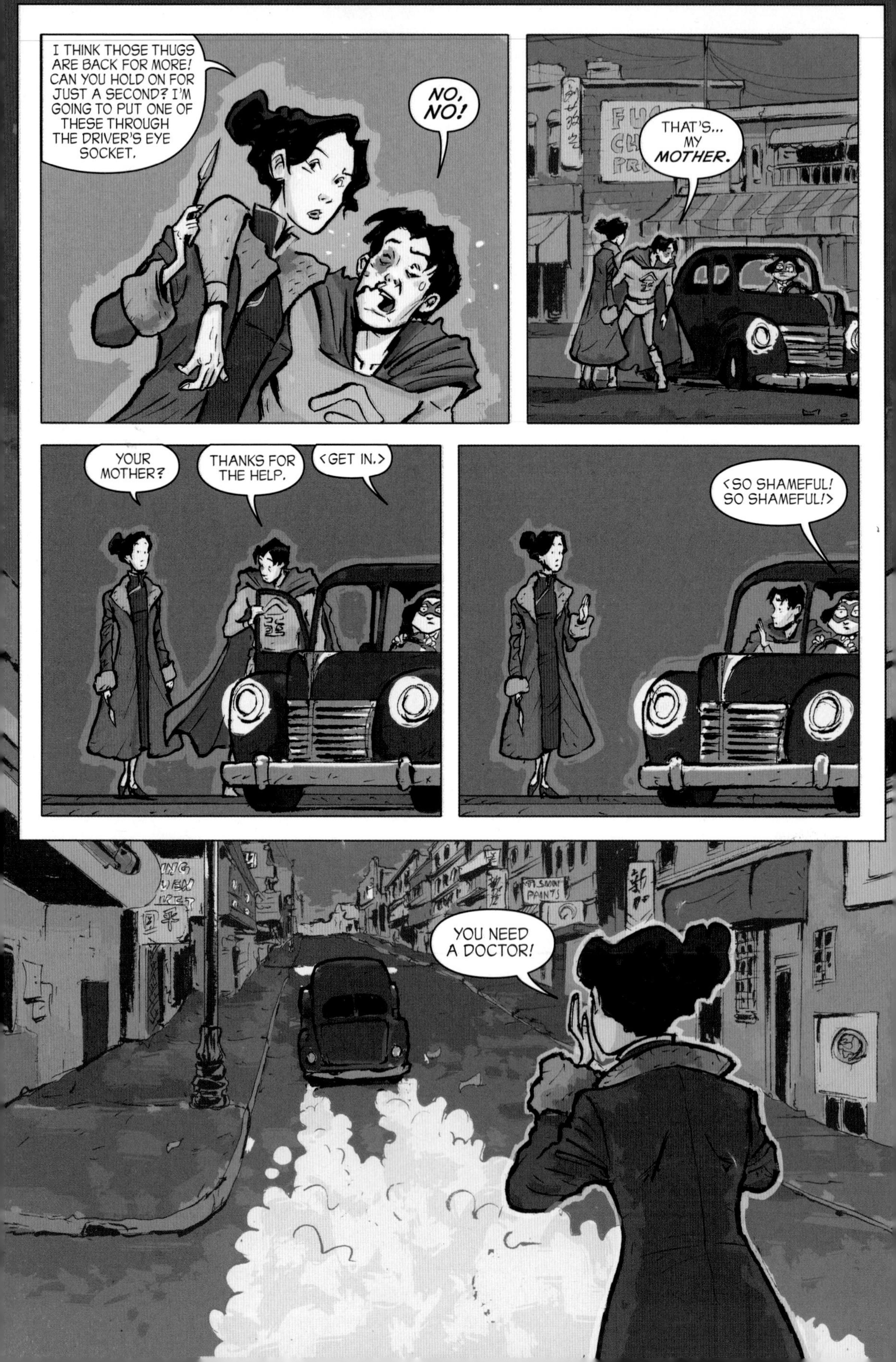
I THINK THOSE THUGS ARE BACK FOR MORE! CAN YOU HOLD ON FOR JUST A SECOND? I'M GOING TO PUT ONE OF THESE THROUGH THE DRIVER'S EYE SOCKET.
NO, NO!
THAT'S... MY MOTHER.
YOUR MOTHER?
THANKS FOR THE HELP.
<GET IN.>
<SO SHAMEFUL! SO SHAMEFUL!>
YOU NEED A DOCTOR!

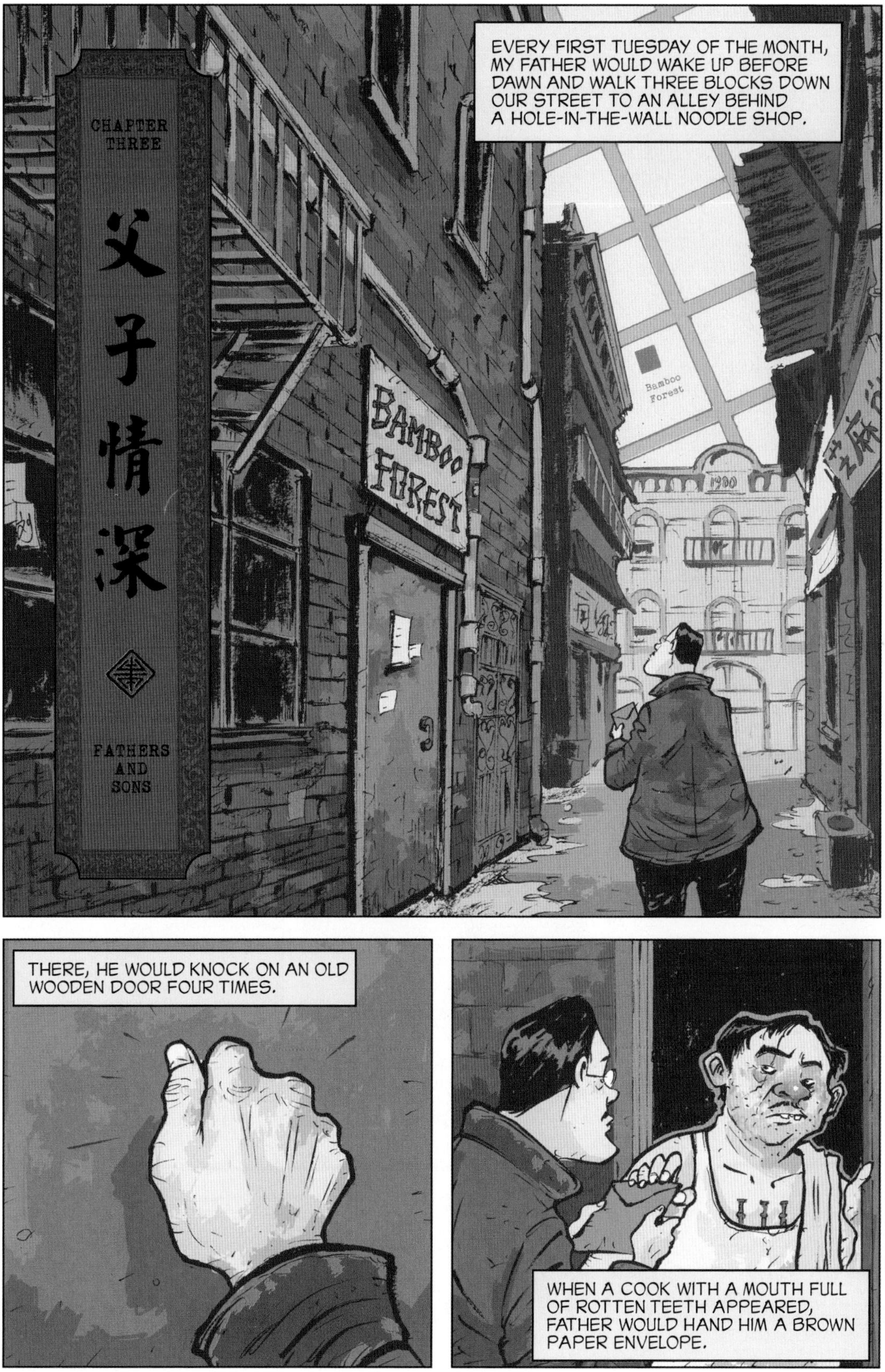
CHAPTER THREE
父子情深
FATHERS AND SONS
EVERY FIRST TUESDAY OF THE MONTH, MY FATHER WOULD WAKE UP BEFORE DAWN AND WALK THREE BLOCKS DOWN OUR STREET TO AN ALLEY BEHIND A HOLE-IN-THE-WALL NOODLE SHOP.
BAMBOO FOREST
Bamboo Forest
1900
THERE, HE WOULD KNOCK ON AN OLD WOODEN DOOR FOUR TIMES.
WHEN A COOK WITH A MOUTH FULL OF ROTTEN TEETH APPEARED, FATHER WOULD HAND HIM A BROWN PAPER ENVELOPE.

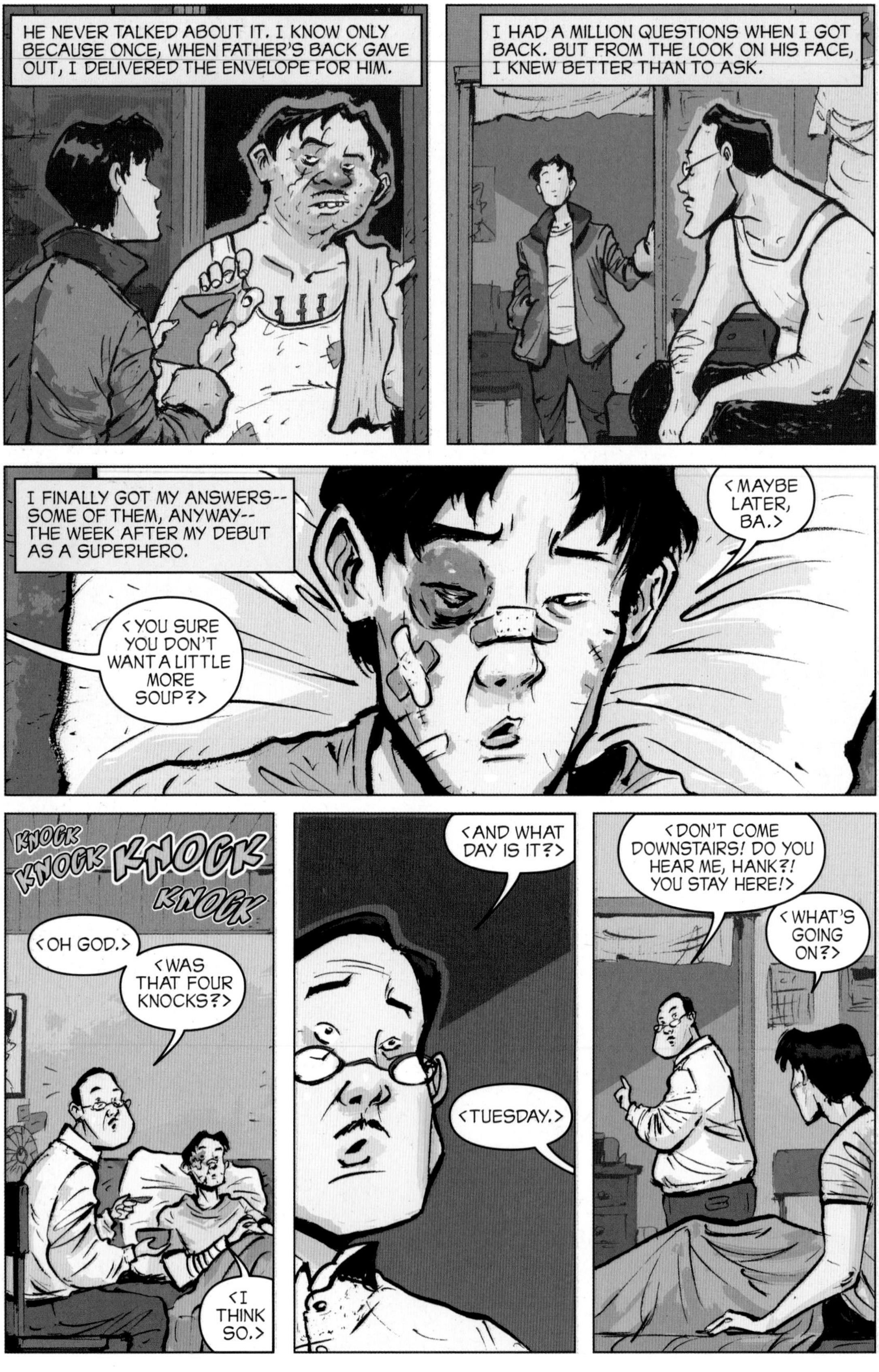
HE NEVER TALKED ABOUT IT. I KNOW ONLY BECAUSE ONCE, WHEN FATHER'S BACK GAVE OUT, I DELIVERED THE ENVELOPE FOR HIM.
I HAD A MILLION QUESTIONS WHEN I GOT BACK. BUT FROM THE LOOK ON HIS FACE, I KNEW BETTER THAN TO ASK.
I FINALLY GOT MY ANSWERS-- SOME OF THEM, ANYWAY-- THE WEEK AFTER MY DEBUT AS A SUPERHERO.
<YOU SURE YOU DON'T WANT A LITTLE MORE SOUP?>
<MAYBE LATER, BA.>
KNOCK KNOCK KNOCK KNOCK
<OH GOD.>
<WAS THAT FOUR KNOCKS?>
<I THINK SO.>
<AND WHAT DAY IS IT?>
<TUESDAY.>
<DON'T COME DOWNSTAIRS! DO YOU HEAR ME, HANK?! YOU STAY HERE!>
<WHAT'S GOING ON?>

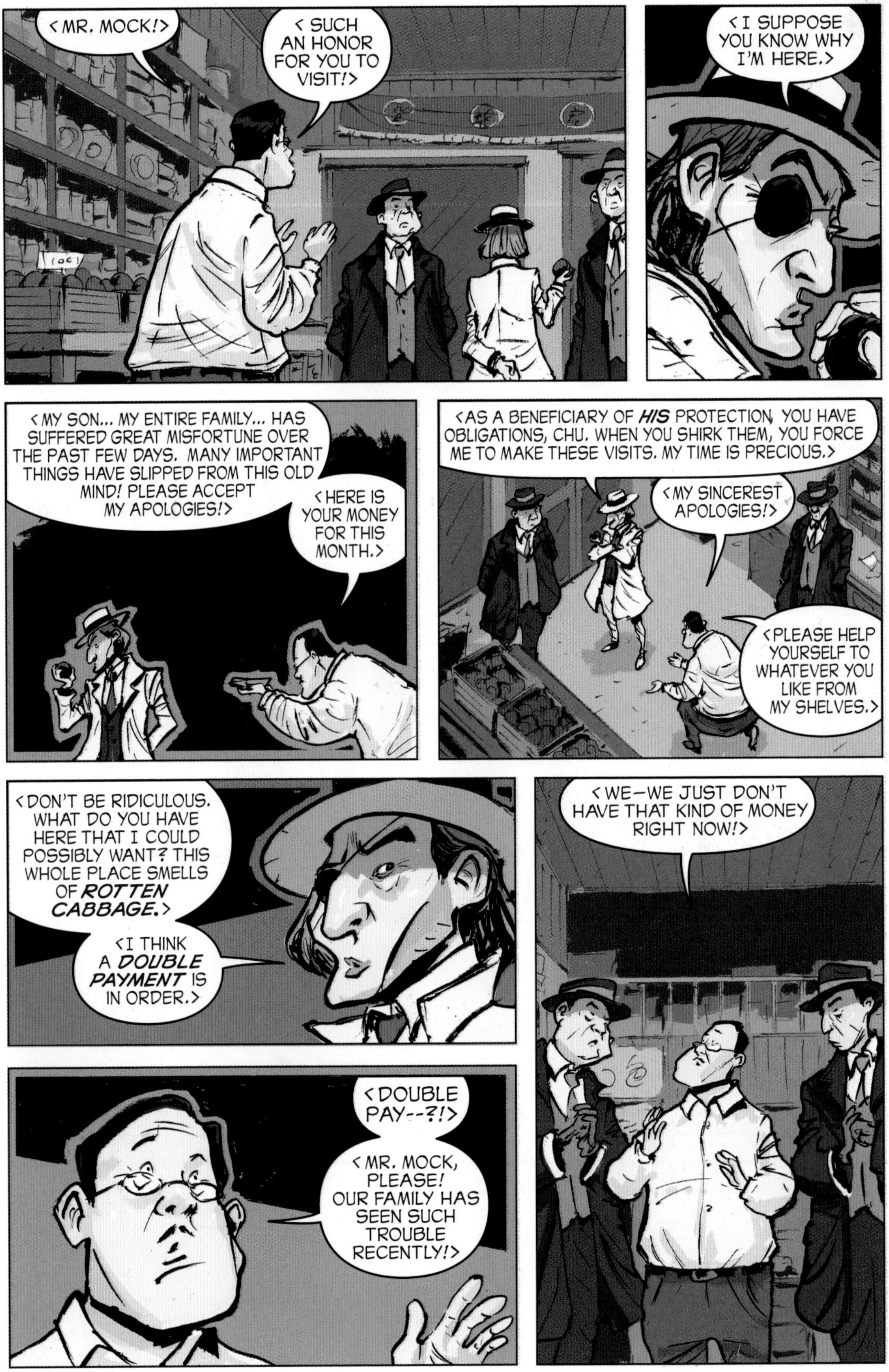

<MR. MOCK!>
<SUCH AN HONOR FOR YOU TO VISIT!>
<I SUPPOSE YOU KNOW WHY I'M HERE.>
<MY SON... MY ENTIRE FAMILY... HAS SUFFERED GREAT MISFORTUNE OVER THE PAST FEW DAYS. MANY IMPORTANT THINGS HAVE SLIPPED FROM THIS OLD MIND! PLEASE ACCEPT MY APOLOGIES!>
<HERE IS YOUR MONEY FOR THIS MONTH.>
<AS A BENEFICIARY OF HIS PROTECTION, YOU HAVE OBLIGATIONS, CHU. WHEN YOU SHIRK THEM, YOU FORCE ME TO MAKE THESE VISITS. MY TIME IS PRECIOUS.>
<MY SINCEREST APOLOGIES!>
<PLEASE HELP YOURSELF TO WHATEVER YOU LIKE FROM MY SHELVES.>
<DON'T BE RIDICULOUS. WHAT DO YOU HAVE HERE THAT I COULD POSSIBLY WANT? THIS WHOLE PLACE SMELLS OF ROTTEN CABBAGE.>
<I THINK A DOUBLE PAYMENT IS IN ORDER.>
<DOUBLE PAY--?!>
<MR. MOCK, PLEASE! OUR FAMILY HAS SEEN SUCH TROUBLE RECENTLY!>
<WE—WE JUST DON'T HAVE THAT KIND OF MONEY RIGHT NOW!>

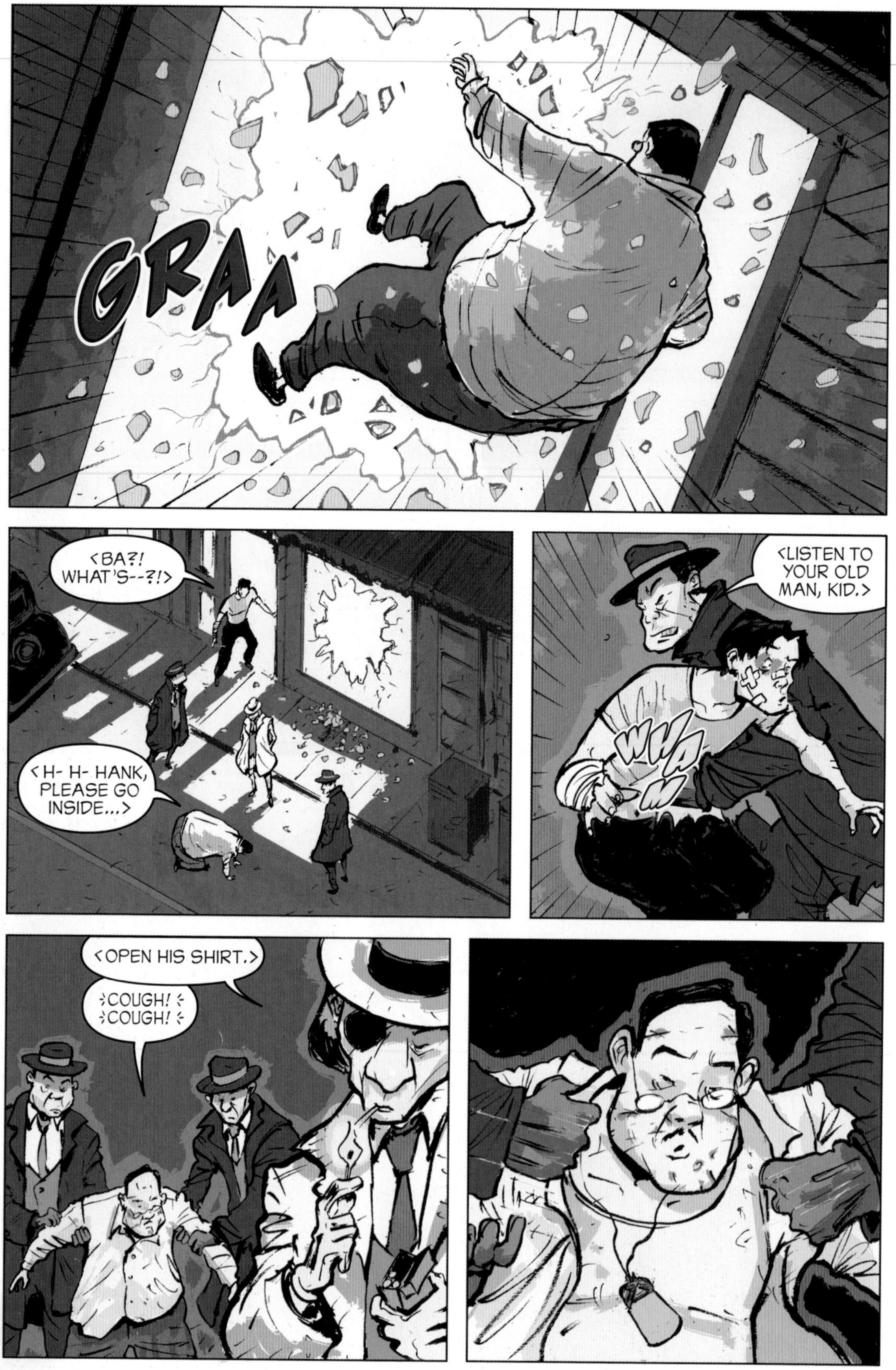
GRAA
<BA?! WHAT'S--?!>
<H- H- HANK, PLEASE GO INSIDE...>
<LISTEN TO YOUR OLD MAN, KID.>
WHAM
<OPEN HIS SHIRT.>
COUGH! COUGH!

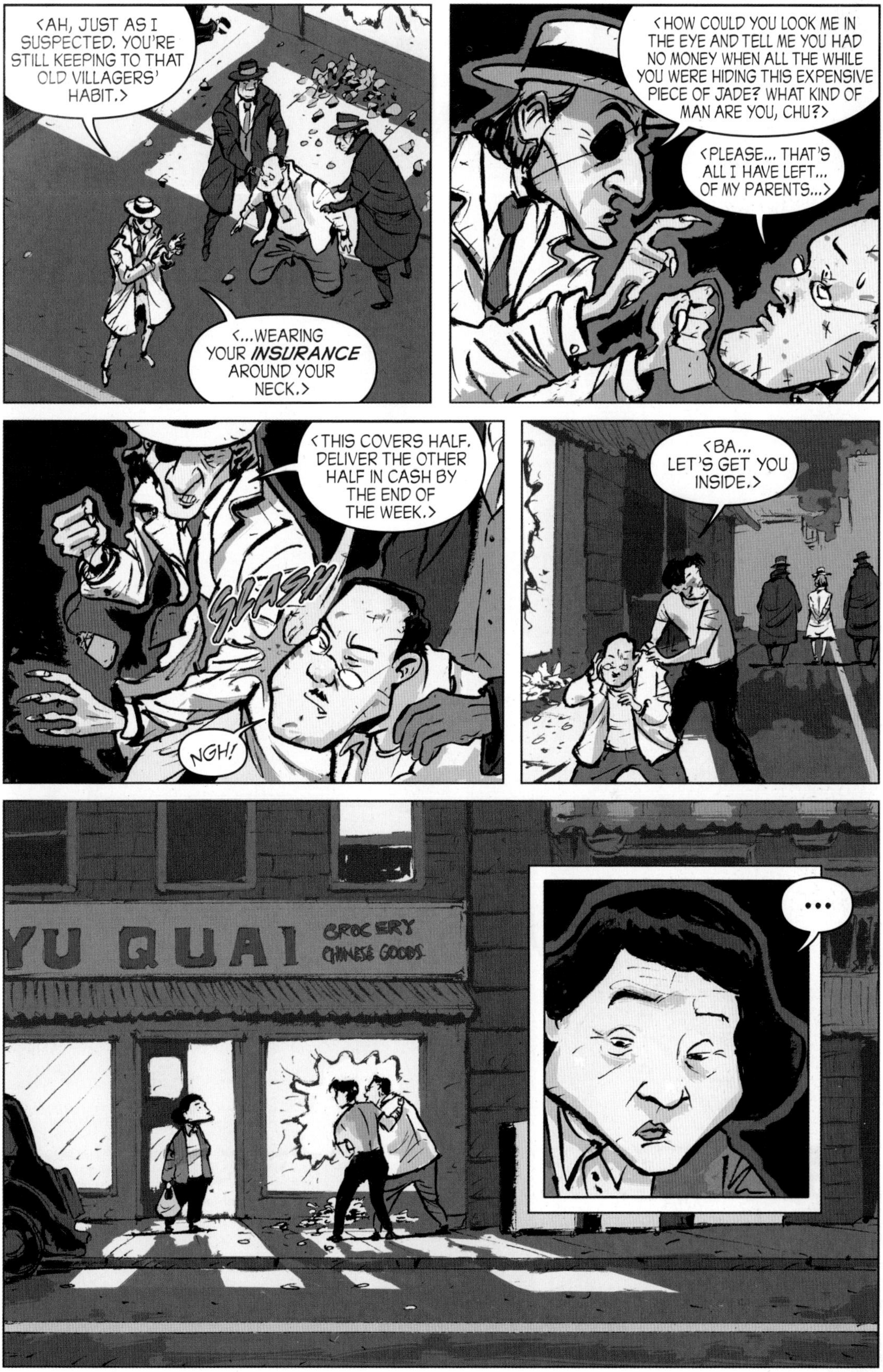
<AH, JUST AS I SUSPECTED. YOU'RE STILL KEEPING TO THAT OLD VILLAGERS' HABIT.>
<...WEARING YOUR *INSURANCE* AROUND YOUR NECK.>
<HOW COULD YOU LOOK ME IN THE EYE AND TELL ME YOU HAD NO MONEY WHEN ALL THE WHILE YOU WERE HIDING THIS EXPENSIVE PIECE OF JADE? WHAT KIND OF MAN ARE YOU, CHU?>
<PLEASE... THAT'S ALL I HAVE LEFT... OF MY PARENTS...>
<THIS COVERS HALF. DELIVER THE OTHER HALF IN CASH BY THE END OF THE WEEK.>
SLASH
NGH!
<BA... LET'S GET YOU INSIDE.>
YU QUAI
GROCERY
CHINESE GOODS
...

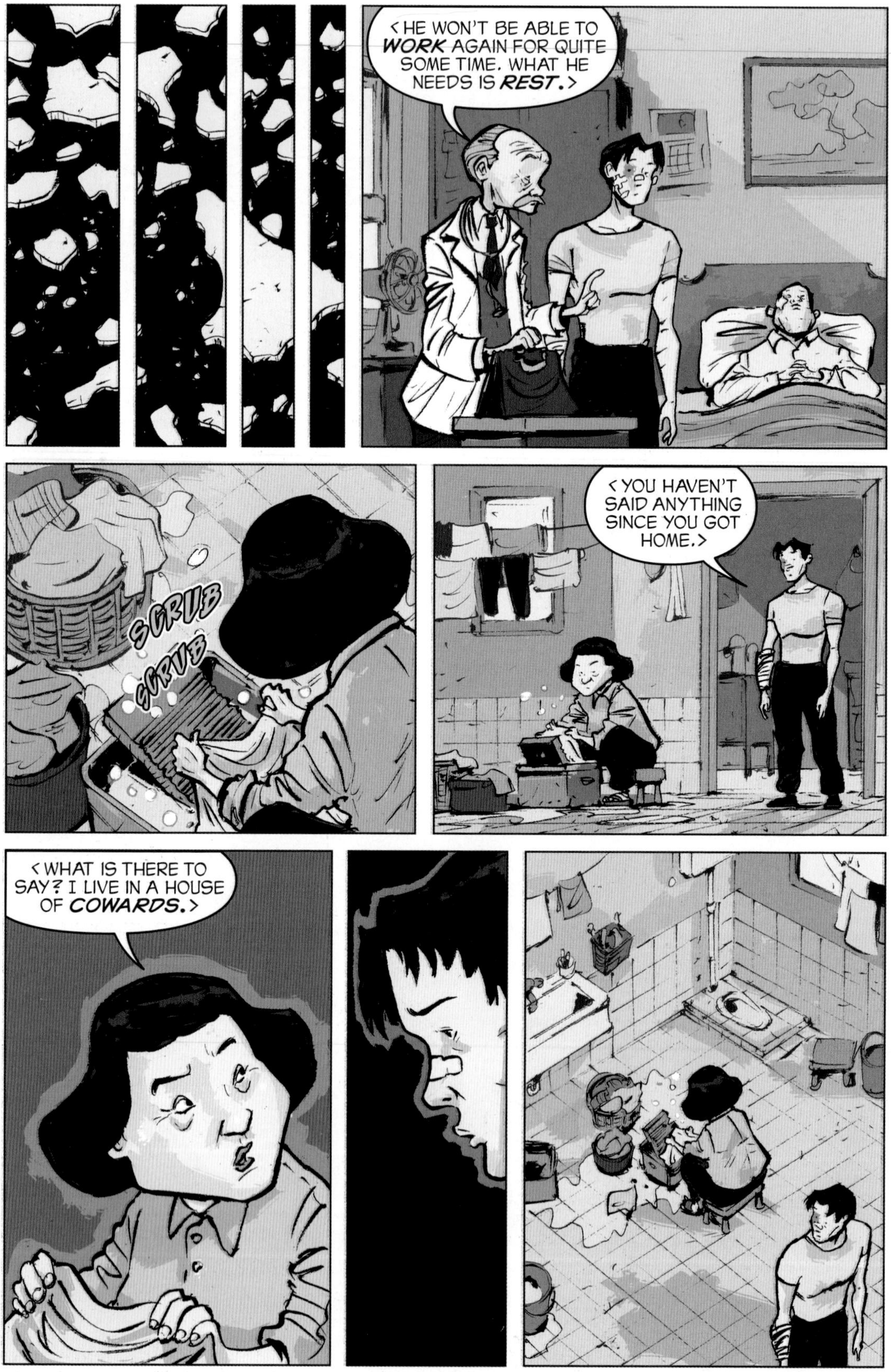

<HE WON'T BE ABLE TO WORK AGAIN FOR QUITE SOME TIME. WHAT HE NEEDS IS REST.>
SCRUB
SCRUB
<YOU HAVEN'T SAID ANYTHING SINCE YOU GOT HOME.>
<WHAT IS THERE TO SAY? I LIVE IN A HOUSE OF COWARDS.>

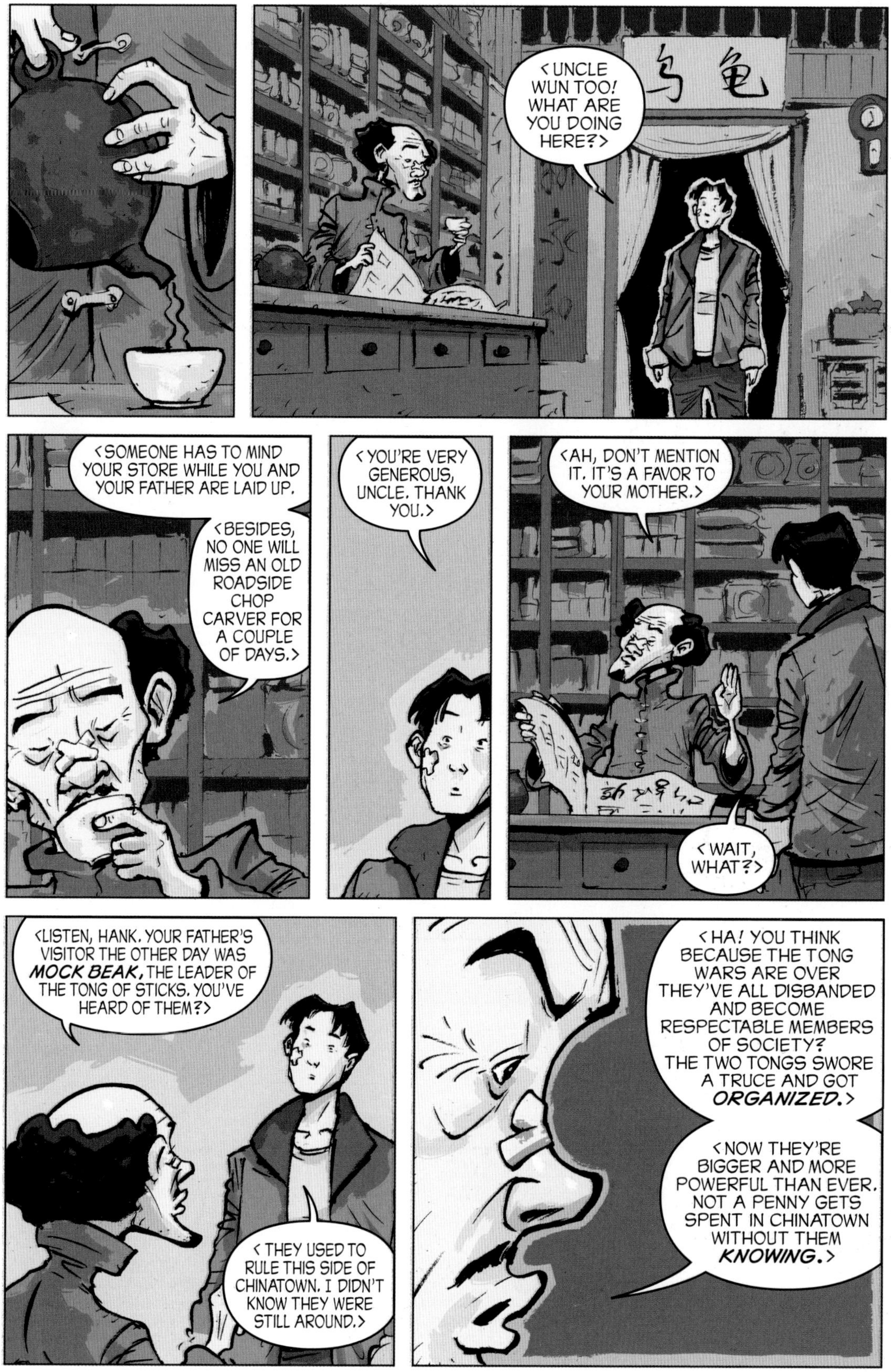
<UNCLE WUN TOO! WHAT ARE YOU DOING HERE?>
<SOMEONE HAS TO MIND YOUR STORE WHILE YOU AND YOUR FATHER ARE LAID UP.
<BESIDES, NO ONE WILL MISS AN OLD ROADSIDE CHOP CARVER FOR A COUPLE OF DAYS.>
<YOU'RE VERY GENEROUS, UNCLE. THANK YOU.>
<AH, DON'T MENTION IT. IT'S A FAVOR TO YOUR MOTHER.>
<WAIT, WHAT?>
<LISTEN, HANK. YOUR FATHER'S VISITOR THE OTHER DAY WAS ***MOCK BEAK,*** THE LEADER OF THE TONG OF STICKS. YOU'VE HEARD OF THEM?>
<THEY USED TO RULE THIS SIDE OF CHINATOWN. I DIDN'T KNOW THEY WERE STILL AROUND.>
<HA! YOU THINK BECAUSE THE TONG WARS ARE OVER THEY'VE ALL DISBANDED AND BECOME RESPECTABLE MEMBERS OF SOCIETY? THE TWO TONGS SWORE A TRUCE AND GOT ***ORGANIZED.***>
<NOW THEY'RE BIGGER AND MORE POWERFUL THAN EVER. NOT A PENNY GETS SPENT IN CHINATOWN WITHOUT THEM ***KNOWING.***>

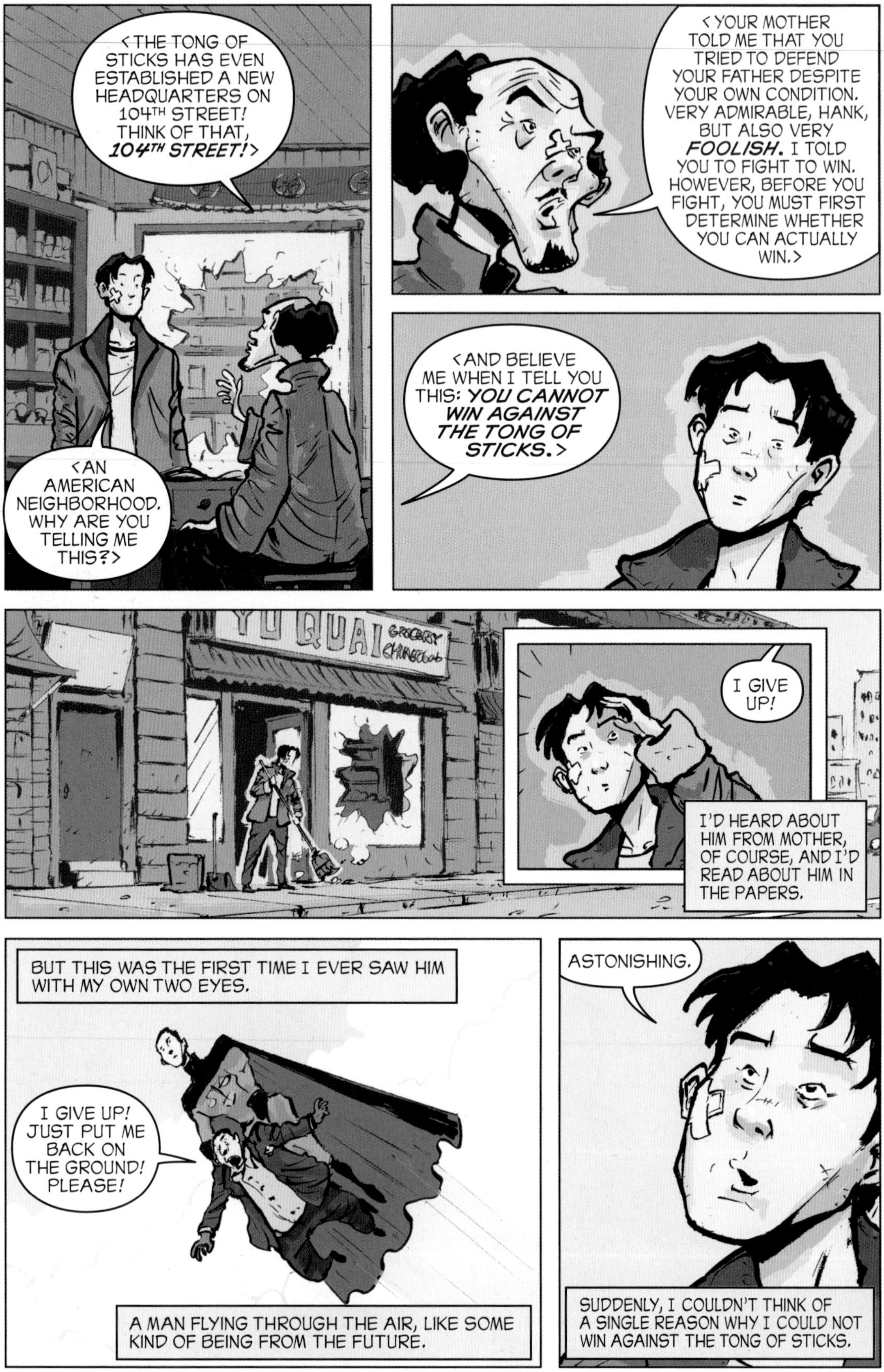

<THE TONG OF STICKS HAS EVEN ESTABLISHED A NEW HEADQUARTERS ON 104TH STREET! THINK OF THAT, **104TH STREET!**>
<AN AMERICAN NEIGHBORHOOD. WHY ARE YOU TELLING ME THIS?>
<YOUR MOTHER TOLD ME THAT YOU TRIED TO DEFEND YOUR FATHER DESPITE YOUR OWN CONDITION. VERY ADMIRABLE, HANK, BUT ALSO VERY **FOOLISH.** I TOLD YOU TO FIGHT TO WIN. HOWEVER, BEFORE YOU FIGHT, YOU MUST FIRST DETERMINE WHETHER YOU CAN ACTUALLY WIN.>
<AND BELIEVE ME WHEN I TELL YOU THIS: ***YOU CANNOT WIN AGAINST THE TONG OF STICKS.***>
YU QUAI
GROCERY
I GIVE UP!
I'D HEARD ABOUT HIM FROM MOTHER, OF COURSE, AND I'D READ ABOUT HIM IN THE PAPERS.
BUT THIS WAS THE FIRST TIME I EVER SAW HIM WITH MY OWN TWO EYES.
I GIVE UP! JUST PUT ME BACK ON THE GROUND! PLEASE!
A MAN FLYING THROUGH THE AIR, LIKE SOME KIND OF BEING FROM THE FUTURE.
ASTONISHING.
SUDDENLY, I COULDN'T THINK OF A SINGLE REASON WHY I COULD NOT WIN AGAINST THE TONG OF STICKS.

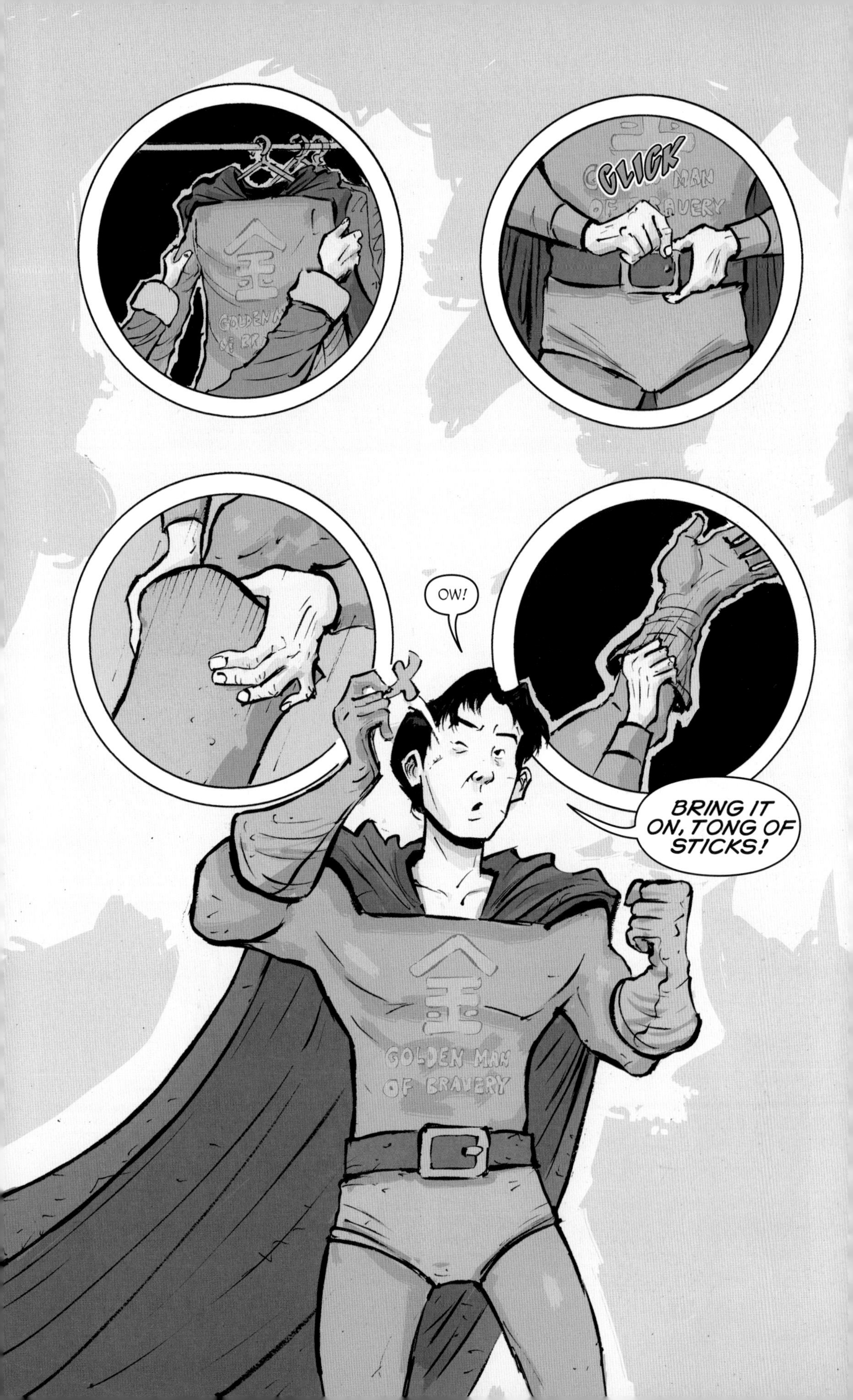
CLICK
OW!
BRING IT ON, TONG OF STICKS!
GOLDEN MAN OF BRAVERY

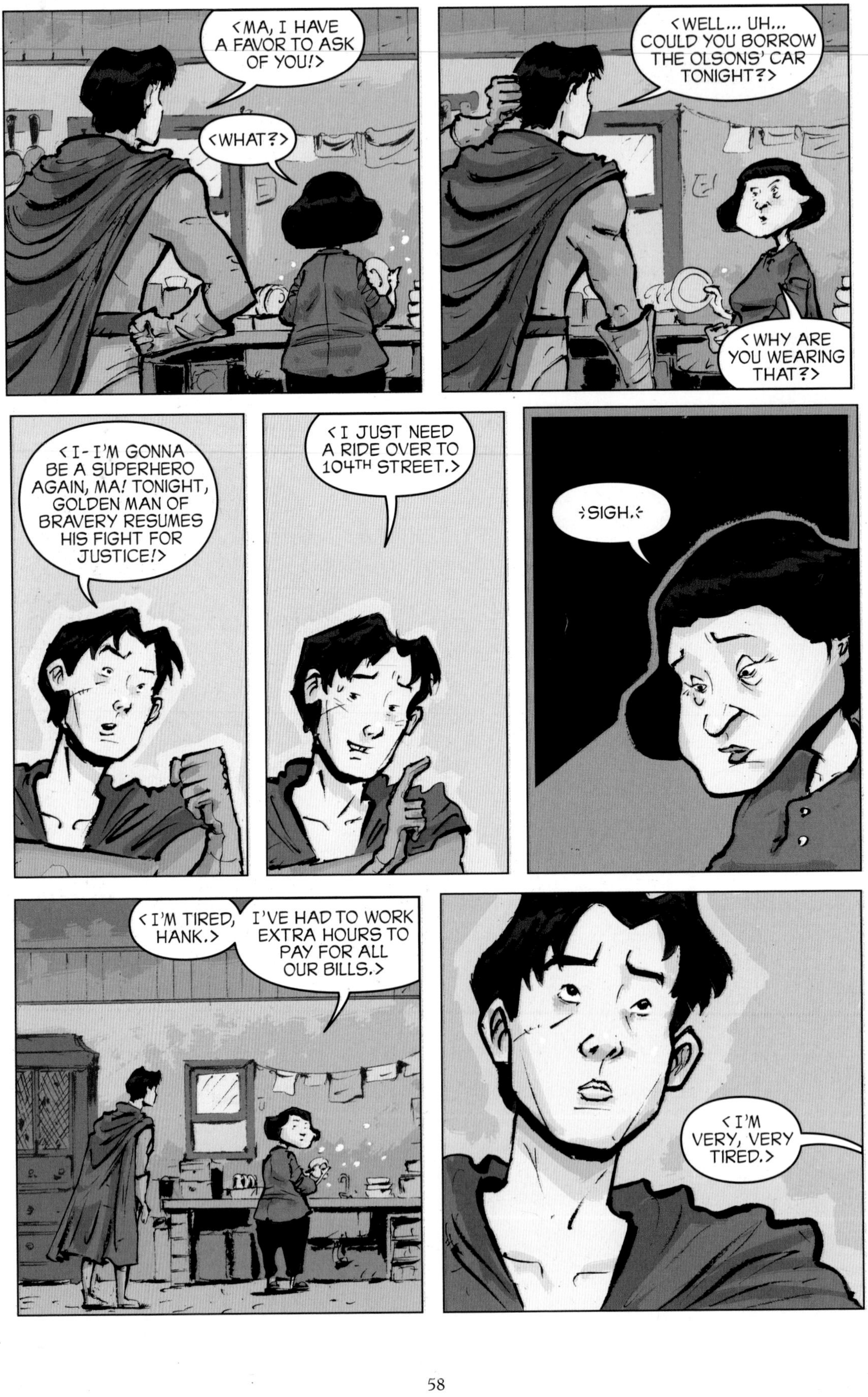
<MA, I HAVE A FAVOR TO ASK OF YOU!>
<WHAT?>
<WELL... UH... COULD YOU BORROW THE OLSONS' CAR TONIGHT?>
<WHY ARE YOU WEARING THAT?>
<I- I'M GONNA BE A SUPERHERO AGAIN, MA! TONIGHT, GOLDEN MAN OF BRAVERY RESUMES HIS FIGHT FOR JUSTICE!>
<I JUST NEED A RIDE OVER TO 104TH STREET.>
SIGH.
<I'M TIRED, HANK.>
I'VE HAD TO WORK EXTRA HOURS TO PAY FOR ALL OUR BILLS.>
<I'M VERY, VERY TIRED.>

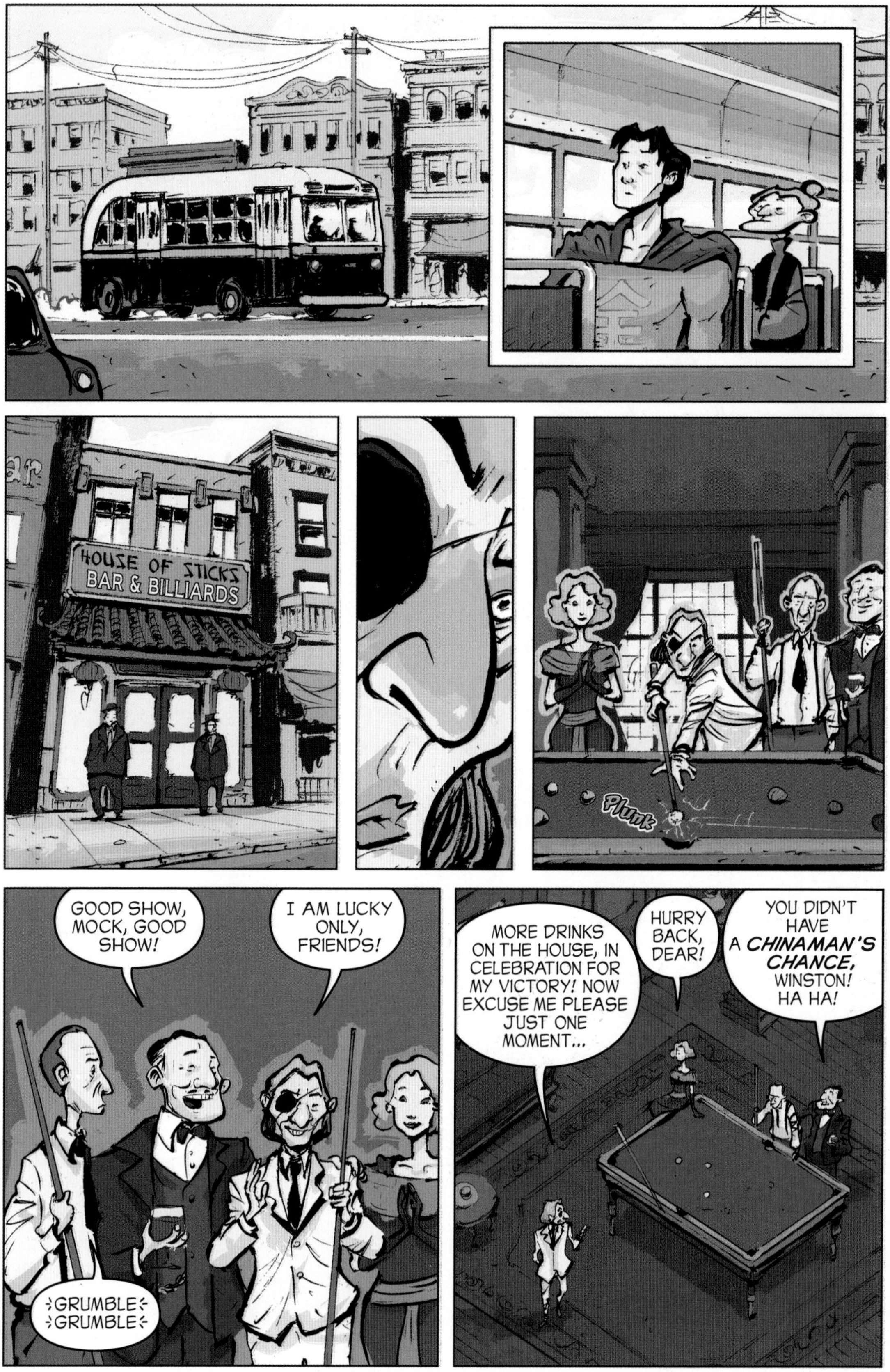
HOUSE OF STICKS
BAR & BILLIARDS
Plunk
GOOD SHOW, MOCK, GOOD SHOW!
I AM LUCKY ONLY, FRIENDS!
GRUMBLE GRUMBLE
MORE DRINKS ON THE HOUSE, IN CELEBRATION FOR MY VICTORY! NOW EXCUSE ME PLEASE JUST ONE MOMENT...
HURRY BACK, DEAR!
YOU DIDN'T HAVE A CHINAMAN'S CHANCE, WINSTON! HA HA!

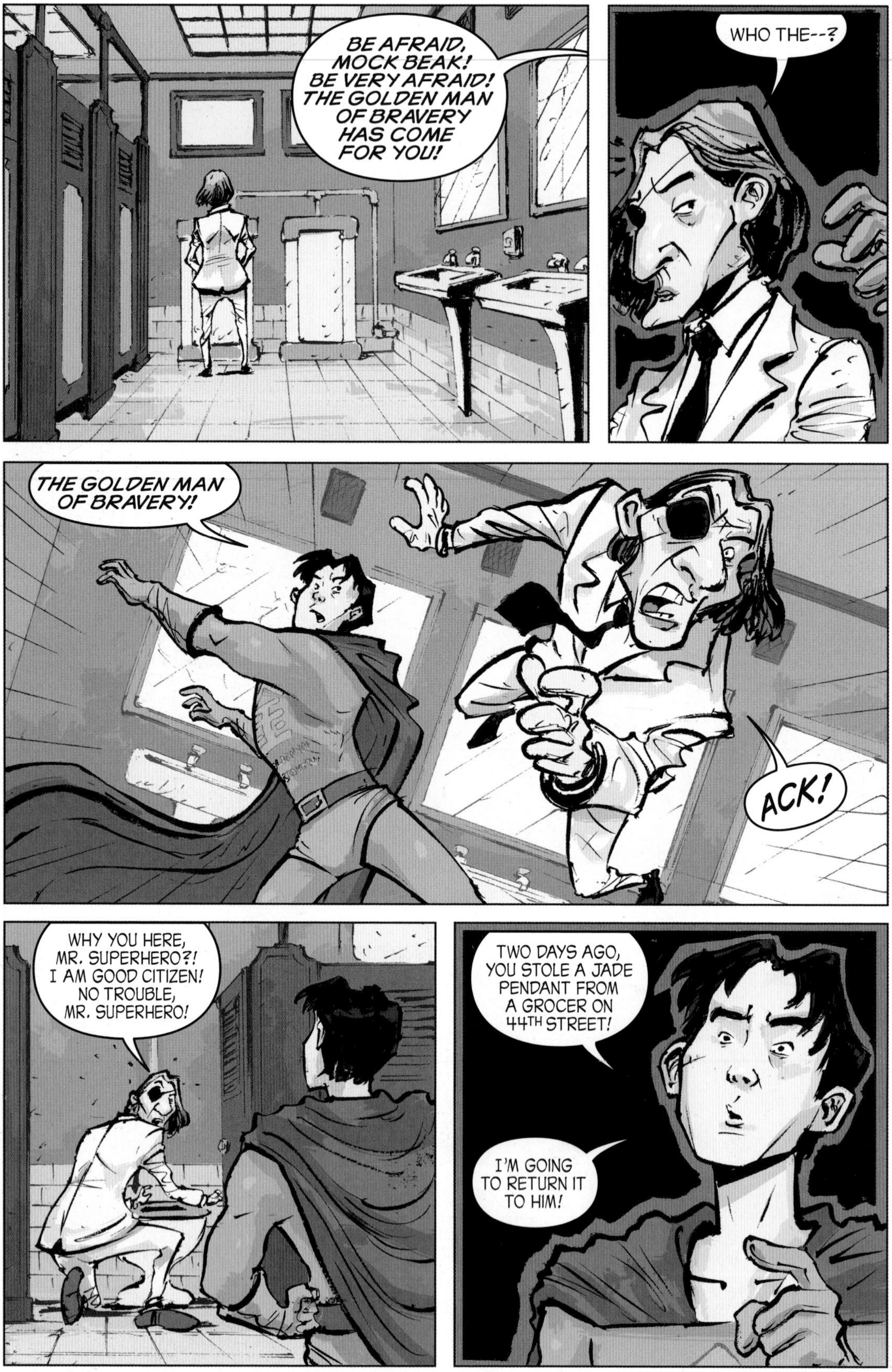
BE AFRAID, MOCK BEAK! BE VERY AFRAID! THE GOLDEN MAN OF BRAVERY HAS COME FOR YOU!
WHO THE--?
THE GOLDEN MAN OF BRAVERY!
ACK!
WHY YOU HERE, MR. SUPERHERO?! I AM GOOD CITIZEN! NO TROUBLE, MR. SUPERHERO!
TWO DAYS AGO, YOU STOLE A JADE PENDANT FROM A GROCER ON 44TH STREET!
I'M GOING TO RETURN IT TO HIM!

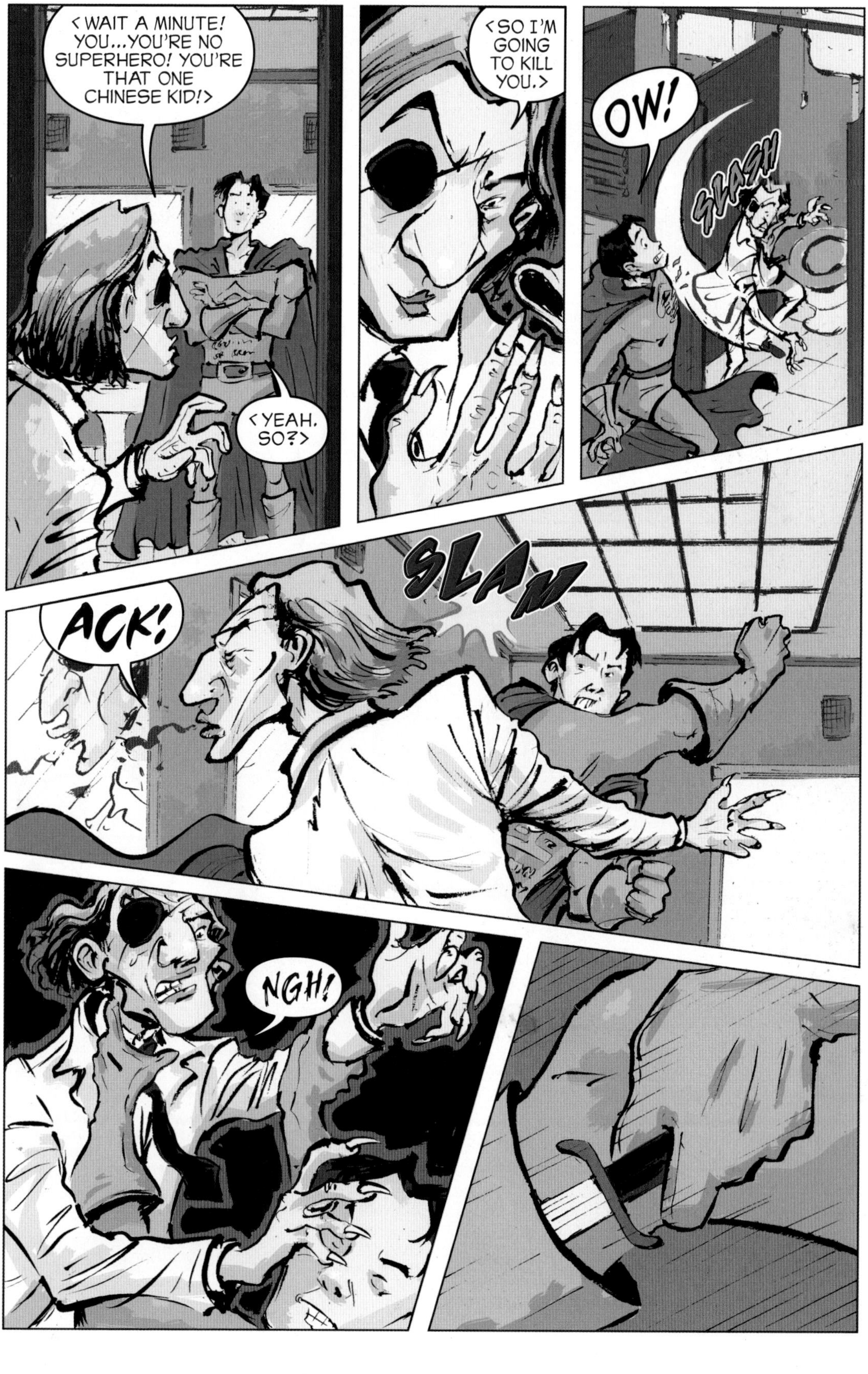
<WAIT A MINUTE! YOU...YOU'RE NO SUPERHERO! YOU'RE THAT ONE CHINESE KID!>
<YEAH. SO?>
<SO I'M GOING TO KILL YOU.>
OW!
SLASH
SLAM
ACK!
NGH!

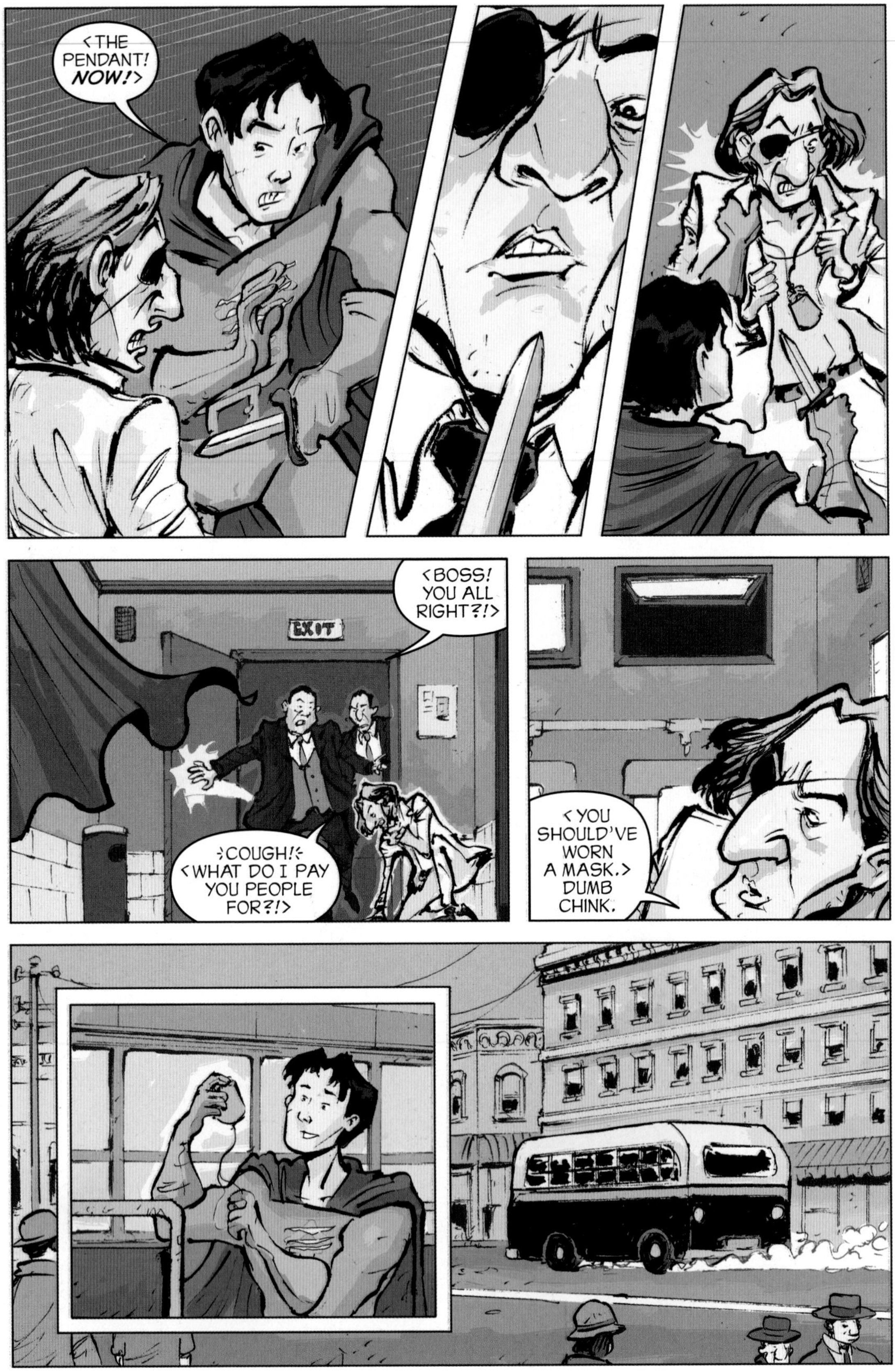

<THE PENDANT! NOW!>
<BOSS! YOU ALL RIGHT?!>
COUGH! <WHAT DO I PAY YOU PEOPLE FOR?!>
<YOU SHOULD'VE WORN A MASK.> DUMB CHINK.

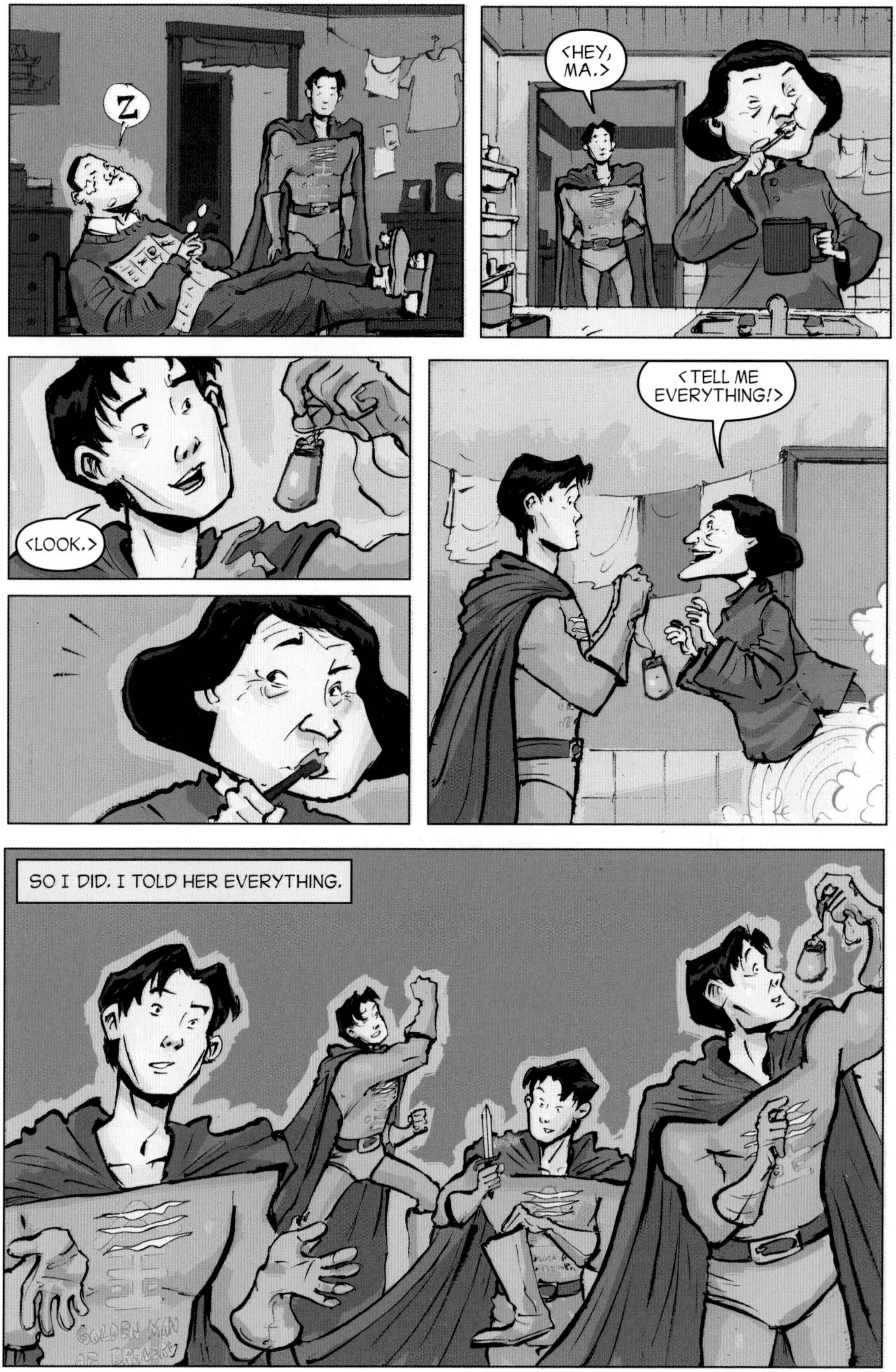
Z
<HEY, MA.>
<LOOK.>
<TELL ME EVERYTHING!>
SO I DID. I TOLD HER EVERYTHING.

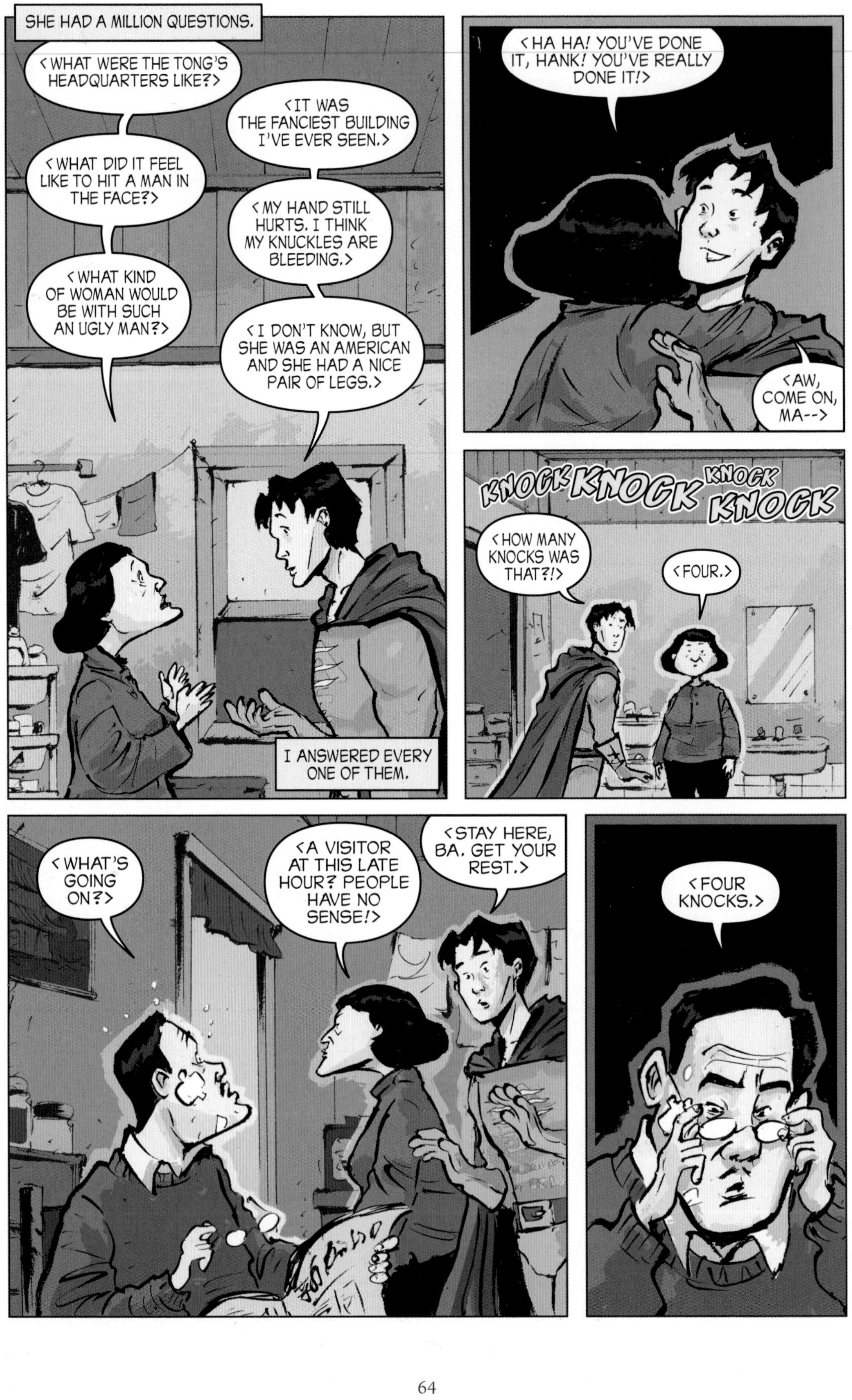
SHE HAD A MILLION QUESTIONS.
<WHAT WERE THE TONG'S HEADQUARTERS LIKE?>
<IT WAS THE FANCIEST BUILDING I'VE EVER SEEN.>
<WHAT DID IT FEEL LIKE TO HIT A MAN IN THE FACE?>
<MY HAND STILL HURTS. I THINK MY KNUCKLES ARE BLEEDING.>
<WHAT KIND OF WOMAN WOULD BE WITH SUCH AN UGLY MAN?>
<I DON'T KNOW, BUT SHE WAS AN AMERICAN AND SHE HAD A NICE PAIR OF LEGS.>
I ANSWERED EVERY ONE OF THEM.
<HA HA! YOU'VE DONE IT, HANK! YOU'VE REALLY DONE IT!>
<AW, COME ON, MA-->
KNOCK KNOCK KNOCK KNOCK
<HOW MANY KNOCKS WAS THAT?!>
<FOUR.>
<WHAT'S GOING ON?>
<A VISITOR AT THIS LATE HOUR? PEOPLE HAVE NO SENSE!>
<STAY HERE, BA. GET YOUR REST.>
<FOUR KNOCKS.>

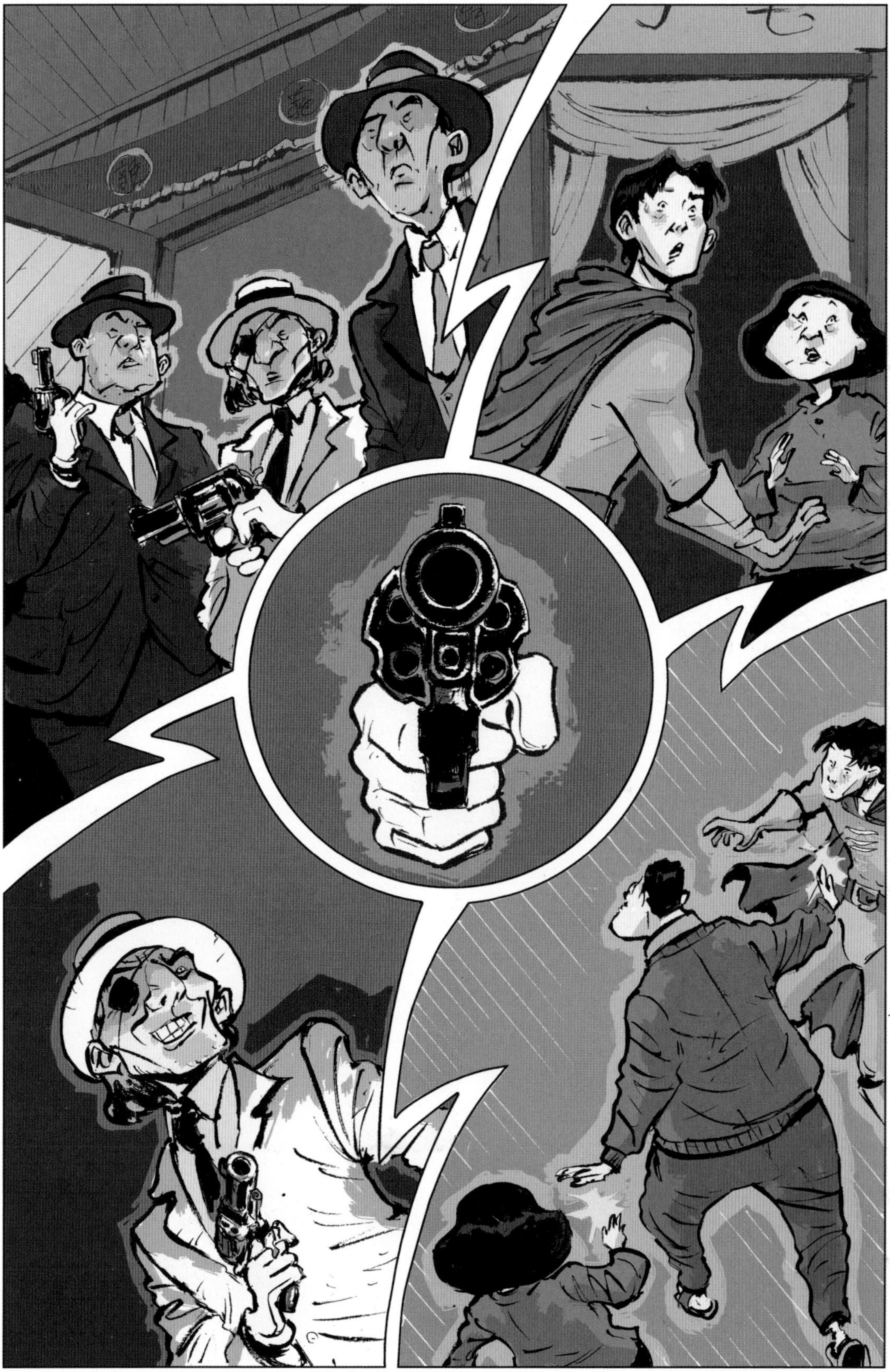

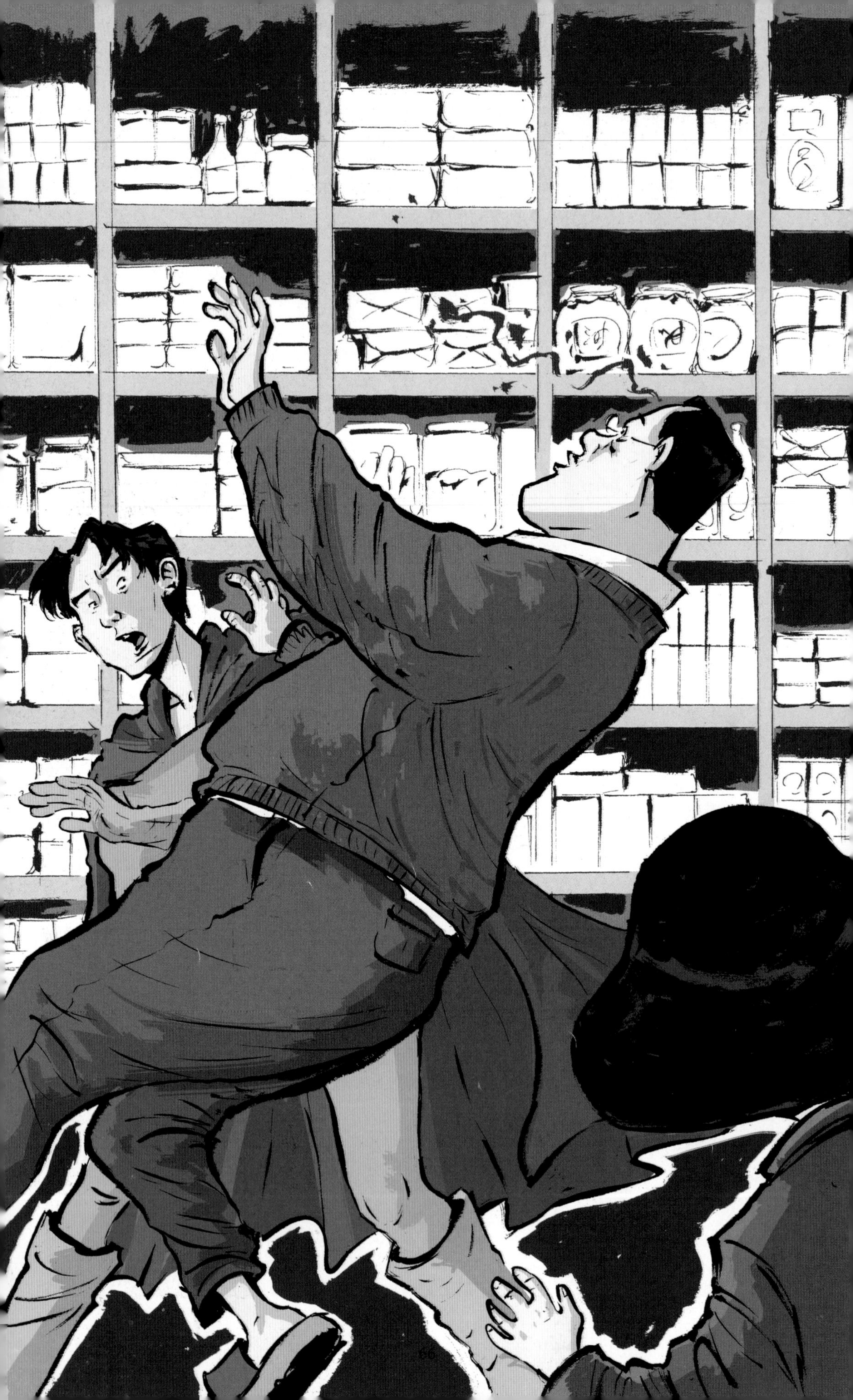

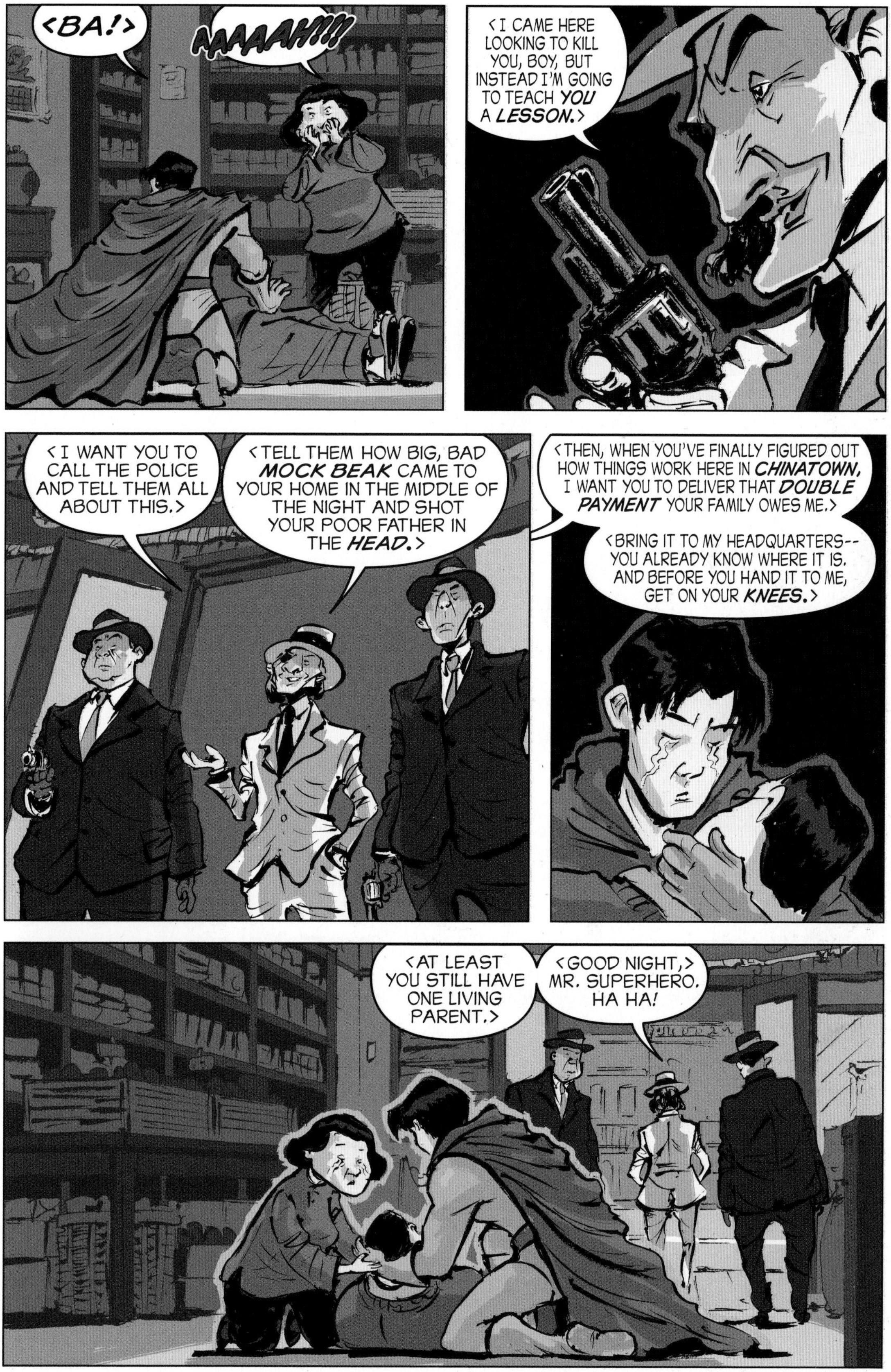
<BA!>
AAAAAH!!!
<I CAME HERE LOOKING TO KILL YOU, BOY, BUT INSTEAD I'M GOING TO TEACH YOU A LESSON.>
<I WANT YOU TO CALL THE POLICE AND TELL THEM ALL ABOUT THIS.>
<TELL THEM HOW BIG, BAD MOCK BEAK CAME TO YOUR HOME IN THE MIDDLE OF THE NIGHT AND SHOT YOUR POOR FATHER IN THE HEAD.>
<THEN, WHEN YOU'VE FINALLY FIGURED OUT HOW THINGS WORK HERE IN CHINATOWN, I WANT YOU TO DELIVER THAT DOUBLE PAYMENT YOUR FAMILY OWES ME.>
<BRING IT TO MY HEADQUARTERS-- YOU ALREADY KNOW WHERE IT IS. AND BEFORE YOU HAND IT TO ME, GET ON YOUR KNEES.>
<AT LEAST YOU STILL HAVE ONE LIVING PARENT.>
<GOOD NIGHT,> MR. SUPERHERO. HA HA!

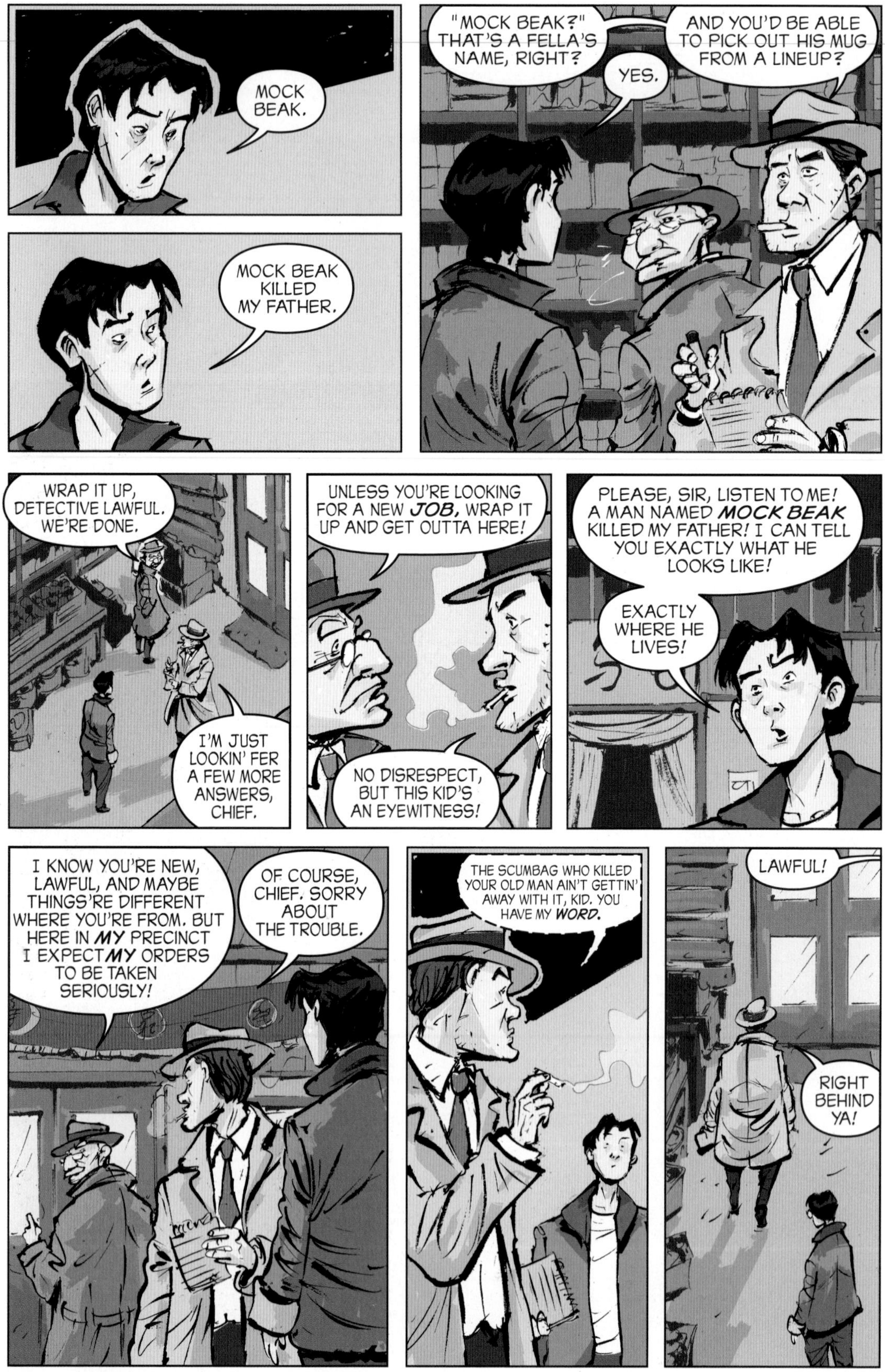
MOCK BEAK.
MOCK BEAK KILLED MY FATHER.
"MOCK BEAK?" THAT'S A FELLA'S NAME, RIGHT?
YES.
AND YOU'D BE ABLE TO PICK OUT HIS MUG FROM A LINEUP?
WRAP IT UP, DETECTIVE LAWFUL. WE'RE DONE.
I'M JUST LOOKIN' FER A FEW MORE ANSWERS, CHIEF.
UNLESS YOU'RE LOOKING FOR A NEW JOB, WRAP IT UP AND GET OUTTA HERE!
NO DISRESPECT, BUT THIS KID'S AN EYEWITNESS!
PLEASE, SIR, LISTEN TO ME! A MAN NAMED MOCK BEAK KILLED MY FATHER! I CAN TELL YOU EXACTLY WHAT HE LOOKS LIKE!
EXACTLY WHERE HE LIVES!
I KNOW YOU'RE NEW, LAWFUL, AND MAYBE THINGS'RE DIFFERENT WHERE YOU'RE FROM. BUT HERE IN MY PRECINCT I EXPECT MY ORDERS TO BE TAKEN SERIOUSLY!
OF COURSE, CHIEF. SORRY ABOUT THE TROUBLE.
THE SCUMBAG WHO KILLED YOUR OLD MAN AIN'T GETTIN' AWAY WITH IT, KID. YOU HAVE MY WORD.
LAWFUL!
RIGHT BEHIND YA!

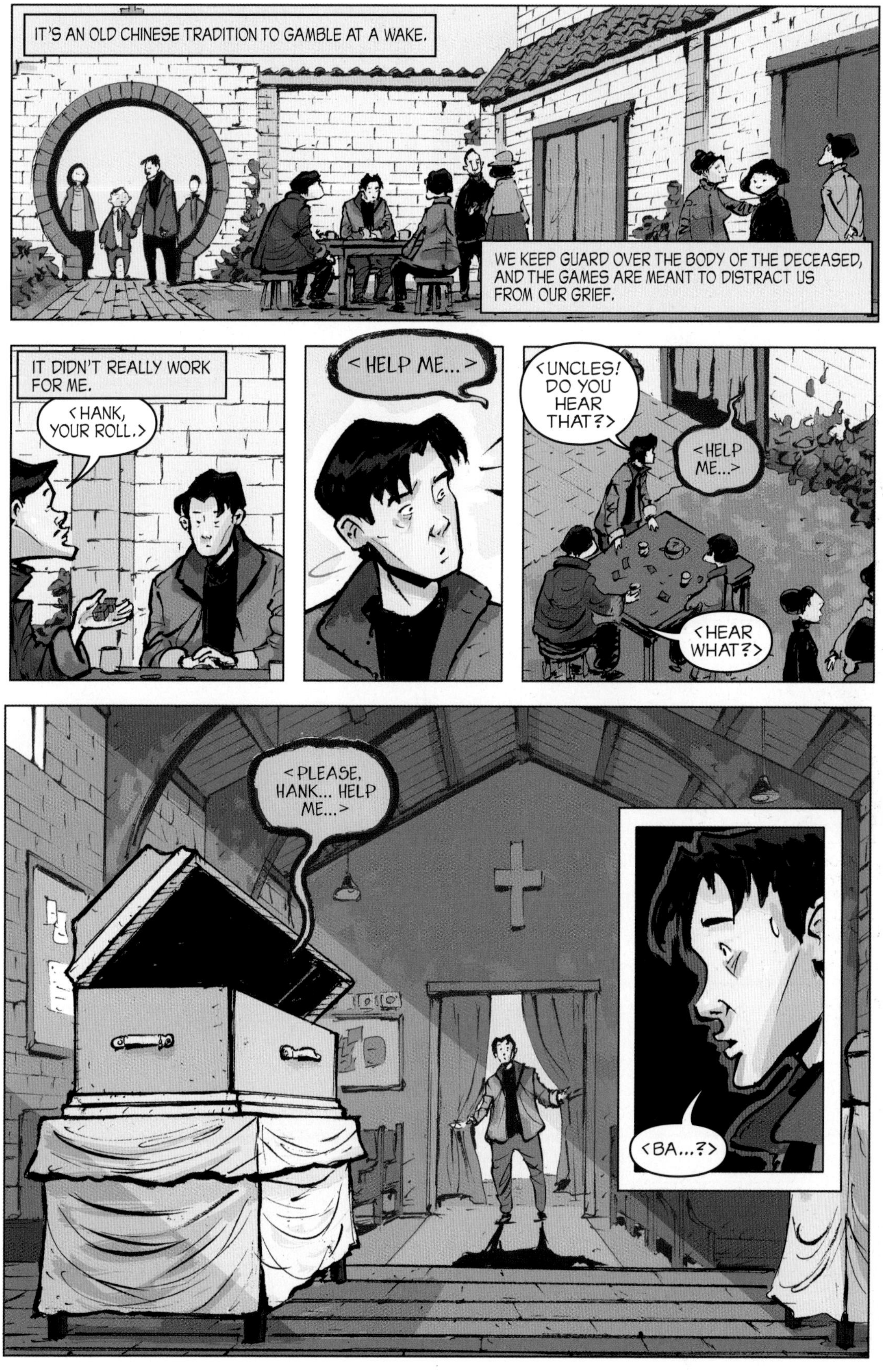
IT'S AN OLD CHINESE TRADITION TO GAMBLE AT A WAKE.
WE KEEP GUARD OVER THE BODY OF THE DECEASED, AND THE GAMES ARE MEANT TO DISTRACT US FROM OUR GRIEF.
IT DIDN'T REALLY WORK FOR ME.
<HANK, YOUR ROLL.>
<HELP ME...>
<UNCLES! DO YOU HEAR THAT?>
<HELP ME...>
<HEAR WHAT?>
<PLEASE, HANK... HELP ME...>
<BA...?>

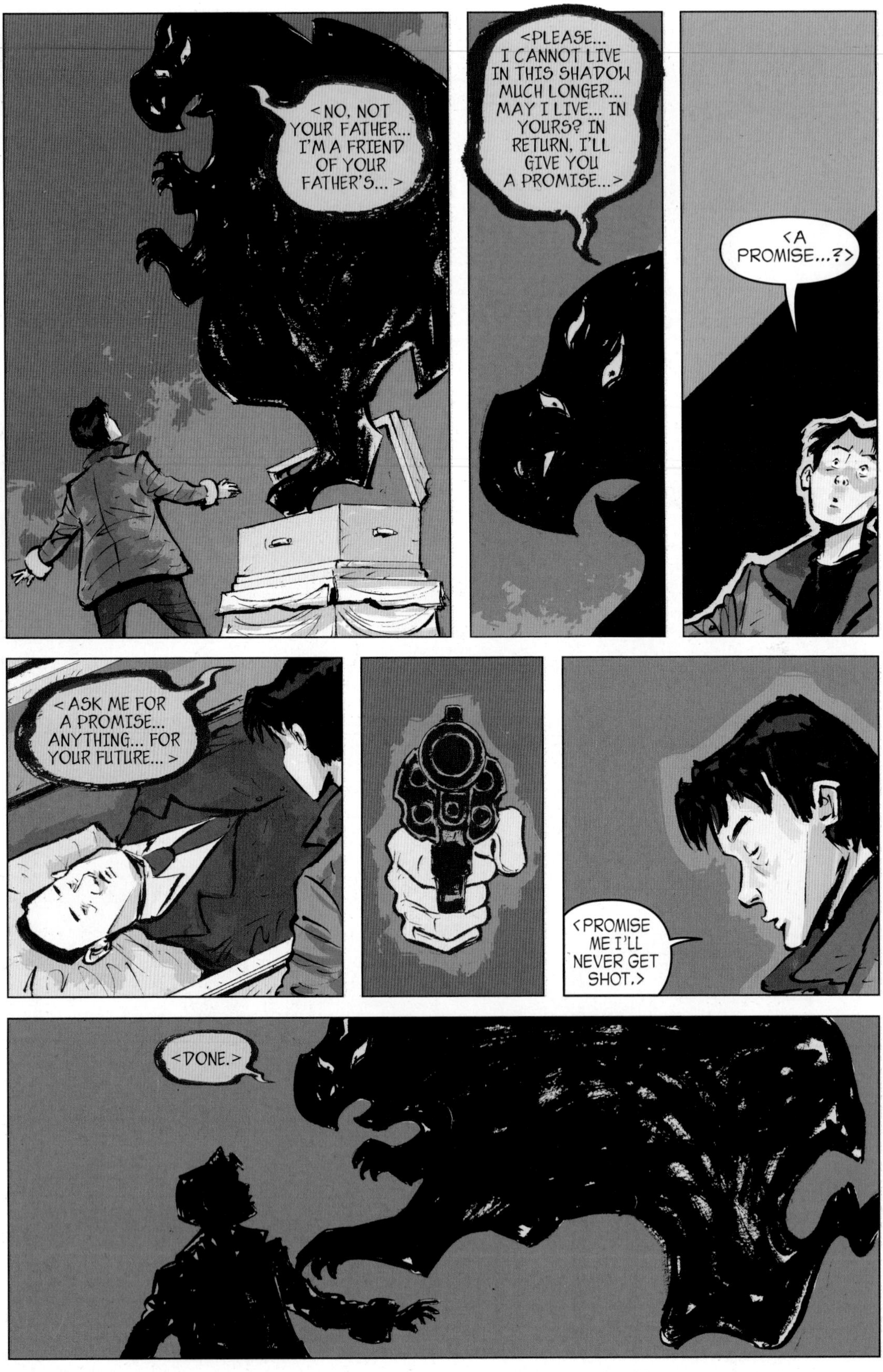
<NO, NOT YOUR FATHER... I'M A FRIEND OF YOUR FATHER'S...>
<PLEASE... I CANNOT LIVE IN THIS SHADOW MUCH LONGER... MAY I LIVE... IN YOURS? IN RETURN, I'LL GIVE YOU A PROMISE...>
<A PROMISE...?>
<ASK ME FOR A PROMISE... ANYTHING... FOR YOUR FUTURE...>
<PROMISE ME I'LL NEVER GET SHOT.>
<DONE.>

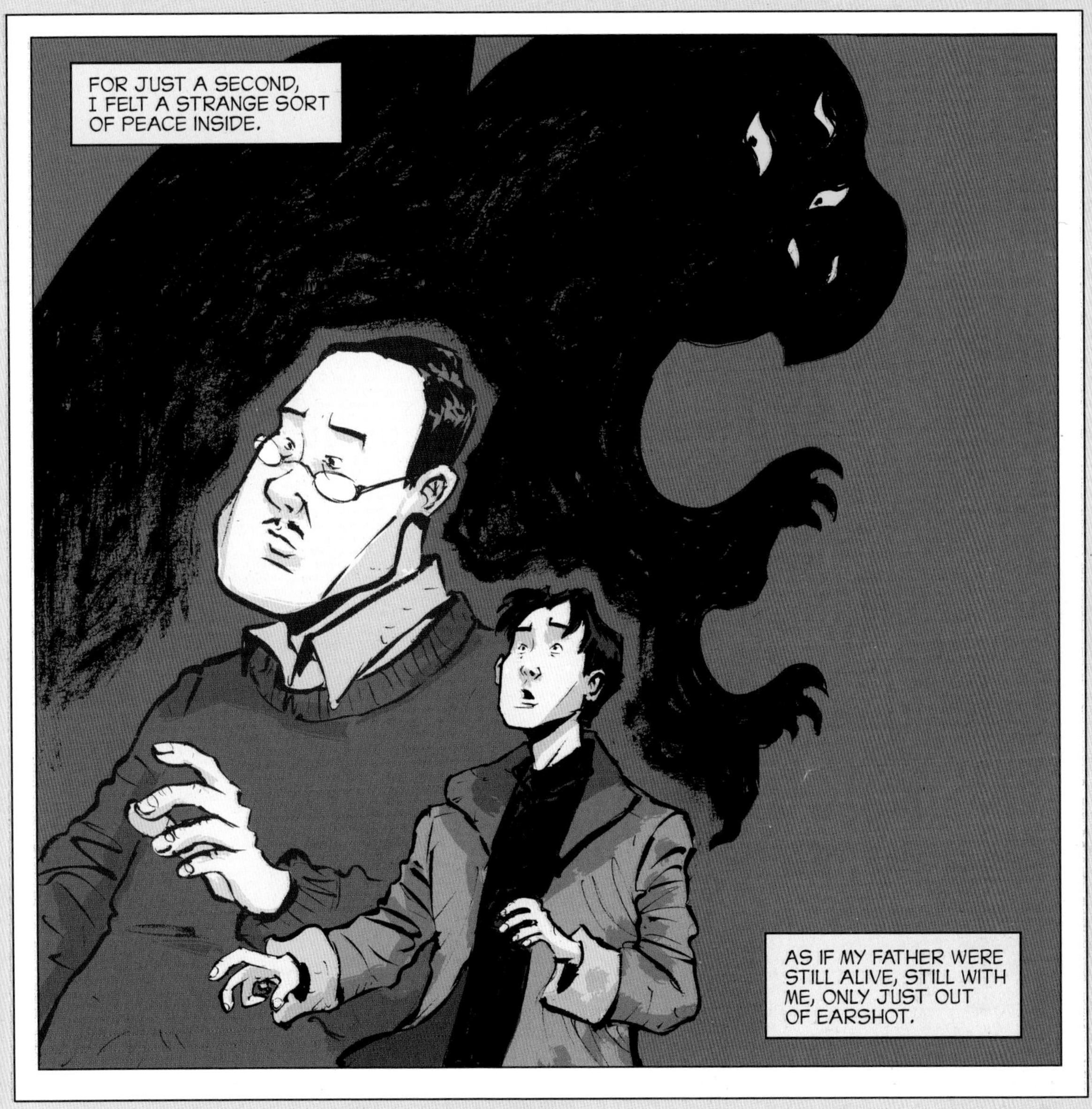
FOR JUST A SECOND, I FELT A STRANGE SORT OF PEACE INSIDE.
AS IF MY FATHER WERE STILL ALIVE, STILL WITH ME, ONLY JUST OUT OF EARSHOT.

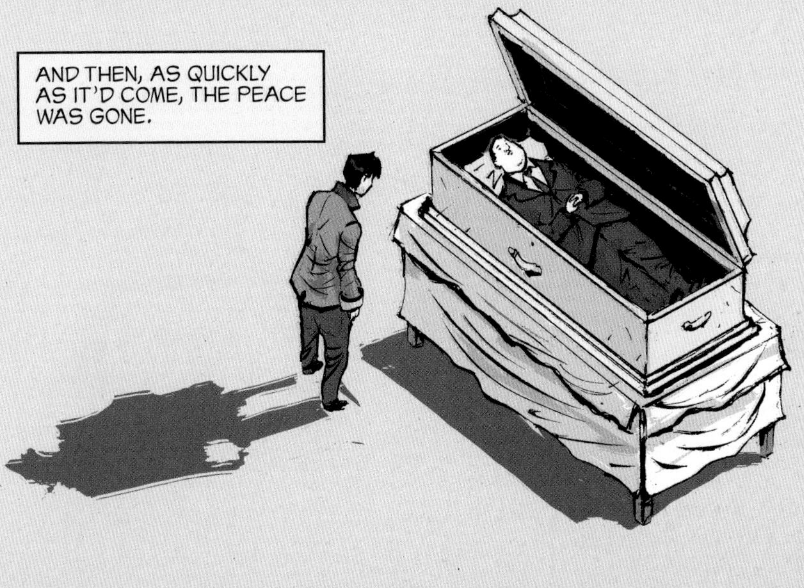
AND THEN, AS QUICKLY AS IT'D COME, THE PEACE WAS GONE.

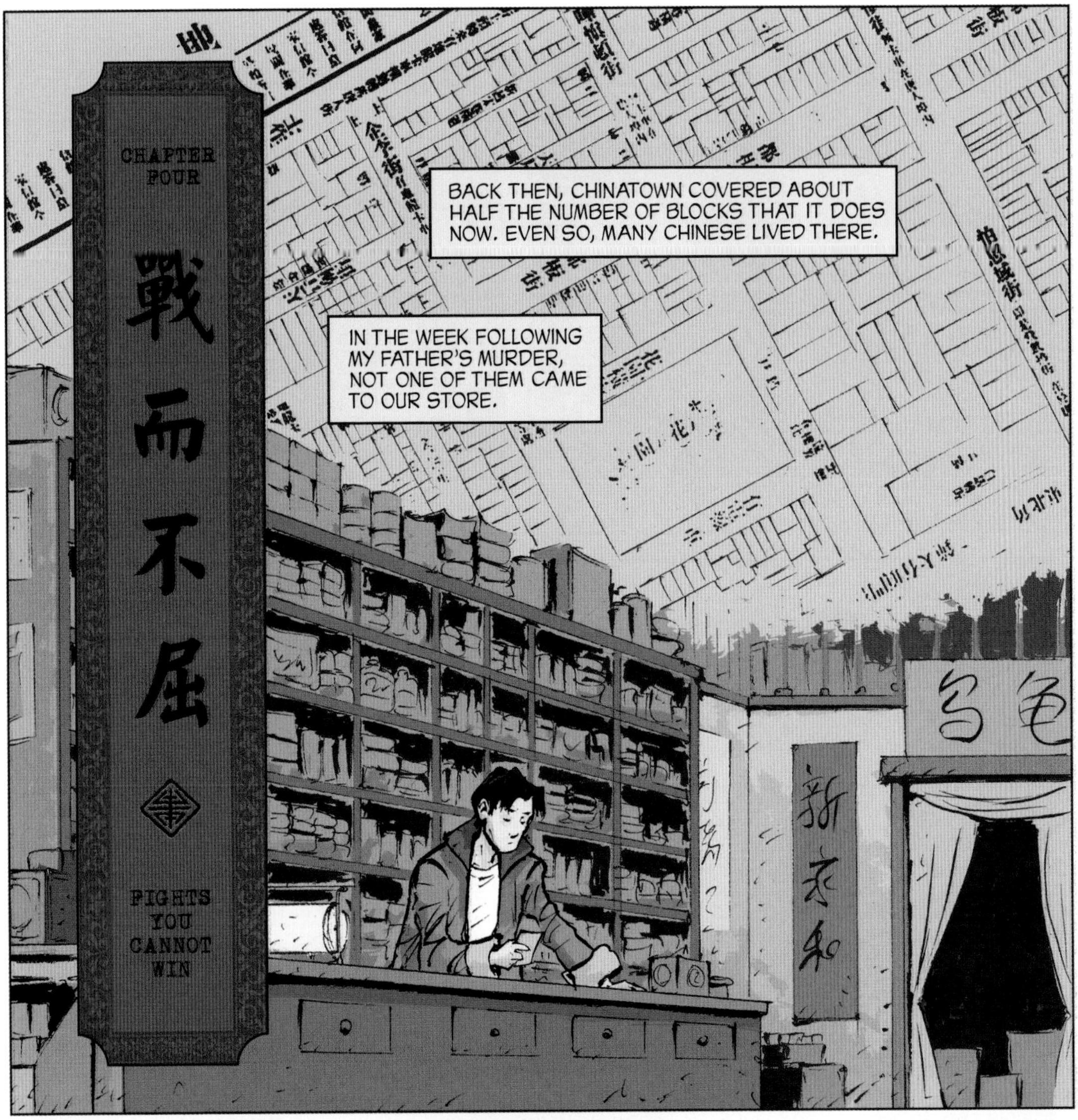
CHAPTER FOUR
戰而不屈
FIGHTS YOU CANNOT WIN
BACK THEN, CHINATOWN COVERED ABOUT HALF THE NUMBER OF BLOCKS THAT IT DOES NOW. EVEN SO, MANY CHINESE LIVED THERE.
IN THE WEEK FOLLOWING MY FATHER'S MURDER, NOT ONE OF THEM CAME TO OUR STORE.

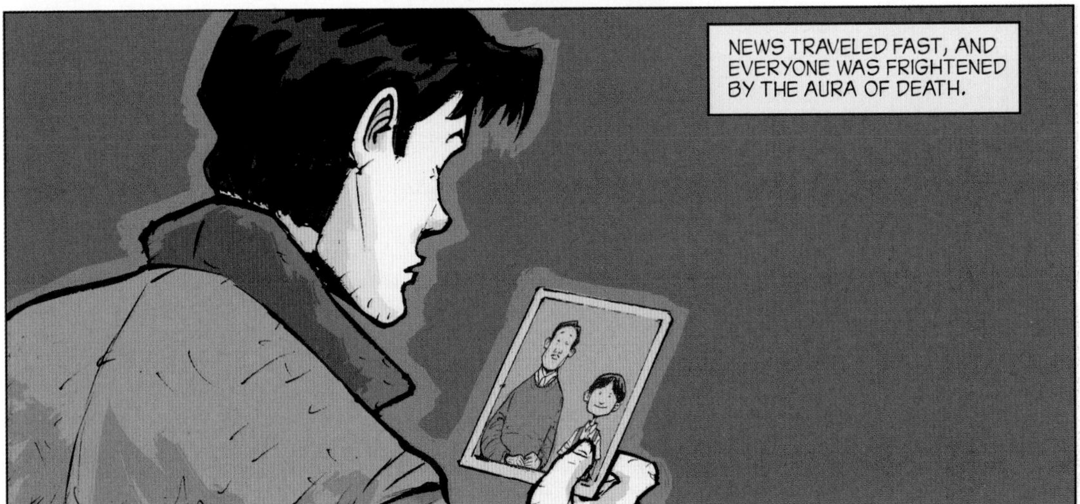
NEWS TRAVELED FAST, AND EVERYONE WAS FRIGHTENED BY THE AURA OF DEATH.

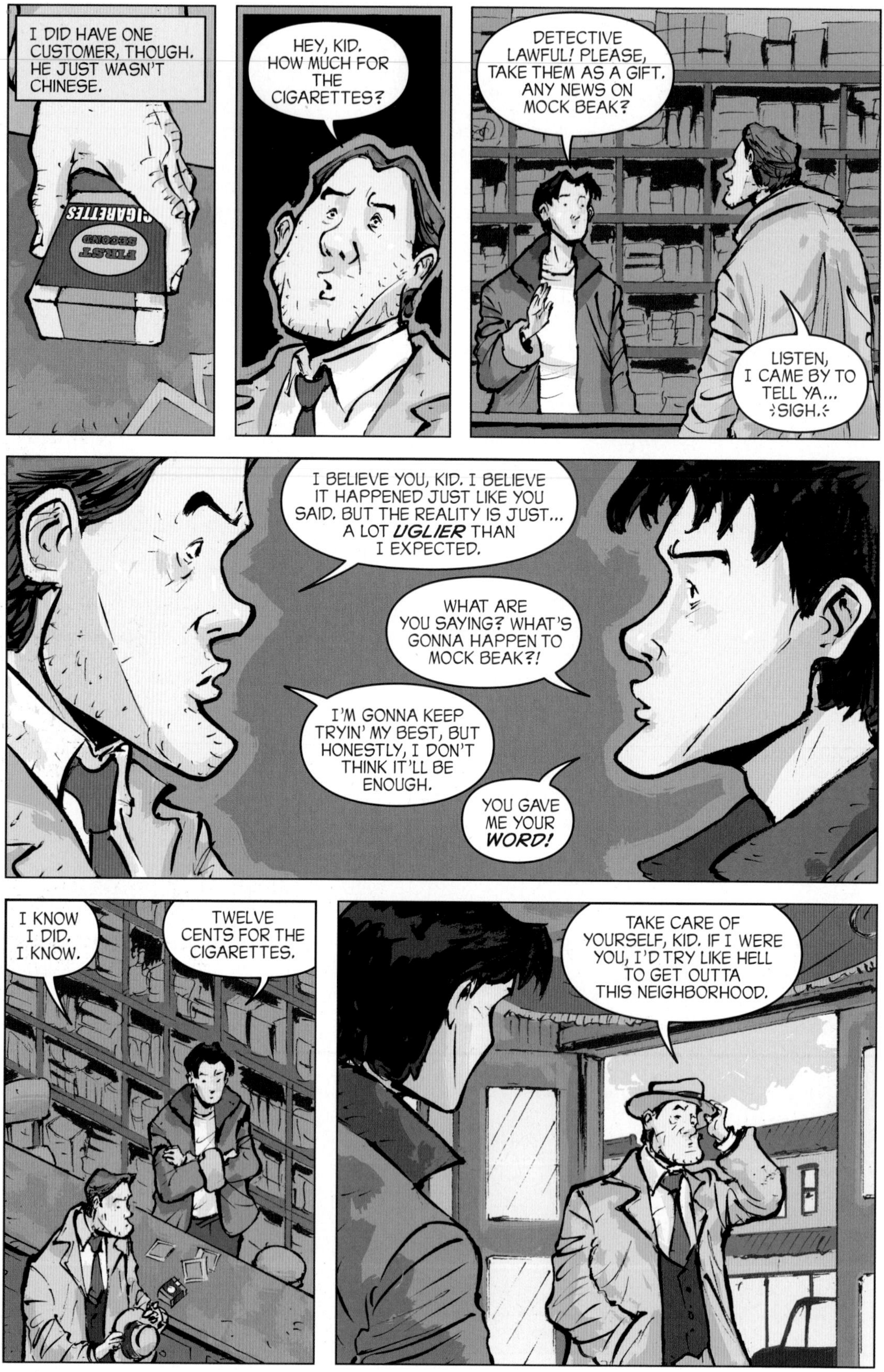
I DID HAVE ONE CUSTOMER, THOUGH. HE JUST WASN'T CHINESE.
FIRST SECOND CIGARETTES
HEY, KID. HOW MUCH FOR THE CIGARETTES?
DETECTIVE LAWFUL! PLEASE, TAKE THEM AS A GIFT. ANY NEWS ON MOCK BEAK?
LISTEN, I CAME BY TO TELL YA... *SIGH.*
I BELIEVE YOU, KID. I BELIEVE IT HAPPENED JUST LIKE YOU SAID. BUT THE REALITY IS JUST... A LOT UGLIER THAN I EXPECTED.
WHAT ARE YOU SAYING? WHAT'S GONNA HAPPEN TO MOCK BEAK?!
I'M GONNA KEEP TRYIN' MY BEST, BUT HONESTLY, I DON'T THINK IT'LL BE ENOUGH.
YOU GAVE ME YOUR WORD!
I KNOW I DID. I KNOW.
TWELVE CENTS FOR THE CIGARETTES.
TAKE CARE OF YOURSELF, KID. IF I WERE YOU, I'D TRY LIKE HELL TO GET OUTTA THIS NEIGHBORHOOD.

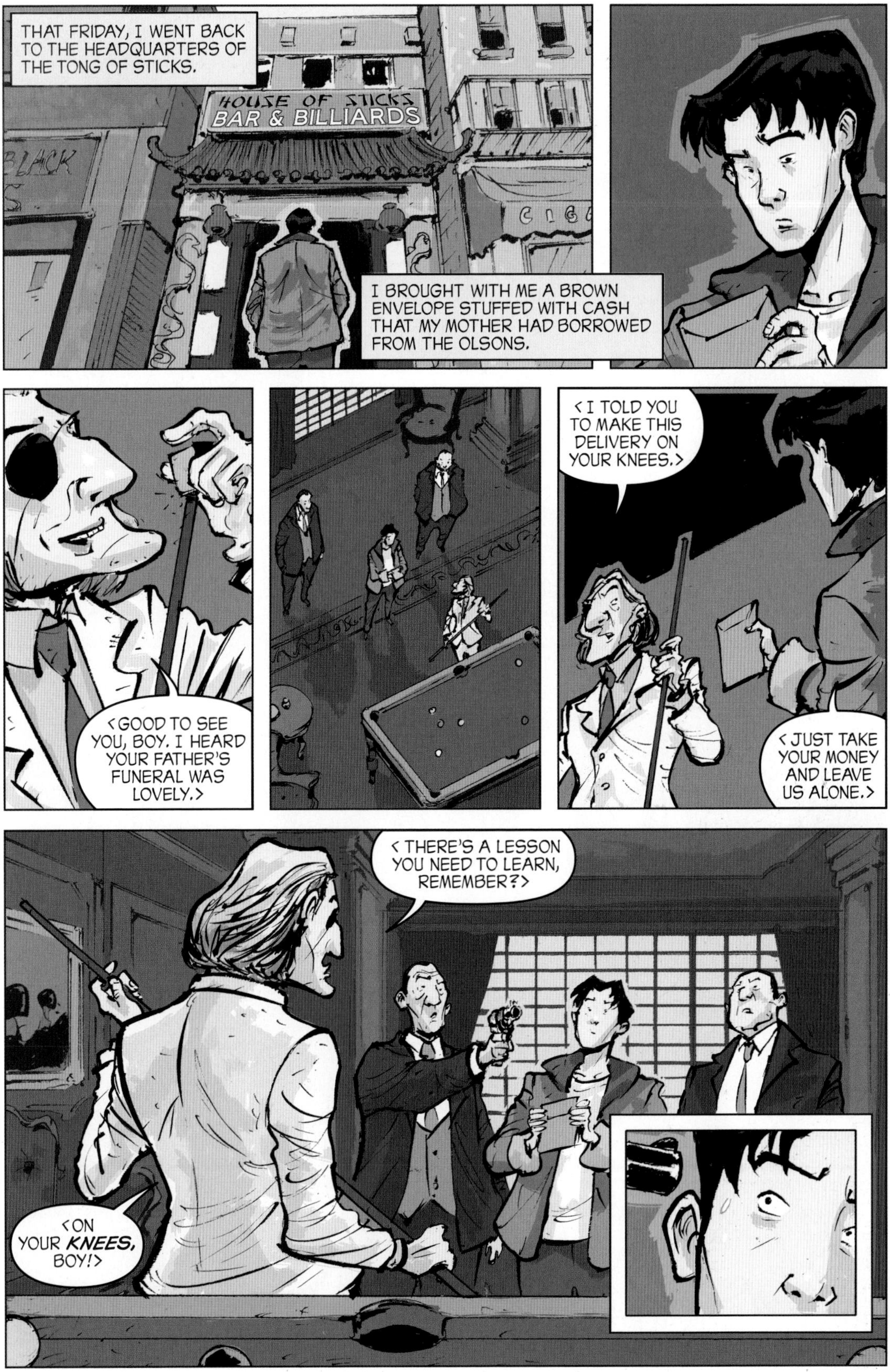

THAT FRIDAY, I WENT BACK TO THE HEADQUARTERS OF THE TONG OF STICKS.
HOUSE OF STICKS
BAR & BILLIARDS
I BROUGHT WITH ME A BROWN ENVELOPE STUFFED WITH CASH THAT MY MOTHER HAD BORROWED FROM THE OLSONS.
<GOOD TO SEE YOU, BOY. I HEARD YOUR FATHER'S FUNERAL WAS LOVELY.>
<I TOLD YOU TO MAKE THIS DELIVERY ON YOUR KNEES.>
<JUST TAKE YOUR MONEY AND LEAVE US ALONE.>
<THERE'S A LESSON YOU NEED TO LEARN, REMEMBER?>
<ON YOUR KNEES, BOY!>

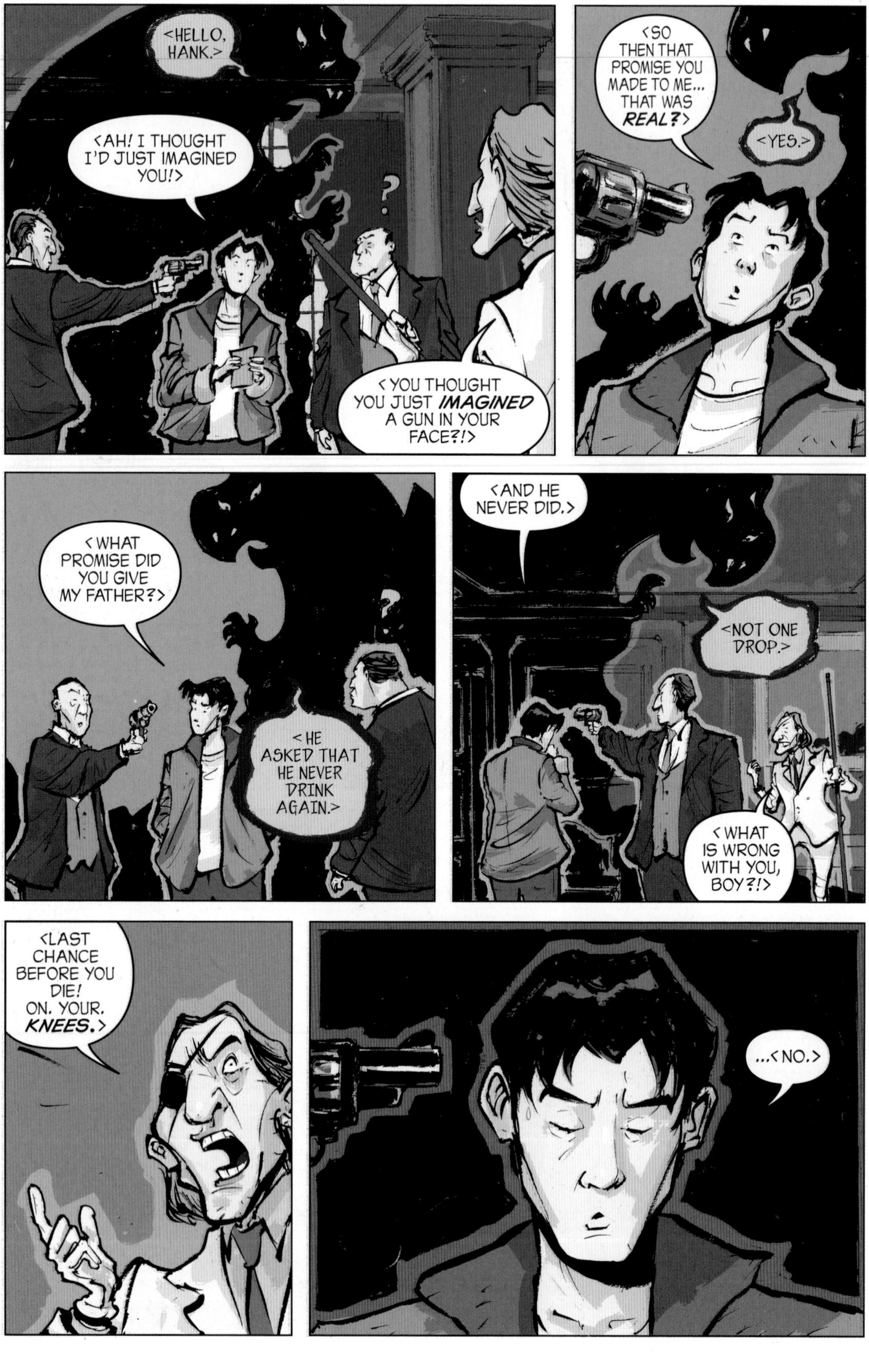
<HELLO, HANK.>
<AH! I THOUGHT I'D JUST IMAGINED YOU!>
?
<YOU THOUGHT YOU JUST IMAGINED A GUN IN YOUR FACE?!>
<SO THEN THAT PROMISE YOU MADE TO ME... THAT WAS REAL?>
<YES.>
<WHAT PROMISE DID YOU GIVE MY FATHER?>
<HE ASKED THAT HE NEVER DRINK AGAIN.>
<AND HE NEVER DID.>
<NOT ONE DROP.>
<WHAT IS WRONG WITH YOU, BOY?!>
<LAST CHANCE BEFORE YOU DIE! ON. YOUR. KNEES.>
...<NO.>

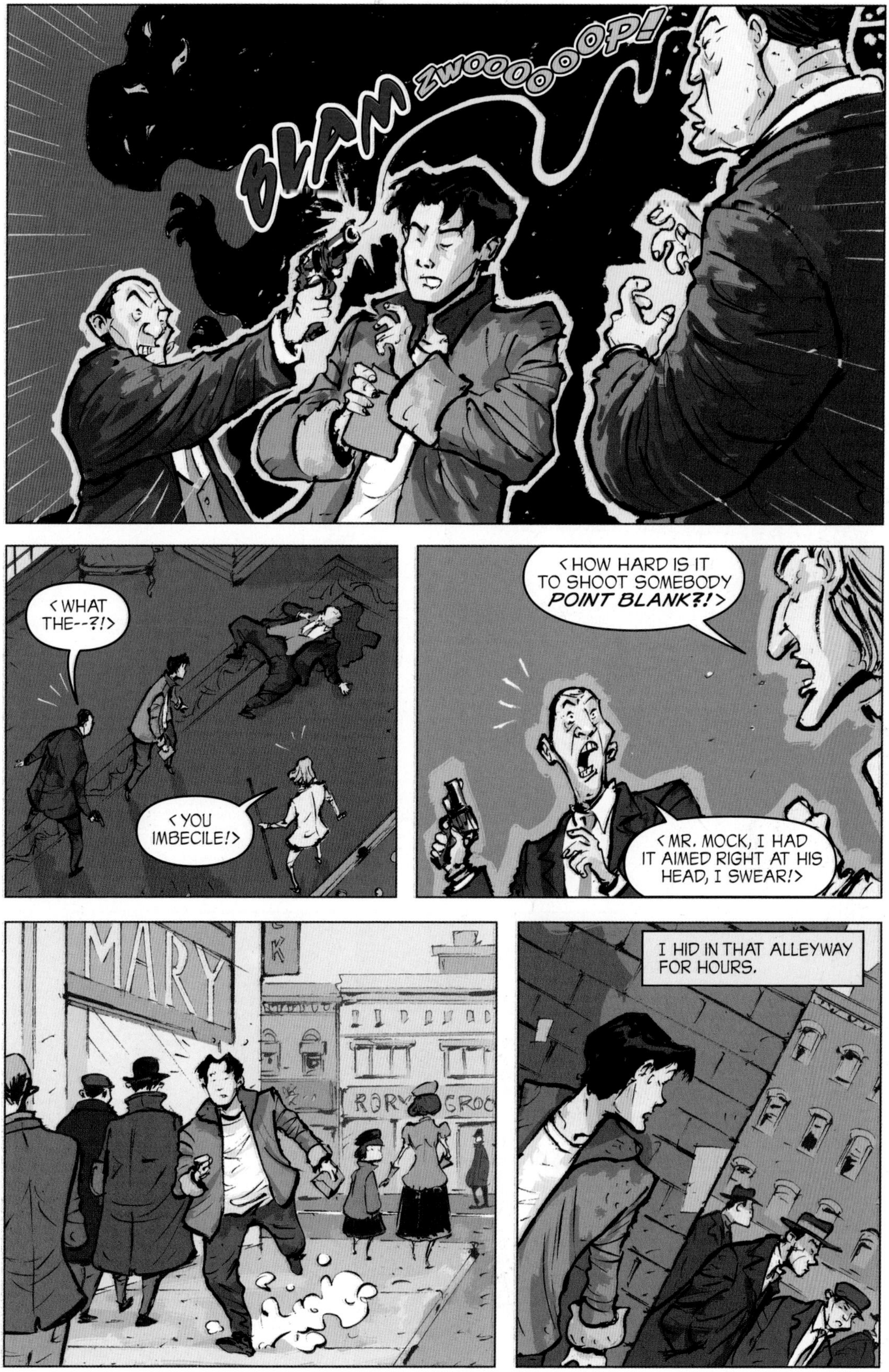
BLAM
ZWOOOOOOOP!
< WHAT THE--?!>
< YOU IMBECILE!>
< HOW HARD IS IT TO SHOOT SOMEBODY POINT BLANK?!>
< MR. MOCK, I HAD IT AIMED RIGHT AT HIS HEAD, I SWEAR!>
MARY
I HID IN THAT ALLEYWAY FOR HOURS.

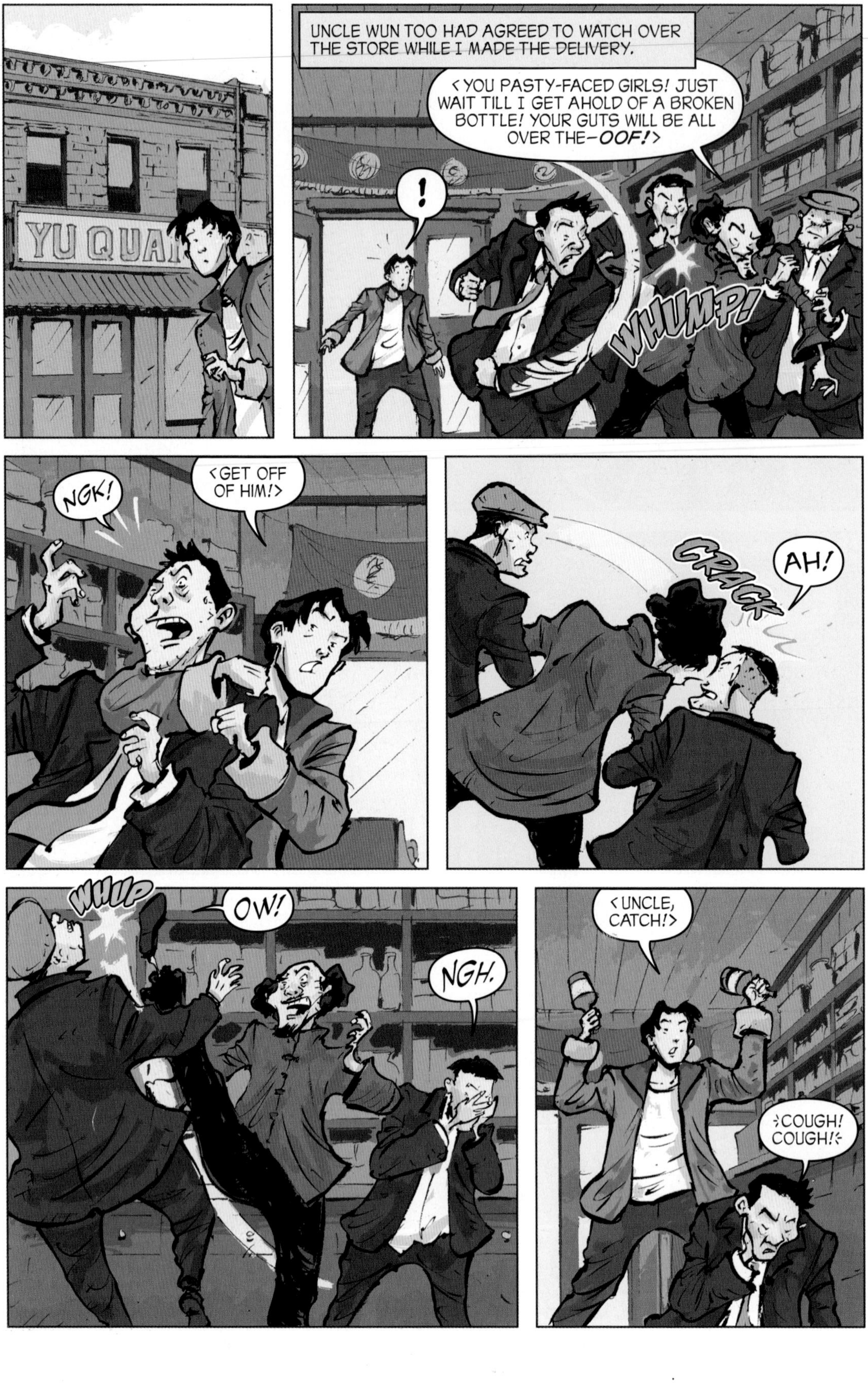
YU QUAI
UNCLE WUN TOO HAD AGREED TO WATCH OVER THE STORE WHILE I MADE THE DELIVERY.
<YOU PASTY-FACED GIRLS! JUST WAIT TILL I GET AHOLD OF A BROKEN BOTTLE! YOUR GUTS WILL BE ALL OVER THE–OOF!>
!
WHUMP!
NGK!
<GET OFF OF HIM!>
CRACK
AH!
WHUP
OW!
NGH.
<UNCLE, CATCH!>
COUGH! COUGH!

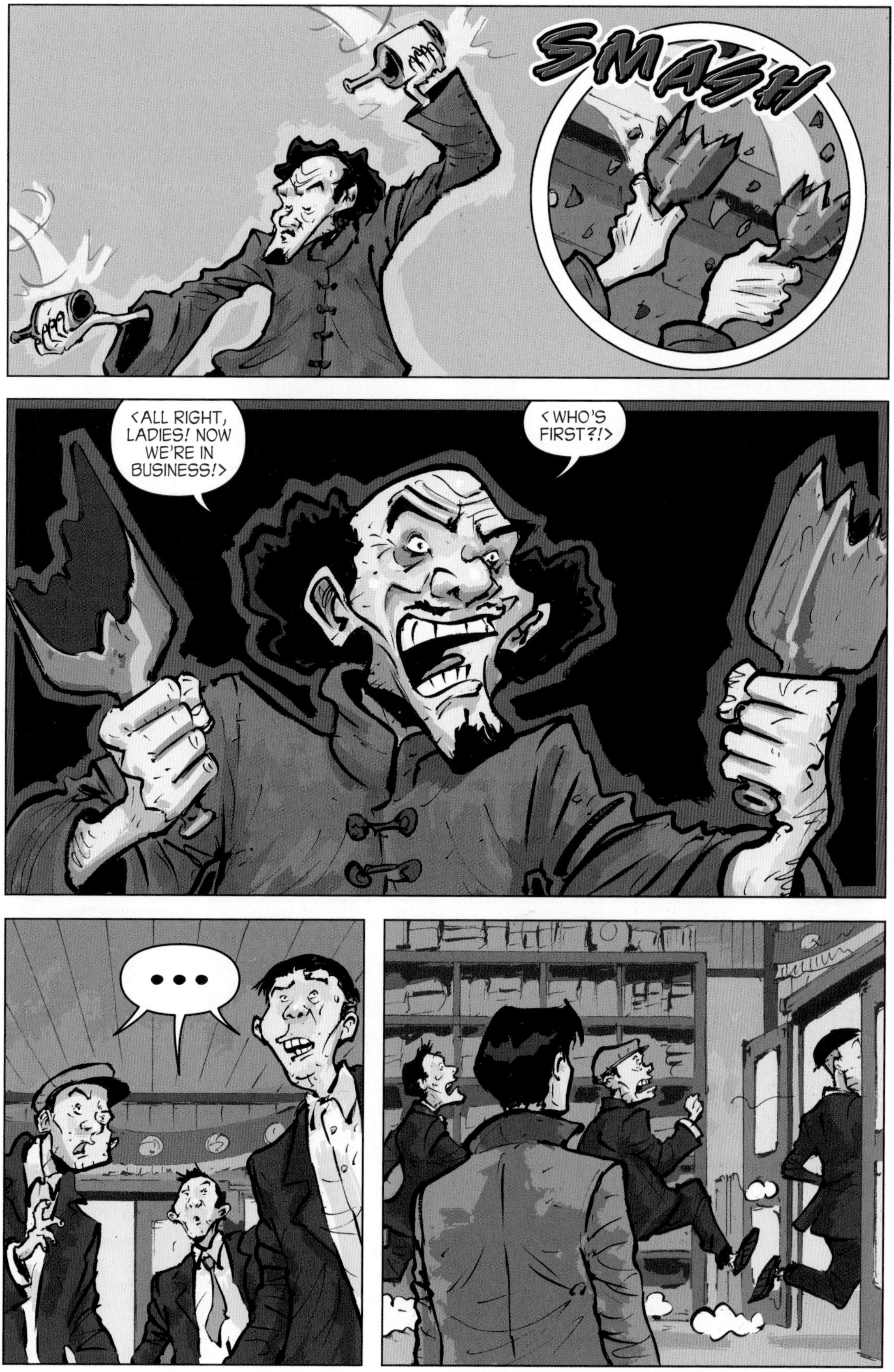
SMASH
<ALL RIGHT, LADIES! NOW WE'RE IN BUSINESS!>
< WHO'S FIRST?!>
...

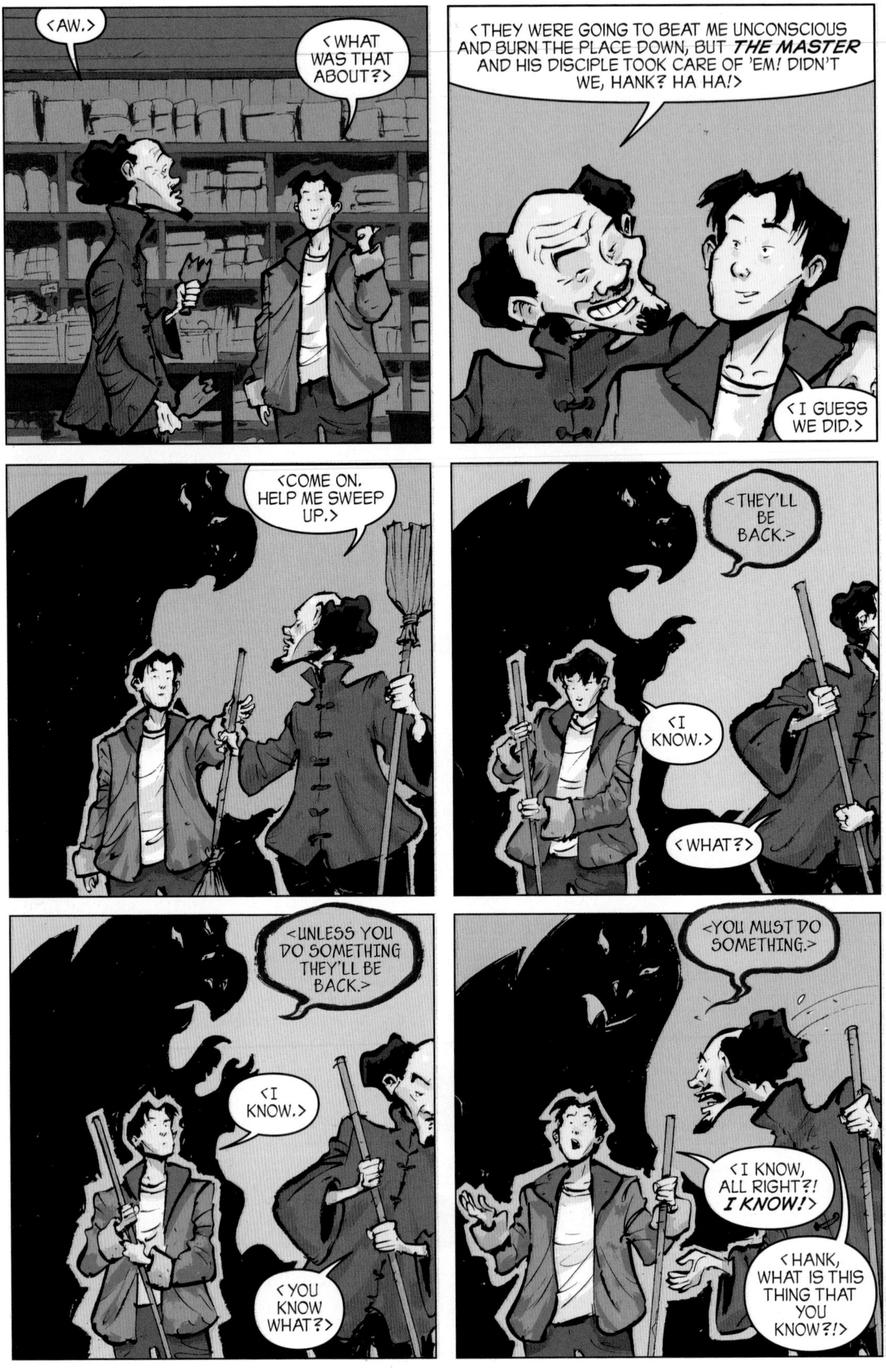
<AW.>
<WHAT WAS THAT ABOUT?>
<THEY WERE GOING TO BEAT ME UNCONSCIOUS AND BURN THE PLACE DOWN, BUT ***THE MASTER*** AND HIS DISCIPLE TOOK CARE OF 'EM! DIDN'T WE, HANK? HA HA!>
<I GUESS WE DID.>
<COME ON. HELP ME SWEEP UP.>
<THEY'LL BE BACK.>
<I KNOW.>
<WHAT?>
<UNLESS YOU DO SOMETHING THEY'LL BE BACK.>
<I KNOW.>
<YOU KNOW WHAT?>
<YOU MUST DO SOMETHING.>
<I KNOW, ALL RIGHT?! ***I KNOW!***>
<HANK, WHAT IS THIS THING THAT YOU KNOW?!>

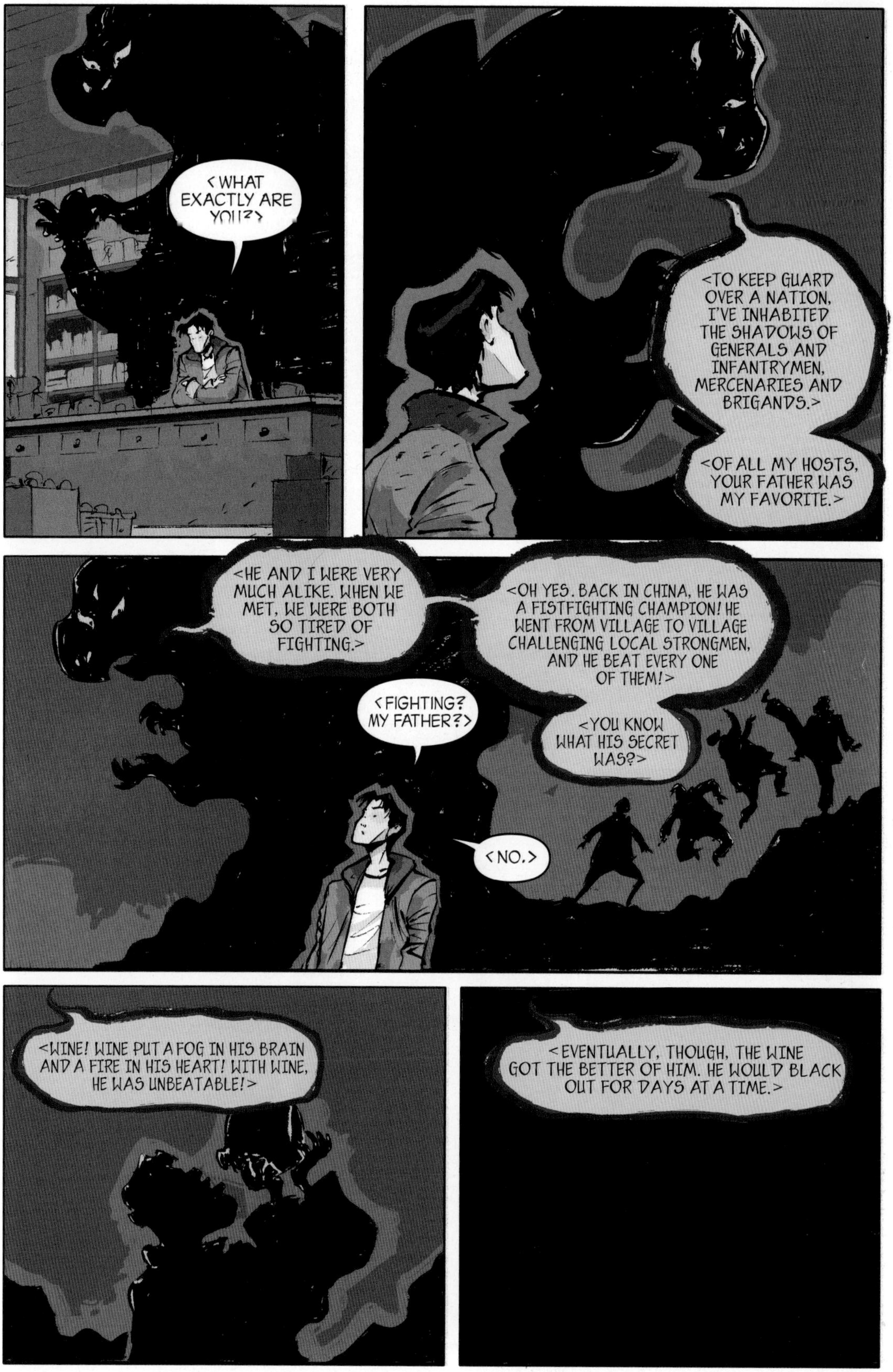

<WHAT EXACTLY ARE YOU?>
<TO KEEP GUARD OVER A NATION, I'VE INHABITED THE SHADOWS OF GENERALS AND INFANTRYMEN, MERCENARIES AND BRIGANDS.>
<OF ALL MY HOSTS, YOUR FATHER WAS MY FAVORITE.>
<HE AND I WERE VERY MUCH ALIKE. WHEN WE MET, WE WERE BOTH SO TIRED OF FIGHTING.>
<FIGHTING? MY FATHER?>
<OH YES. BACK IN CHINA, HE WAS A FISTFIGHTING CHAMPION! HE WENT FROM VILLAGE TO VILLAGE CHALLENGING LOCAL STRONGMEN, AND HE BEAT EVERY ONE OF THEM!>
<YOU KNOW WHAT HIS SECRET WAS?>
<NO.>
<WINE! WINE PUT A FOG IN HIS BRAIN AND A FIRE IN HIS HEART! WITH WINE, HE WAS UNBEATABLE!>
<EVENTUALLY, THOUGH, THE WINE GOT THE BETTER OF HIM. HE WOULD BLACK OUT FOR DAYS AT A TIME.>

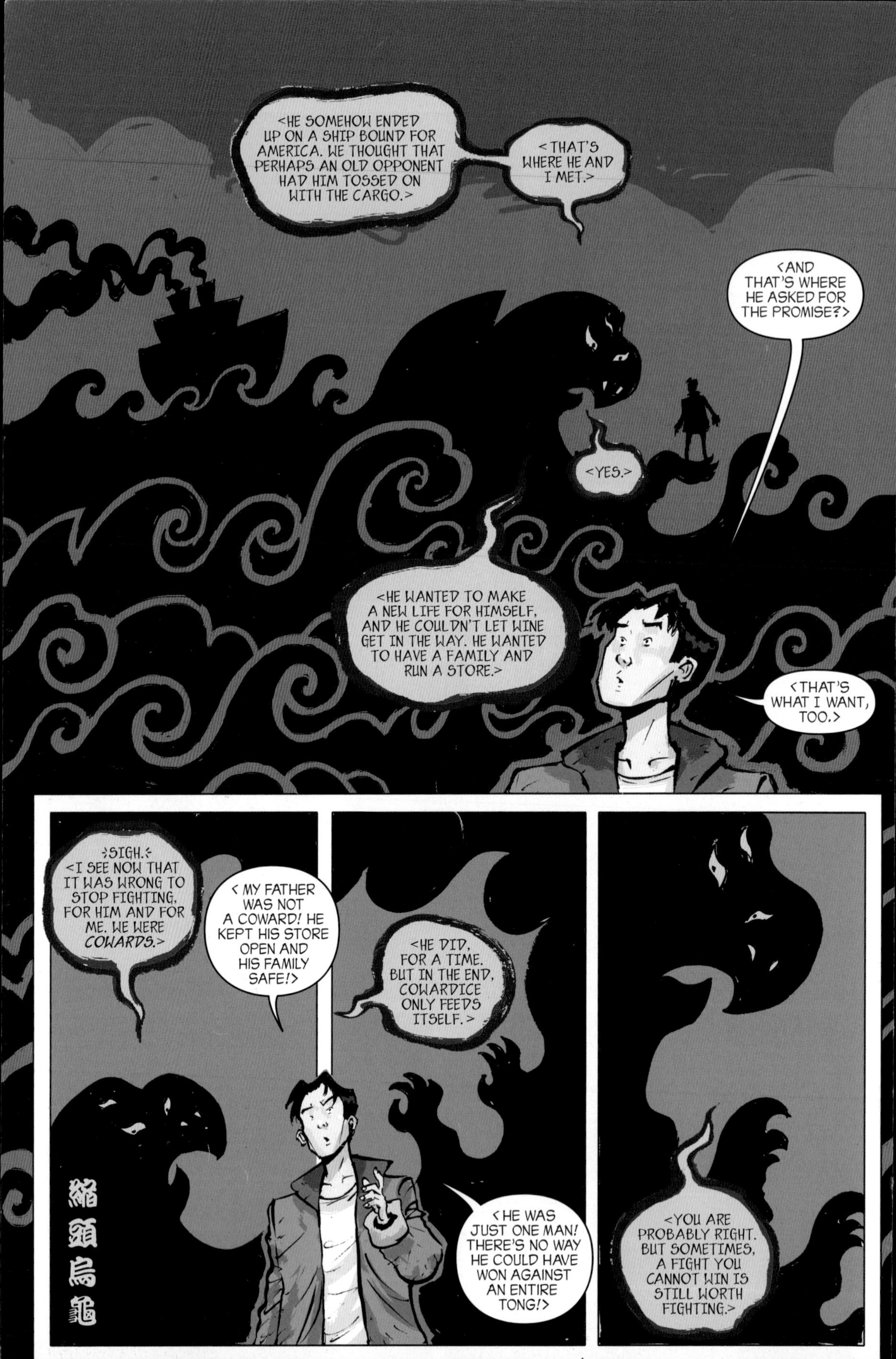
<HE SOMEHOW ENDED UP ON A SHIP BOUND FOR AMERICA. WE THOUGHT THAT PERHAPS AN OLD OPPONENT HAD HIM TOSSED ON WITH THE CARGO.>
<THAT'S WHERE HE AND I MET.>
<AND THAT'S WHERE HE ASKED FOR THE PROMISE?>
<YES.>
<HE WANTED TO MAKE A NEW LIFE FOR HIMSELF, AND HE COULDN'T LET WINE GET IN THE WAY. HE WANTED TO HAVE A FAMILY AND RUN A STORE.>
<THAT'S WHAT I WANT, TOO.>
SIGH. <I SEE NOW THAT IT WAS WRONG TO STOP FIGHTING, FOR HIM AND FOR ME. WE WERE *COWARDS.*>
<MY FATHER WAS NOT A COWARD! HE KEPT HIS STORE OPEN AND HIS FAMILY SAFE!>
<HE DID, FOR A TIME. BUT IN THE END, COWARDICE ONLY FEEDS ITSELF.>
縮頭烏龜
<HE WAS JUST ONE MAN! THERE'S NO WAY HE COULD HAVE WON AGAINST AN ENTIRE TONG!>
<YOU ARE PROBABLY RIGHT. BUT SOMETIMES, A FIGHT YOU CANNOT WIN IS STILL WORTH FIGHTING.>

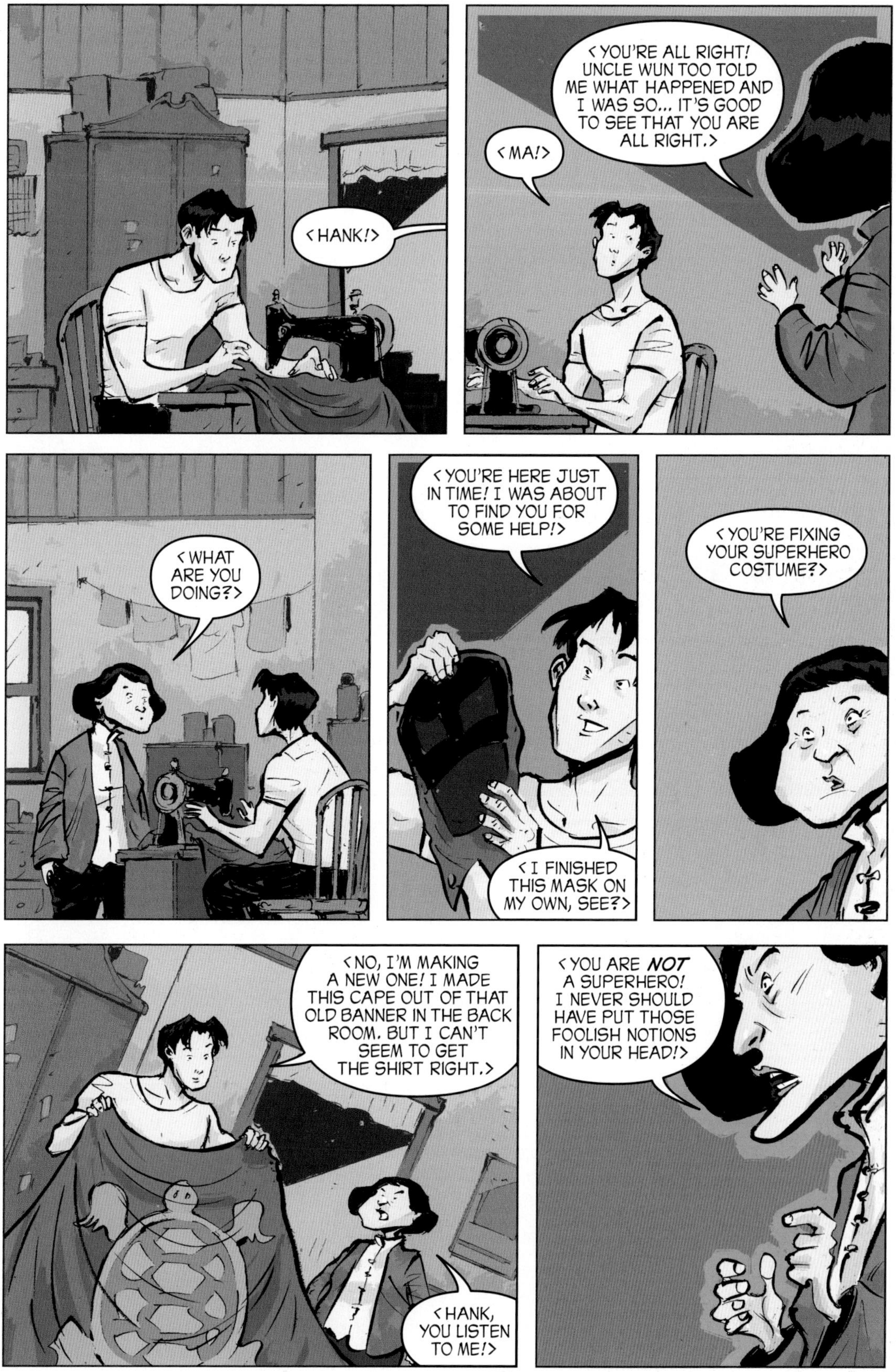

<HANK!>
<MA!>
<YOU'RE ALL RIGHT! UNCLE WUN TOO TOLD ME WHAT HAPPENED AND I WAS SO... IT'S GOOD TO SEE THAT YOU ARE ALL RIGHT.>
<WHAT ARE YOU DOING?>
<YOU'RE HERE JUST IN TIME! I WAS ABOUT TO FIND YOU FOR SOME HELP!>
<I FINISHED THIS MASK ON MY OWN, SEE?>
<YOU'RE FIXING YOUR SUPERHERO COSTUME?>
<NO, I'M MAKING A NEW ONE! I MADE THIS CAPE OUT OF THAT OLD BANNER IN THE BACK ROOM. BUT I CAN'T SEEM TO GET THE SHIRT RIGHT.>
<HANK, YOU LISTEN TO ME!>
<YOU ARE ***NOT*** A SUPERHERO! I NEVER SHOULD HAVE PUT THOSE FOOLISH NOTIONS IN YOUR HEAD!>

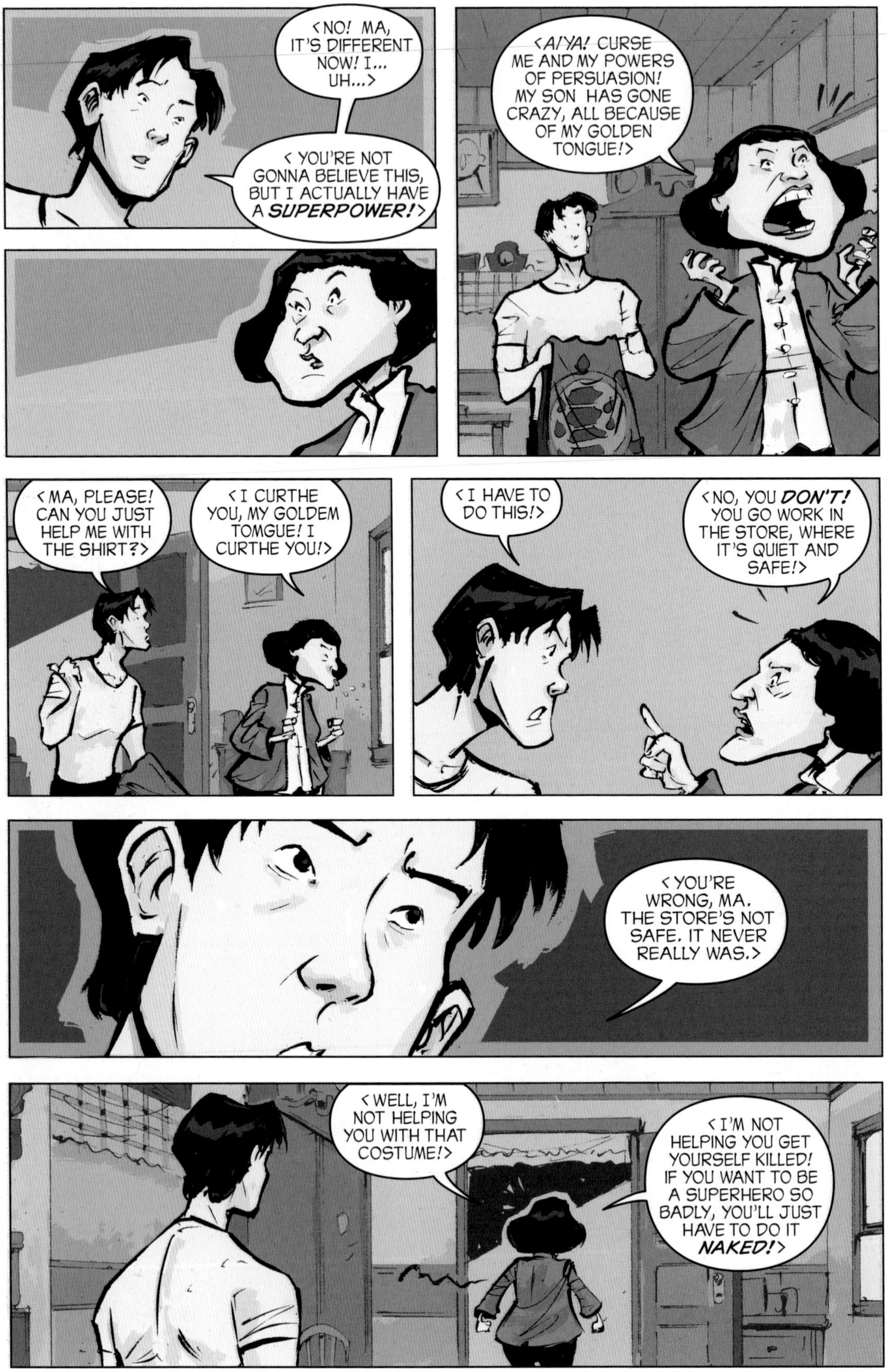
<NO! MA, IT'S DIFFERENT NOW! I... UH...>
< YOU'RE NOT GONNA BELIEVE THIS, BUT I ACTUALLY HAVE A SUPERPOWER!>
<AIYA! CURSE ME AND MY POWERS OF PERSUASION! MY SON HAS GONE CRAZY, ALL BECAUSE OF MY GOLDEN TONGUE!>
<MA, PLEASE! CAN YOU JUST HELP ME WITH THE SHIRT?>
<I CURTHE YOU, MY GOLDEM TOMGUE! I CURTHE YOU!>
<I HAVE TO DO THIS!>
<NO, YOU DON'T! YOU GO WORK IN THE STORE, WHERE IT'S QUIET AND SAFE!>
<YOU'RE WRONG, MA. THE STORE'S NOT SAFE. IT NEVER REALLY WAS.>
<WELL, I'M NOT HELPING YOU WITH THAT COSTUME!>
<I'M NOT HELPING YOU GET YOURSELF KILLED! IF YOU WANT TO BE A SUPERHERO SO BADLY, YOU'LL JUST HAVE TO DO IT NAKED!>

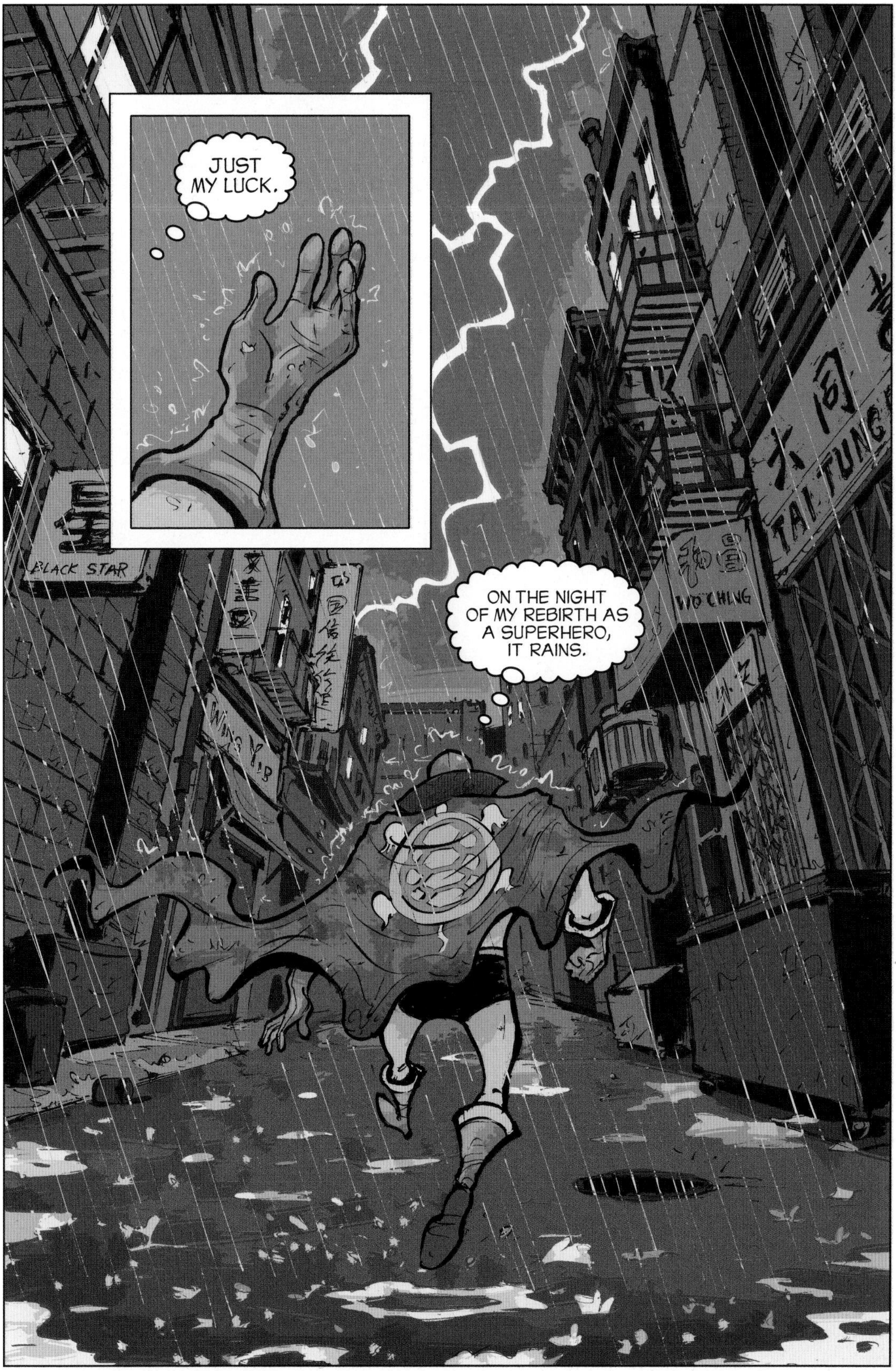
JUST MY LUCK.
ON THE NIGHT OF MY REBIRTH AS A SUPERHERO, IT RAINS.
BLACK STAR
WO CHING
TAI TUNG

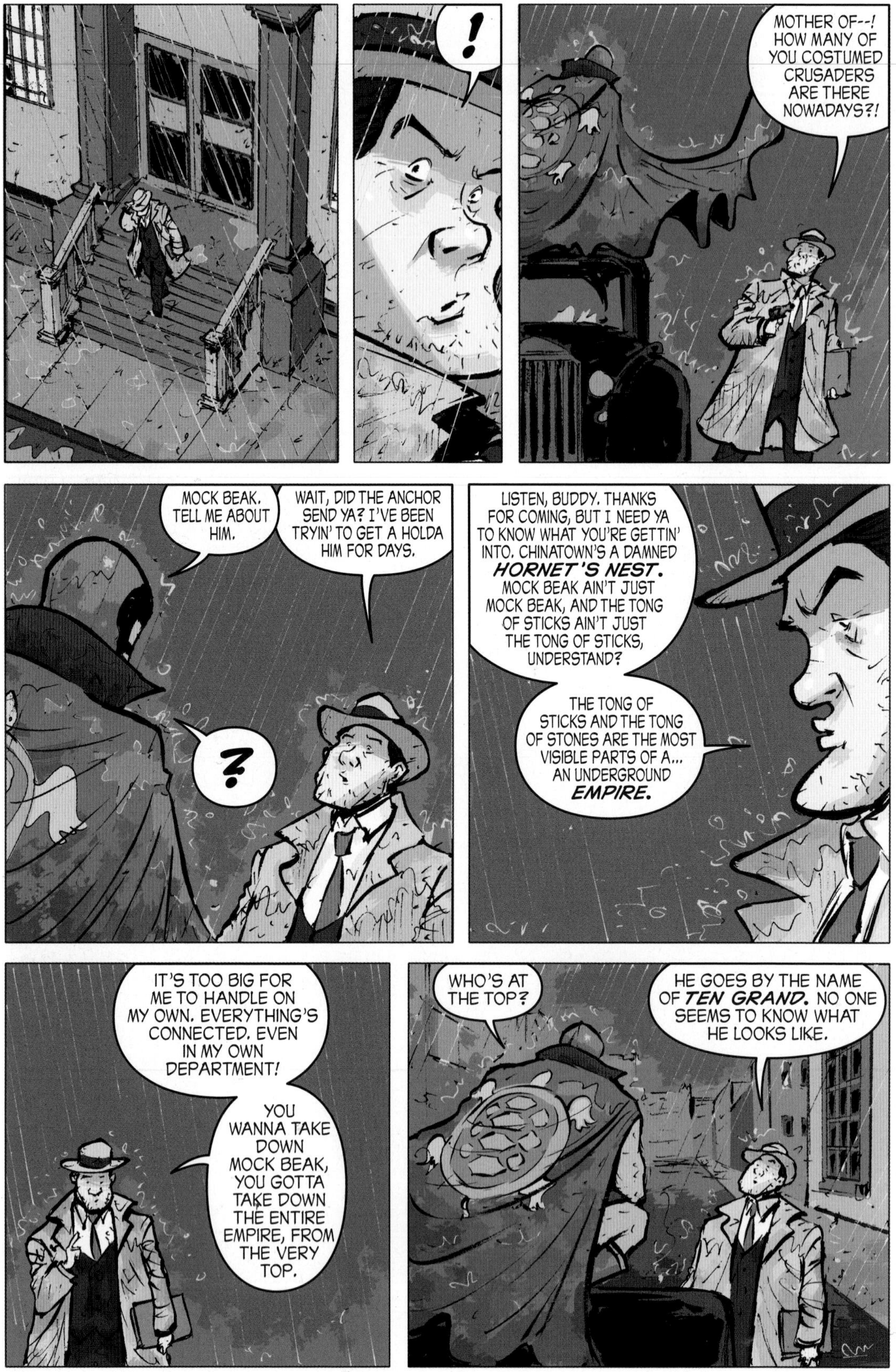
!
MOTHER OF--! HOW MANY OF YOU COSTUMED CRUSADERS ARE THERE NOWADAYS?!
MOCK BEAK. TELL ME ABOUT HIM.
WAIT, DID THE ANCHOR SEND YA? I'VE BEEN TRYIN' TO GET A HOLDA HIM FOR DAYS.
?
LISTEN, BUDDY. THANKS FOR COMING, BUT I NEED YA TO KNOW WHAT YOU'RE GETTIN' INTO. CHINATOWN'S A DAMNED HORNET'S NEST. MOCK BEAK AIN'T JUST MOCK BEAK, AND THE TONG OF STICKS AIN'T JUST THE TONG OF STICKS, UNDERSTAND?
THE TONG OF STICKS AND THE TONG OF STONES ARE THE MOST VISIBLE PARTS OF A... AN UNDERGROUND EMPIRE.
IT'S TOO BIG FOR ME TO HANDLE ON MY OWN. EVERYTHING'S CONNECTED. EVEN IN MY OWN DEPARTMENT!
YOU WANNA TAKE DOWN MOCK BEAK, YOU GOTTA TAKE DOWN THE ENTIRE EMPIRE, FROM THE VERY TOP.
WHO'S AT THE TOP?
HE GOES BY THE NAME OF TEN GRAND. NO ONE SEEMS TO KNOW WHAT HE LOOKS LIKE.

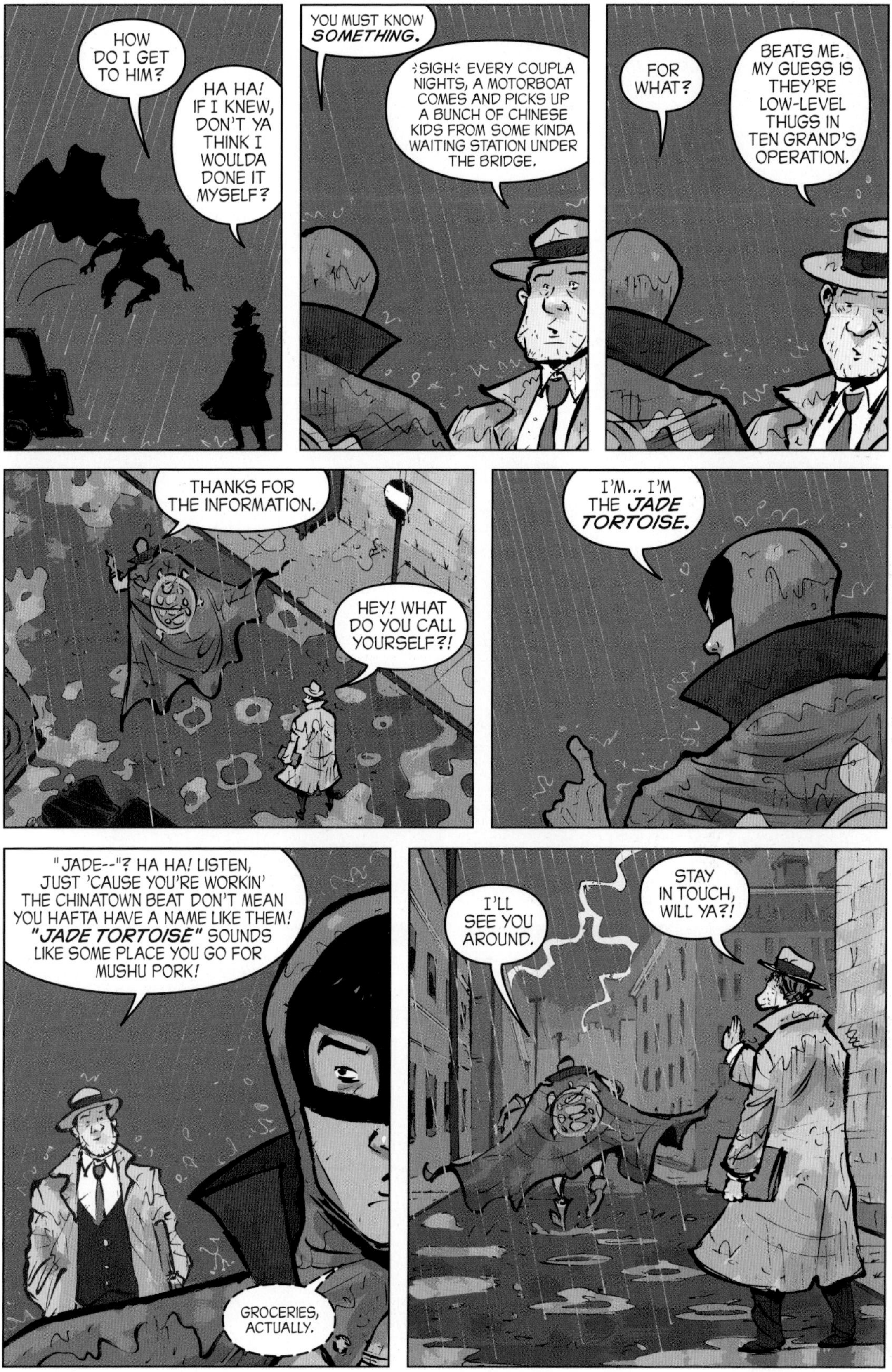
HOW DO I GET TO HIM?
HA HA! IF I KNEW, DON'T YA THINK I WOULDA DONE IT MYSELF?
YOU MUST KNOW SOMETHING.
SIGH EVERY COUPLA NIGHTS, A MOTORBOAT COMES AND PICKS UP A BUNCH OF CHINESE KIDS FROM SOME KINDA WAITING STATION UNDER THE BRIDGE.
FOR WHAT?
BEATS ME. MY GUESS IS THEY'RE LOW-LEVEL THUGS IN TEN GRAND'S OPERATION.
THANKS FOR THE INFORMATION.
HEY! WHAT DO YOU CALL YOURSELF?!
I'M... I'M THE JADE TORTOISE.
"JADE--"? HA HA! LISTEN, JUST 'CAUSE YOU'RE WORKIN' THE CHINATOWN BEAT DON'T MEAN YOU HAFTA HAVE A NAME LIKE THEM! "JADE TORTOISE" SOUNDS LIKE SOME PLACE YOU GO FOR MUSHU PORK!
GROCERIES, ACTUALLY.
I'LL SEE YOU AROUND.
STAY IN TOUCH, WILL YA?!

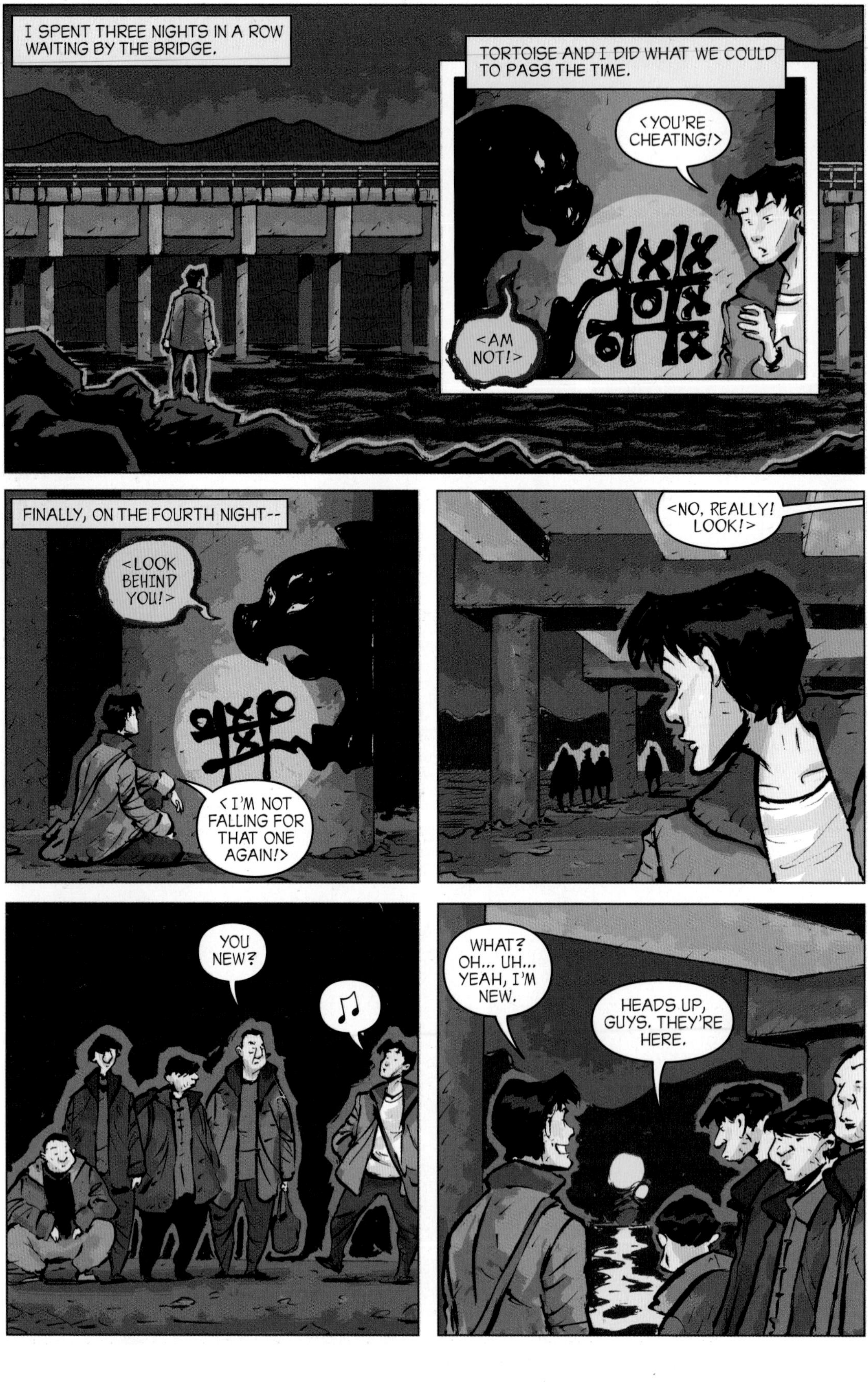
I SPENT THREE NIGHTS IN A ROW WAITING BY THE BRIDGE.
TORTOISE AND I DID WHAT WE COULD TO PASS THE TIME.
<YOU'RE CHEATING!>
<AM NOT!>
FINALLY, ON THE FOURTH NIGHT--
<LOOK BEHIND YOU!>
<I'M NOT FALLING FOR THAT ONE AGAIN!>
<NO, REALLY! LOOK!>
YOU NEW?
♫
WHAT? OH... UH... YEAH, I'M NEW.
HEADS UP, GUYS. THEY'RE HERE.

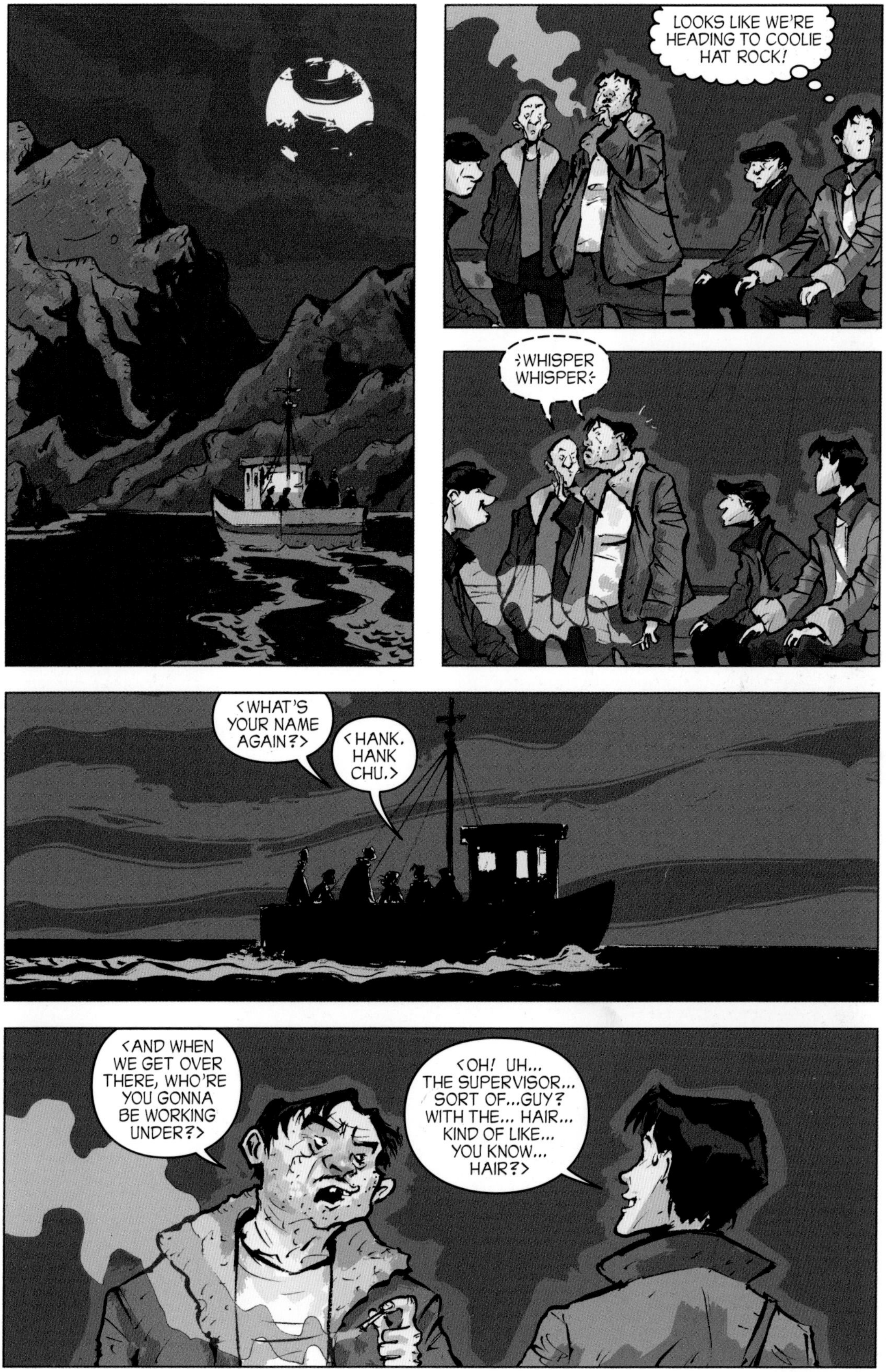
LOOKS LIKE WE'RE HEADING TO COOLIE HAT ROCK!
WHISPER WHISPER
<WHAT'S YOUR NAME AGAIN?>
<HANK. HANK CHU.>
<AND WHEN WE GET OVER THERE, WHO'RE YOU GONNA BE WORKING UNDER?>
<OH! UH... THE SUPERVISOR... SORT OF...GUY? WITH THE... HAIR... KIND OF LIKE... YOU KNOW... HAIR?>

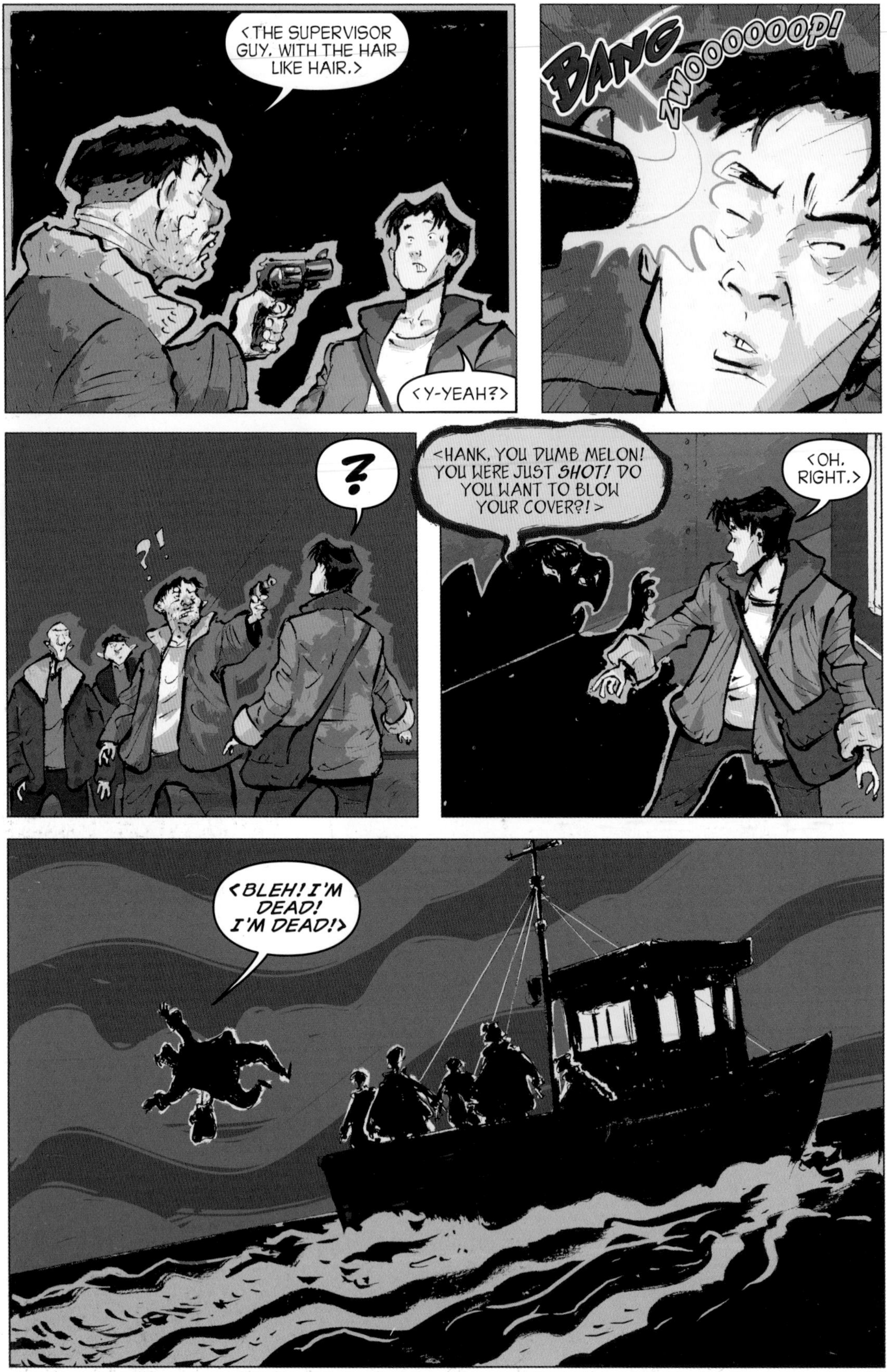
<THE SUPERVISOR GUY. WITH THE HAIR LIKE HAIR.>
<Y-YEAH?>
BANG
ZWOOOOOOOP!
?
?!
<HANK, YOU DUMB MELON! YOU WERE JUST SHOT! DO YOU WANT TO BLOW YOUR COVER?!>
<OH. RIGHT.>
<BLEH! I'M DEAD! I'M DEAD!>

<WHAT THE HELL WAS THAT?!>
<HEADS UP! WE'RE LANDING!>
<HURRY UP! YOU'RE ALREADY LATE!>
CANIFF
CANIFF

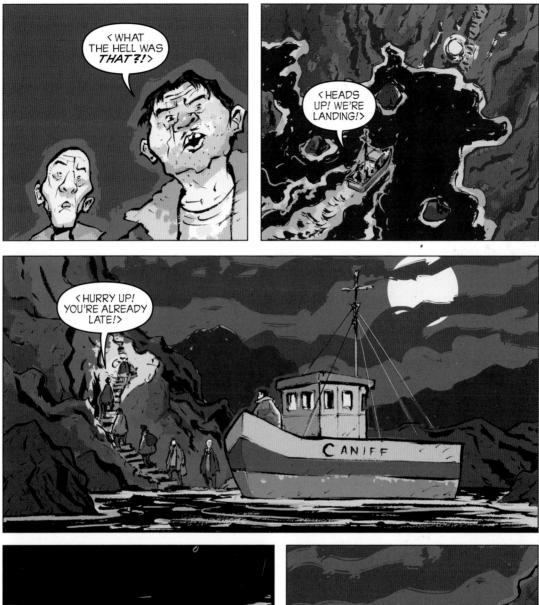

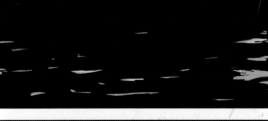

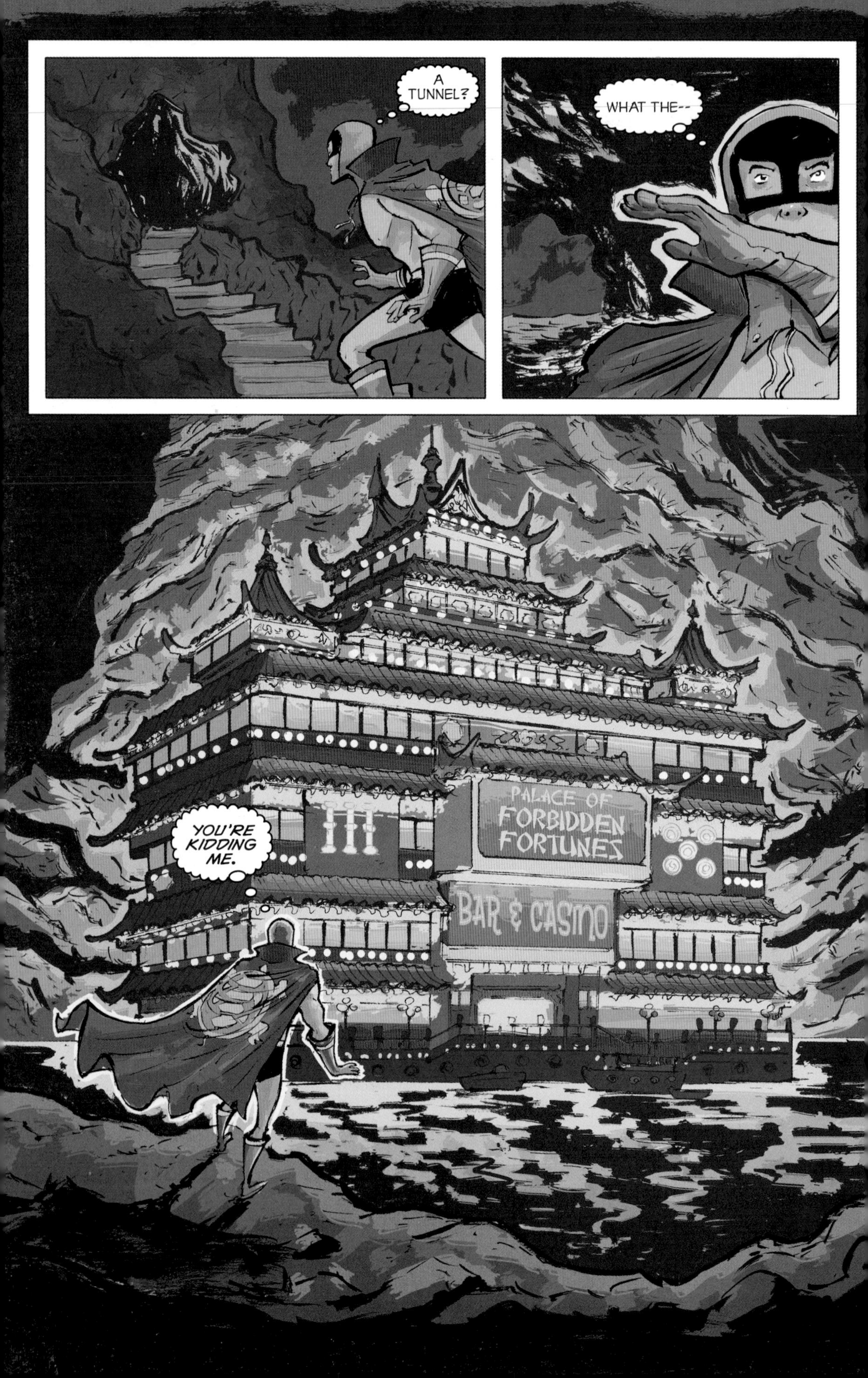
A TUNNEL?
WHAT THE--
YOU'RE KIDDING ME.
PALACE OF FORBIDDEN FORTUNES
BAR & CASINO

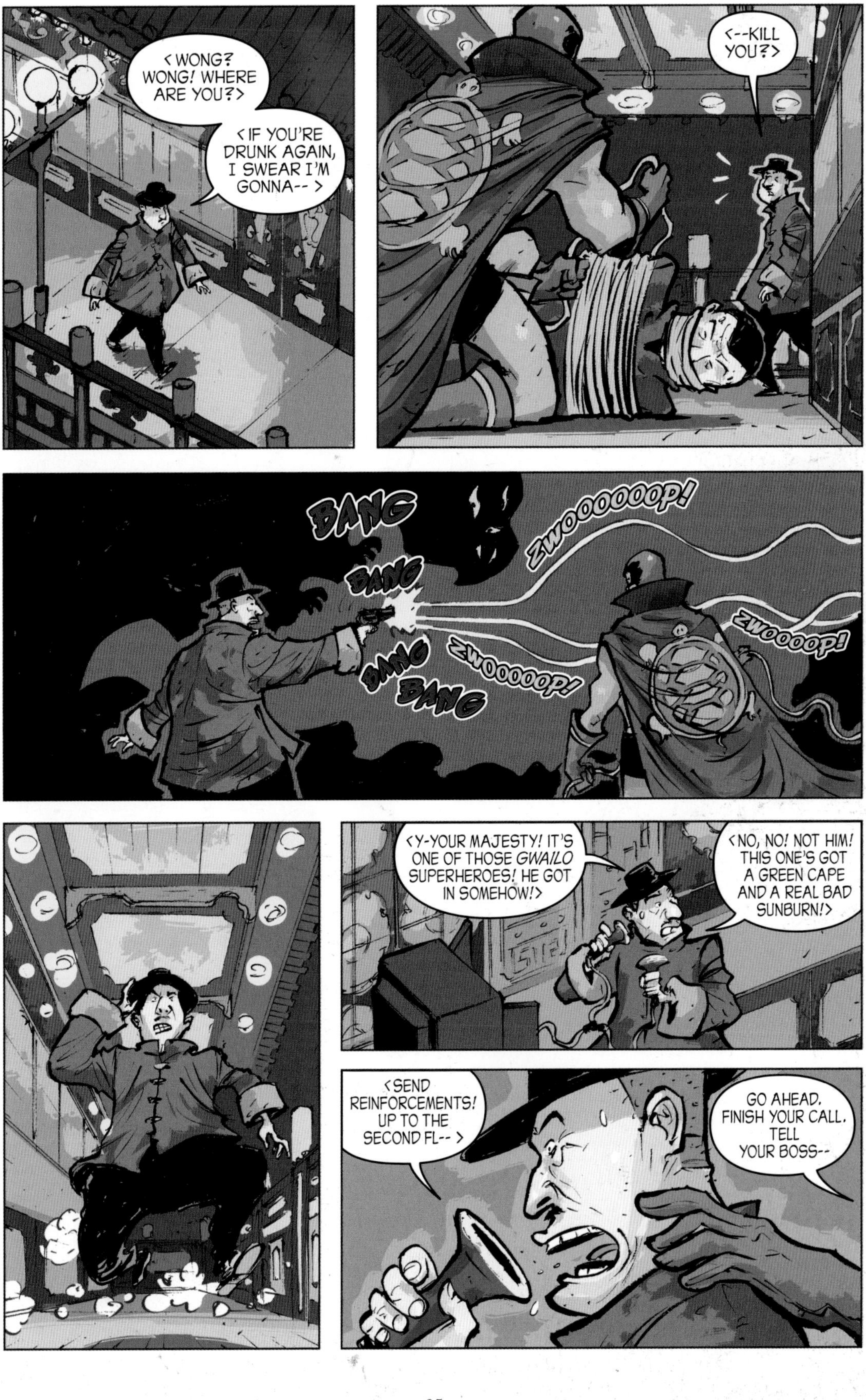
<WONG? WONG! WHERE ARE YOU?>
<IF YOU'RE DRUNK AGAIN, I SWEAR I'M GONNA-- >
<--KILL YOU?>
BANG
BANG
BANG
BANG
ZWOOOOOOOP!
ZWOOOOP!
ZWOOOOOOP!
<Y-YOUR MAJESTY! IT'S ONE OF THOSE *GWAILO* SUPERHEROES! HE GOT IN SOMEHOW!>
<NO, NO! NOT HIM! THIS ONE'S GOT A GREEN CAPE AND A REAL BAD SUNBURN!>
<SEND REINFORCEMENTS! UP TO THE SECOND FL-- >
GO AHEAD. FINISH YOUR CALL. TELL YOUR BOSS--

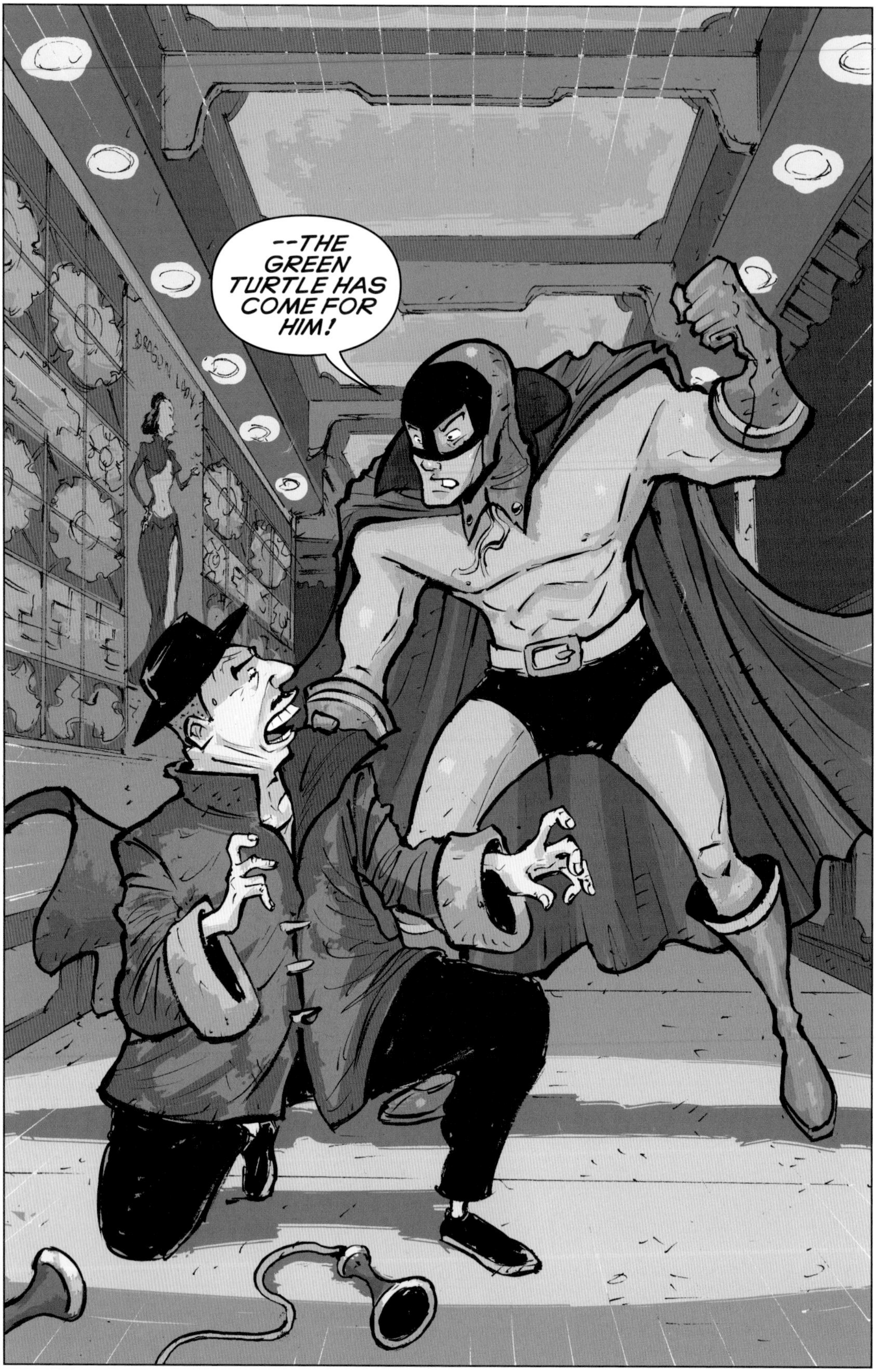
--THE GREEN TURTLE HAS COME FOR HIM!

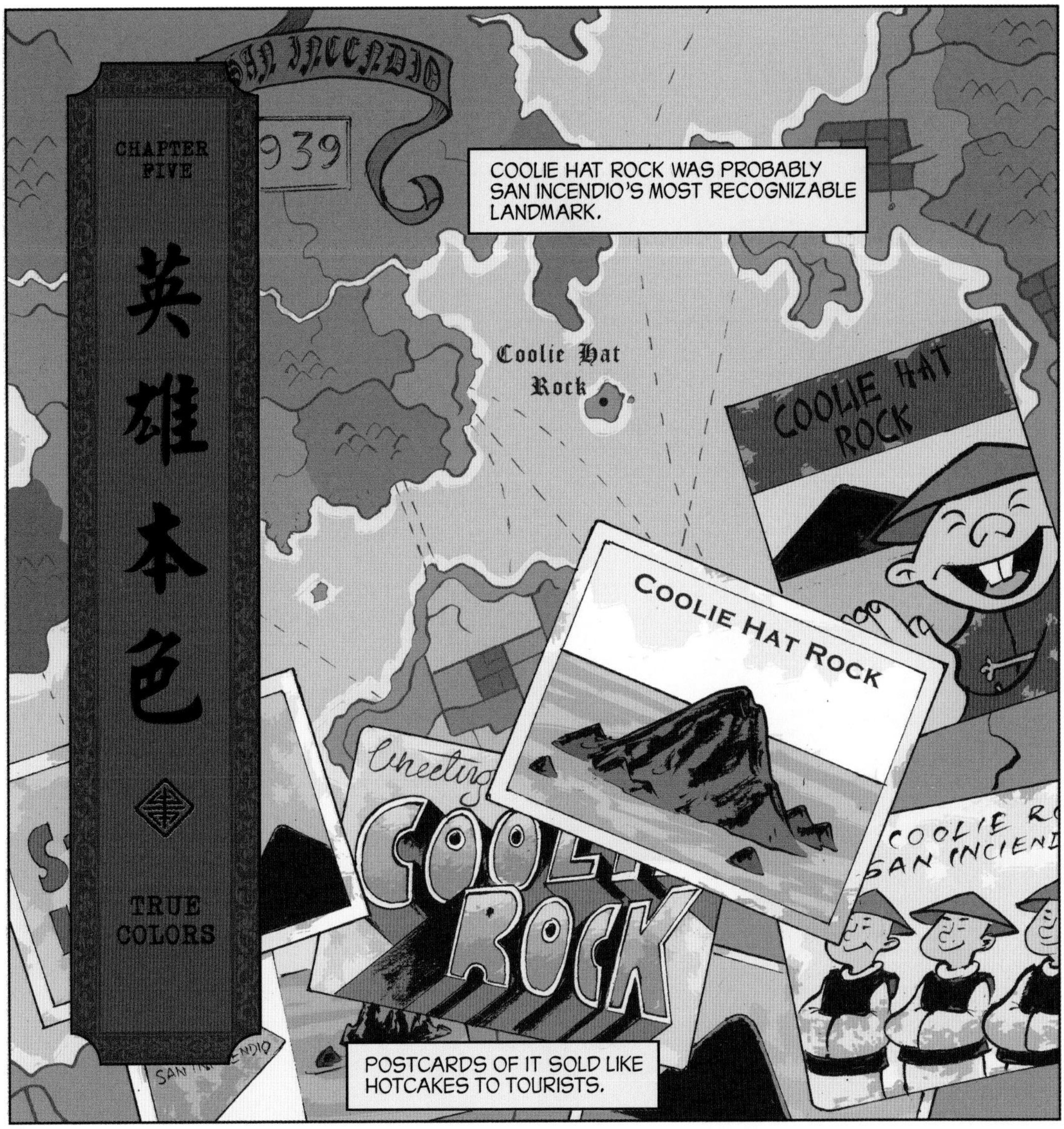
SAN INCENDIO
1939
CHAPTER FIVE
英雄本色
TRUE COLORS
COOLIE HAT ROCK WAS PROBABLY SAN INCENDIO'S MOST RECOGNIZABLE LANDMARK.
Coolie Hat Rock
COOLIE HAT ROCK
COOLIE HAT ROCK
COOLIE ROCK
POSTCARDS OF IT SOLD LIKE HOTCAKES TO TOURISTS.

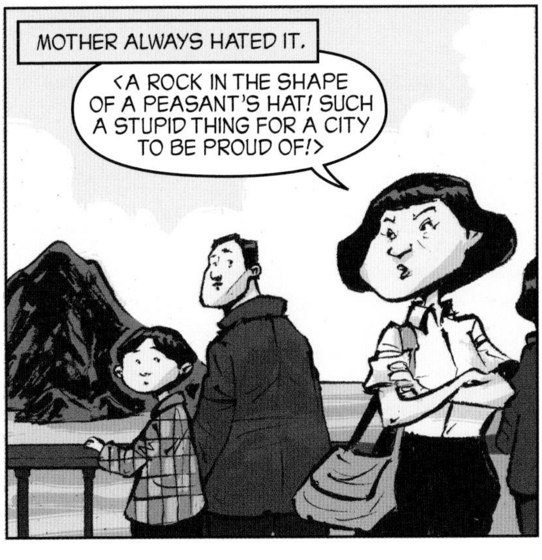
MOTHER ALWAYS HATED IT.
<A ROCK IN THE SHAPE OF A PEASANT'S HAT! SUCH A STUPID THING FOR A CITY TO BE PROUD OF!>

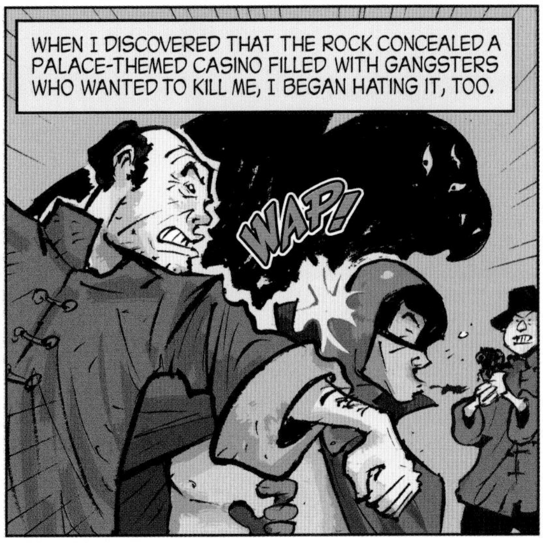
WHEN I DISCOVERED THAT THE ROCK CONCEALED A PALACE-THEMED CASINO FILLED WITH GANGSTERS WHO WANTED TO KILL ME, I BEGAN HATING IT, TOO.
WAP!

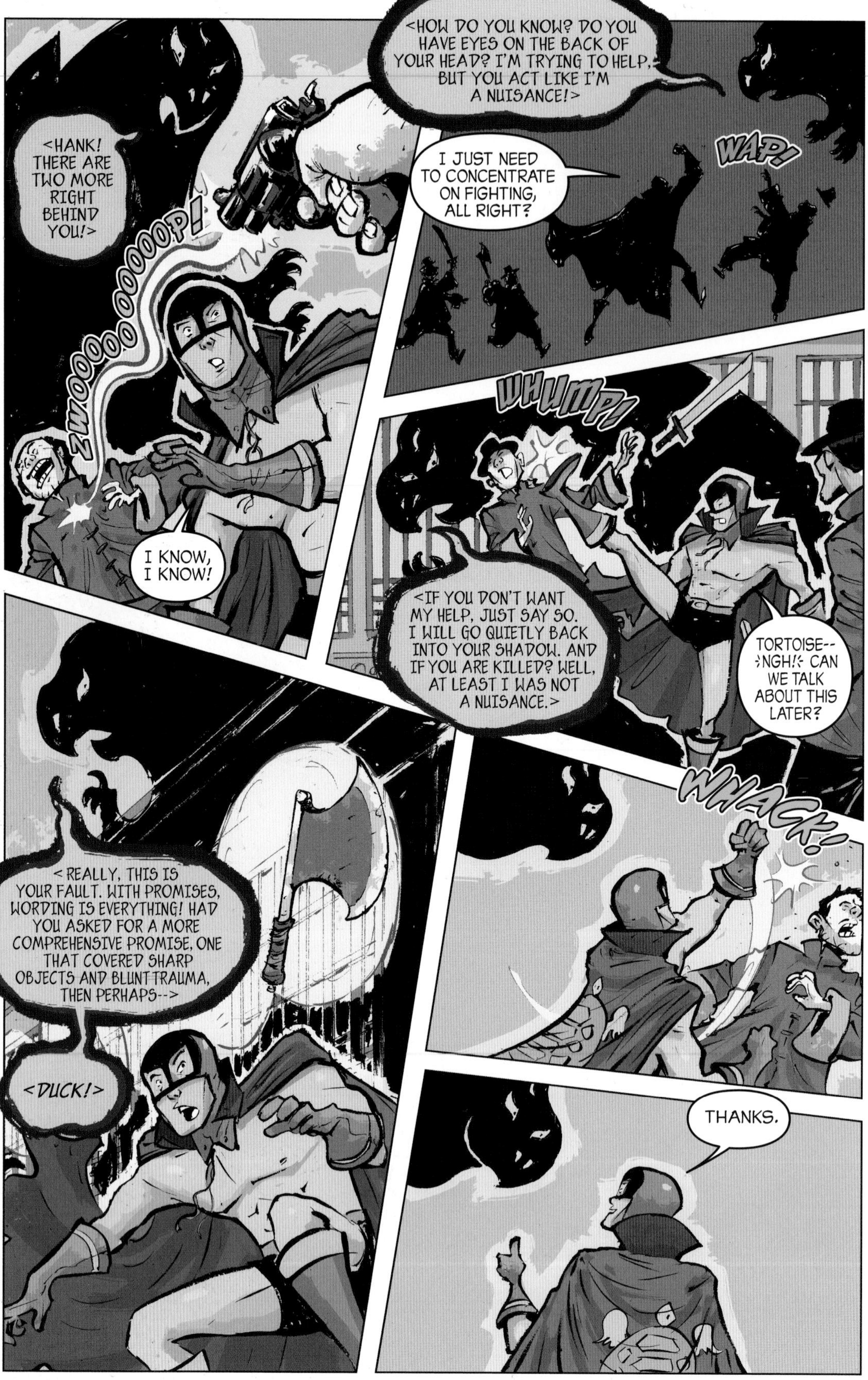

<HANK! THERE ARE TWO MORE RIGHT BEHIND YOU!>
ZWOOOOOOOOOOP!
I KNOW, I KNOW!
<HOW DO YOU KNOW? DO YOU HAVE EYES ON THE BACK OF YOUR HEAD? I'M TRYING TO HELP, BUT YOU ACT LIKE I'M A NUISANCE!>
I JUST NEED TO CONCENTRATE ON FIGHTING, ALL RIGHT?
WAP!
WHUMP!
<IF YOU DON'T WANT MY HELP, JUST SAY SO. I WILL GO QUIETLY BACK INTO YOUR SHADOW. AND IF YOU ARE KILLED? WELL, AT LEAST I WAS NOT A NUISANCE.>
TORTOISE-- -NGH!- CAN WE TALK ABOUT THIS LATER?
<REALLY, THIS IS YOUR FAULT. WITH PROMISES, WORDING IS EVERYTHING! HAD YOU ASKED FOR A MORE COMPREHENSIVE PROMISE, ONE THAT COVERED SHARP OBJECTS AND BLUNT TRAUMA, THEN PERHAPS-->
<DUCK!>
WHACK!
THANKS.

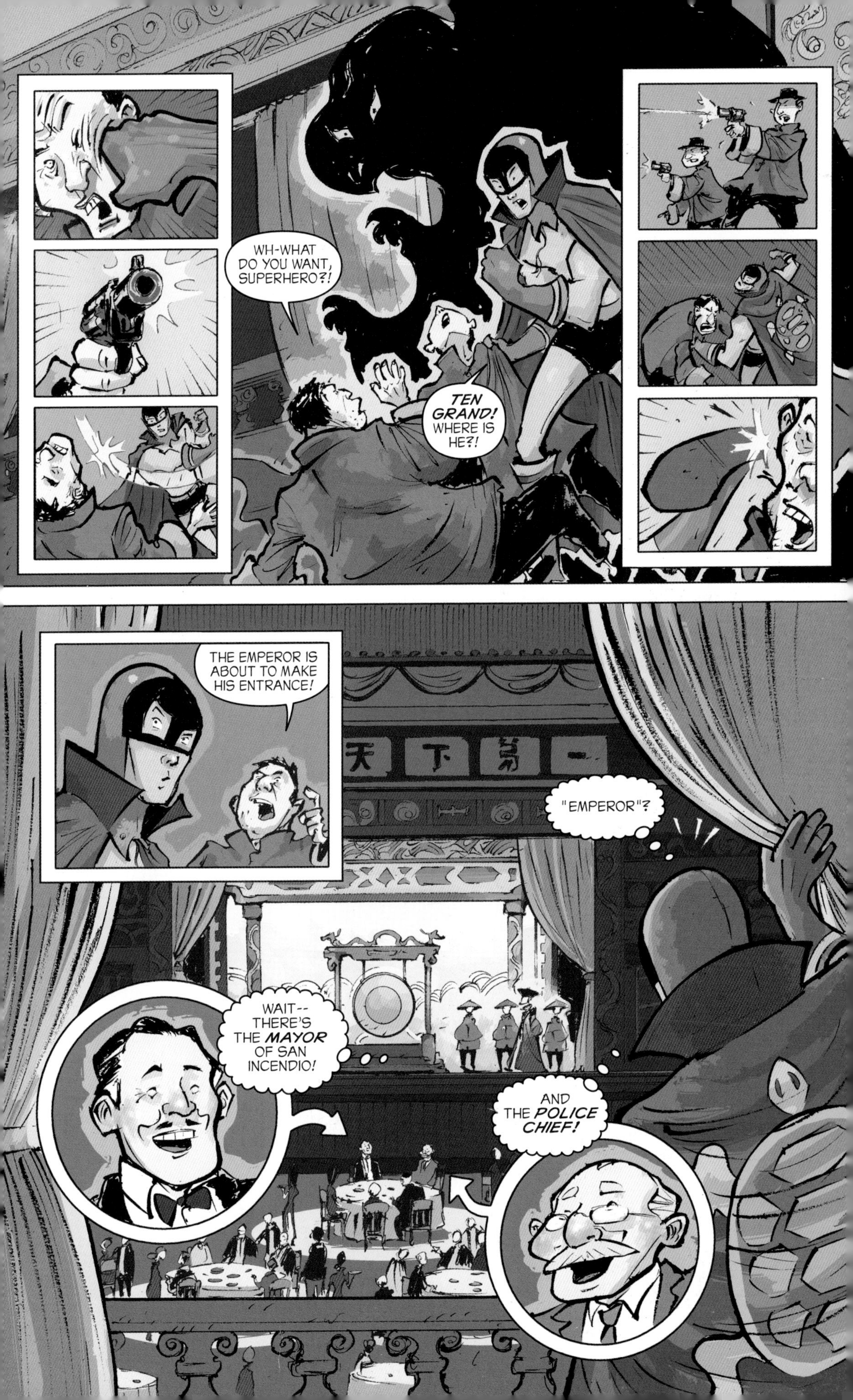
WH-WHAT DO YOU WANT, SUPERHERO?!
TEN GRAND! WHERE IS HE?!
THE EMPEROR IS ABOUT TO MAKE HIS ENTRANCE!
"EMPEROR"?
WAIT-- THERE'S THE MAYOR OF SAN INCENDIO!
AND THE POLICE CHIEF!

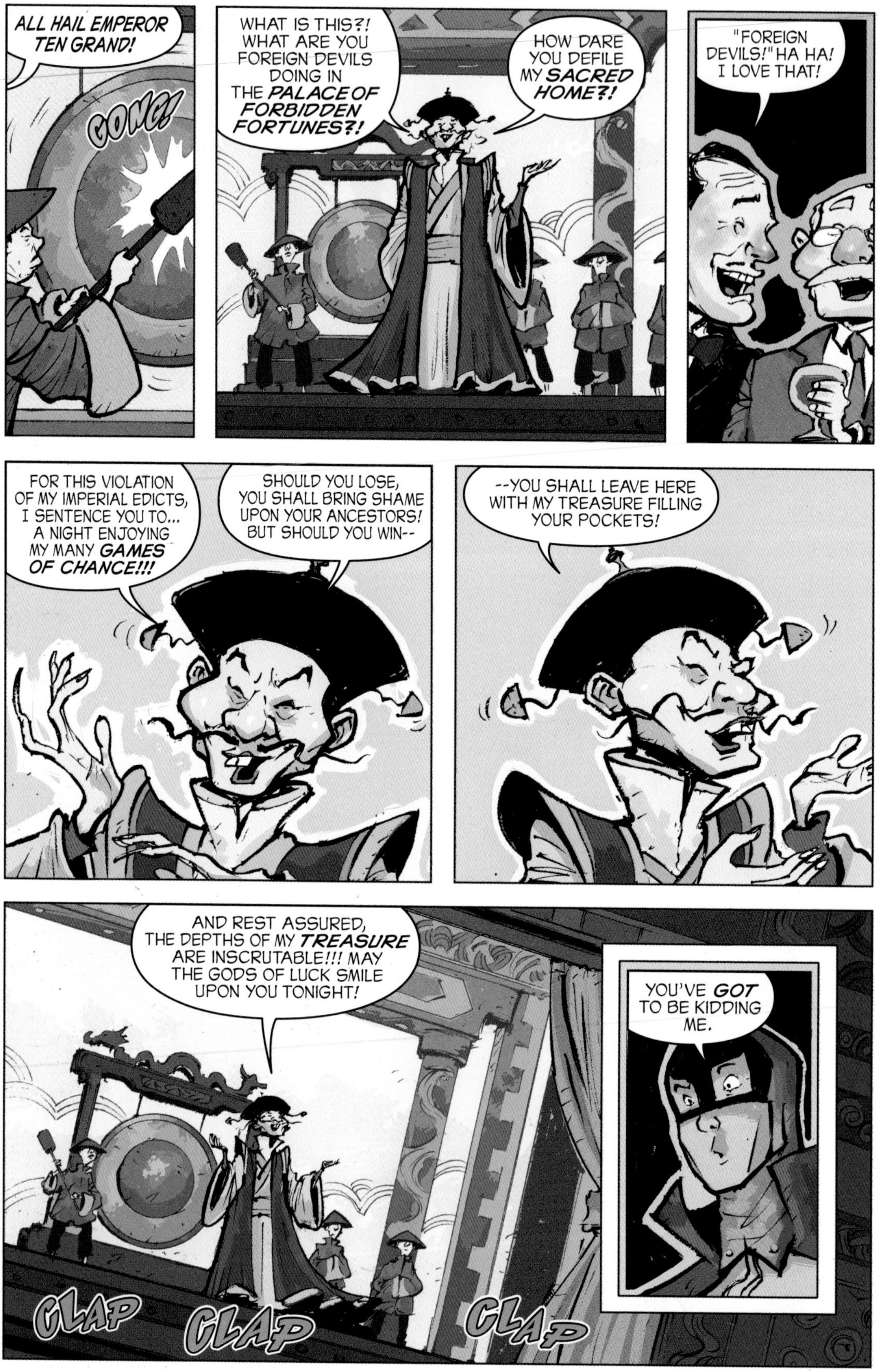
ALL HAIL EMPEROR TEN GRAND!
GONG!
WHAT IS THIS?! WHAT ARE YOU FOREIGN DEVILS DOING IN THE PALACE OF FORBIDDEN FORTUNES?!
HOW DARE YOU DEFILE MY SACRED HOME?!
"FOREIGN DEVILS!" HA HA! I LOVE THAT!
FOR THIS VIOLATION OF MY IMPERIAL EDICTS, I SENTENCE YOU TO... A NIGHT ENJOYING MY MANY GAMES OF CHANCE!!!
SHOULD YOU LOSE, YOU SHALL BRING SHAME UPON YOUR ANCESTORS! BUT SHOULD YOU WIN--
--YOU SHALL LEAVE HERE WITH MY TREASURE FILLING YOUR POCKETS!
AND REST ASSURED, THE DEPTHS OF MY TREASURE ARE INSCRUTABLE!!! MAY THE GODS OF LUCK SMILE UPON YOU TONIGHT!
YOU'VE GOT TO BE KIDDING ME.
CLAP
CLAP
CLAP

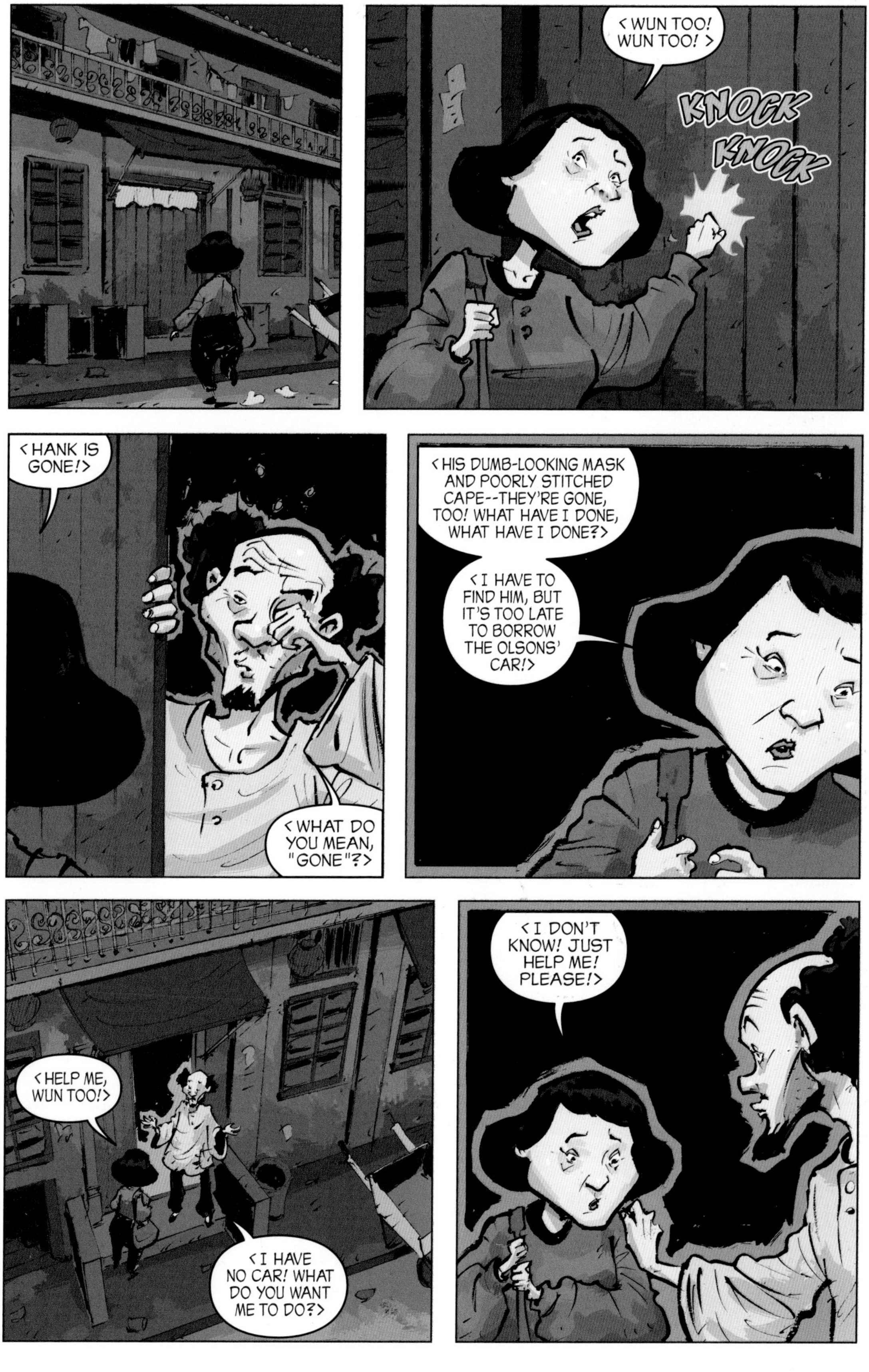
< WUN TOO! WUN TOO! >
KNOCK KNOCK
< HANK IS GONE! >
< WHAT DO YOU MEAN, "GONE"? >
< HIS DUMB-LOOKING MASK AND POORLY STITCHED CAPE--THEY'RE GONE, TOO! WHAT HAVE I DONE, WHAT HAVE I DONE? >
< I HAVE TO FIND HIM, BUT IT'S TOO LATE TO BORROW THE OLSONS' CAR! >
< HELP ME, WUN TOO! >
< I HAVE NO CAR! WHAT DO YOU WANT ME TO DO? >
< I DON'T KNOW! JUST HELP ME! PLEASE! >

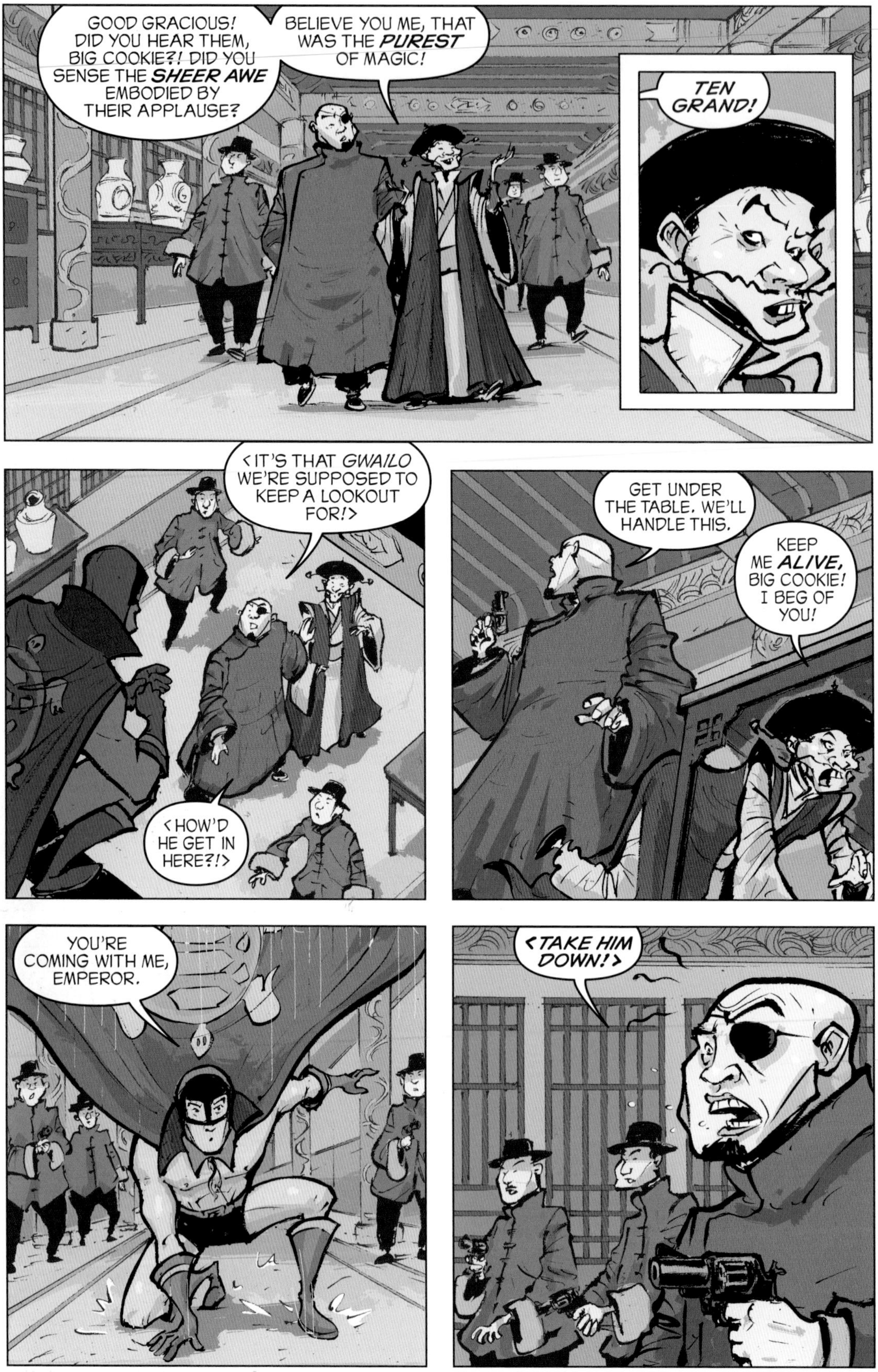
GOOD GRACIOUS! DID YOU HEAR THEM, BIG COOKIE?! DID YOU SENSE THE SHEER AWE EMBODIED BY THEIR APPLAUSE?
BELIEVE YOU ME, THAT WAS THE PUREST OF MAGIC!
TEN GRAND!
<IT'S THAT GWAILO WE'RE SUPPOSED TO KEEP A LOOKOUT FOR!>
<HOW'D HE GET IN HERE?!>
GET UNDER THE TABLE. WE'LL HANDLE THIS.
KEEP ME ALIVE, BIG COOKIE! I BEG OF YOU!
YOU'RE COMING WITH ME, EMPEROR.
<TAKE HIM DOWN!>

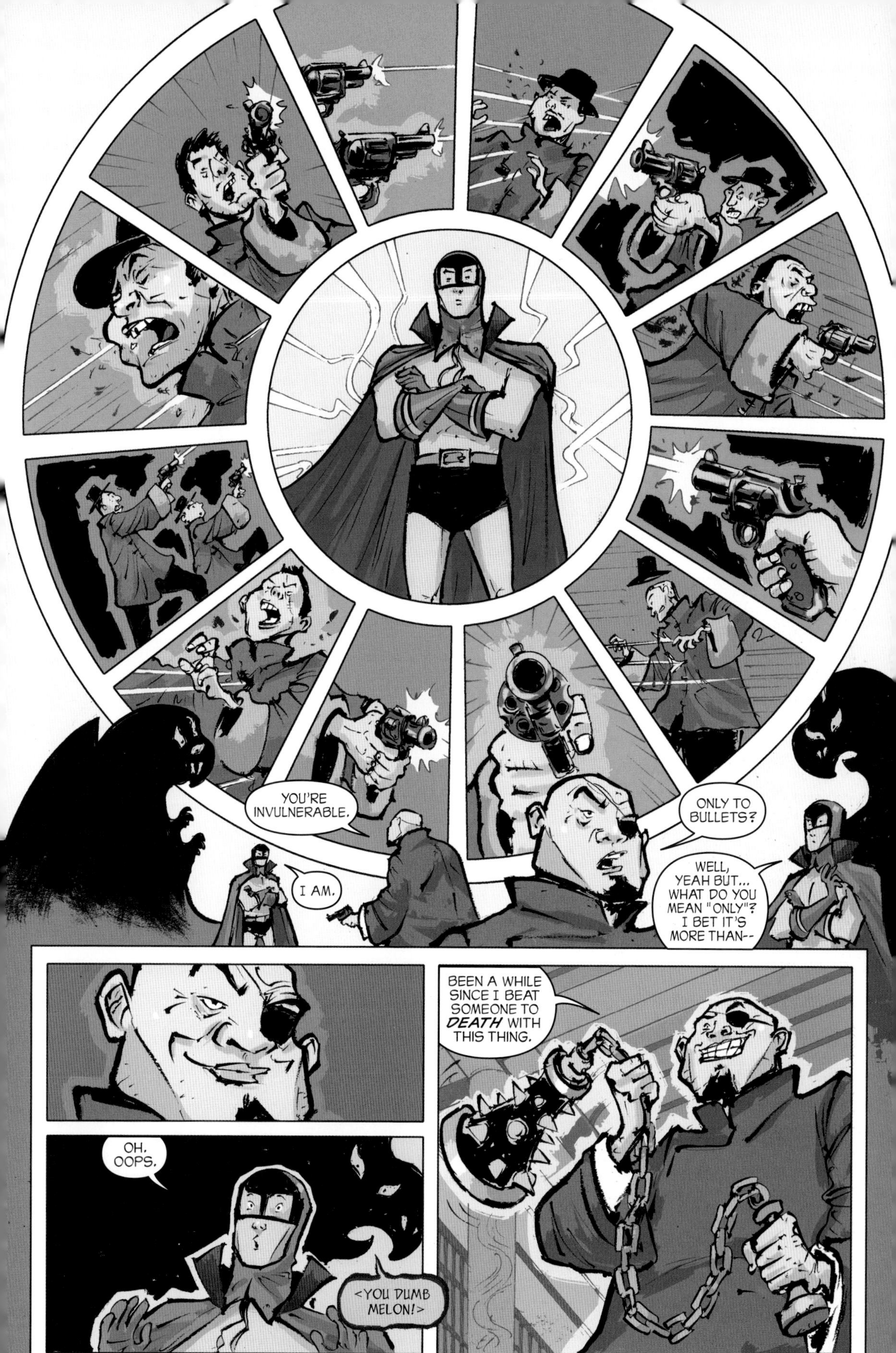
YOU'RE INVULNERABLE.
I AM.
ONLY TO BULLETS?
WELL, YEAH BUT... WHAT DO YOU MEAN "ONLY"? I BET IT'S MORE THAN--
BEEN A WHILE SINCE I BEAT SOMEONE TO DEATH WITH THIS THING.
OH. OOPS.
<YOU DUMB MELON!>

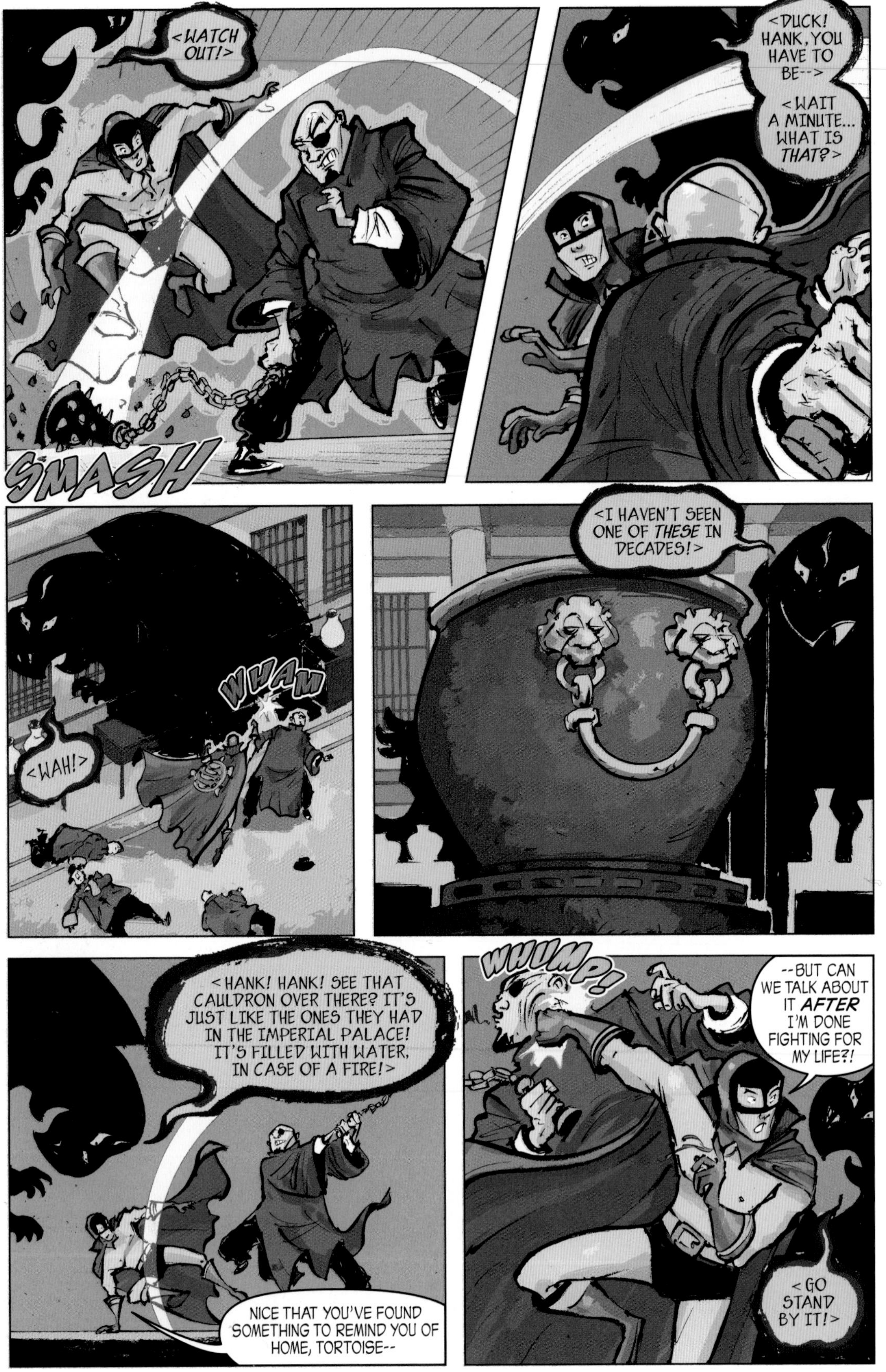

<WATCH OUT!>
SMASH
<DUCK! HANK, YOU HAVE TO BE-->
<WAIT A MINUTE... WHAT IS THAT?>
WHAM
<WAH!>
<I HAVEN'T SEEN ONE OF THESE IN DECADES!>
<HANK! HANK! SEE THAT CAULDRON OVER THERE? IT'S JUST LIKE THE ONES THEY HAD IN THE IMPERIAL PALACE! IT'S FILLED WITH WATER, IN CASE OF A FIRE!>
NICE THAT YOU'VE FOUND SOMETHING TO REMIND YOU OF HOME, TORTOISE--
WHUMP!
--BUT CAN WE TALK ABOUT IT AFTER I'M DONE FIGHTING FOR MY LIFE?!
<GO STAND BY IT!>

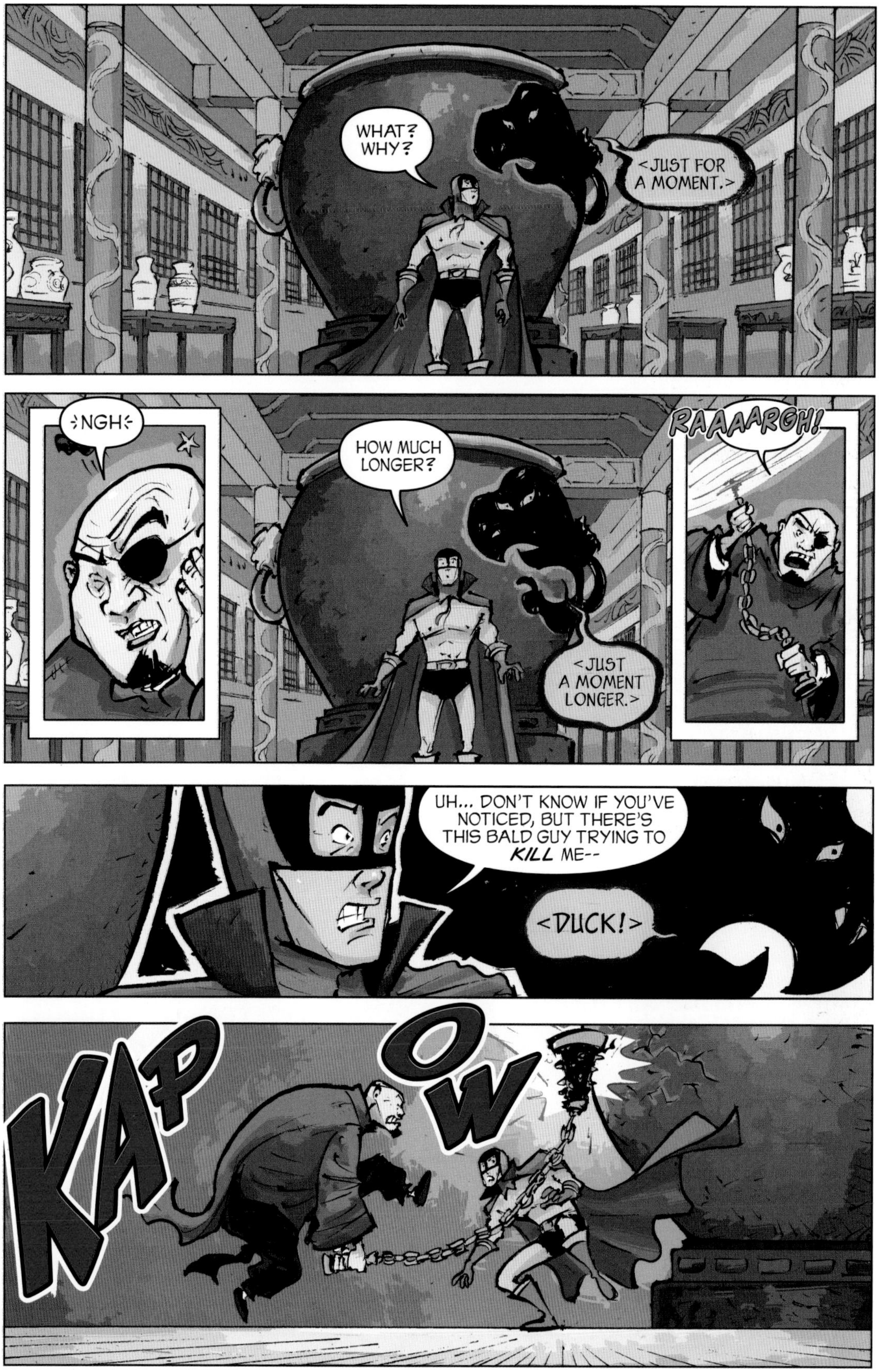
WHAT? WHY?
<JUST FOR A MOMENT.>
NGH
HOW MUCH LONGER?
RAAAARGH!
<JUST A MOMENT LONGER.>
UH... DON'T KNOW IF YOU'VE NOTICED, BUT THERE'S THIS BALD GUY TRYING TO KILL ME--
<DUCK!>
KAPOW

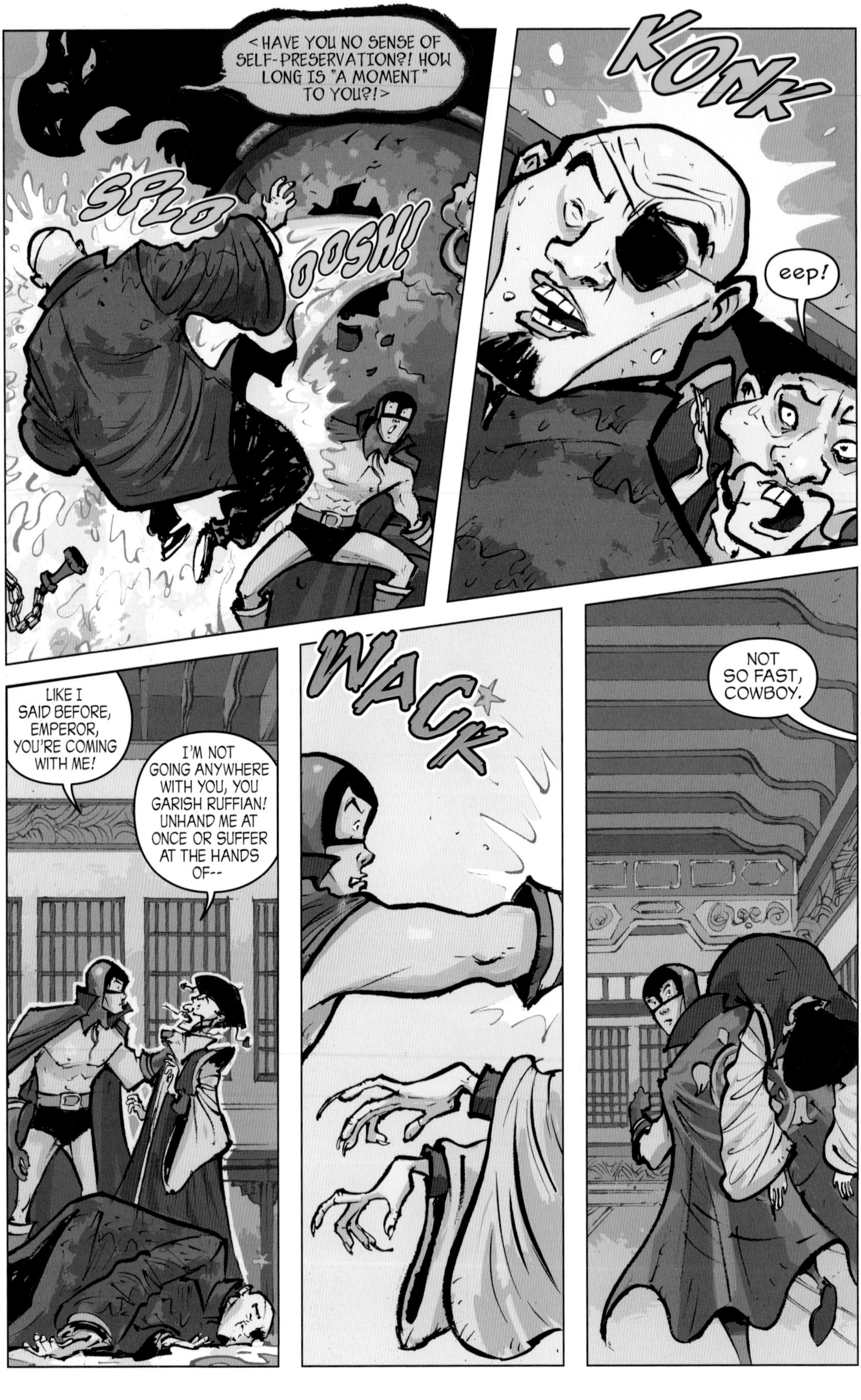
<HAVE YOU NO SENSE OF SELF-PRESERVATION?! HOW LONG IS "A MOMENT" TO YOU?!>
SPLO
OOSH!
KONK
eep!
LIKE I SAID BEFORE, EMPEROR, YOU'RE COMING WITH ME!
I'M NOT GOING ANYWHERE WITH YOU, YOU GARISH RUFFIAN! UNHAND ME AT ONCE OR SUFFER AT THE HANDS OF--
WACK
NOT SO FAST, COWBOY.

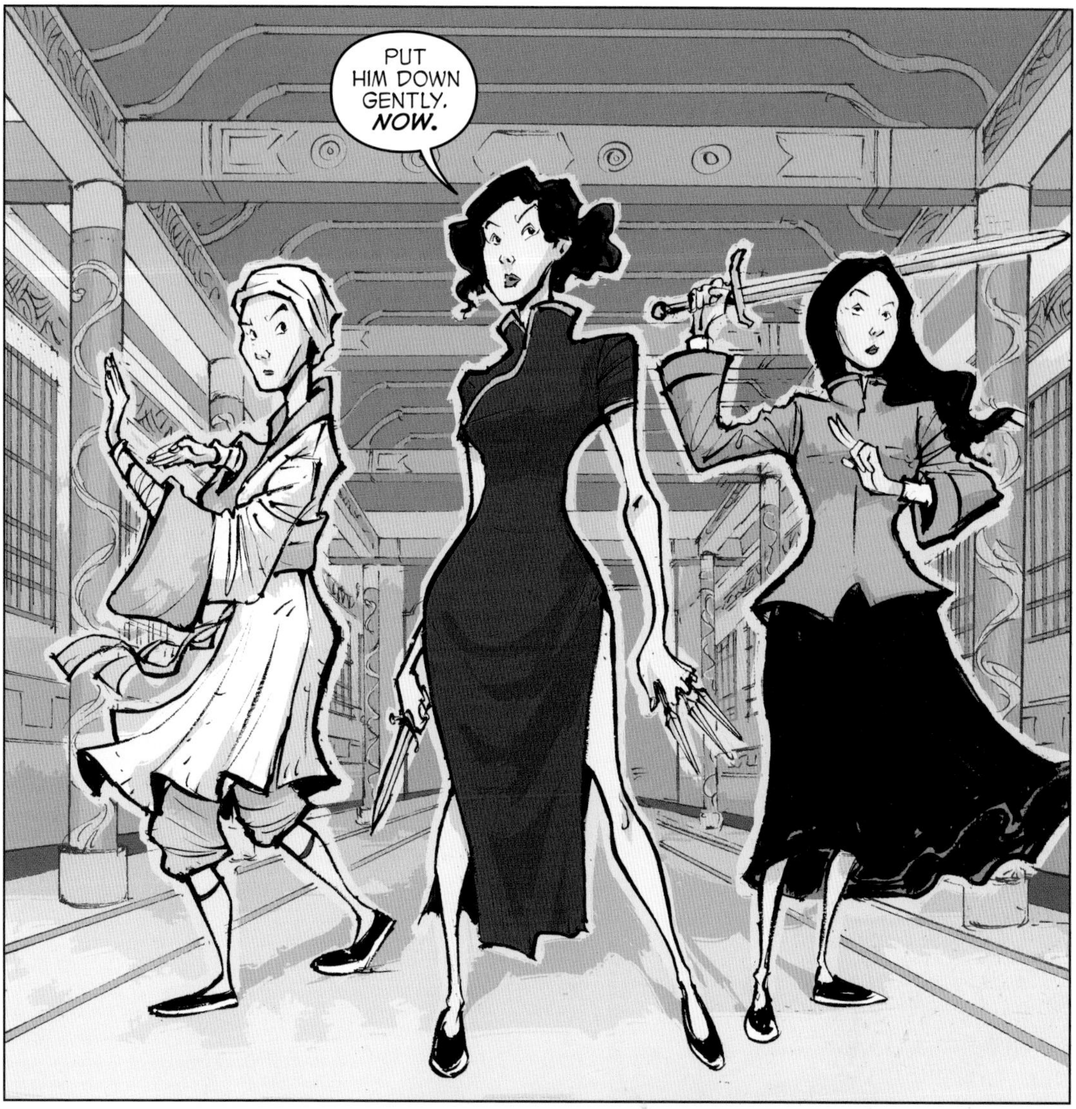
PUT HIM DOWN GENTLY. *NOW.*

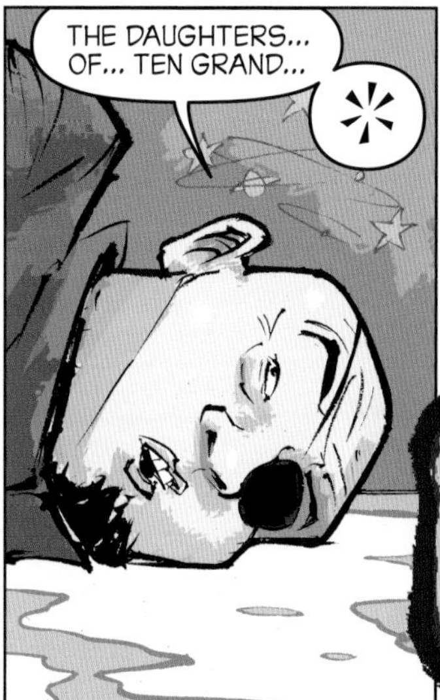
THE DAUGHTERS... OF... TEN GRAND...

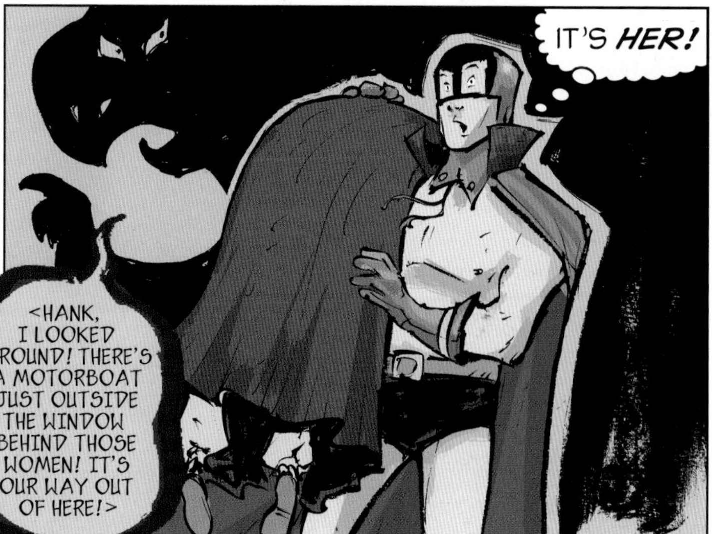
IT'S *HER!*
<HANK, I LOOKED AROUND! THERE'S A MOTORBOAT JUST OUTSIDE THE WINDOW BEHIND THOSE WOMEN! IT'S OUR WAY OUT OF HERE!>

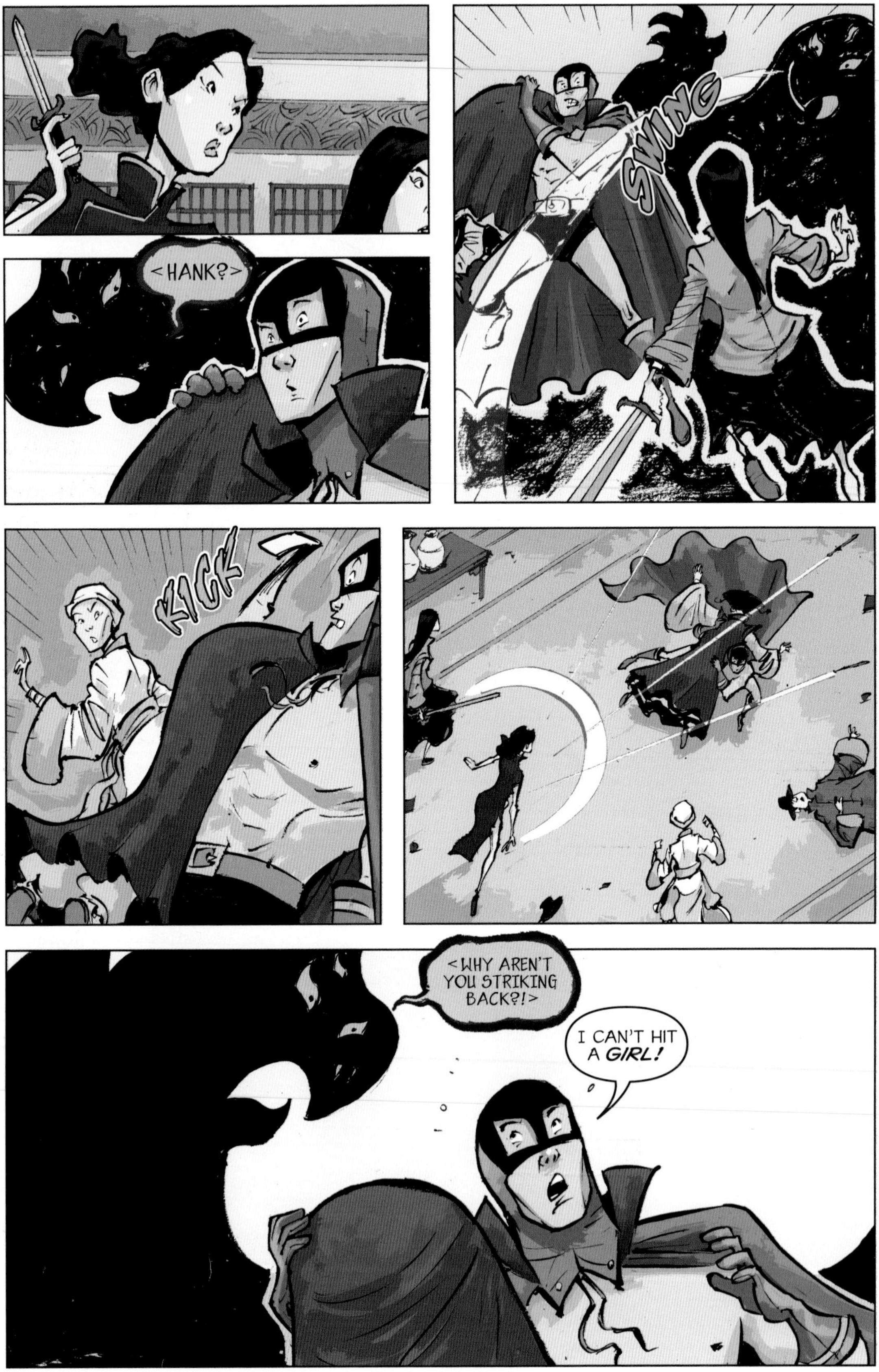
SWING
<HANK?>
KICK
<WHY AREN'T YOU STRIKING BACK?!>
I CAN'T HIT A *GIRL!*

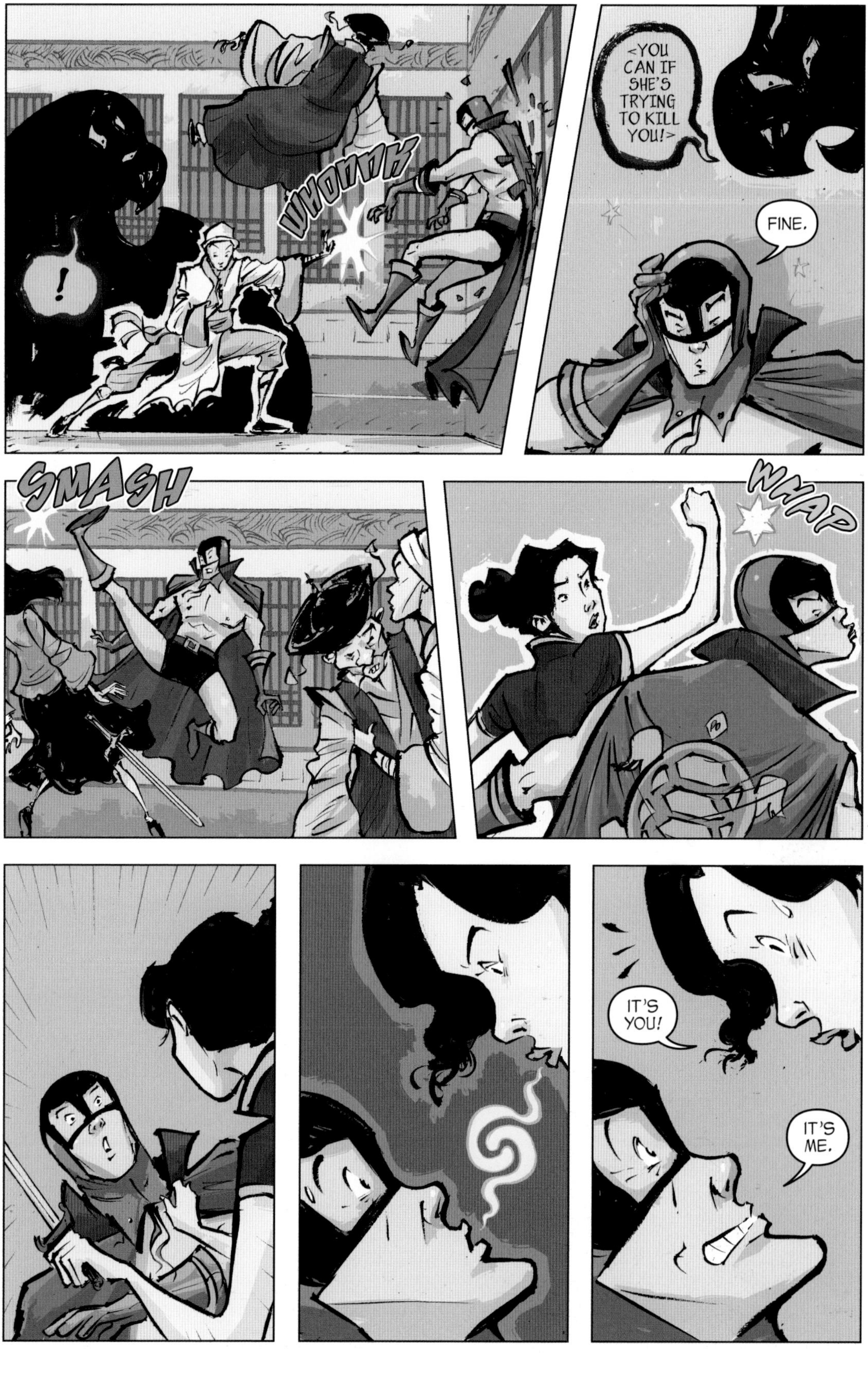
WHOOOSH
!
<YOU CAN IF SHE'S TRYING TO KILL YOU!>
FINE.
SMASH
WHAP
IT'S YOU!
IT'S ME.

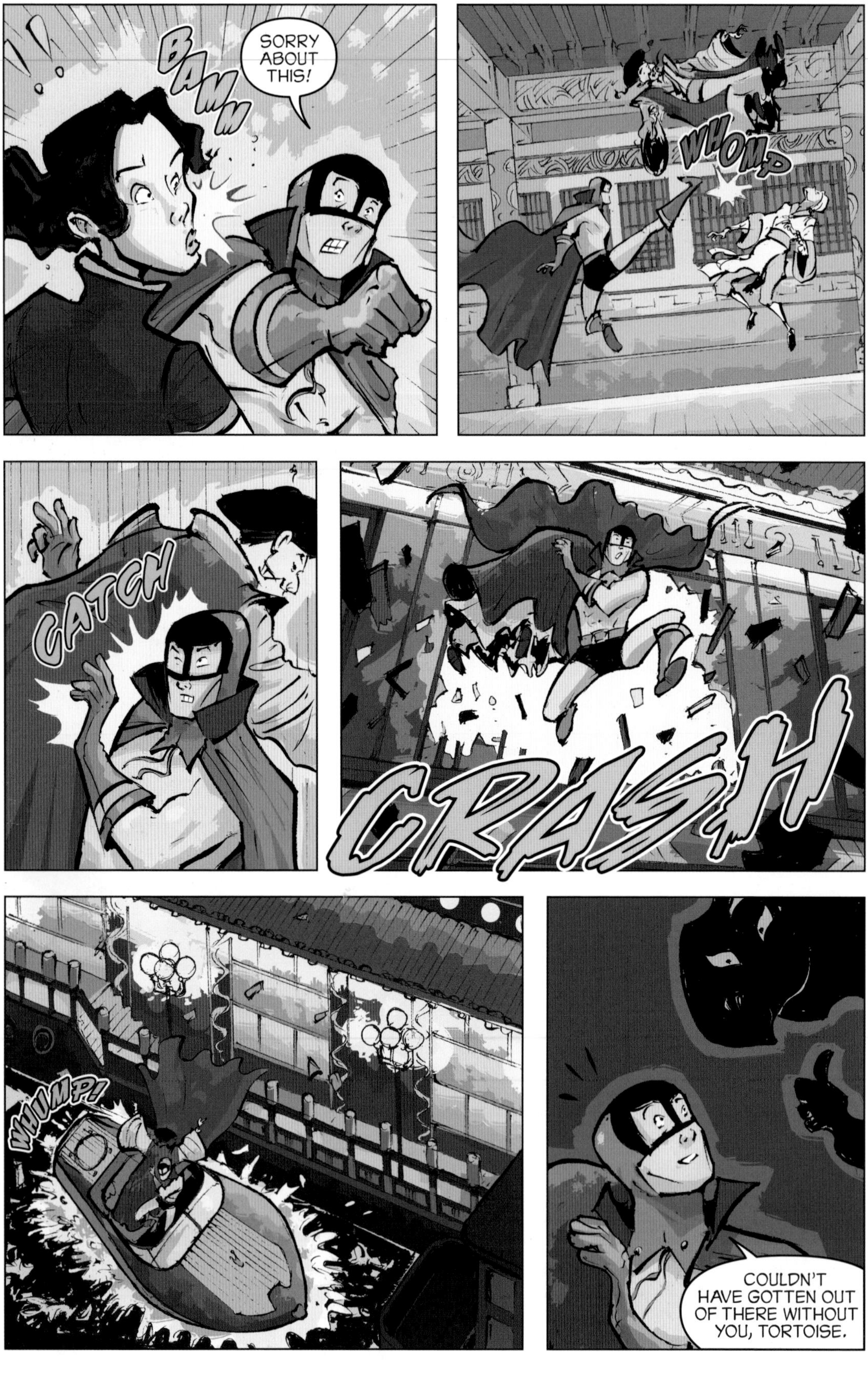
BAMM
SORRY ABOUT THIS!
WHOMP
CATCH
CRASH
WHUMP!
COULDN'T HAVE GOTTEN OUT OF THERE WITHOUT YOU, TORTOISE.

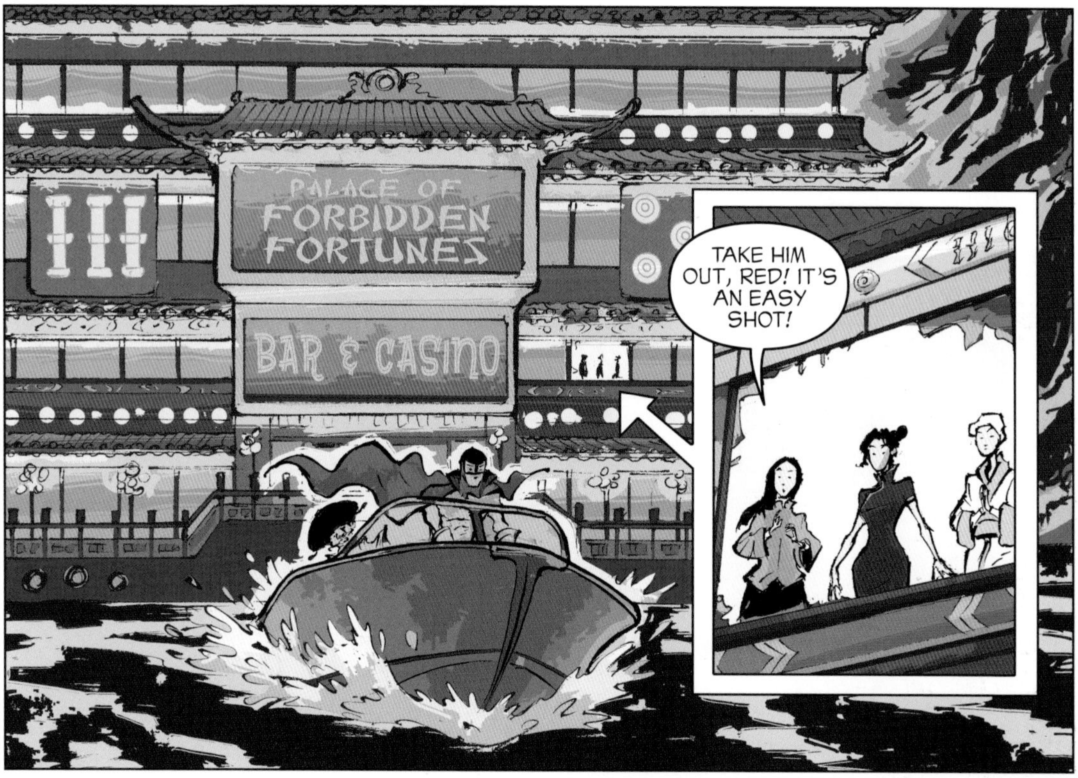
PALACE OF
FORBIDDEN
FORTUNES
BAR & CASINO
TAKE HIM OUT, RED! IT'S AN EASY SHOT!

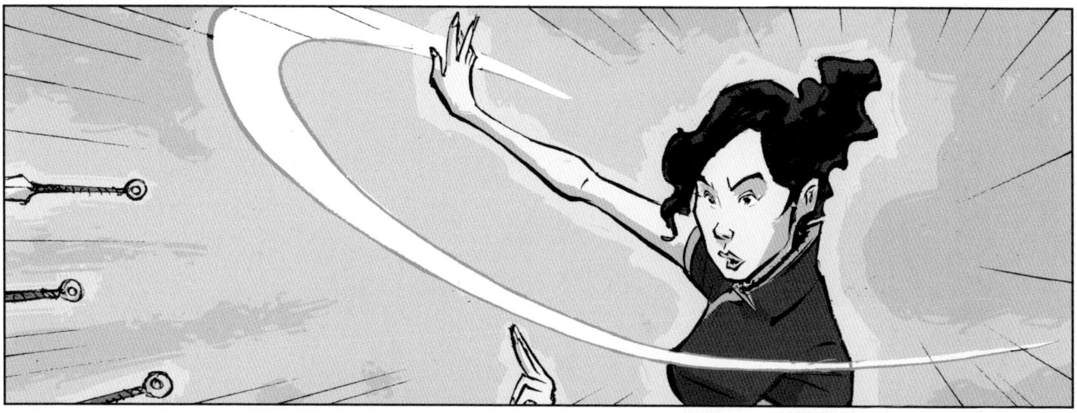

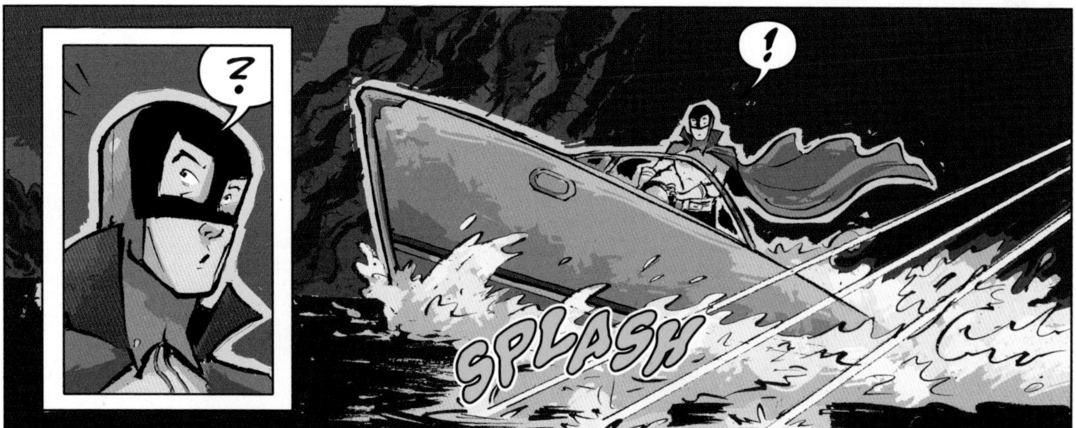
?
!
SPLASH

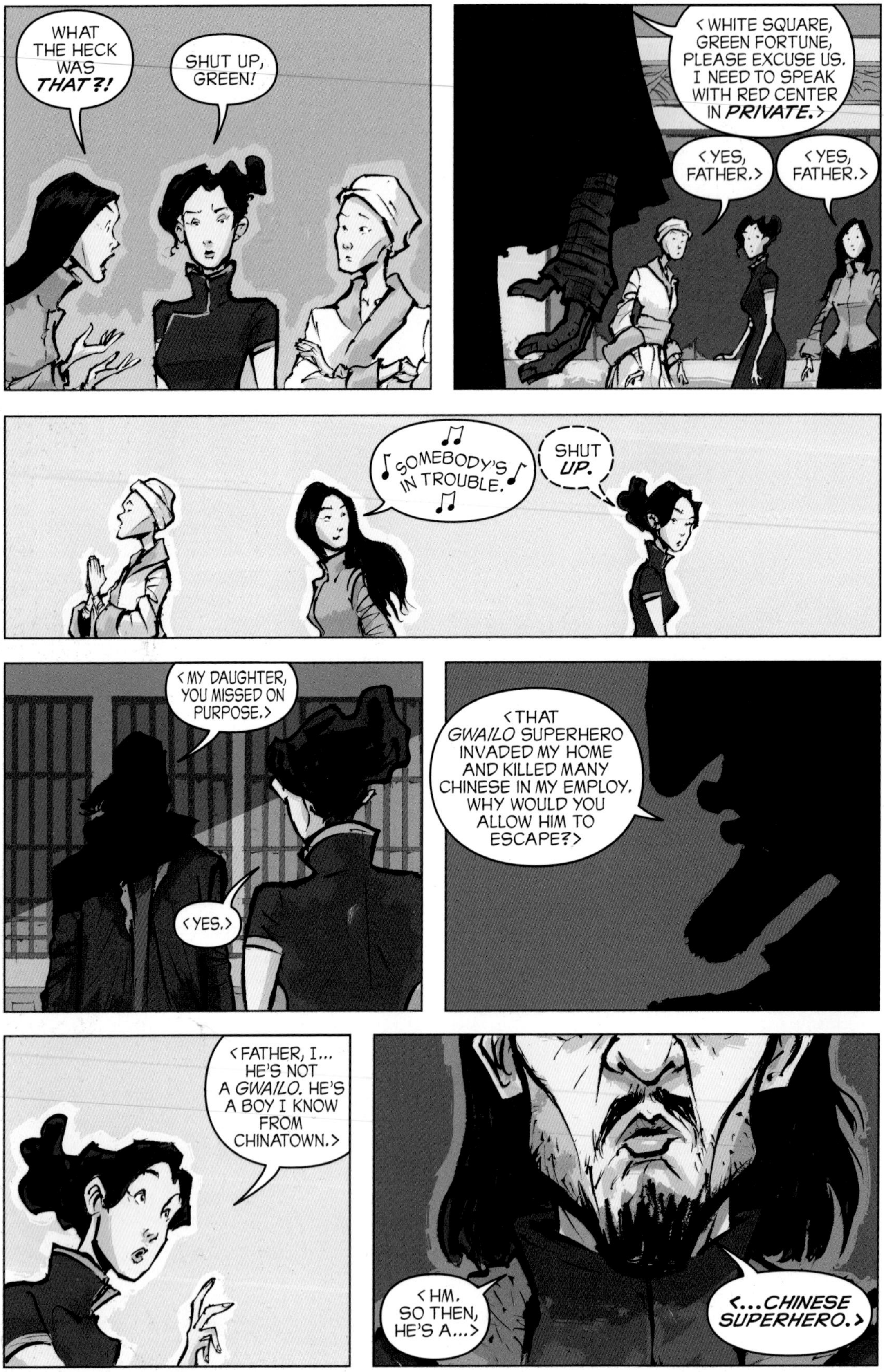
WHAT THE HECK WAS *THAT?!*
SHUT UP, GREEN!
< WHITE SQUARE, GREEN FORTUNE, PLEASE EXCUSE US. I NEED TO SPEAK WITH RED CENTER IN *PRIVATE.* >
< YES, FATHER. >
< YES, FATHER. >
SOMEBODY'S IN TROUBLE.
SHUT *UP.*
< MY DAUGHTER, YOU MISSED ON PURPOSE. >
< YES. >
< THAT *GWAILO* SUPERHERO INVADED MY HOME AND KILLED MANY CHINESE IN MY EMPLOY. WHY WOULD YOU ALLOW HIM TO ESCAPE? >
< FATHER, I... HE'S NOT A *GWAILO.* HE'S A BOY I KNOW FROM CHINATOWN. >
< HM. SO THEN, HE'S A... >
<...CHINESE SUPERHERO.>

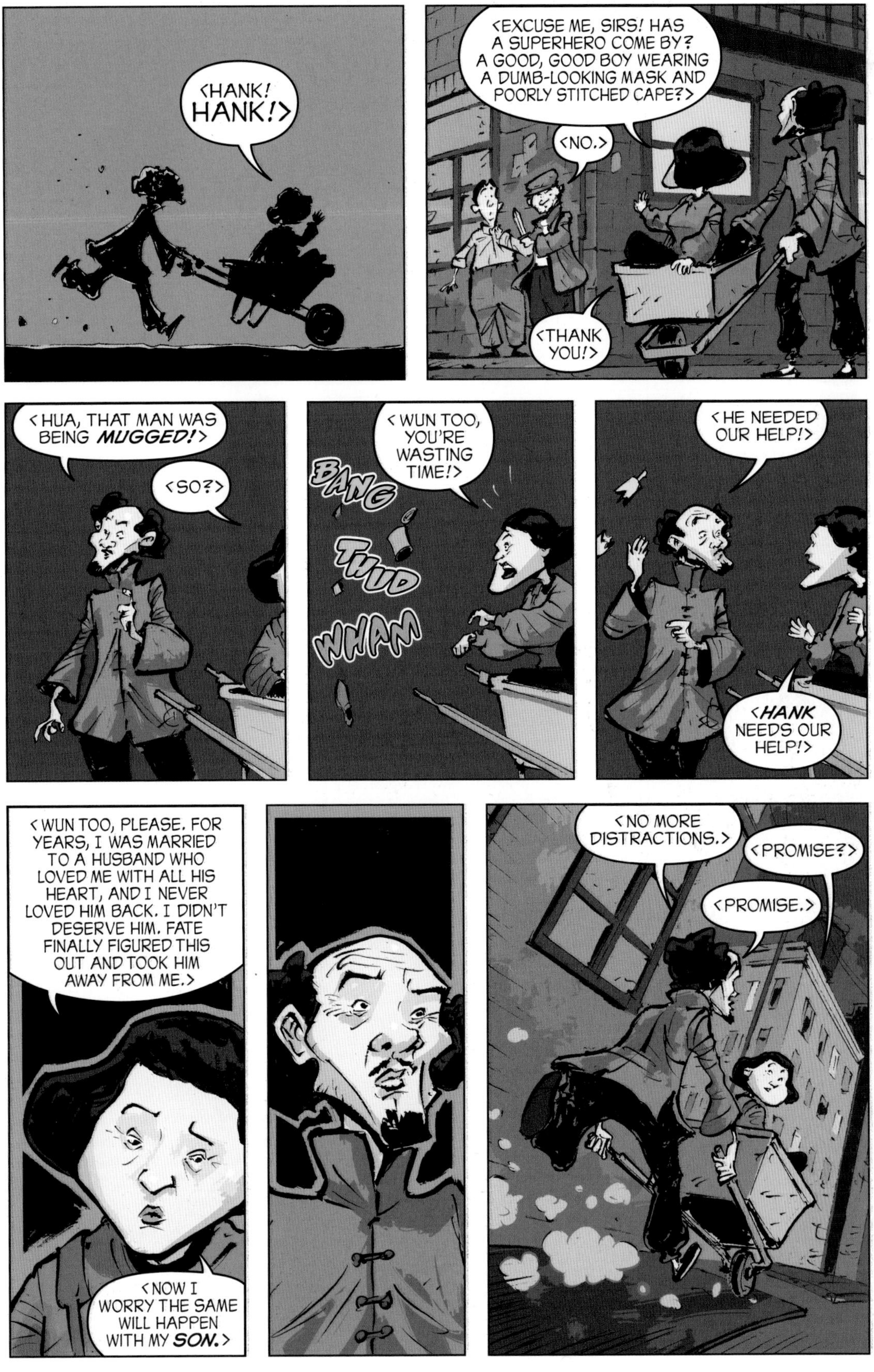
<HANK! HANK!>
<EXCUSE ME, SIRS! HAS A SUPERHERO COME BY? A GOOD, GOOD BOY WEARING A DUMB-LOOKING MASK AND POORLY STITCHED CAPE?>
<NO.>
<THANK YOU!>
<HUA, THAT MAN WAS BEING MUGGED!>
<SO?>
<WUN TOO, YOU'RE WASTING TIME!>
BANG
THUD
WHAM
<HE NEEDED OUR HELP!>
<HANK NEEDS OUR HELP!>
<WUN TOO, PLEASE. FOR YEARS, I WAS MARRIED TO A HUSBAND WHO LOVED ME WITH ALL HIS HEART, AND I NEVER LOVED HIM BACK. I DIDN'T DESERVE HIM. FATE FINALLY FIGURED THIS OUT AND TOOK HIM AWAY FROM ME.>
<NOW I WORRY THE SAME WILL HAPPEN WITH MY SON.>
<NO MORE DISTRACTIONS.>
<PROMISE?>
<PROMISE.>

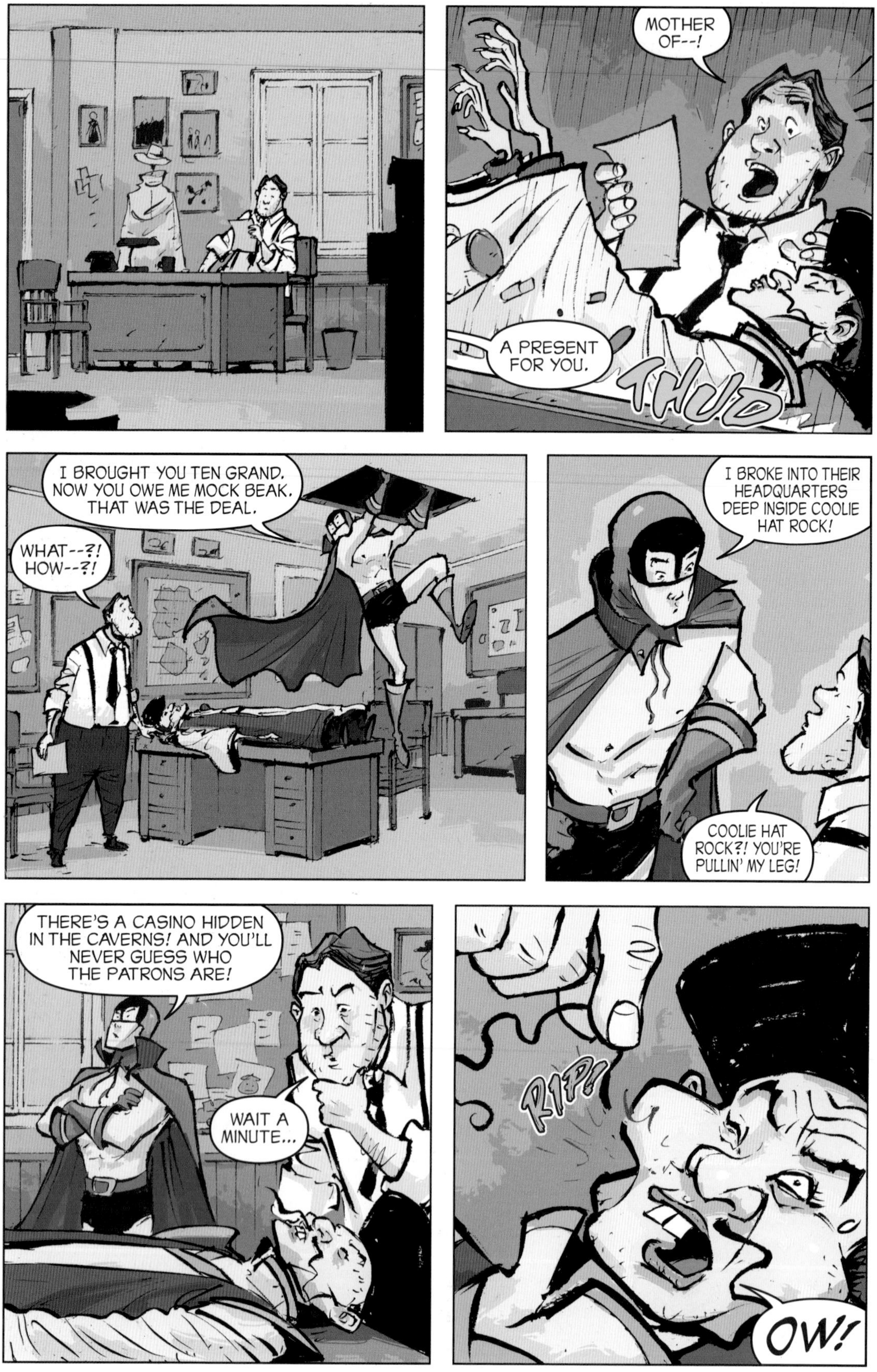
MOTHER OF--!
A PRESENT FOR YOU.
THUD
I BROUGHT YOU TEN GRAND. NOW YOU OWE ME MOCK BEAK. THAT WAS THE DEAL.
WHAT--?! HOW--?!
I BROKE INTO THEIR HEADQUARTERS DEEP INSIDE COOLIE HAT ROCK!
COOLIE HAT ROCK?! YOU'RE PULLIN' MY LEG!
THERE'S A CASINO HIDDEN IN THE CAVERNS! AND YOU'LL NEVER GUESS WHO THE PATRONS ARE!
WAIT A MINUTE...
RIP!
OW!

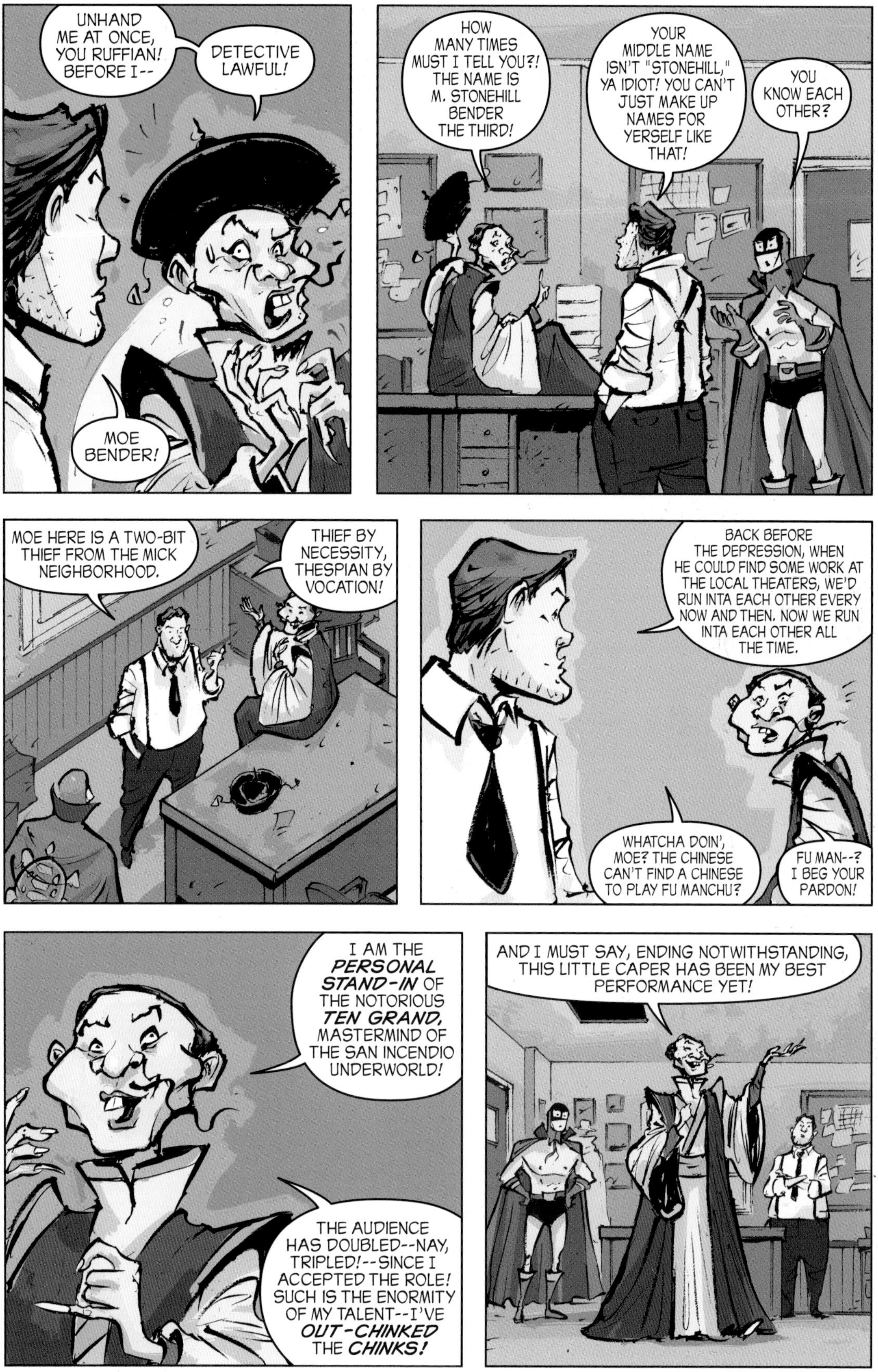
UNHAND ME AT ONCE, YOU RUFFIAN! BEFORE I--
DETECTIVE LAWFUL!
MOE BENDER!
HOW MANY TIMES MUST I TELL YOU?! THE NAME IS M. STONEHILL BENDER THE THIRD!
YOUR MIDDLE NAME ISN'T "STONEHILL," YA IDIOT! YOU CAN'T JUST MAKE UP NAMES FOR YERSELF LIKE THAT!
YOU KNOW EACH OTHER?
MOE HERE IS A TWO-BIT THIEF FROM THE MICK NEIGHBORHOOD.
THIEF BY NECESSITY, THESPIAN BY VOCATION!
BACK BEFORE THE DEPRESSION, WHEN HE COULD FIND SOME WORK AT THE LOCAL THEATERS, WE'D RUN INTA EACH OTHER EVERY NOW AND THEN. NOW WE RUN INTA EACH OTHER ALL THE TIME.
WHATCHA DOIN', MOE? THE CHINESE CAN'T FIND A CHINESE TO PLAY FU MANCHU?
FU MAN--? I BEG YOUR PARDON!
I AM THE PERSONAL STAND-IN OF THE NOTORIOUS TEN GRAND, MASTERMIND OF THE SAN INCENDIO UNDERWORLD!
THE AUDIENCE HAS DOUBLED--NAY, TRIPLED!--SINCE I ACCEPTED THE ROLE! SUCH IS THE ENORMITY OF MY TALENT--I'VE OUT-CHINKED THE CHINKS!
AND I MUST SAY, ENDING NOTWITHSTANDING, THIS LITTLE CAPER HAS BEEN MY BEST PERFORMANCE YET!

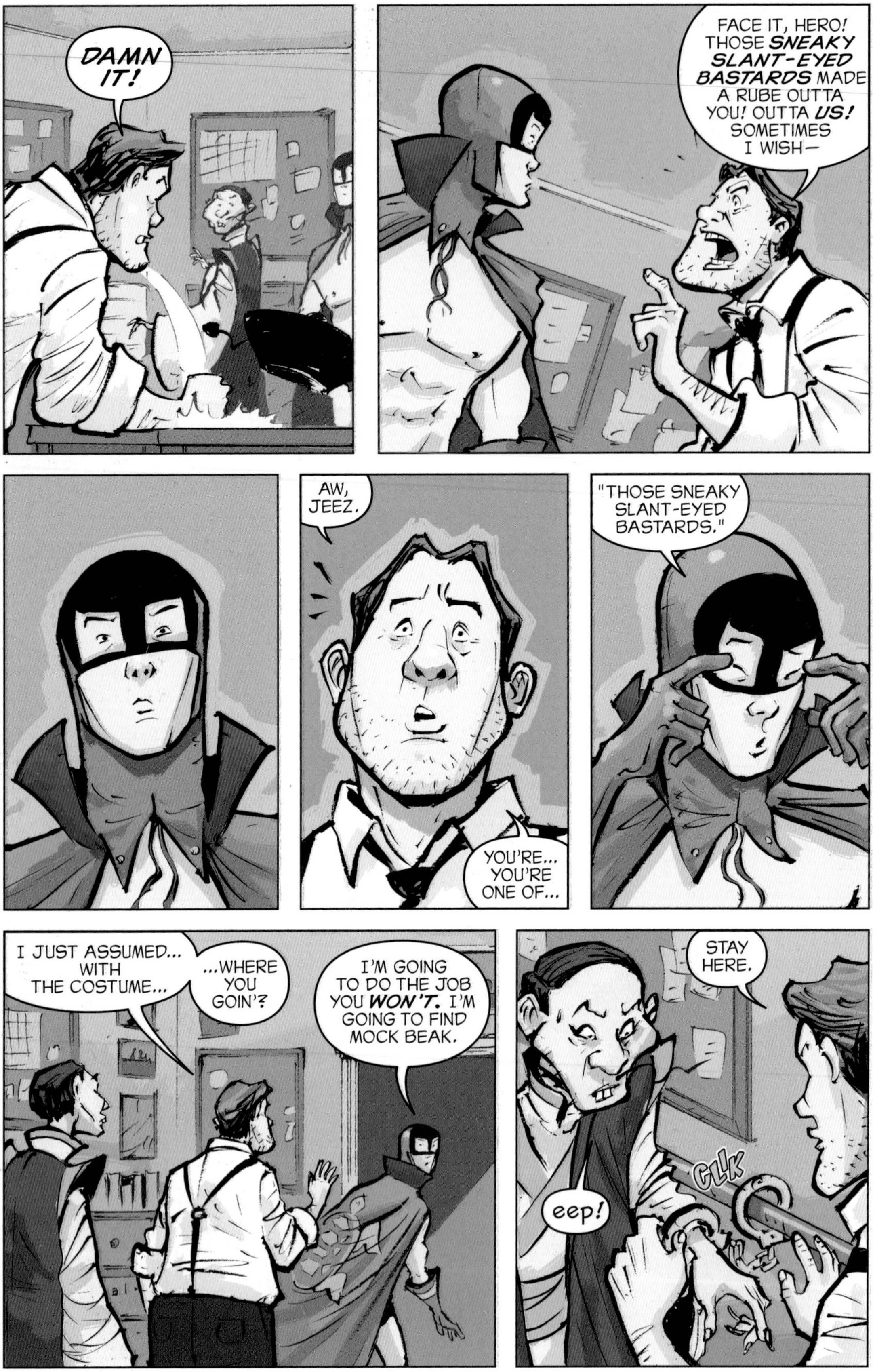
DAMN IT!
FACE IT, HERO! THOSE SNEAKY SLANT-EYED BASTARDS MADE A RUBE OUTTA YOU! OUTTA US! SOMETIMES I WISH—
AW, JEEZ.
YOU'RE... YOU'RE ONE OF...
"THOSE SNEAKY SLANT-EYED BASTARDS."
I JUST ASSUMED... WITH THE COSTUME...
...WHERE YOU GOIN'?
I'M GOING TO DO THE JOB YOU WON'T. I'M GOING TO FIND MOCK BEAK.
STAY HERE.
CLIK
eep!

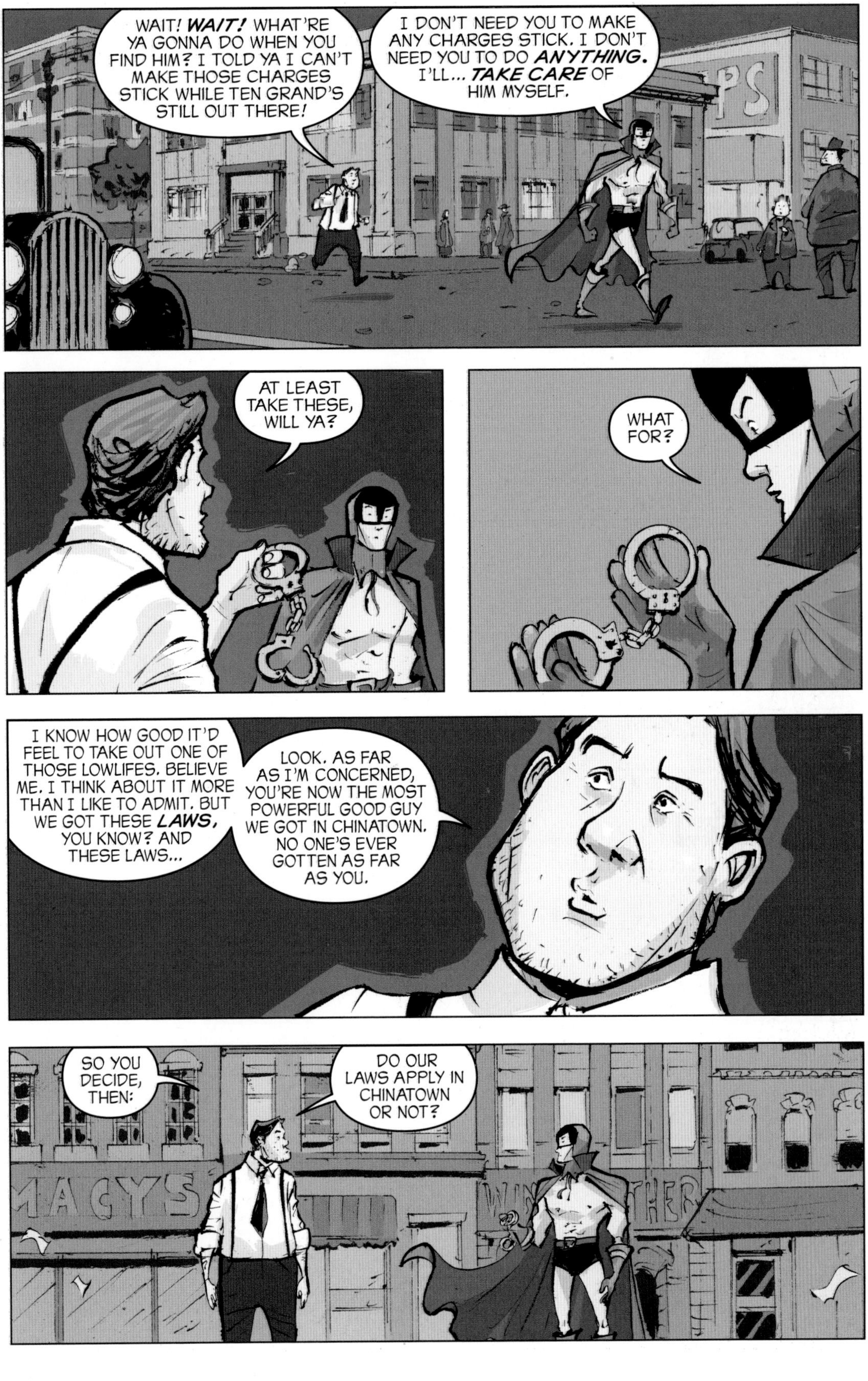
WAIT! ***WAIT!*** WHAT'RE YA GONNA DO WHEN YOU FIND HIM? I TOLD YA I CAN'T MAKE THOSE CHARGES STICK WHILE TEN GRAND'S STILL OUT THERE!
I DON'T NEED YOU TO MAKE ANY CHARGES STICK. I DON'T NEED YOU TO DO ***ANYTHING.*** I'LL... ***TAKE CARE*** OF HIM MYSELF.
AT LEAST TAKE THESE, WILL YA?
WHAT FOR?
I KNOW HOW GOOD IT'D FEEL TO TAKE OUT ONE OF THOSE LOWLIFES. BELIEVE ME. I THINK ABOUT IT MORE THAN I LIKE TO ADMIT. BUT WE GOT THESE ***LAWS,*** YOU KNOW? AND THESE LAWS...
LOOK. AS FAR AS I'M CONCERNED, YOU'RE NOW THE MOST POWERFUL GOOD GUY WE GOT IN CHINATOWN. NO ONE'S EVER GOTTEN AS FAR AS YOU.
SO YOU DECIDE, THEN:
DO OUR LAWS APPLY IN CHINATOWN OR NOT?
MACYS

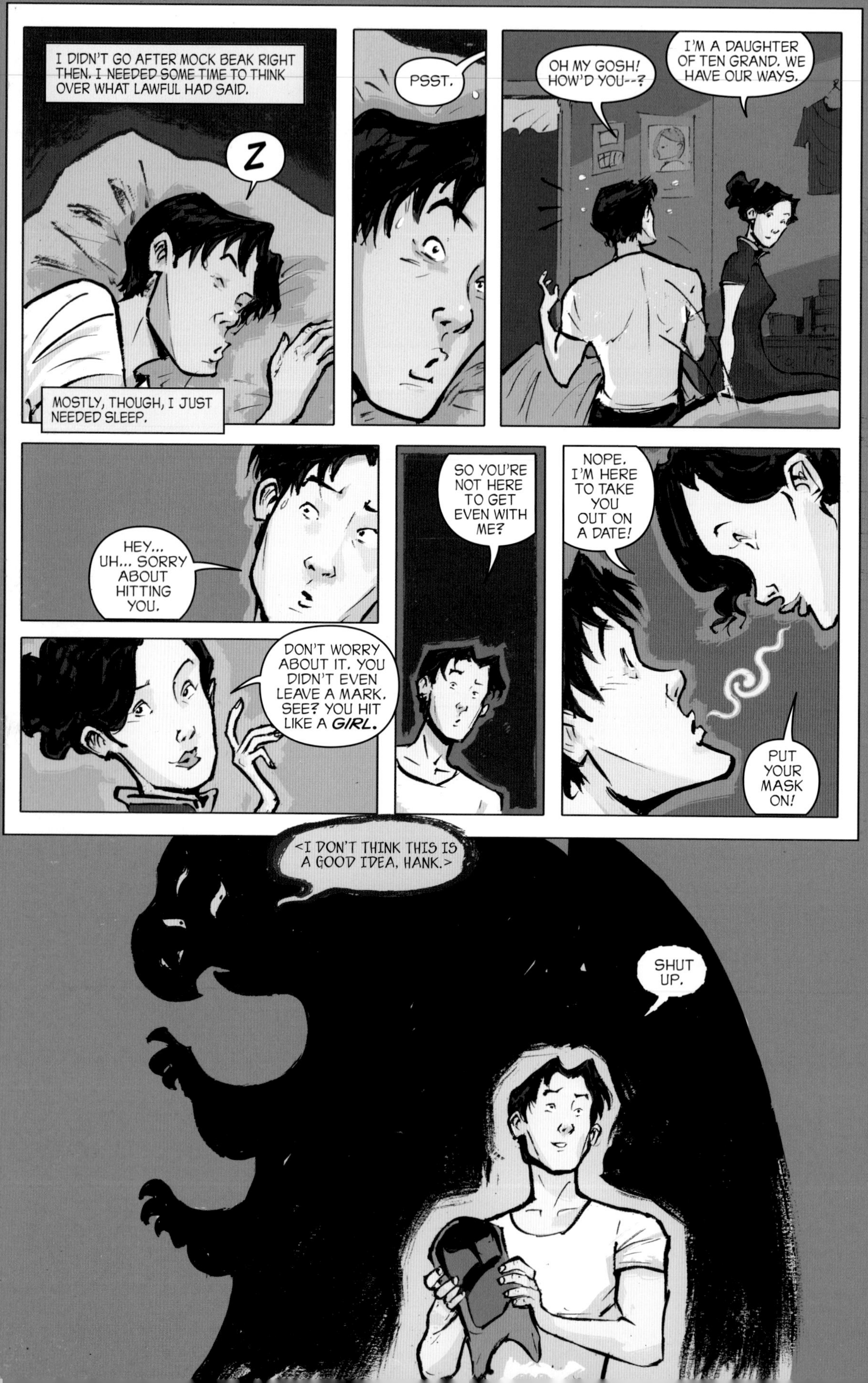
I DIDN'T GO AFTER MOCK BEAK RIGHT THEN. I NEEDED SOME TIME TO THINK OVER WHAT LAWFUL HAD SAID.
Z
MOSTLY, THOUGH, I JUST NEEDED SLEEP.
PSST.
OH MY GOSH! HOW'D YOU--?
I'M A DAUGHTER OF TEN GRAND. WE HAVE OUR WAYS.
HEY... UH... SORRY ABOUT HITTING YOU.
DON'T WORRY ABOUT IT. YOU DIDN'T EVEN LEAVE A MARK. SEE? YOU HIT LIKE A GIRL.
SO YOU'RE NOT HERE TO GET EVEN WITH ME?
NOPE. I'M HERE TO TAKE YOU OUT ON A DATE!
PUT YOUR MASK ON!
<I DON'T THINK THIS IS A GOOD IDEA, HANK.>
SHUT UP.

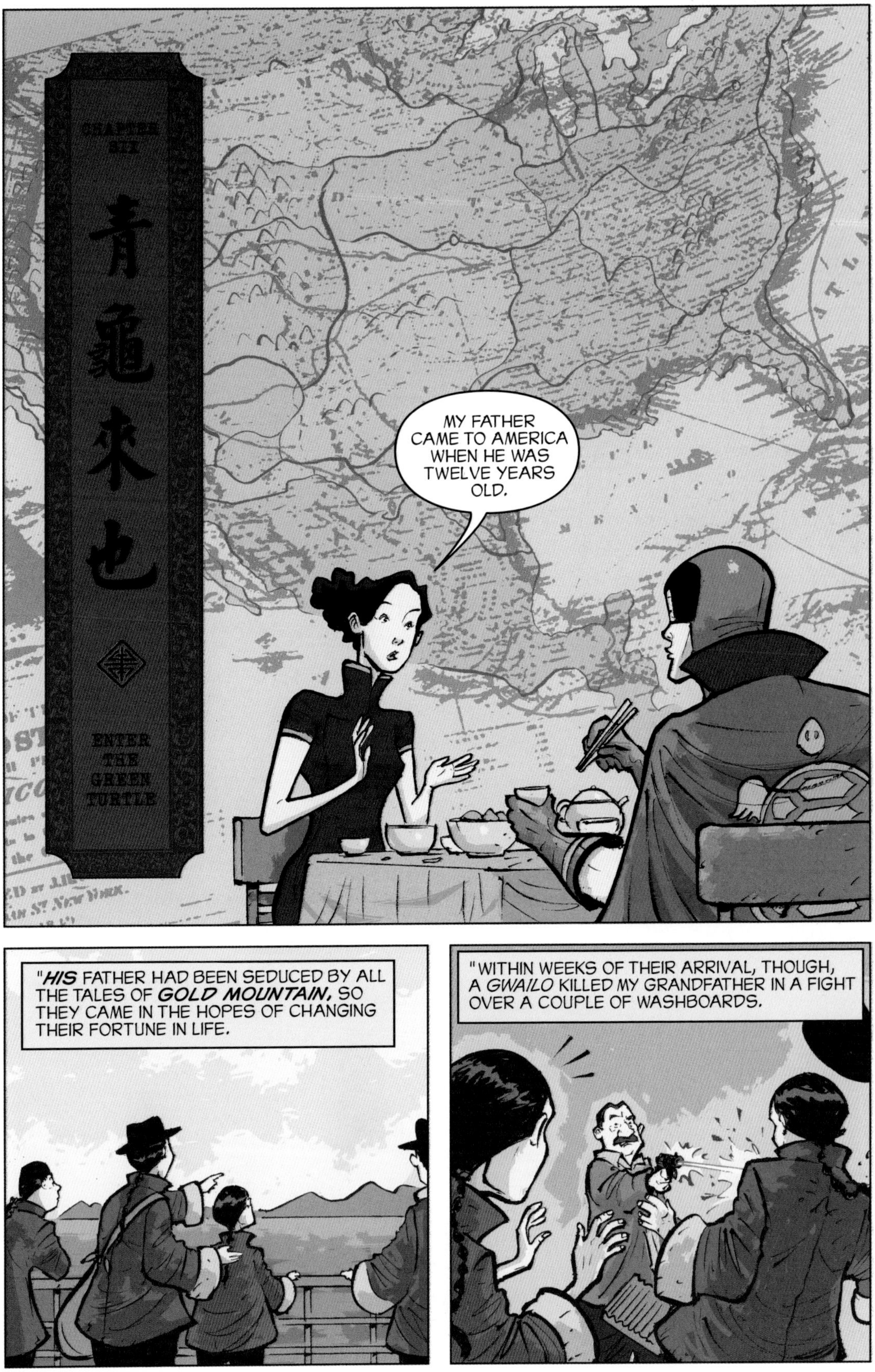
CHAPTER SIX
青龜來也
ENTER THE GREEN TURTLE
MY FATHER CAME TO AMERICA WHEN HE WAS TWELVE YEARS OLD.
"*HIS* FATHER HAD BEEN SEDUCED BY ALL THE TALES OF *GOLD MOUNTAIN*, SO THEY CAME IN THE HOPES OF CHANGING THEIR FORTUNE IN LIFE.
"WITHIN WEEKS OF THEIR ARRIVAL, THOUGH, A *GWAILO* KILLED MY GRANDFATHER IN A FIGHT OVER A COUPLE OF WASHBOARDS.

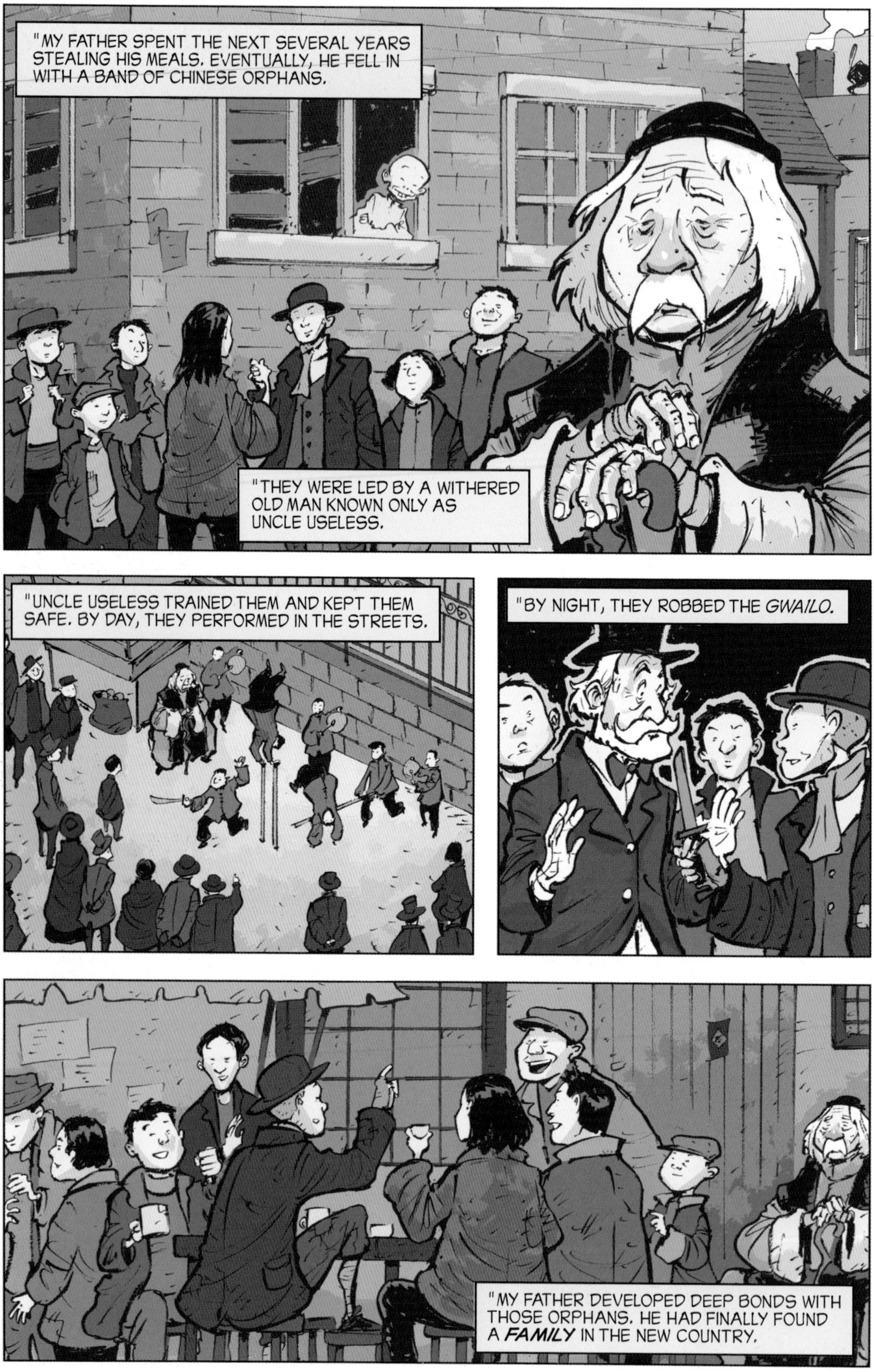
"MY FATHER SPENT THE NEXT SEVERAL YEARS STEALING HIS MEALS. EVENTUALLY, HE FELL IN WITH A BAND OF CHINESE ORPHANS.
"THEY WERE LED BY A WITHERED OLD MAN KNOWN ONLY AS UNCLE USELESS.
"UNCLE USELESS TRAINED THEM AND KEPT THEM SAFE. BY DAY, THEY PERFORMED IN THE STREETS.
"BY NIGHT, THEY ROBBED THE *GWAILO*.
"MY FATHER DEVELOPED DEEP BONDS WITH THOSE ORPHANS. HE HAD FINALLY FOUND A ***FAMILY*** IN THE NEW COUNTRY.

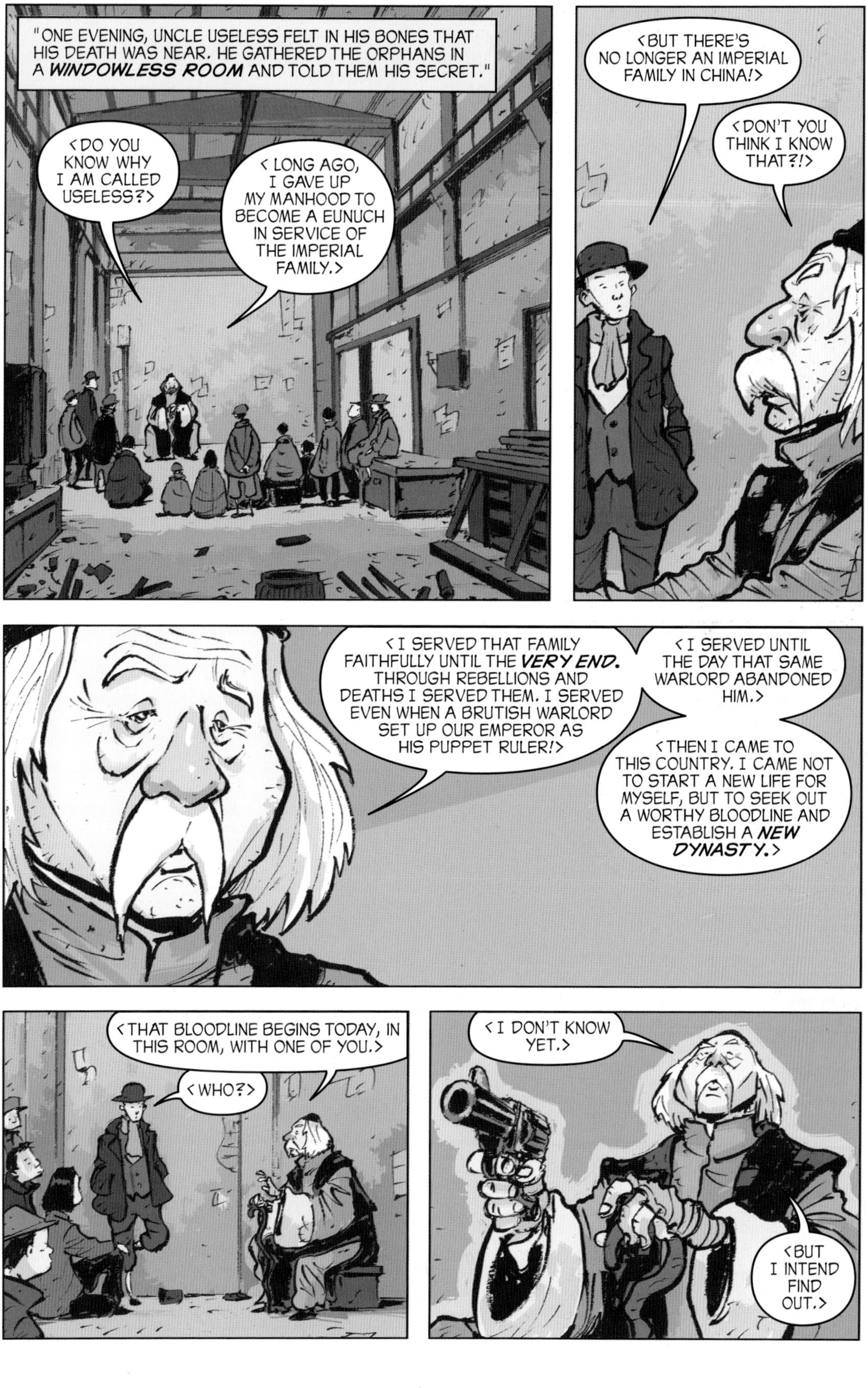
"ONE EVENING, UNCLE USELESS FELT IN HIS BONES THAT HIS DEATH WAS NEAR. HE GATHERED THE ORPHANS IN A WINDOWLESS ROOM AND TOLD THEM HIS SECRET."
<DO YOU KNOW WHY I AM CALLED USELESS?>
<LONG AGO, I GAVE UP MY MANHOOD TO BECOME A EUNUCH IN SERVICE OF THE IMPERIAL FAMILY.>
<BUT THERE'S NO LONGER AN IMPERIAL FAMILY IN CHINA!>
<DON'T YOU THINK I KNOW THAT?!>
<I SERVED THAT FAMILY FAITHFULLY UNTIL THE VERY END. THROUGH REBELLIONS AND DEATHS I SERVED THEM. I SERVED EVEN WHEN A BRUTISH WARLORD SET UP OUR EMPEROR AS HIS PUPPET RULER!>
<I SERVED UNTIL THE DAY THAT SAME WARLORD ABANDONED HIM.>
<THEN I CAME TO THIS COUNTRY. I CAME NOT TO START A NEW LIFE FOR MYSELF, BUT TO SEEK OUT A WORTHY BLOODLINE AND ESTABLISH A NEW DYNASTY.>
<THAT BLOODLINE BEGINS TODAY, IN THIS ROOM, WITH ONE OF YOU.>
<WHO?>
<I DON'T KNOW YET.>
<BUT I INTEND FIND OUT.>

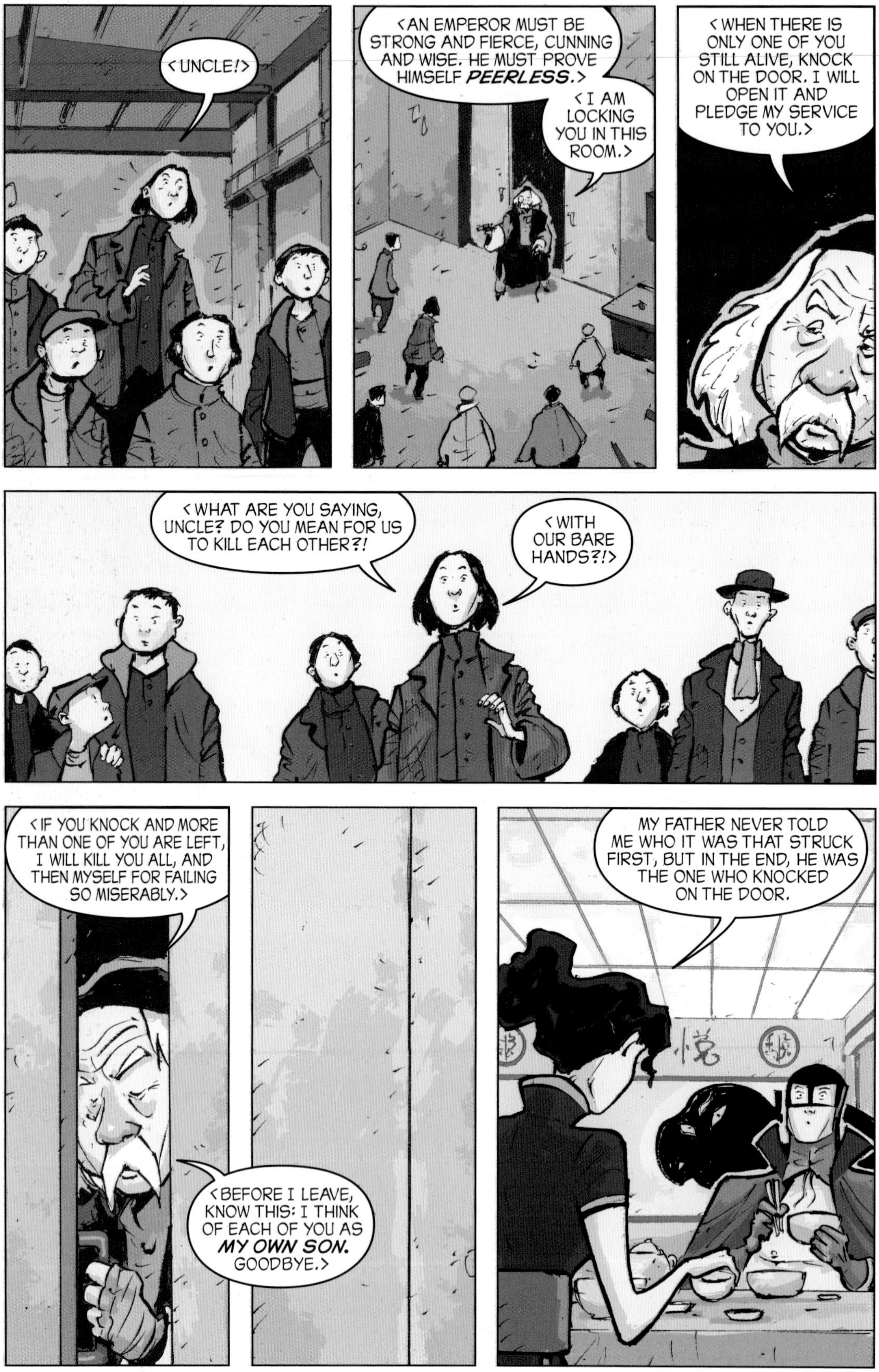
<UNCLE!>
<AN EMPEROR MUST BE STRONG AND FIERCE, CUNNING AND WISE. HE MUST PROVE HIMSELF **PEERLESS.**>
<I AM LOCKING YOU IN THIS ROOM.>
<WHEN THERE IS ONLY ONE OF YOU STILL ALIVE, KNOCK ON THE DOOR. I WILL OPEN IT AND PLEDGE MY SERVICE TO YOU.>
<WHAT ARE YOU SAYING, UNCLE? DO YOU MEAN FOR US TO KILL EACH OTHER?!
<WITH OUR BARE HANDS?!>
<IF YOU KNOCK AND MORE THAN ONE OF YOU ARE LEFT, I WILL KILL YOU ALL, AND THEN MYSELF FOR FAILING SO MISERABLY.>
<BEFORE I LEAVE, KNOW THIS: I THINK OF EACH OF YOU AS ***MY OWN SON.*** GOODBYE.>
MY FATHER NEVER TOLD ME WHO IT WAS THAT STRUCK FIRST, BUT IN THE END, HE WAS THE ONE WHO KNOCKED ON THE DOOR.

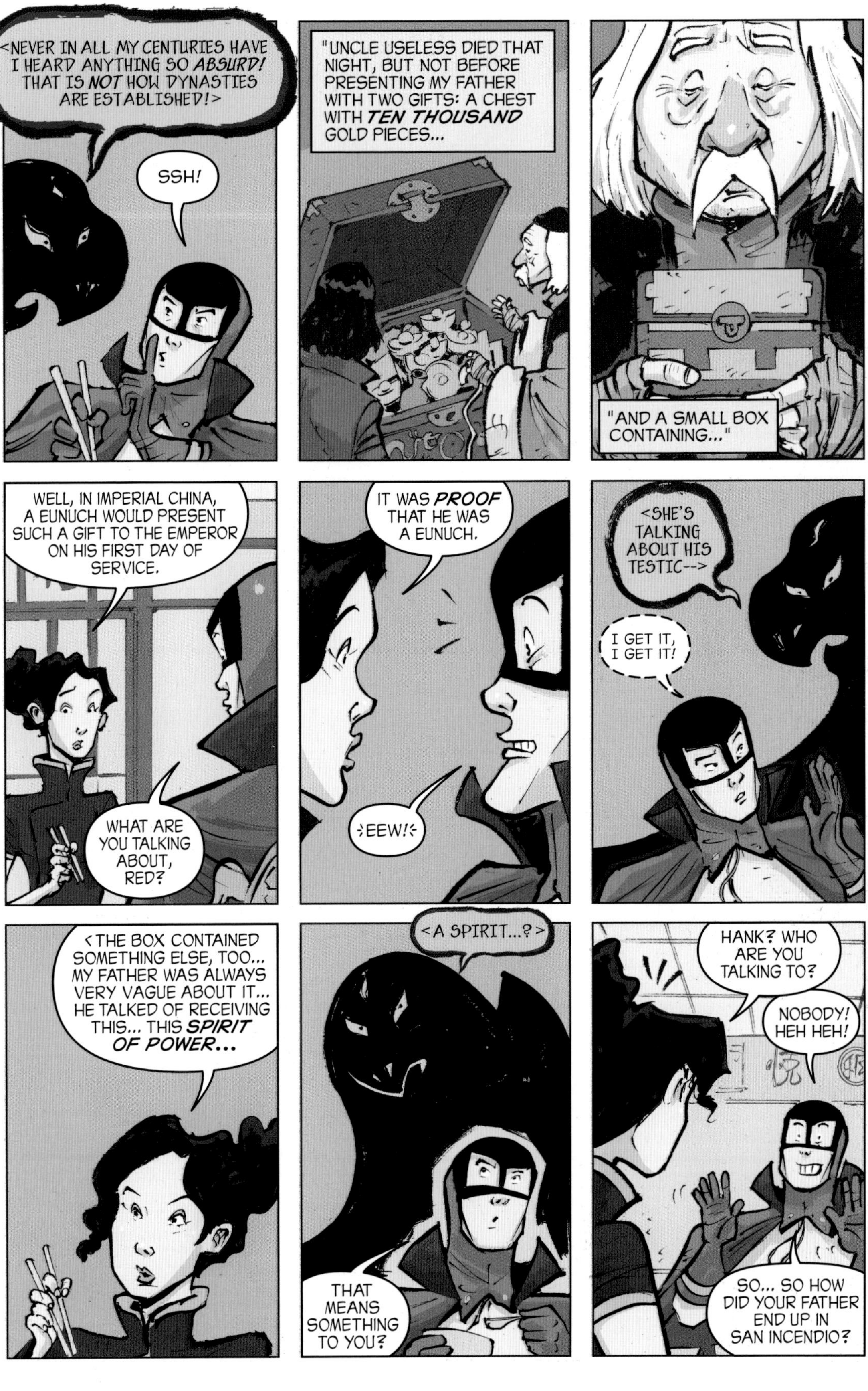
<NEVER IN ALL MY CENTURIES HAVE I HEARD ANYTHING SO *ABSURD!* THAT IS *NOT* HOW DYNASTIES ARE ESTABLISHED!>
SSH!
"UNCLE USELESS DIED THAT NIGHT, BUT NOT BEFORE PRESENTING MY FATHER WITH TWO GIFTS: A CHEST WITH ***TEN THOUSAND*** GOLD PIECES...
"AND A SMALL BOX CONTAINING..."
WELL, IN IMPERIAL CHINA, A EUNUCH WOULD PRESENT SUCH A GIFT TO THE EMPEROR ON HIS FIRST DAY OF SERVICE.
WHAT ARE YOU TALKING ABOUT, RED?
IT WAS ***PROOF*** THAT HE WAS A EUNUCH.
EEW!
<SHE'S TALKING ABOUT HIS TESTIC-->
I GET IT, I GET IT!
<THE BOX CONTAINED SOMETHING ELSE, TOO... MY FATHER WAS ALWAYS VERY VAGUE ABOUT IT... HE TALKED OF RECEIVING THIS... THIS ***SPIRIT OF POWER...***
<A SPIRIT...?>
THAT MEANS SOMETHING TO YOU?
HANK? WHO ARE YOU TALKING TO?
NOBODY! HEH HEH!
SO... SO HOW DID YOUR FATHER END UP IN SAN INCENDIO?

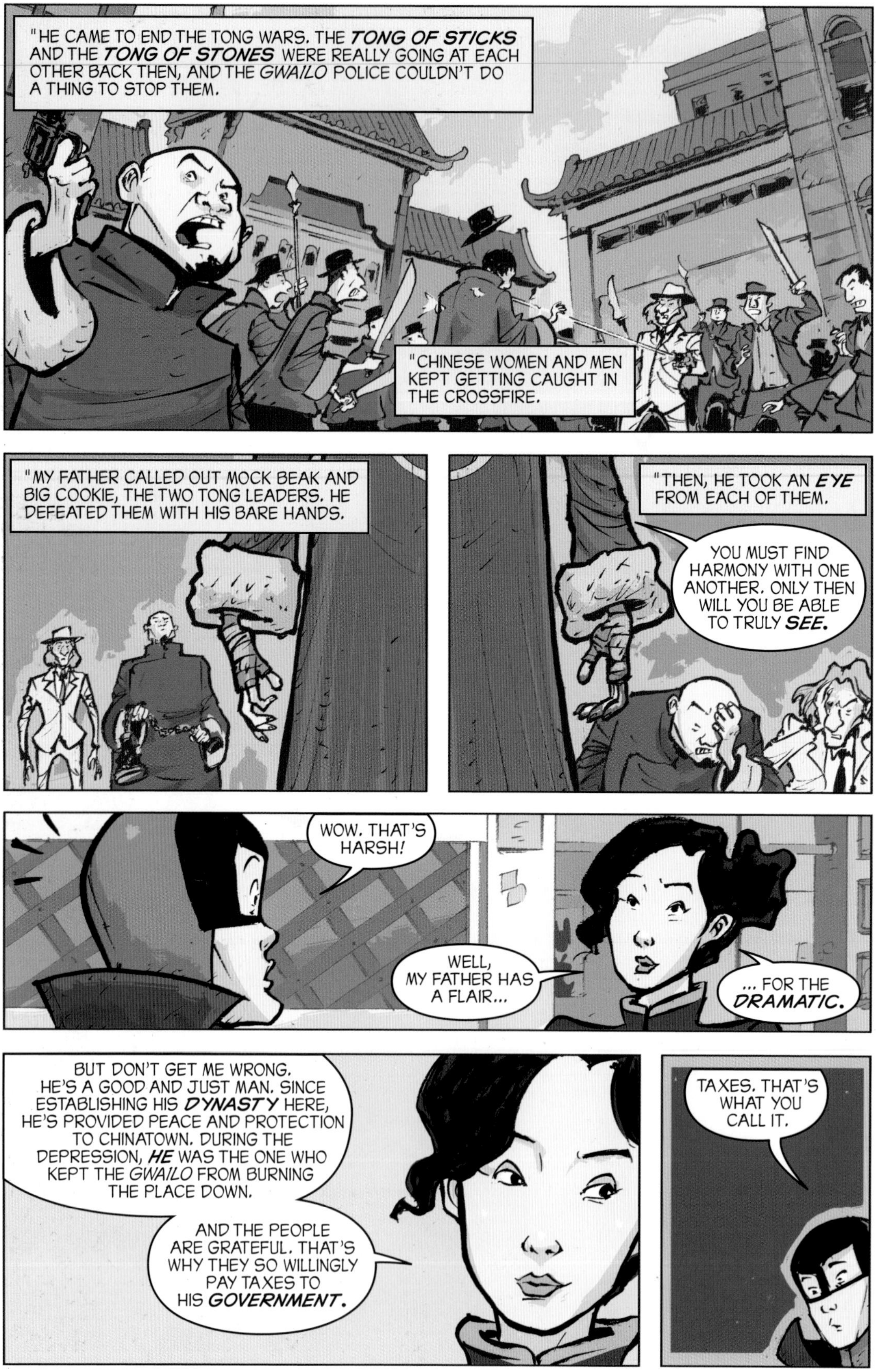
"HE CAME TO END THE TONG WARS. THE TONG OF STICKS AND THE TONG OF STONES WERE REALLY GOING AT EACH OTHER BACK THEN, AND THE GWAILO POLICE COULDN'T DO A THING TO STOP THEM.
"CHINESE WOMEN AND MEN KEPT GETTING CAUGHT IN THE CROSSFIRE.
"MY FATHER CALLED OUT MOCK BEAK AND BIG COOKIE, THE TWO TONG LEADERS. HE DEFEATED THEM WITH HIS BARE HANDS.
"THEN, HE TOOK AN EYE FROM EACH OF THEM.
YOU MUST FIND HARMONY WITH ONE ANOTHER. ONLY THEN WILL YOU BE ABLE TO TRULY SEE.
WOW. THAT'S HARSH!
WELL, MY FATHER HAS A FLAIR...
... FOR THE DRAMATIC.
BUT DON'T GET ME WRONG. HE'S A GOOD AND JUST MAN. SINCE ESTABLISHING HIS DYNASTY HERE, HE'S PROVIDED PEACE AND PROTECTION TO CHINATOWN. DURING THE DEPRESSION, HE WAS THE ONE WHO KEPT THE GWAILO FROM BURNING THE PLACE DOWN.
AND THE PEOPLE ARE GRATEFUL. THAT'S WHY THEY SO WILLINGLY PAY TAXES TO HIS GOVERNMENT.
TAXES. THAT'S WHAT YOU CALL IT.

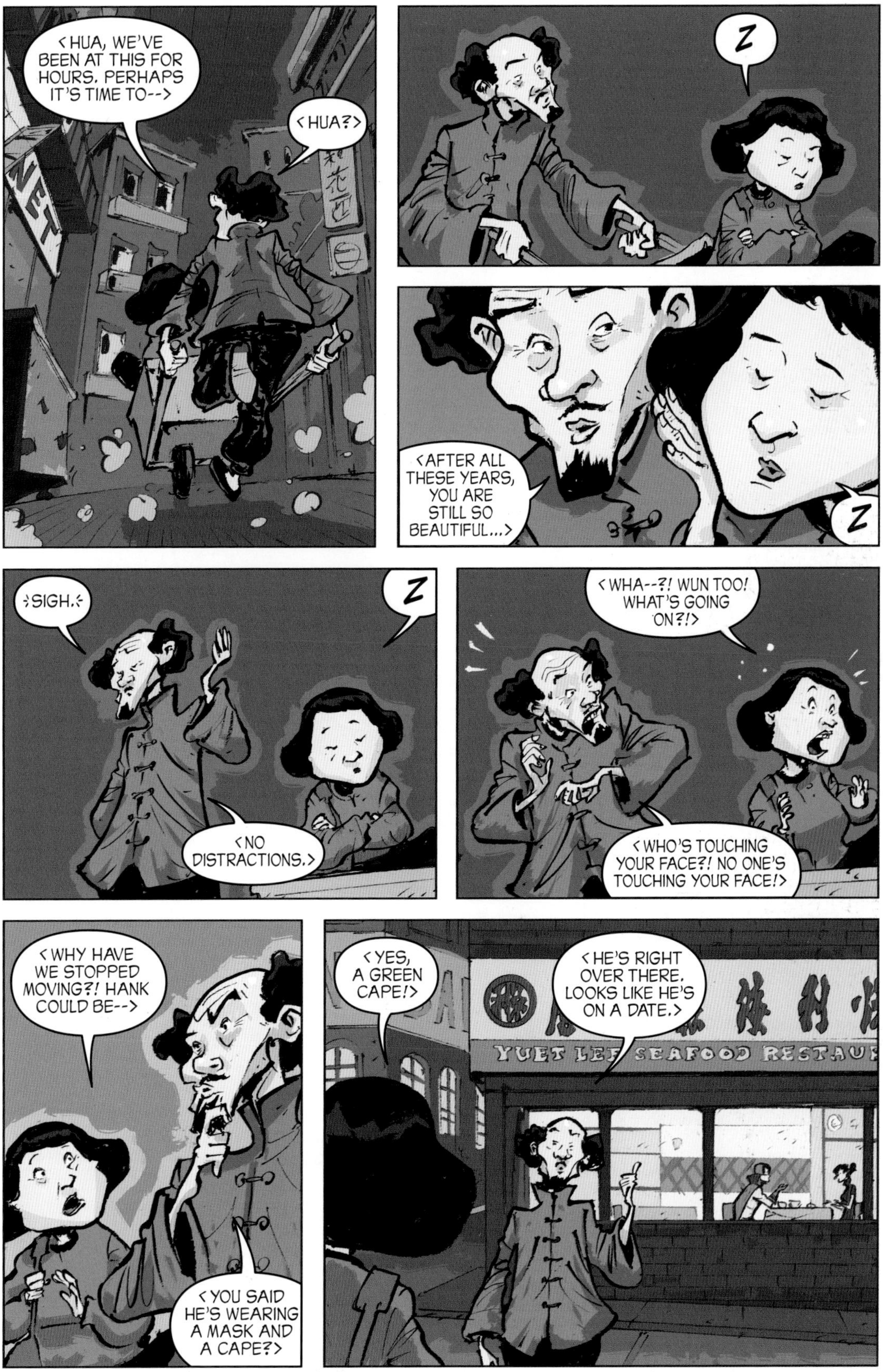
<HUA, WE'VE BEEN AT THIS FOR HOURS. PERHAPS IT'S TIME TO-->
<HUA?>
Z
<AFTER ALL THESE YEARS, YOU ARE STILL SO BEAUTIFUL...>
Z
SIGH.
Z
<NO DISTRACTIONS.>
<WHA--?! WUN TOO! WHAT'S GOING ON?!>
<WHO'S TOUCHING YOUR FACE?! NO ONE'S TOUCHING YOUR FACE!>
<WHY HAVE WE STOPPED MOVING?! HANK COULD BE-->
<YOU SAID HE'S WEARING A MASK AND A CAPE?>
<YES, A GREEN CAPE!>
<HE'S RIGHT OVER THERE. LOOKS LIKE HE'S ON A DATE.>

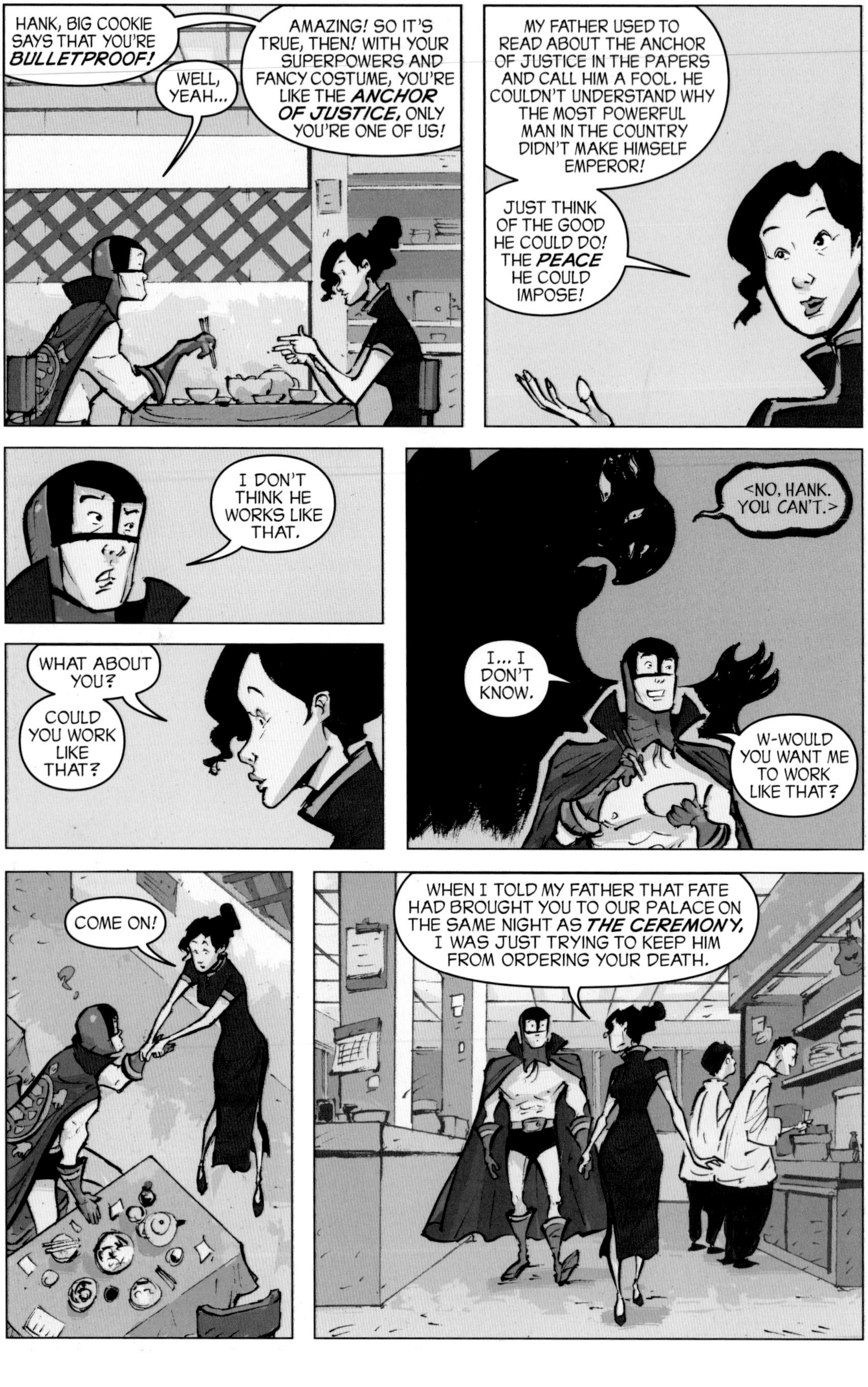
HANK, BIG COOKIE SAYS THAT YOU'RE BULLETPROOF!
WELL, YEAH...
AMAZING! SO IT'S TRUE, THEN! WITH YOUR SUPERPOWERS AND FANCY COSTUME, YOU'RE LIKE THE ANCHOR OF JUSTICE, ONLY YOU'RE ONE OF US!
MY FATHER USED TO READ ABOUT THE ANCHOR OF JUSTICE IN THE PAPERS AND CALL HIM A FOOL. HE COULDN'T UNDERSTAND WHY THE MOST POWERFUL MAN IN THE COUNTRY DIDN'T MAKE HIMSELF EMPEROR!
JUST THINK OF THE GOOD HE COULD DO! THE PEACE HE COULD IMPOSE!
I DON'T THINK HE WORKS LIKE THAT.
WHAT ABOUT YOU?
COULD YOU WORK LIKE THAT?
<NO, HANK. YOU CAN'T.>
I... I DON'T KNOW.
W-WOULD YOU WANT ME TO WORK LIKE THAT?
COME ON!
WHEN I TOLD MY FATHER THAT FATE HAD BROUGHT YOU TO OUR PALACE ON THE SAME NIGHT AS THE CEREMONY, I WAS JUST TRYING TO KEEP HIM FROM ORDERING YOUR DEATH.

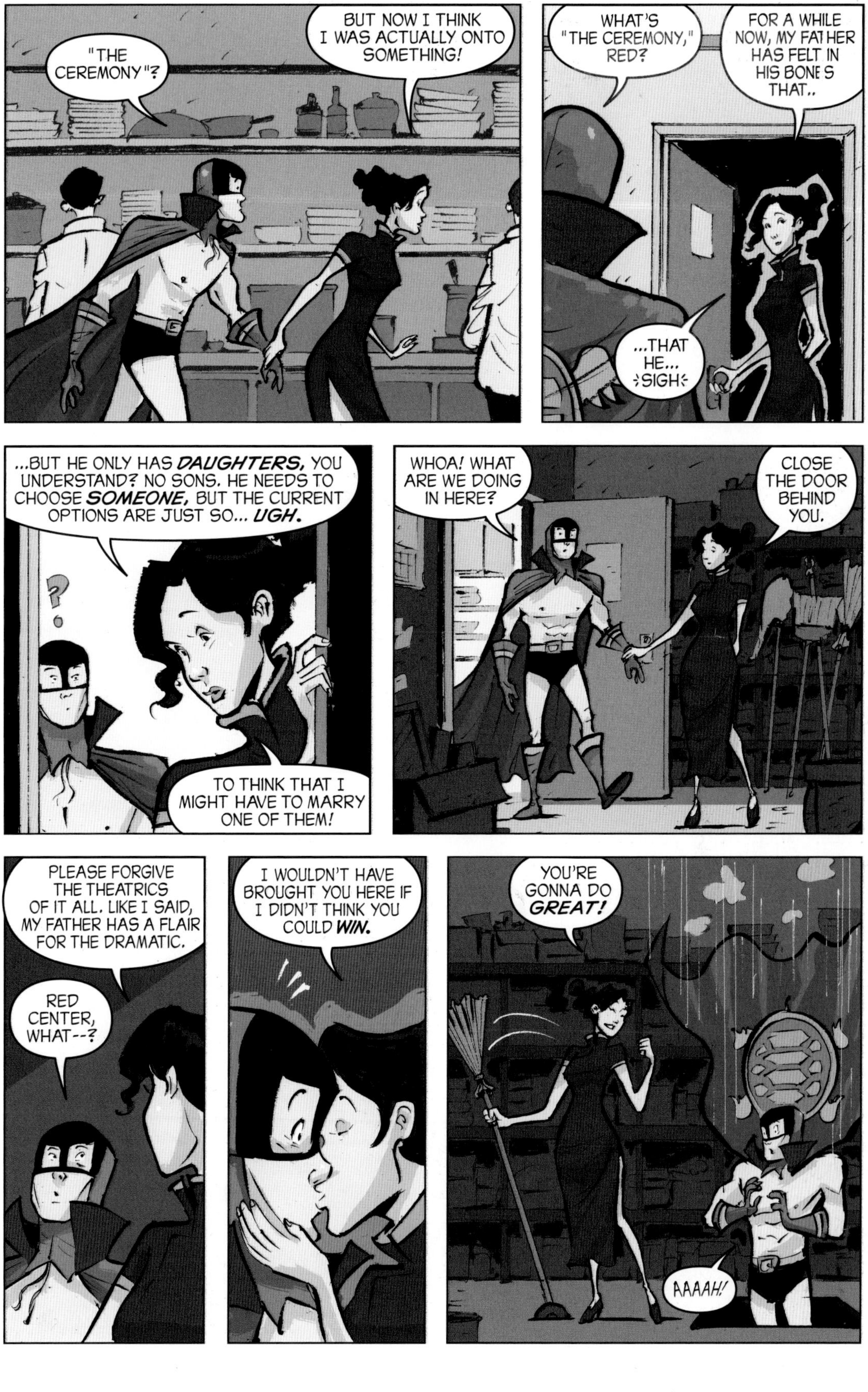
"THE CEREMONY"?
BUT NOW I THINK I WAS ACTUALLY ONTO SOMETHING!
WHAT'S "THE CEREMONY," RED?
FOR A WHILE NOW, MY FATHER HAS FELT IN HIS BONES THAT..
...THAT HE... ⁘SIGH⁘
...BUT HE ONLY HAS DAUGHTERS, YOU UNDERSTAND? NO SONS. HE NEEDS TO CHOOSE SOMEONE, BUT THE CURRENT OPTIONS ARE JUST SO... UGH.
TO THINK THAT I MIGHT HAVE TO MARRY ONE OF THEM!
WHOA! WHAT ARE WE DOING IN HERE?
CLOSE THE DOOR BEHIND YOU.
PLEASE FORGIVE THE THEATRICS OF IT ALL. LIKE I SAID, MY FATHER HAS A FLAIR FOR THE DRAMATIC.
RED CENTER, WHAT--?
I WOULDN'T HAVE BROUGHT YOU HERE IF I DIDN'T THINK YOU COULD WIN.
YOU'RE GONNA DO GREAT!
AAAAH!

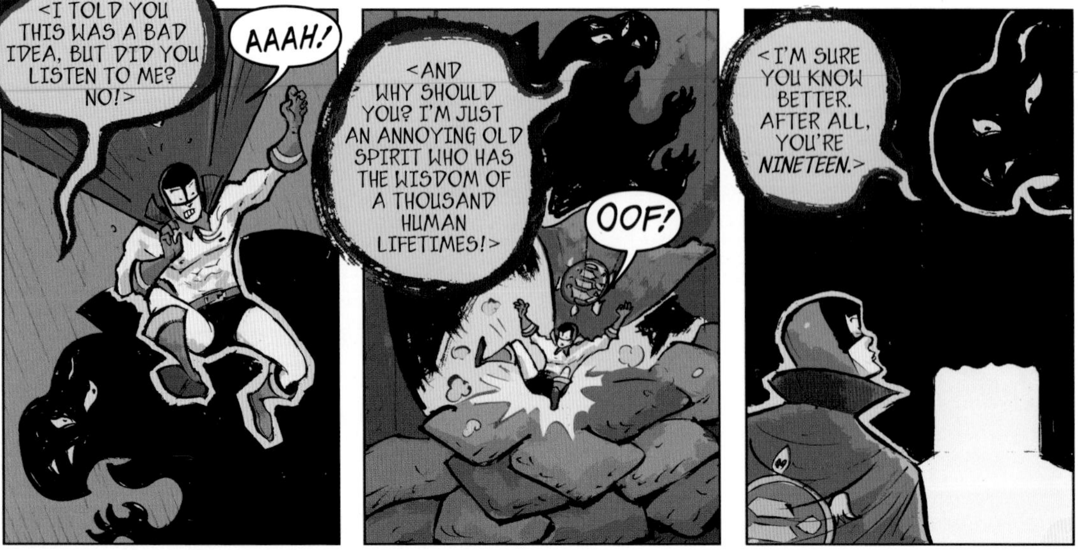
<I TOLD YOU THIS WAS A BAD IDEA, BUT DID YOU LISTEN TO ME? NO!>
AAAH!
<AND WHY SHOULD YOU? I'M JUST AN ANNOYING OLD SPIRIT WHO HAS THE WISDOM OF A THOUSAND HUMAN LIFETIMES!>
OOF!
<I'M SURE YOU KNOW BETTER. AFTER ALL, YOU'RE *NINETEEN.*>

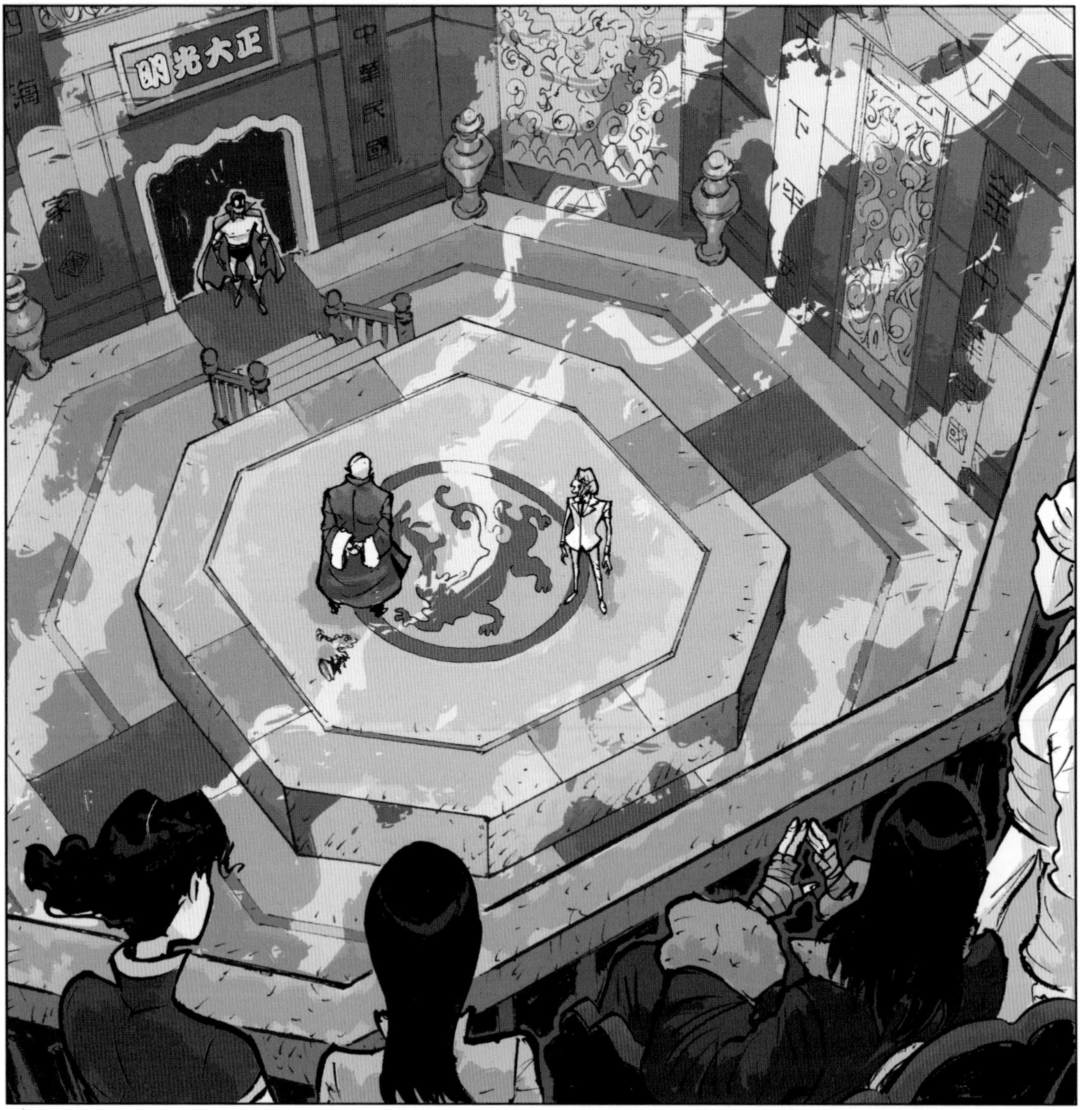
正大光明

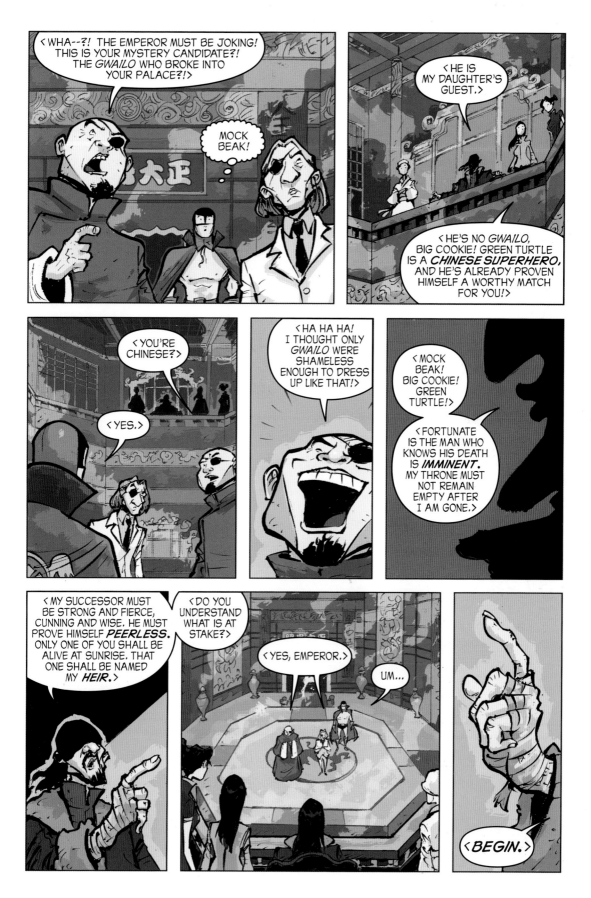

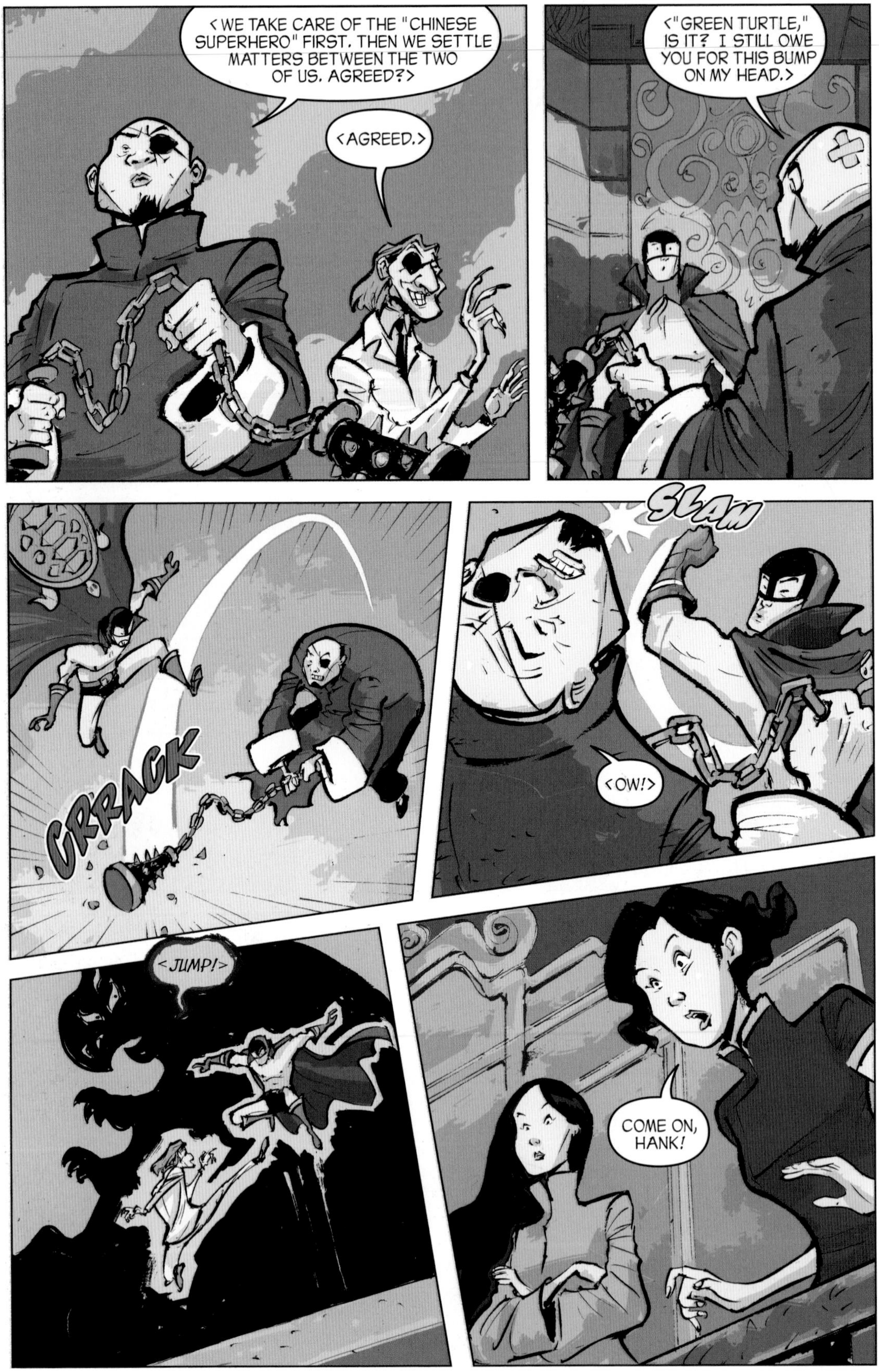

< WE TAKE CARE OF THE "CHINESE SUPERHERO" FIRST. THEN WE SETTLE MATTERS BETWEEN THE TWO OF US. AGREED?>
<AGREED.>
<"GREEN TURTLE," IS IT? I STILL OWE YOU FOR THIS BUMP ON MY HEAD.>
CRRACK
SLAM
<OW!>
<JUMP!>
COME ON, HANK!

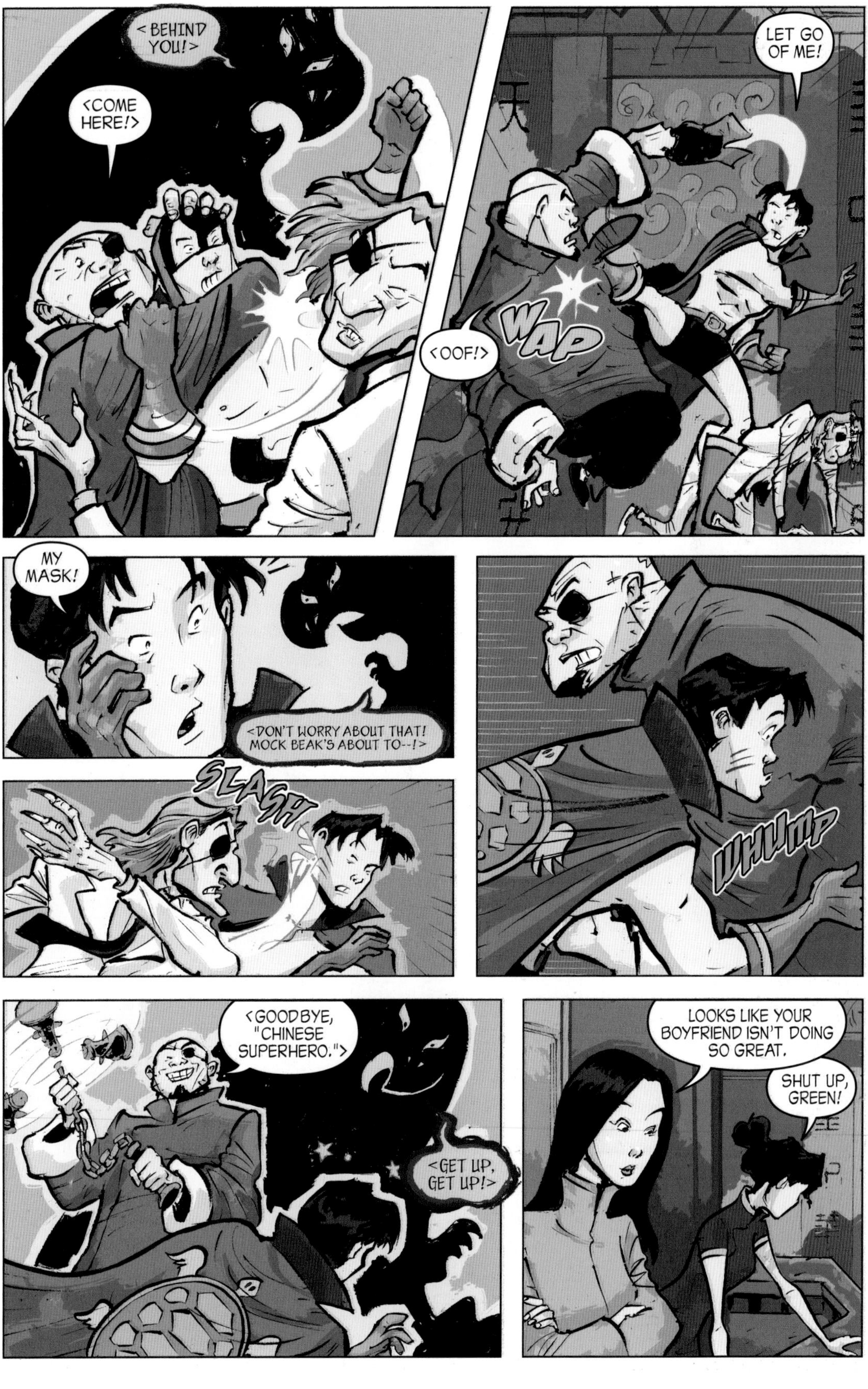

<BEHIND YOU!>
<COME HERE!>
LET GO OF ME!
<OOF!>
WAP
MY MASK!
<DON'T WORRY ABOUT THAT! MOCK BEAK'S ABOUT TO--!>
SLASH
WHUMP
<GOODBYE, "CHINESE SUPERHERO.">
<GET UP, GET UP!>
LOOKS LIKE YOUR BOYFRIEND ISN'T DOING SO GREAT.
SHUT UP, GREEN!

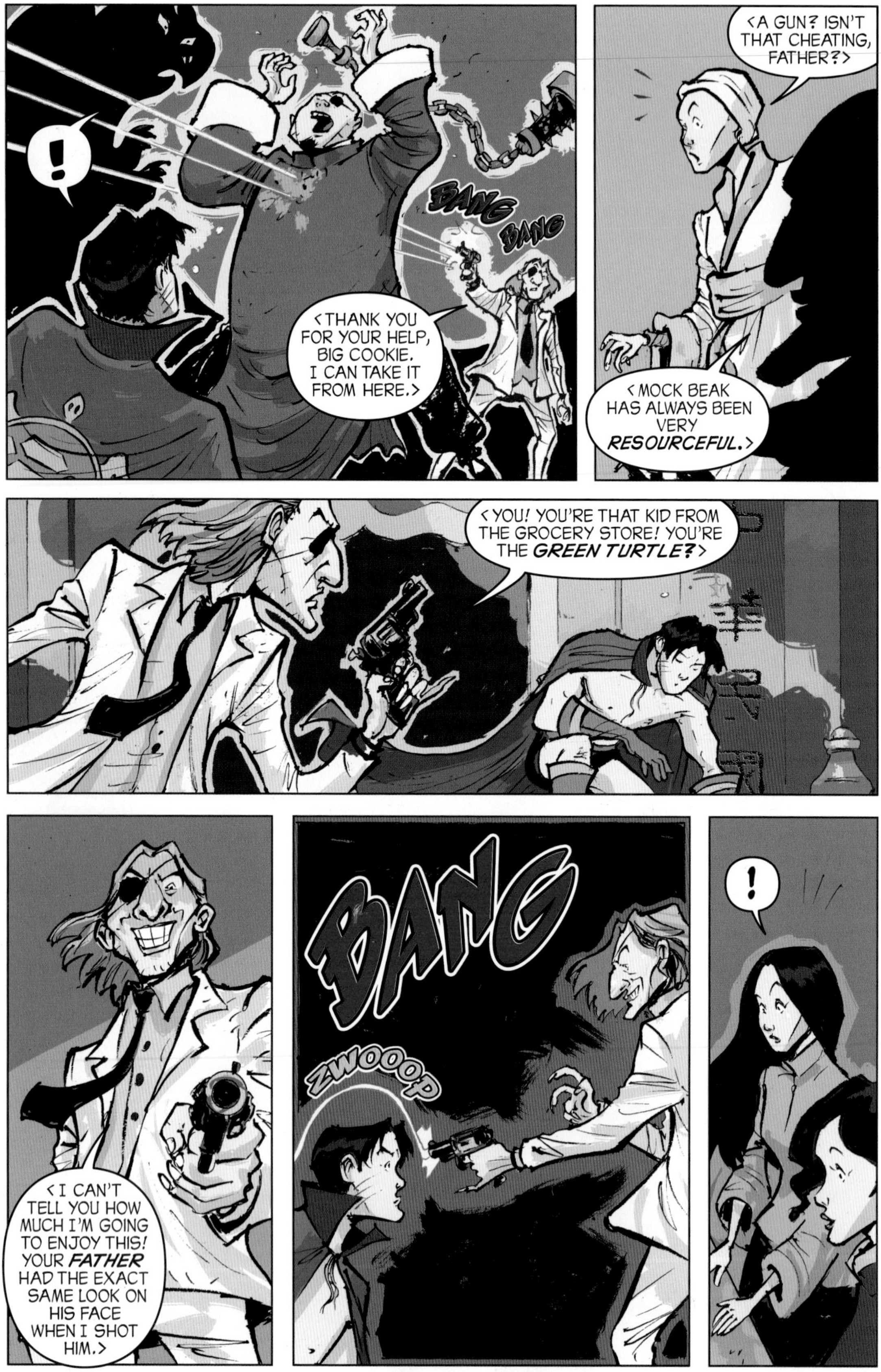
!
BANG
BANG
<THANK YOU FOR YOUR HELP, BIG COOKIE. I CAN TAKE IT FROM HERE.>
<A GUN? ISN'T THAT CHEATING, FATHER?>
<MOCK BEAK HAS ALWAYS BEEN VERY *RESOURCEFUL*.>
<YOU! YOU'RE THAT KID FROM THE GROCERY STORE! YOU'RE THE *GREEN TURTLE*?>
<I CAN'T TELL YOU HOW MUCH I'M GOING TO ENJOY THIS! YOUR *FATHER* HAD THE EXACT SAME LOOK ON HIS FACE WHEN I SHOT HIM.>
BANG
ZWOOOP
!

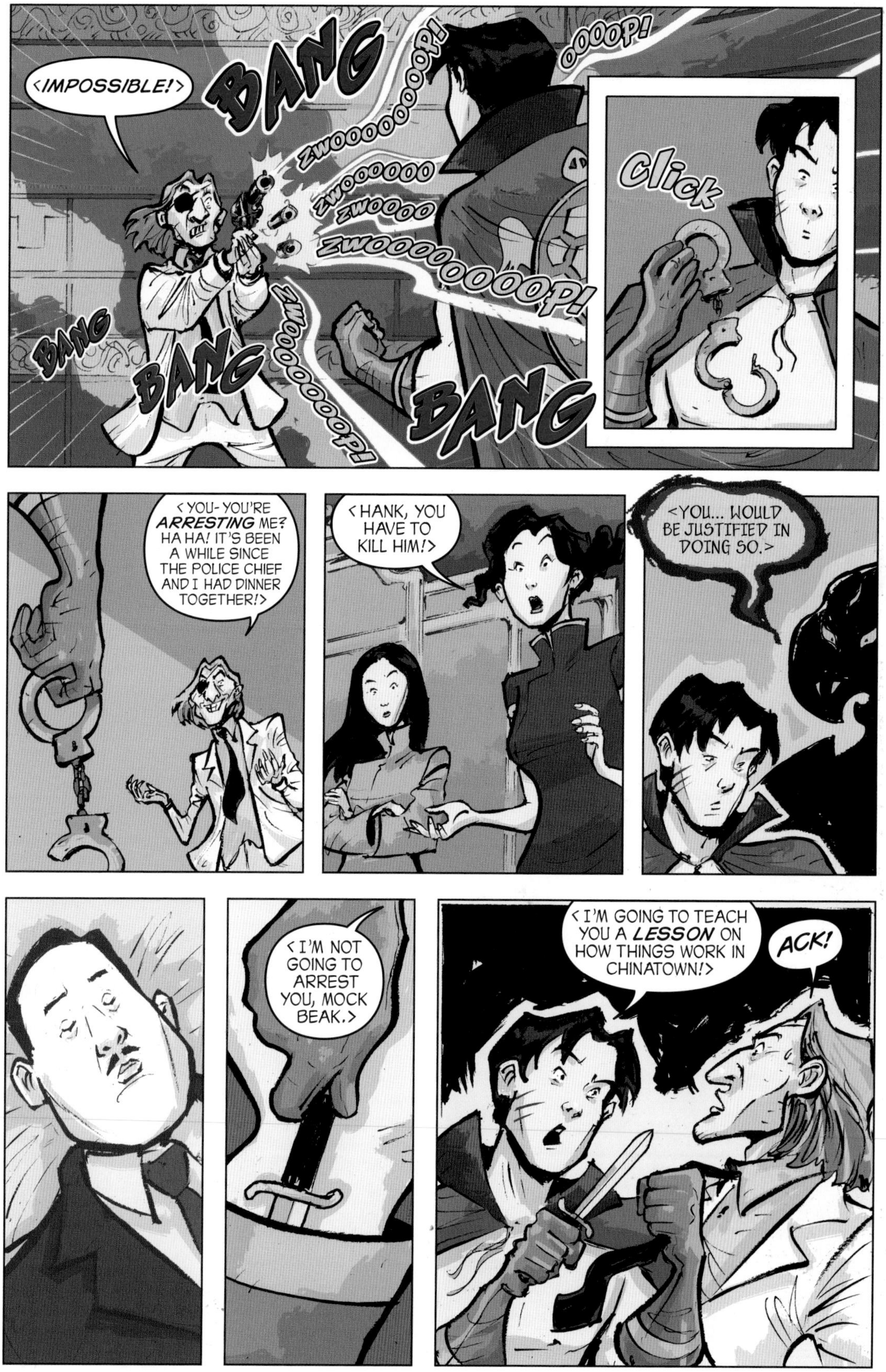

<IMPOSSIBLE!>
BANG
ZWOOOOOOOOOOOP!
OOOOP!
ZWOOOOOOO
ZWOOOO
ZWOOOOOOOOOOOP!
Click
BANG
BANG
ZWOOOOOOOOOOP!
BANG
<YOU- YOU'RE ARRESTING ME? HA HA! IT'S BEEN A WHILE SINCE THE POLICE CHIEF AND I HAD DINNER TOGETHER!>
<HANK, YOU HAVE TO KILL HIM!>
<YOU... WOULD BE JUSTIFIED IN DOING SO.>
<I'M NOT GOING TO ARREST YOU, MOCK BEAK.>
<I'M GOING TO TEACH YOU A LESSON ON HOW THINGS WORK IN CHINATOWN!>
ACK!

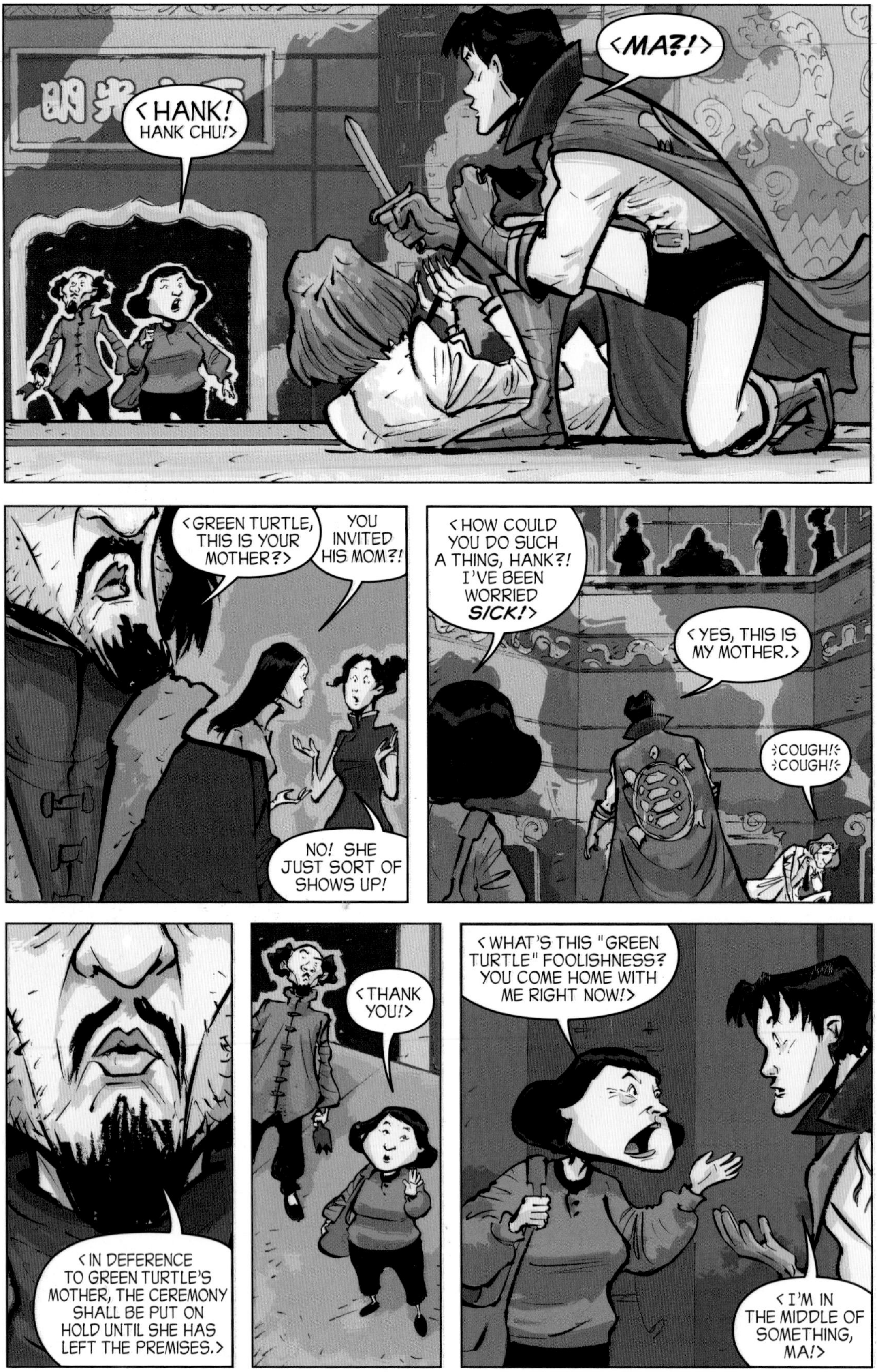

<HANK! HANK CHU!>
<MA?!>
<GREEN TURTLE, THIS IS YOUR MOTHER?>
YOU INVITED HIS MOM?!
NO! SHE JUST SORT OF SHOWS UP!
<HOW COULD YOU DO SUCH A THING, HANK?! I'VE BEEN WORRIED SICK!>
<YES, THIS IS MY MOTHER.>
COUGH! COUGH!
<IN DEFERENCE TO GREEN TURTLE'S MOTHER, THE CEREMONY SHALL BE PUT ON HOLD UNTIL SHE HAS LEFT THE PREMISES.>
<THANK YOU!>
<WHAT'S THIS "GREEN TURTLE" FOOLISHNESS? YOU COME HOME WITH ME RIGHT NOW!>
<I'M IN THE MIDDLE OF SOMETHING, MA!>

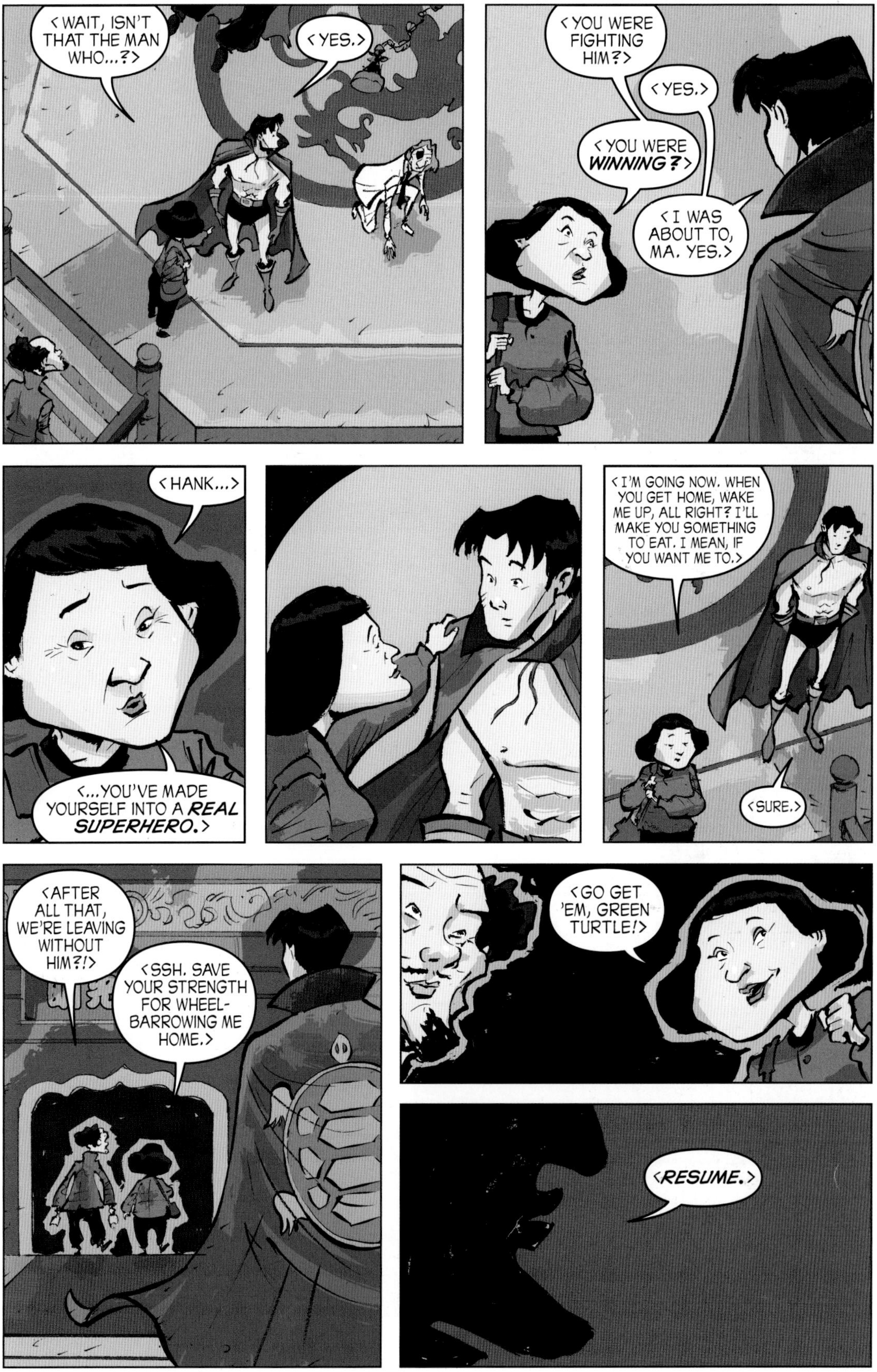
<WAIT, ISN'T THAT THE MAN WHO...?>
<YES.>
<YOU WERE FIGHTING HIM?>
<YES.>
<YOU WERE *WINNING?*>
<I WAS ABOUT TO, MA. YES.>
<HANK...>
<...YOU'VE MADE YOURSELF INTO A *REAL SUPERHERO.*>
<I'M GOING NOW. WHEN YOU GET HOME, WAKE ME UP, ALL RIGHT? I'LL MAKE YOU SOMETHING TO EAT. I MEAN, IF YOU WANT ME TO.>
<SURE.>
<AFTER ALL THAT, WE'RE LEAVING WITHOUT HIM?!>
<SSH. SAVE YOUR STRENGTH FOR WHEEL-BARROWING ME HOME.>
<GO GET 'EM, GREEN TURTLE!>
<*RESUME.*>

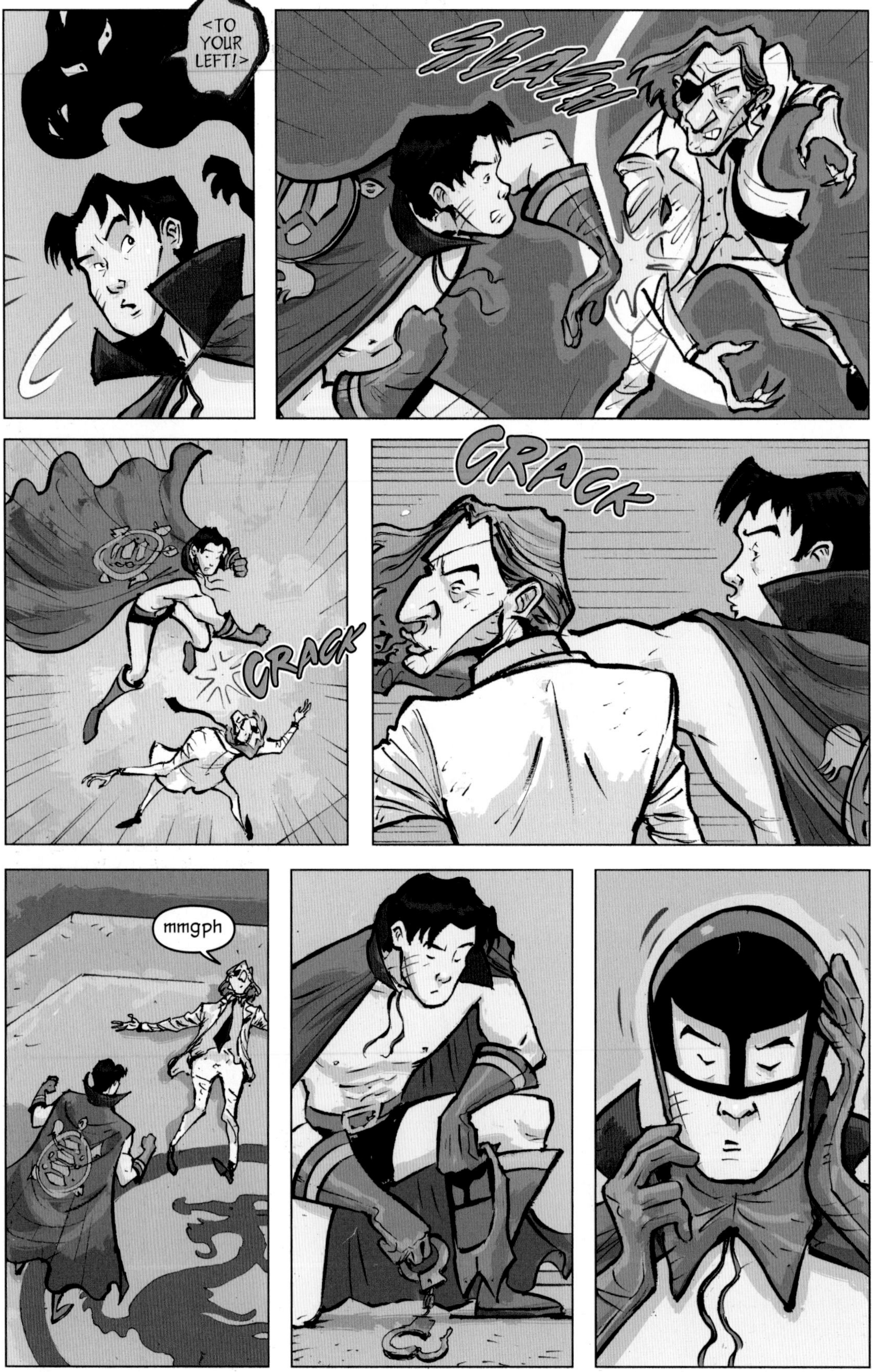
<TO YOUR LEFT!>
SLASH
CRACK
CRACK
mmgph

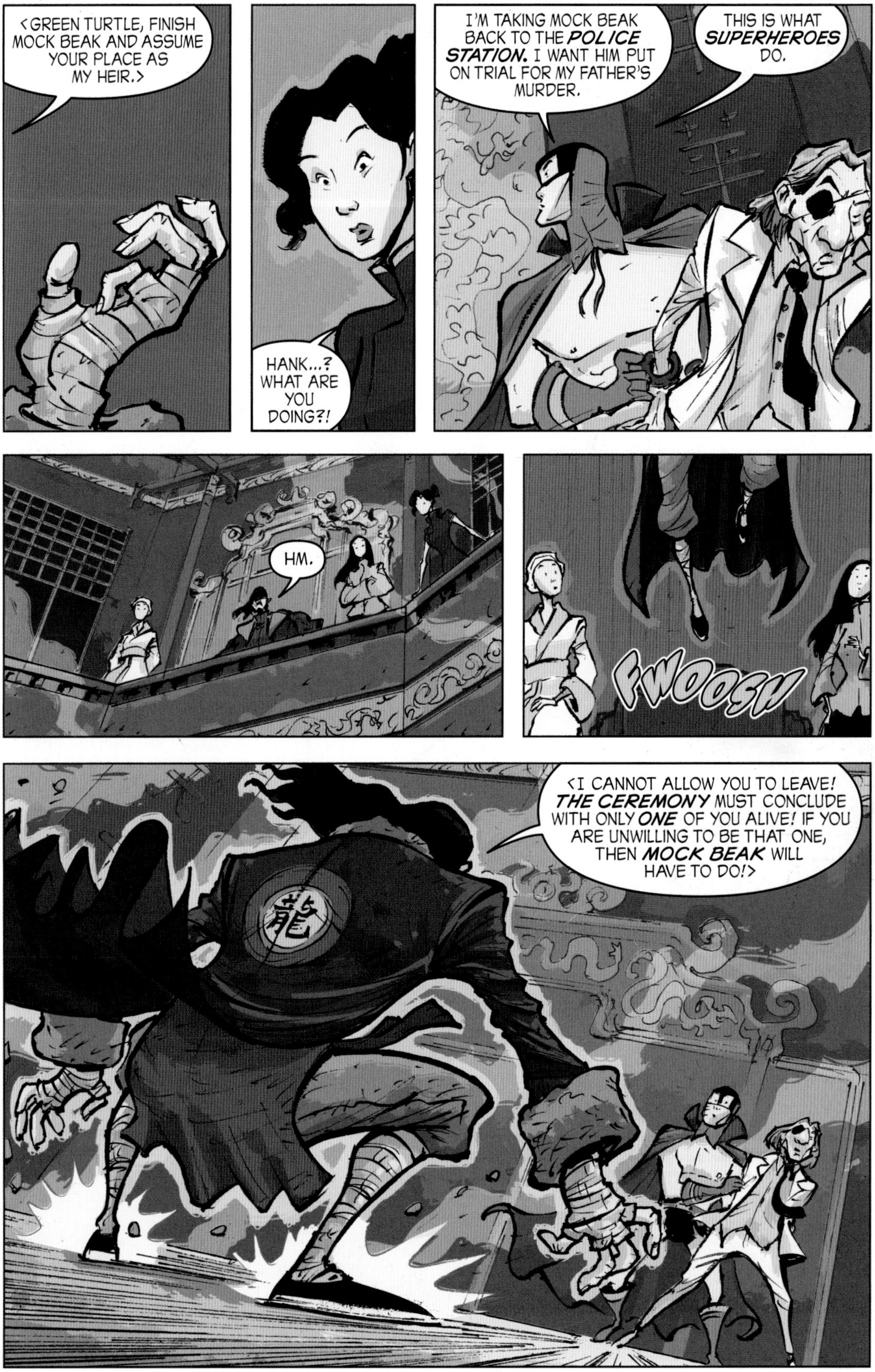

<GREEN TURTLE, FINISH MOCK BEAK AND ASSUME YOUR PLACE AS MY HEIR.>
HANK...? WHAT ARE YOU DOING?!
I'M TAKING MOCK BEAK BACK TO THE *POLICE STATION.* I WANT HIM PUT ON TRIAL FOR MY FATHER'S MURDER.
THIS IS WHAT *SUPERHEROES* DO.
HM.
FWOOSH
<I CANNOT ALLOW YOU TO LEAVE! *THE CEREMONY* MUST CONCLUDE WITH ONLY *ONE* OF YOU ALIVE! IF YOU ARE UNWILLING TO BE THAT ONE, THEN *MOCK BEAK* WILL HAVE TO DO!>

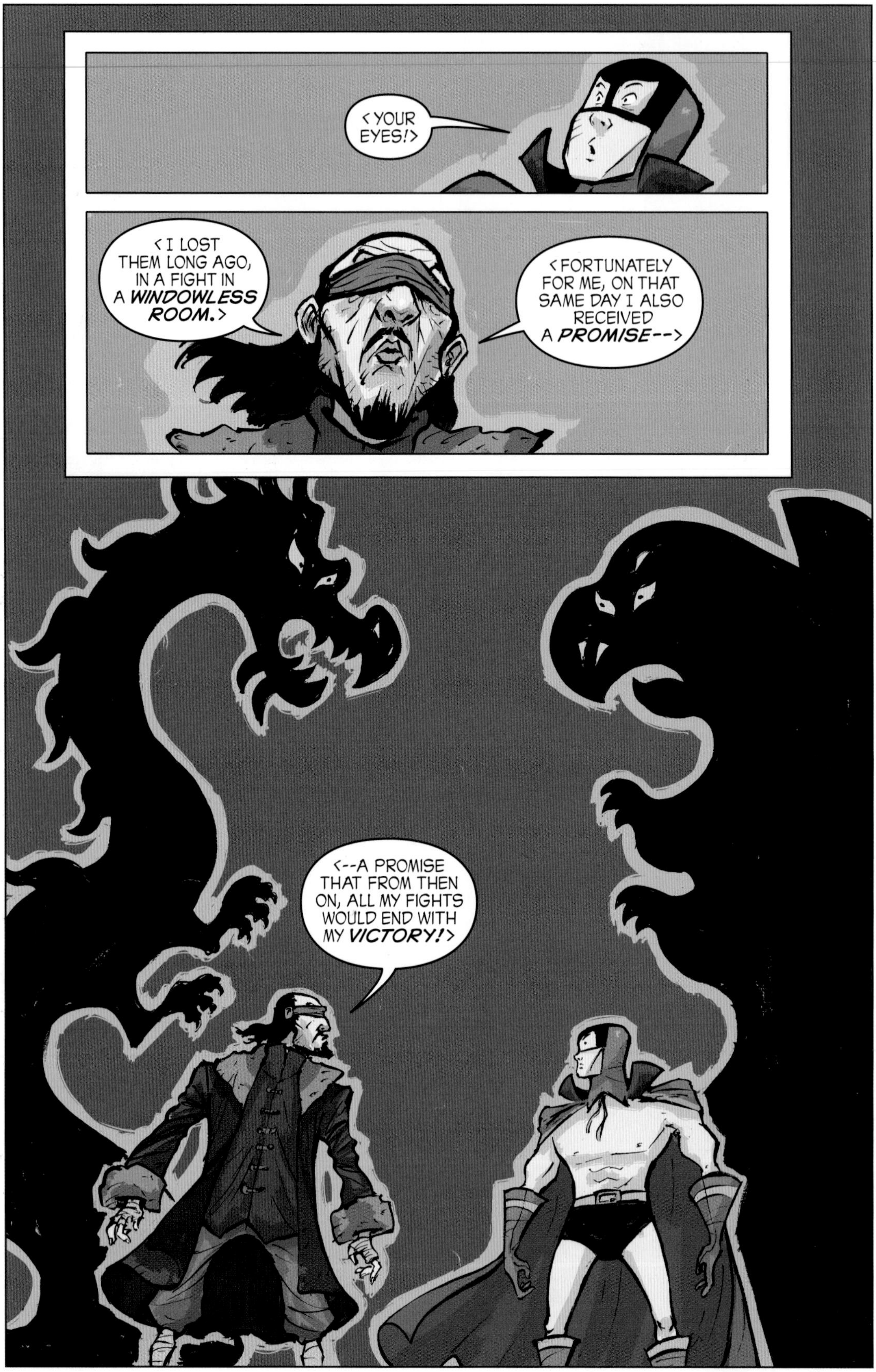
<YOUR EYES!>
<I LOST THEM LONG AGO, IN A FIGHT IN A WINDOWLESS ROOM.>
<FORTUNATELY FOR ME, ON THAT SAME DAY I ALSO RECEIVED A PROMISE-->
<--A PROMISE THAT FROM THEN ON, ALL MY FIGHTS WOULD END WITH MY VICTORY!>

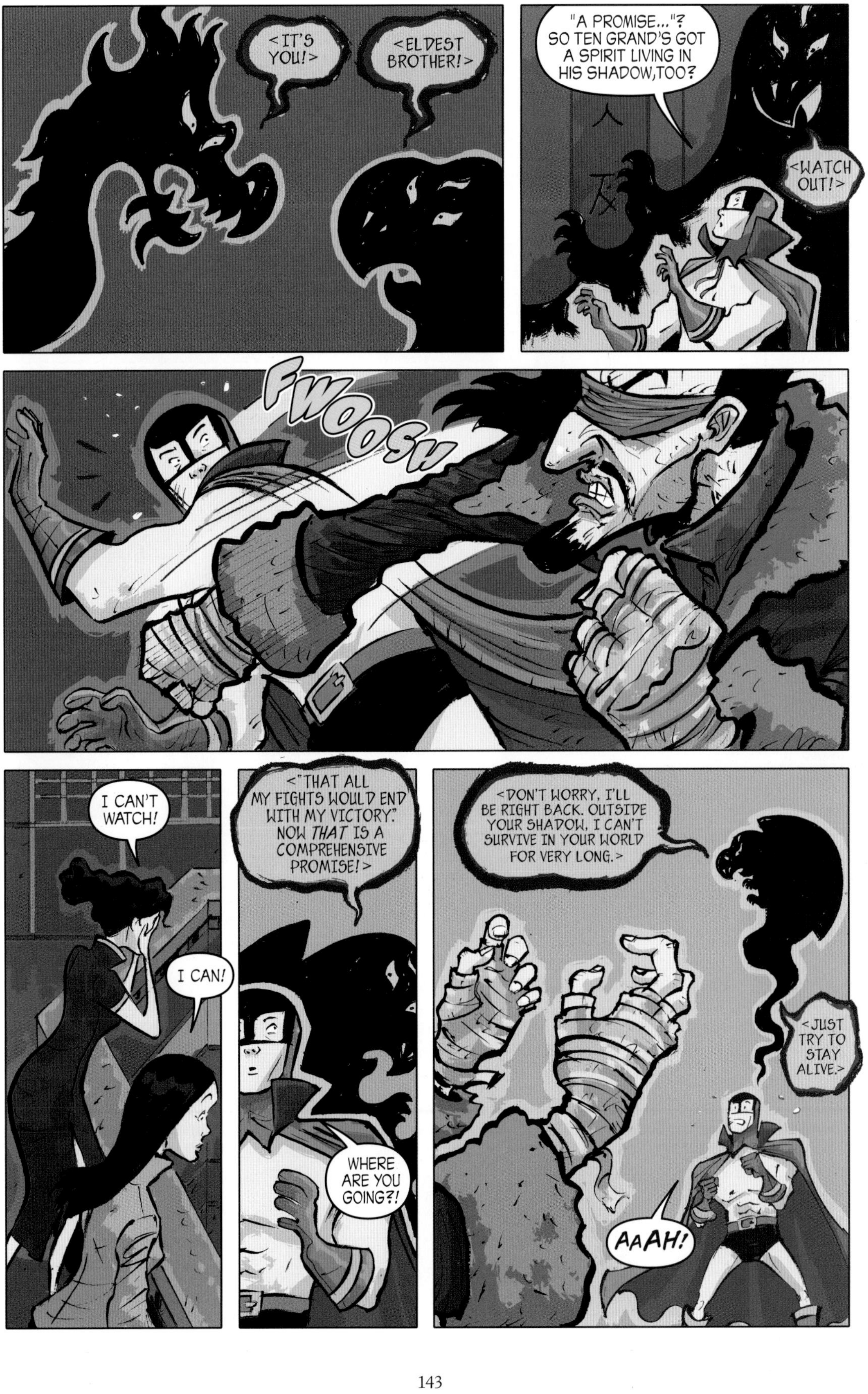
<IT'S YOU!>
<ELDEST BROTHER!>
"A PROMISE..."? SO TEN GRAND'S GOT A SPIRIT LIVING IN HIS SHADOW,TOO?
<WATCH OUT!>
FWOOSH
I CAN'T WATCH!
I CAN!
<"THAT ALL MY FIGHTS WOULD END WITH MY VICTORY." NOW *THAT* IS A COMPREHENSIVE PROMISE!>
WHERE ARE YOU GOING?!
<DON'T WORRY, I'LL BE RIGHT BACK. OUTSIDE YOUR SHADOW, I CAN'T SURVIVE IN YOUR WORLD FOR VERY LONG.>
<JUST TRY TO STAY ALIVE.>
AAAH!

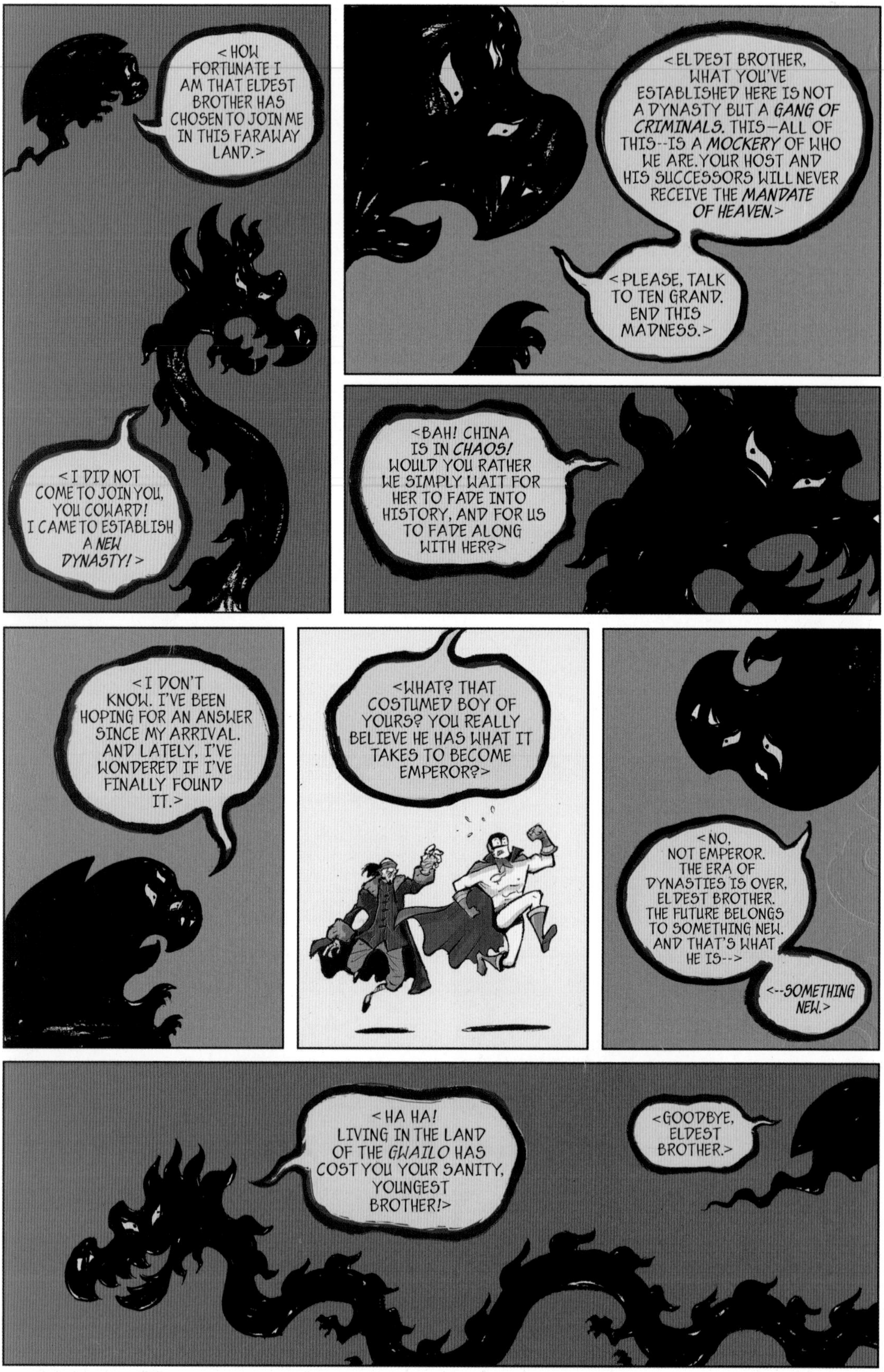
<HOW FORTUNATE I AM THAT ELDEST BROTHER HAS CHOSEN TO JOIN ME IN THIS FARAWAY LAND.>
<I DID NOT COME TO JOIN YOU, YOU COWARD! I CAME TO ESTABLISH A *NEW DYNASTY!*>
<ELDEST BROTHER, WHAT YOU'VE ESTABLISHED HERE IS NOT A DYNASTY BUT A *GANG OF CRIMINALS.* THIS—ALL OF THIS--IS A *MOCKERY* OF WHO WE ARE. YOUR HOST AND HIS SUCCESSORS WILL NEVER RECEIVE THE *MANDATE OF HEAVEN.*>
<PLEASE, TALK TO TEN GRAND. END THIS MADNESS.>
<BAH! CHINA IS IN *CHAOS!* WOULD YOU RATHER WE SIMPLY WAIT FOR HER TO FADE INTO HISTORY, AND FOR US TO FADE ALONG WITH HER?>
<I DON'T KNOW. I'VE BEEN HOPING FOR AN ANSWER SINCE MY ARRIVAL. AND LATELY, I'VE WONDERED IF I'VE FINALLY FOUND IT.>
<WHAT? THAT COSTUMED BOY OF YOURS? YOU REALLY BELIEVE HE HAS WHAT IT TAKES TO BECOME EMPEROR?>
<NO, NOT EMPEROR. THE ERA OF DYNASTIES IS OVER, ELDEST BROTHER. THE FUTURE BELONGS TO SOMETHING NEW. AND THAT'S WHAT HE IS-->
<--*SOMETHING NEW.*>
<HA HA! LIVING IN THE LAND OF THE *GWAILO* HAS COST YOU YOUR SANITY, YOUNGEST BROTHER!>
<GOODBYE, ELDEST BROTHER.>

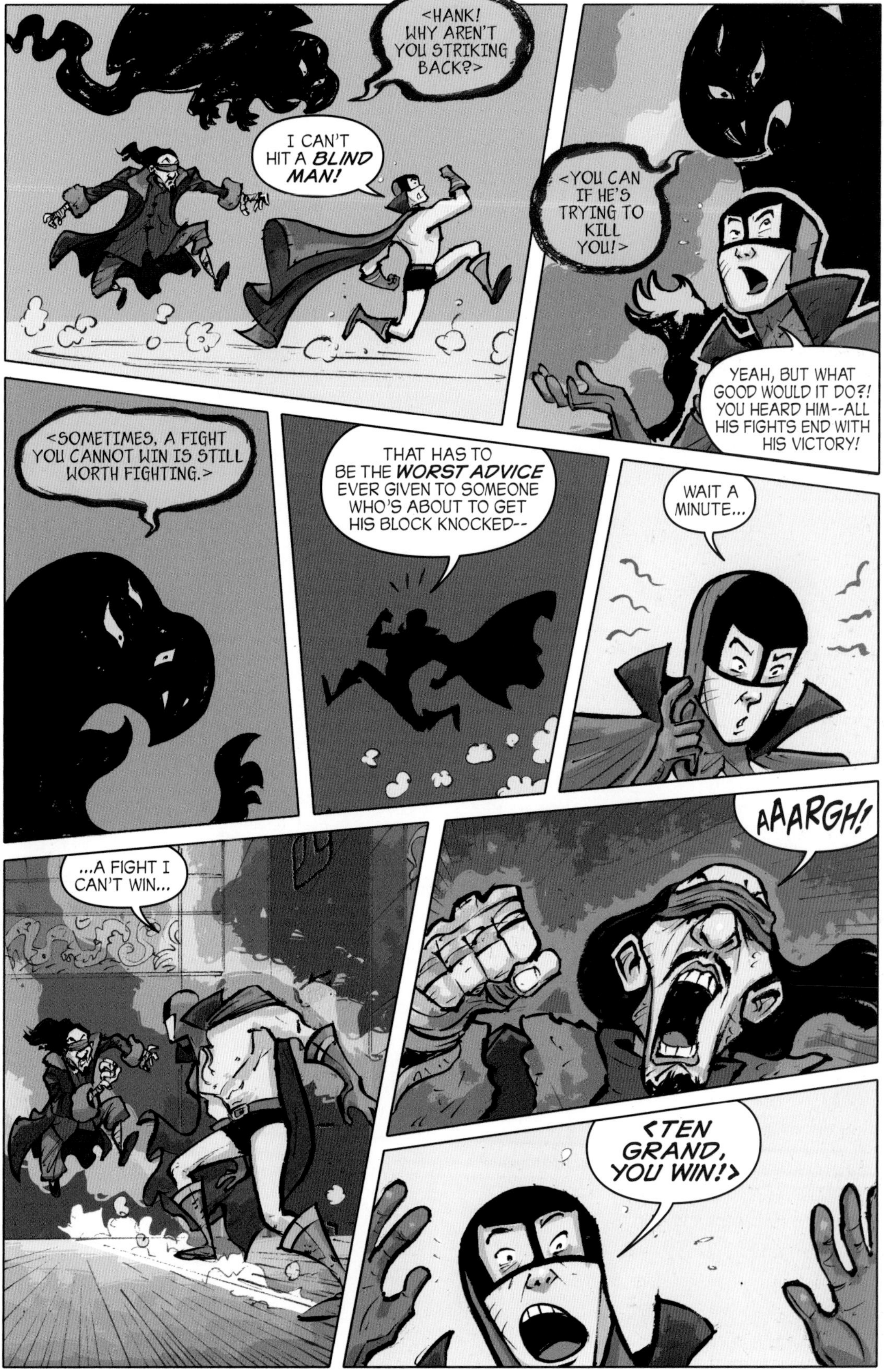
<HANK! WHY AREN'T YOU STRIKING BACK?>
I CAN'T HIT A BLIND MAN!
<YOU CAN IF HE'S TRYING TO KILL YOU!>
YEAH, BUT WHAT GOOD WOULD IT DO?! YOU HEARD HIM--ALL HIS FIGHTS END WITH HIS VICTORY!
<SOMETIMES, A FIGHT YOU CANNOT WIN IS STILL WORTH FIGHTING.>
THAT HAS TO BE THE WORST ADVICE EVER GIVEN TO SOMEONE WHO'S ABOUT TO GET HIS BLOCK KNOCKED--
WAIT A MINUTE...
...A FIGHT I CAN'T WIN...
AAARGH!
<TEN GRAND, YOU WIN!>

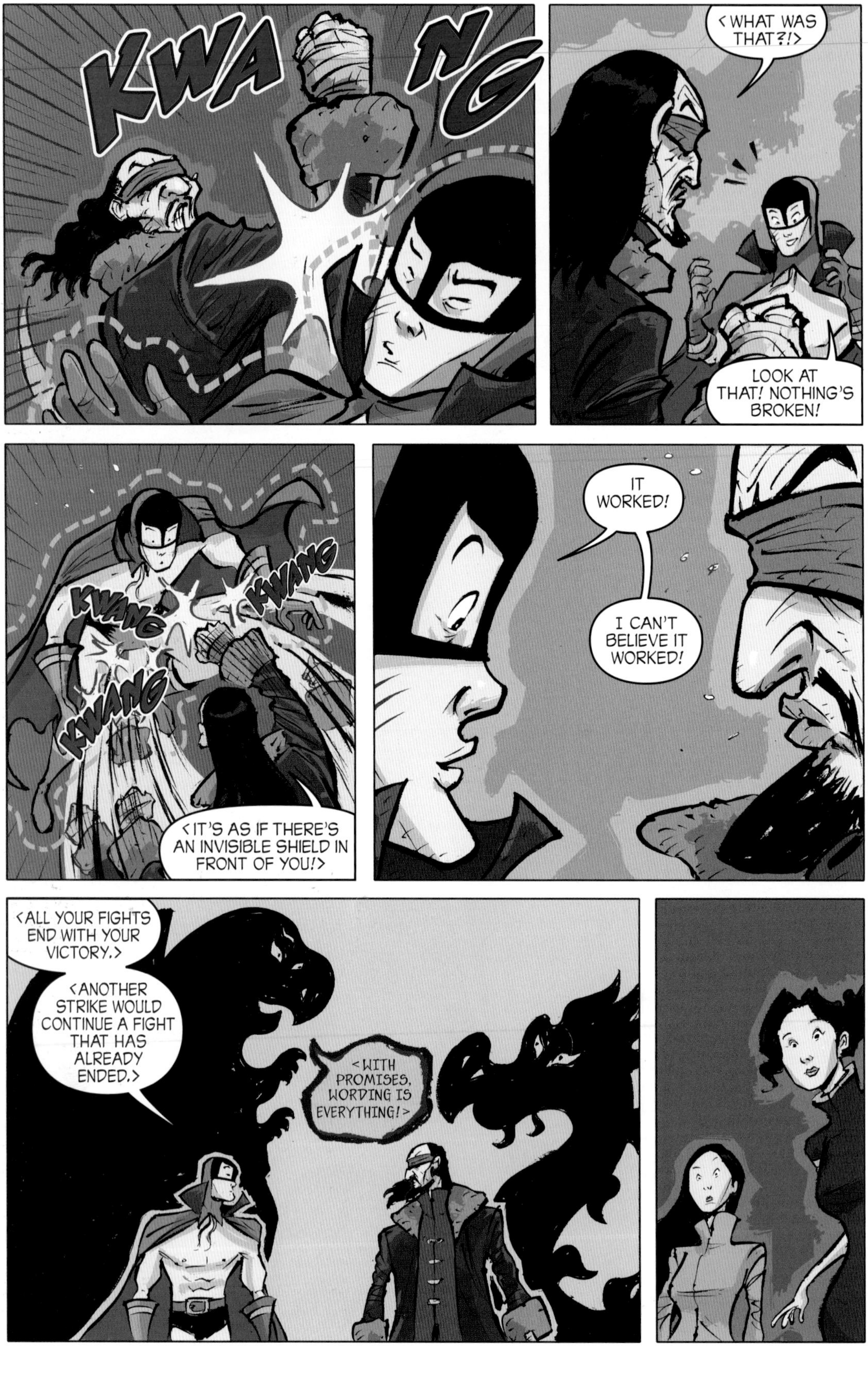
KWANG
<WHAT WAS THAT?!>
LOOK AT THAT! NOTHING'S BROKEN!
KWANG
KWANG
KWANG
<IT'S AS IF THERE'S AN INVISIBLE SHIELD IN FRONT OF YOU!>
IT WORKED!
I CAN'T BELIEVE IT WORKED!
<ALL YOUR FIGHTS END WITH YOUR VICTORY.>
<ANOTHER STRIKE WOULD CONTINUE A FIGHT THAT HAS ALREADY ENDED.>
<WITH PROMISES, WORDING IS EVERYTHING!>

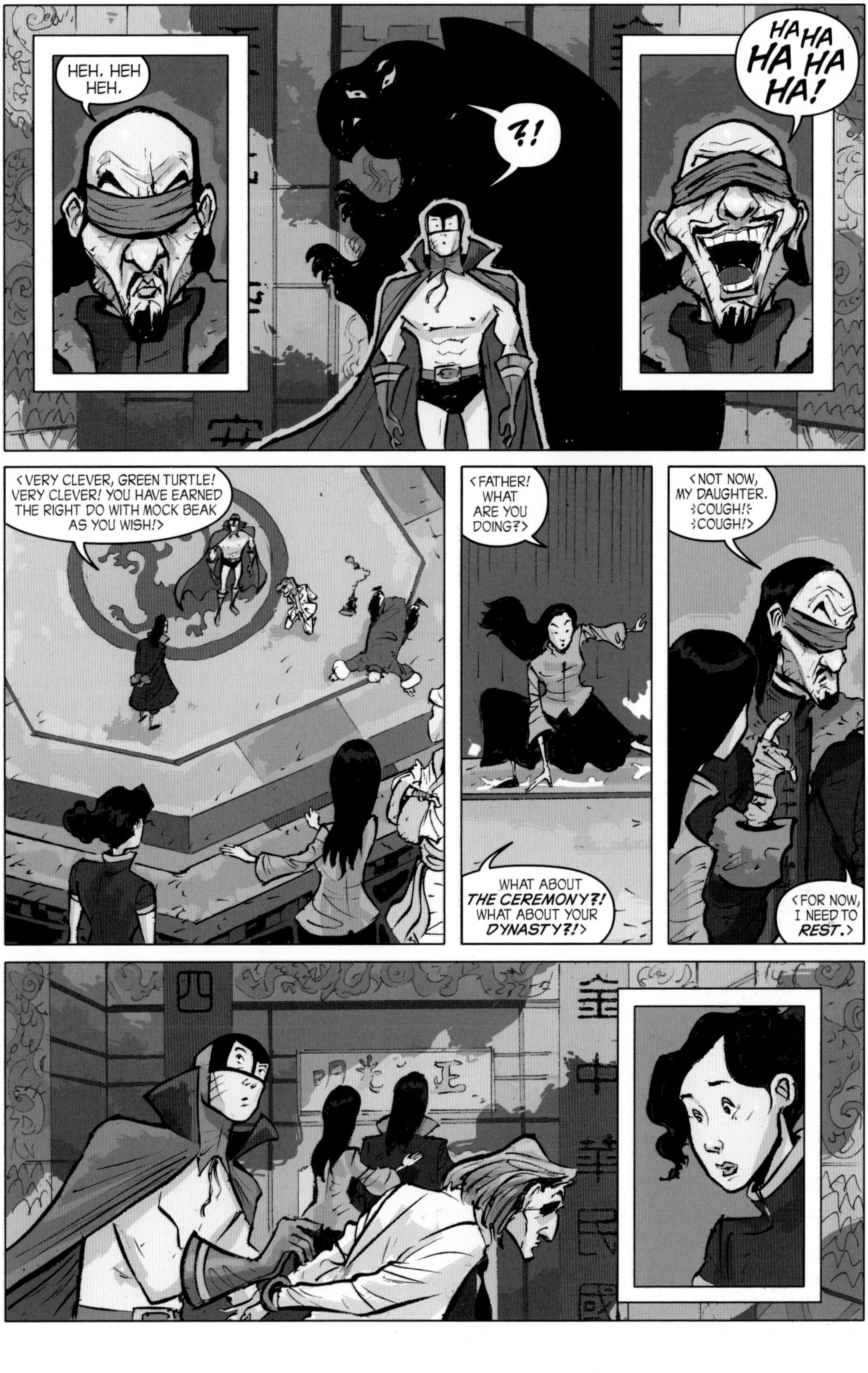
HEH. HEH
HEH.
?!
HA HA HA HA HA!
<VERY CLEVER, GREEN TURTLE! VERY CLEVER! YOU HAVE EARNED THE RIGHT DO WITH MOCK BEAK AS YOU WISH!>
<FATHER! WHAT ARE YOU DOING?>
WHAT ABOUT THE CEREMONY?! WHAT ABOUT YOUR DYNASTY?!>
<NOT NOW, MY DAUGHTER. COUGH! COUGH!>
<FOR NOW, I NEED TO REST.>

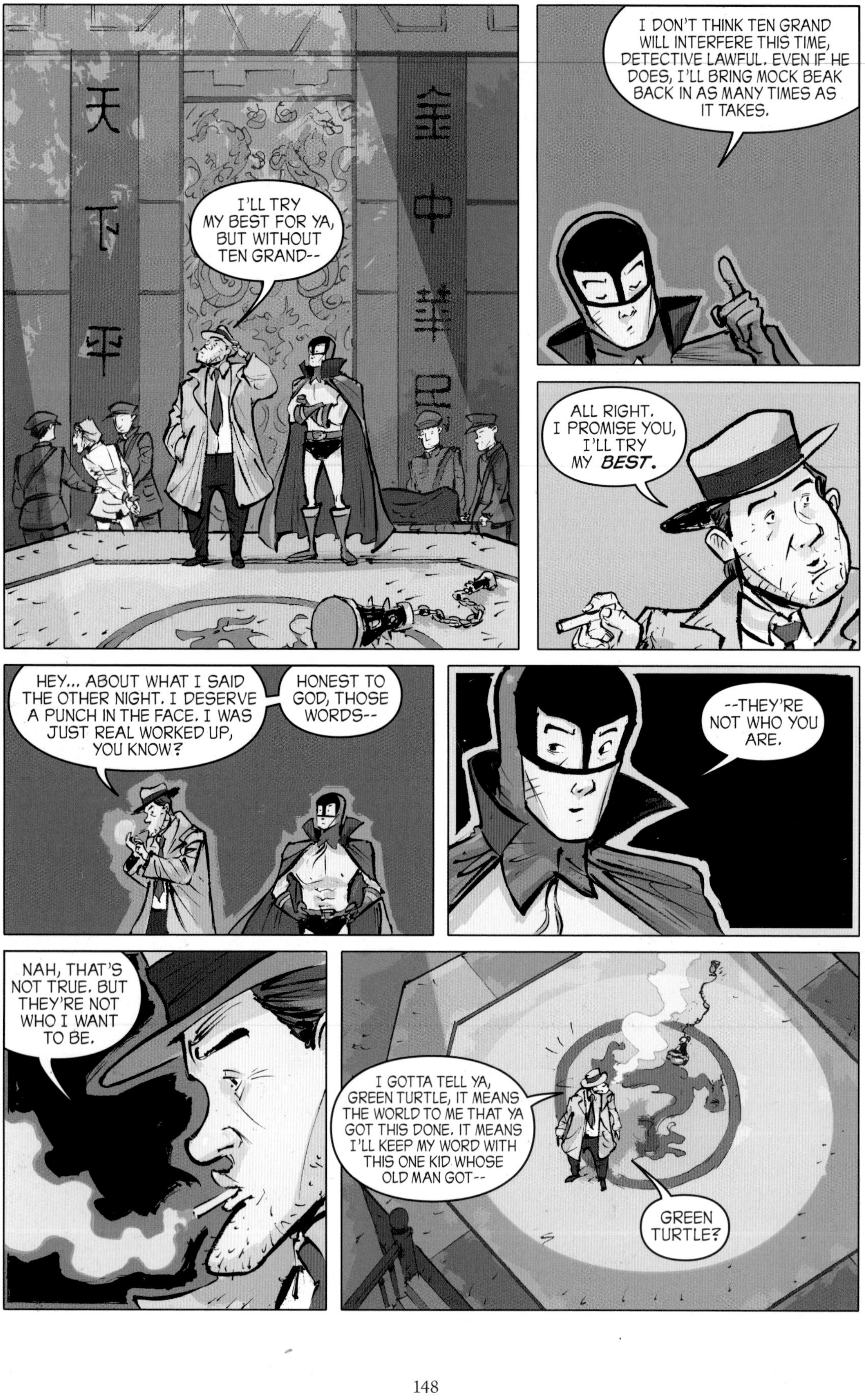
天下平
I'LL TRY MY BEST FOR YA, BUT WITHOUT TEN GRAND--
I DON'T THINK TEN GRAND WILL INTERFERE THIS TIME, DETECTIVE LAWFUL. EVEN IF HE DOES, I'LL BRING MOCK BEAK BACK IN AS MANY TIMES AS IT TAKES.
ALL RIGHT. I PROMISE YOU, I'LL TRY MY BEST.
HEY... ABOUT WHAT I SAID THE OTHER NIGHT. I DESERVE A PUNCH IN THE FACE. I WAS JUST REAL WORKED UP, YOU KNOW?
HONEST TO GOD, THOSE WORDS--
--THEY'RE NOT WHO YOU ARE.
NAH, THAT'S NOT TRUE. BUT THEY'RE NOT WHO I WANT TO BE.
I GOTTA TELL YA, GREEN TURTLE, IT MEANS THE WORLD TO ME THAT YA GOT THIS DONE. IT MEANS I'LL KEEP MY WORD WITH THIS ONE KID WHOSE OLD MAN GOT--
GREEN TURTLE?

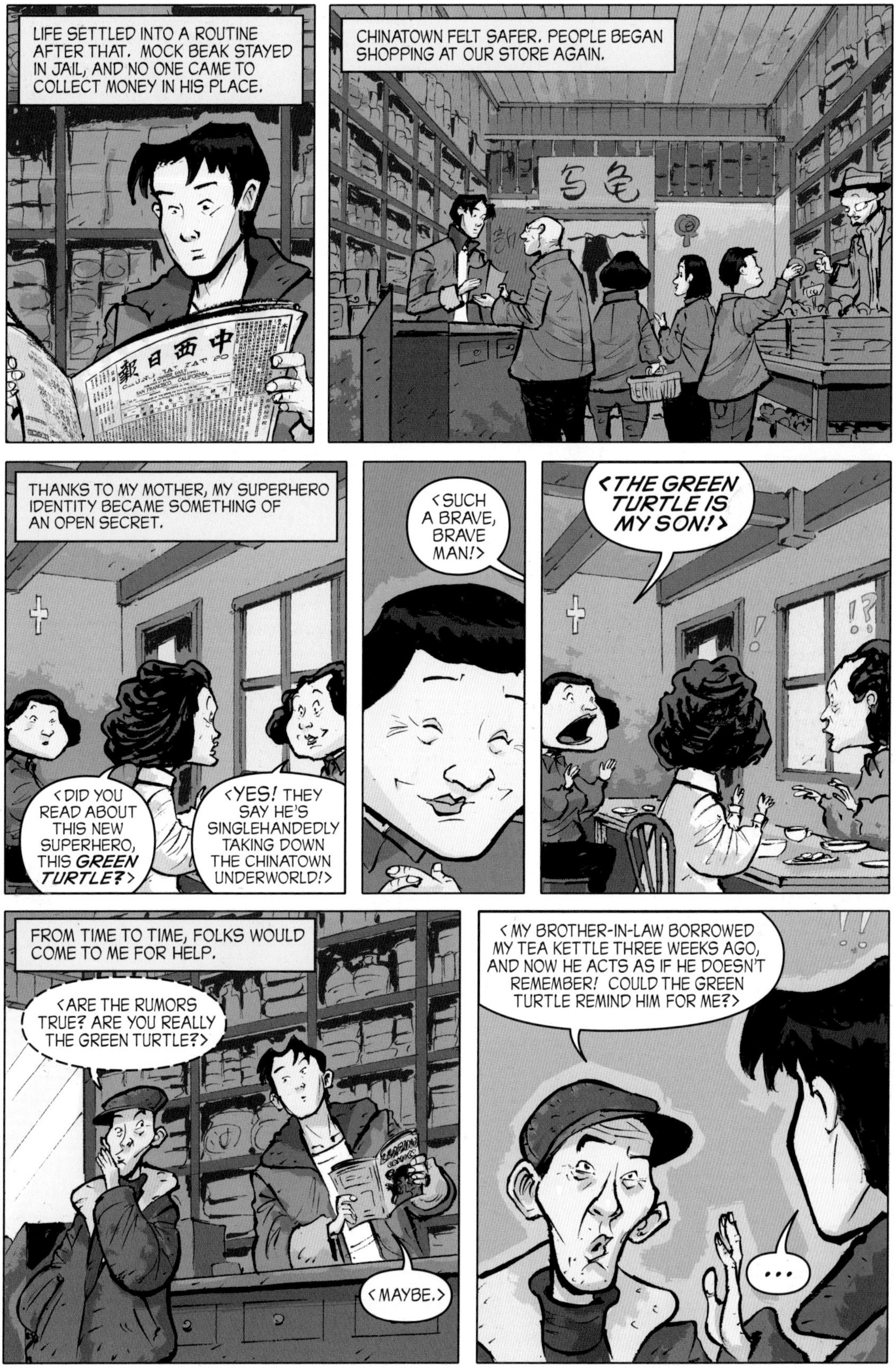
LIFE SETTLED INTO A ROUTINE AFTER THAT. MOCK BEAK STAYED IN JAIL, AND NO ONE CAME TO COLLECT MONEY IN HIS PLACE.
CHINATOWN FELT SAFER. PEOPLE BEGAN SHOPPING AT OUR STORE AGAIN.
THANKS TO MY MOTHER, MY SUPERHERO IDENTITY BECAME SOMETHING OF AN OPEN SECRET.
<DID YOU READ ABOUT THIS NEW SUPERHERO, THIS *GREEN TURTLE?*>
<*YES!* THEY SAY HE'S SINGLEHANDEDLY TAKING DOWN THE CHINATOWN UNDERWORLD!>
<SUCH A BRAVE, BRAVE MAN!>
<*THE GREEN TURTLE IS MY SON!*>
!
!?
FROM TIME TO TIME, FOLKS WOULD COME TO ME FOR HELP.
<ARE THE RUMORS TRUE? ARE YOU REALLY THE GREEN TURTLE?>
<MAYBE.>
<MY BROTHER-IN-LAW BORROWED MY TEA KETTLE THREE WEEKS AGO, AND NOW HE ACTS AS IF HE DOESN'T REMEMBER! COULD THE GREEN TURTLE REMIND HIM FOR ME?>
!!
...

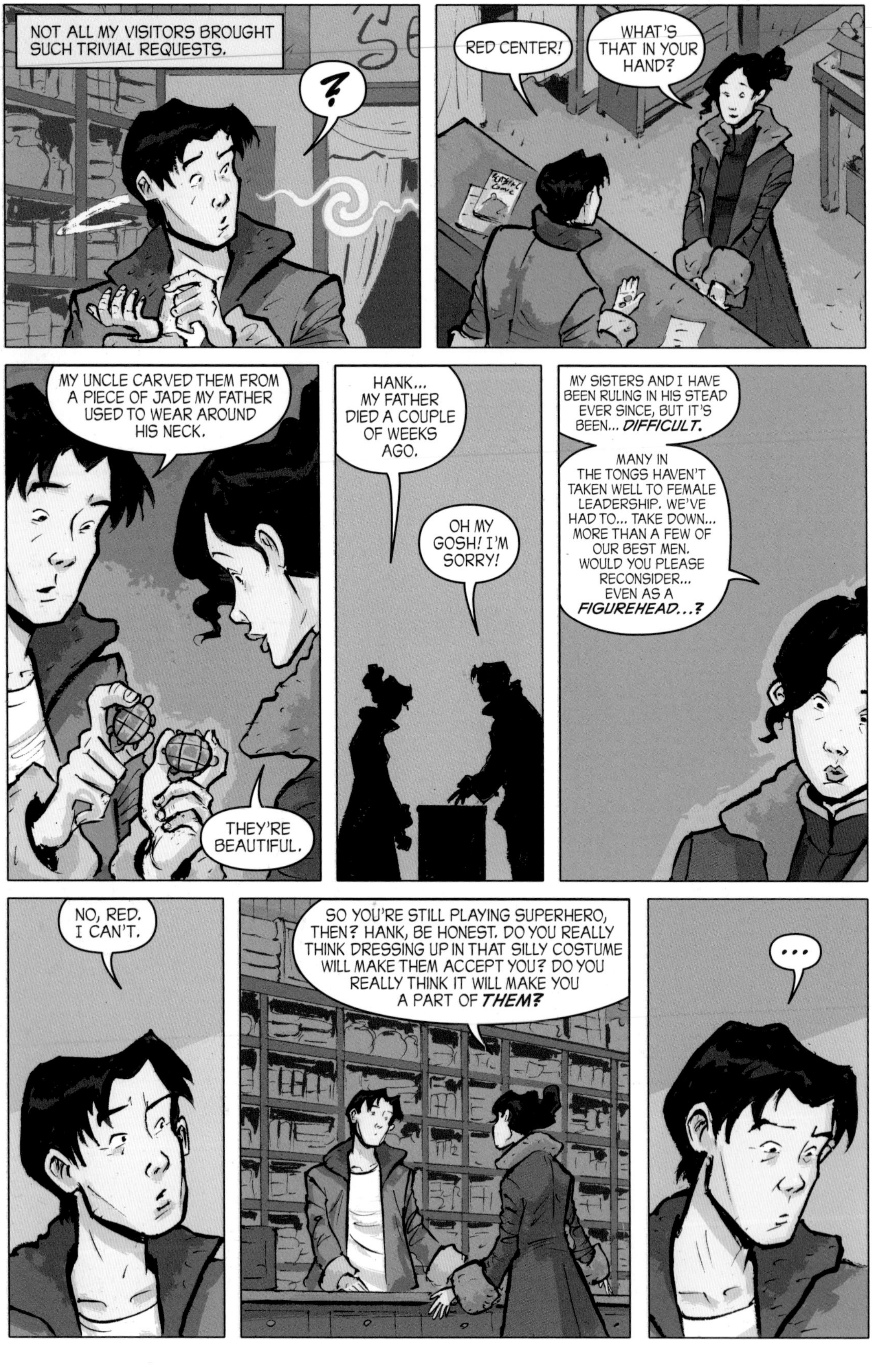
NOT ALL MY VISITORS BROUGHT SUCH TRIVIAL REQUESTS.
?
RED CENTER!
WHAT'S THAT IN YOUR HAND?
MY UNCLE CARVED THEM FROM A PIECE OF JADE MY FATHER USED TO WEAR AROUND HIS NECK.
THEY'RE BEAUTIFUL.
HANK... MY FATHER DIED A COUPLE OF WEEKS AGO.
OH MY GOSH! I'M SORRY!
MY SISTERS AND I HAVE BEEN RULING IN HIS STEAD EVER SINCE, BUT IT'S BEEN... DIFFICULT.
MANY IN THE TONGS HAVEN'T TAKEN WELL TO FEMALE LEADERSHIP. WE'VE HAD TO... TAKE DOWN... MORE THAN A FEW OF OUR BEST MEN. WOULD YOU PLEASE RECONSIDER... EVEN AS A FIGUREHEAD...?
NO, RED. I CAN'T.
SO YOU'RE STILL PLAYING SUPERHERO, THEN? HANK, BE HONEST. DO YOU REALLY THINK DRESSING UP IN THAT SILLY COSTUME WILL MAKE THEM ACCEPT YOU? DO YOU REALLY THINK IT WILL MAKE YOU A PART OF THEM?
...

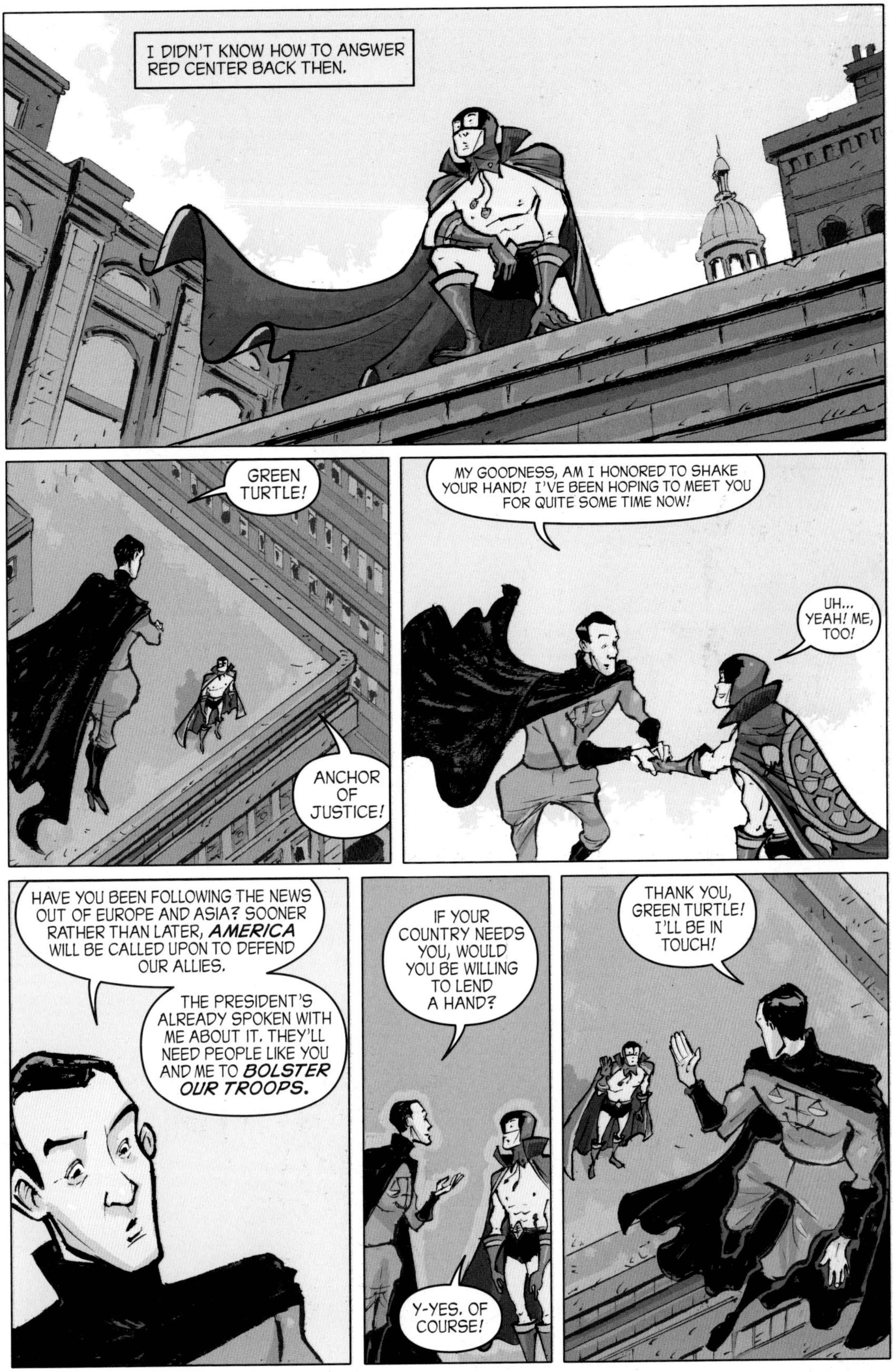
I DIDN'T KNOW HOW TO ANSWER RED CENTER BACK THEN.
GREEN TURTLE!
ANCHOR OF JUSTICE!
MY GOODNESS, AM I HONORED TO SHAKE YOUR HAND! I'VE BEEN HOPING TO MEET YOU FOR QUITE SOME TIME NOW!
UH... YEAH! ME, TOO!
HAVE YOU BEEN FOLLOWING THE NEWS OUT OF EUROPE AND ASIA? SOONER RATHER THAN LATER, AMERICA WILL BE CALLED UPON TO DEFEND OUR ALLIES.
THE PRESIDENT'S ALREADY SPOKEN WITH ME ABOUT IT. THEY'LL NEED PEOPLE LIKE YOU AND ME TO BOLSTER OUR TROOPS.
IF YOUR COUNTRY NEEDS YOU, WOULD YOU BE WILLING TO LEND A HAND?
Y-YES. OF COURSE!
THANK YOU, GREEN TURTLE! I'LL BE IN TOUCH!

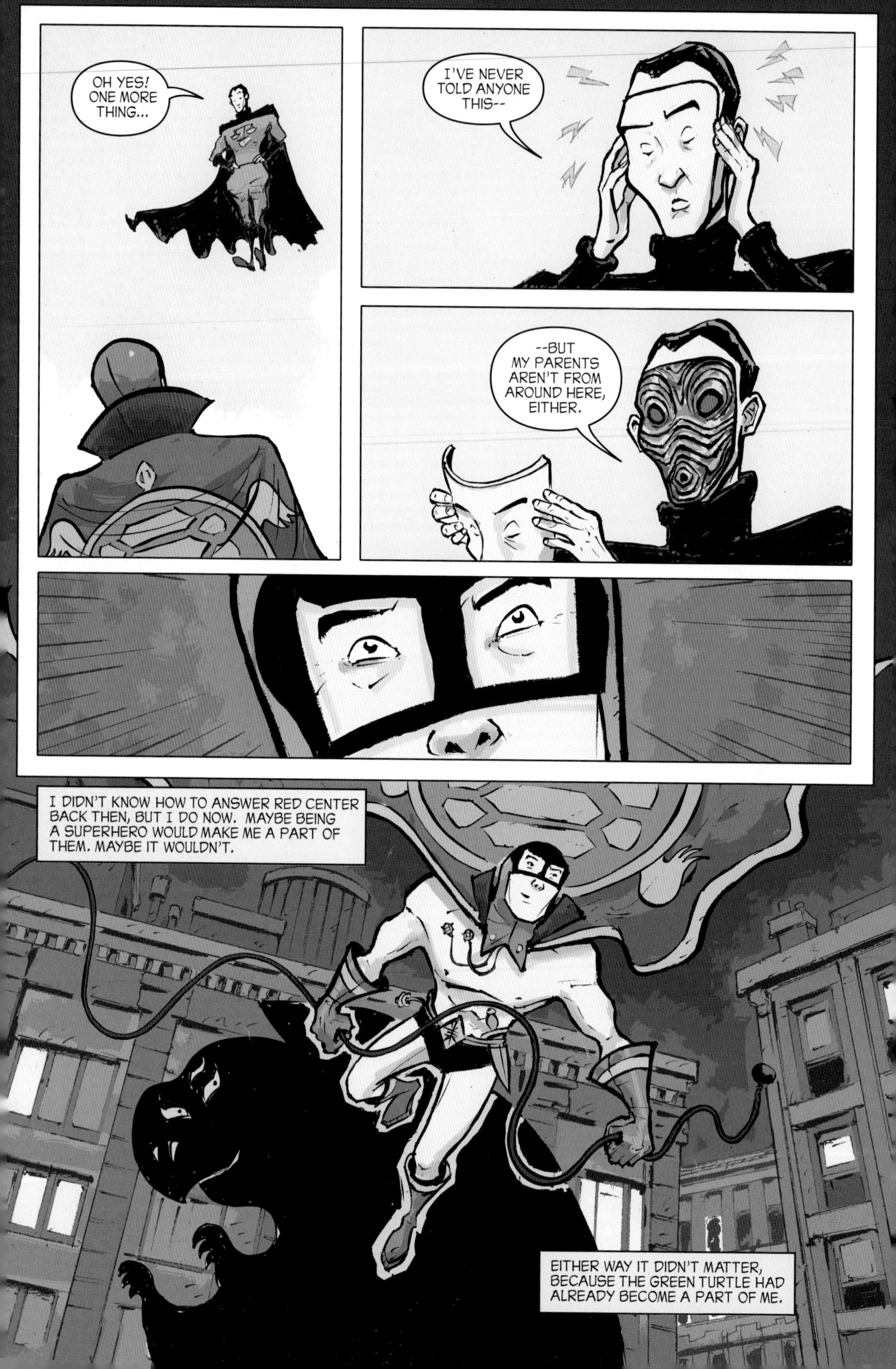
OH YES! ONE MORE THING...
I'VE NEVER TOLD ANYONE THIS--
--BUT MY PARENTS AREN'T FROM AROUND HERE, EITHER.
I DIDN'T KNOW HOW TO ANSWER RED CENTER BACK THEN, BUT I DO NOW. MAYBE BEING A SUPERHERO WOULD MAKE ME A PART OF THEM. MAYBE IT WOULDN'T.
EITHER WAY IT DIDN'T MATTER, BECAUSE THE GREEN TURTLE HAD ALREADY BECOME A PART OF ME.

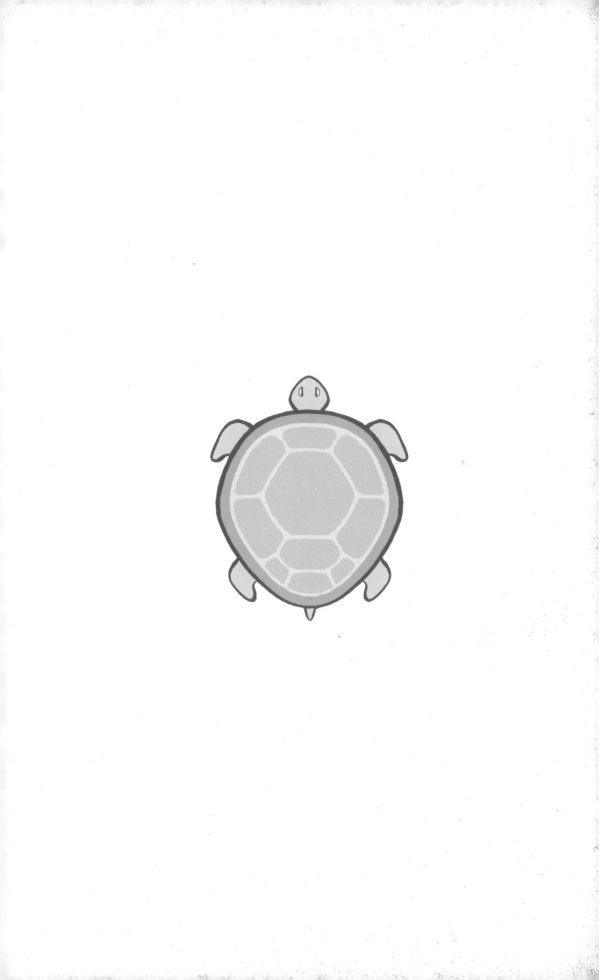

LET'S START WITH THE FACTS. THEN WE'LL GET TO THE RUMORS.

Fact: The 1940s were a crazy time for American comics. There's a reason we call that era the Golden Age. The comic book format had just been invented, and America was in love. Popular titles like *Action Comics* and *Whiz Comics* sold in the millions each month, making their publishers overnight tycoons.

Everyone wanted in. Dozens of tiny, fly-by-night publishers blinked into existence and pushed to the public as many outlandish ideas as their young cartoonists could dream up. Characters were like lottery tickets. Come up with enough of them and sooner or later, one of them had to hit.

In 1944, right in the middle of that frenzied decade, an unknown publisher named Rural Home asked an unknown cartoonist named Chu Hing to create a lead feature for their series *Blazing Comics*. Hing would eventually go on to work for Marvel Comics, but he never gained any sort of prominence. Nowadays, even the most hardcore comic book fans don't remember him.

Hing was among the first Asian Americans working in the American comic book industry. This was decades before the Asian American movement, though, so he wouldn't have self-identified as such. Most likely, he would have just called himself Chinese.

For Rural Home, Chu Hing created a World War II superhero called the Green Turtle. The Green Turtle wore a mask over his face and a cape over his shoulders. He defended China, America's ally, against the invading Japanese army. He had no obvious superpowers, though he did seem to have a knack for avoiding bullets.

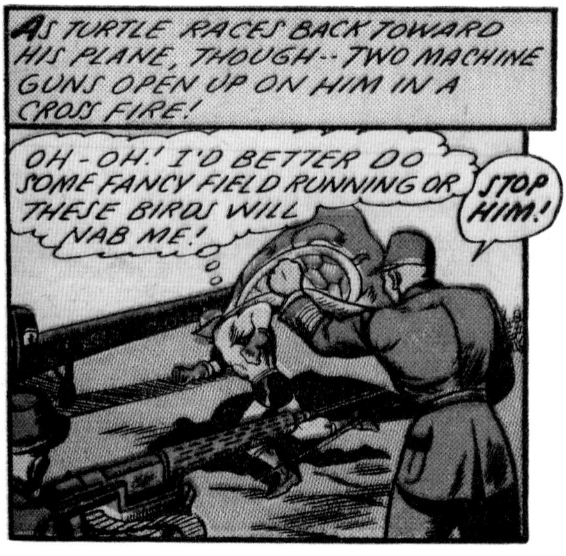
AS TURTLE RACES BACK TOWARD HIS PLANE, THOUGH--TWO MACHINE GUNS OPEN UP ON HIM IN A CROSS FIRE!
OH-OH! I'D BETTER DO SOME FANCY FIELD RUNNING OR THESE BIRDS WILL NAB ME!
STOP HIM!

So those are the facts. Here are the rumors.

Supposedly, Hing wanted his character to be Chinese.

Supposedly, his publisher didn't think a Chinese superhero would sell and told Hing to make his character white.

Supposedly, Hing rebelled right there on the page. Throughout the Green Turtle's adventures, we almost never get to see his face. Most of the time, the hero has his back to us.

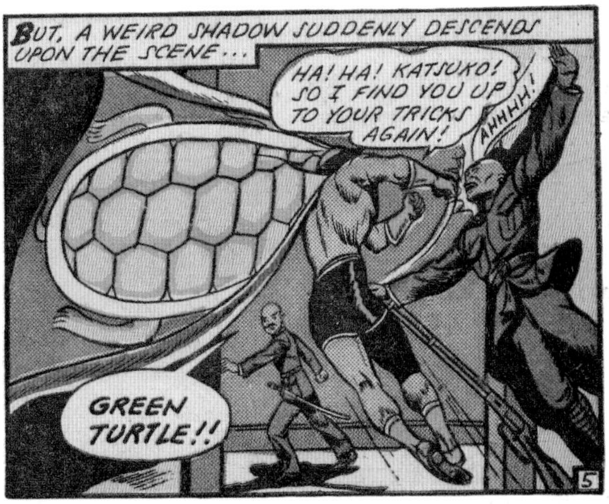

BUT, A WEIRD SHADOW SUDDENLY DESCENDS UPON THE SCENE...
HA! HA! KATSUKO! SO I FIND YOU UP TO YOUR TRICKS AGAIN!
AHHHH!
GREEN TURTLE!!
5

When he does turn around, his visage is almost always obscured by something—a combatant or a shadow or even his own arm.

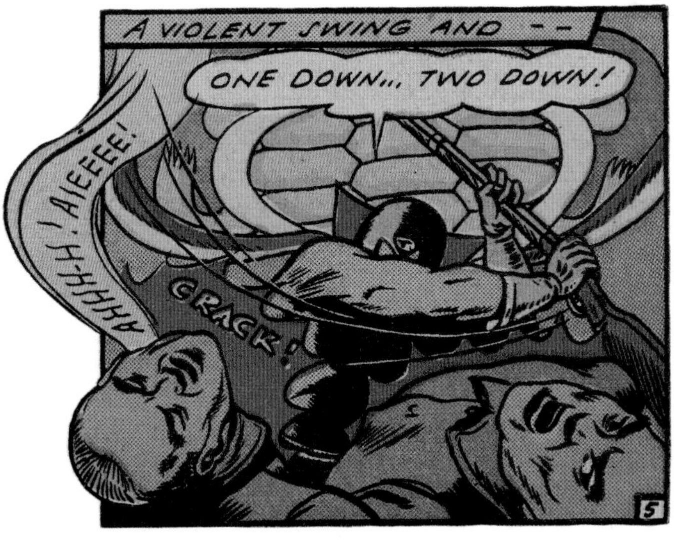

A VIOLENT SWING AND --
ONE DOWN... TWO DOWN!
AHHHH-H! AIEEEE!
CRACK!
5

What we get instead of his face is a strange, turtle-shaped shadow that looms over the Green Turtle's enemies, smirking at them. (And at us? And at the publisher?) The shadow is never explained or commented upon. It's just there.

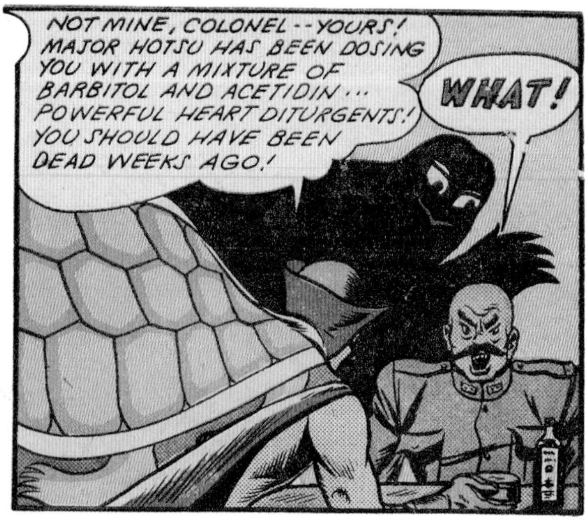
NOT MINE, COLONEL--YOURS! MAJOR HOTSU HAS BEEN DOSING YOU WITH A MIXTURE OF BARBITOL AND ACETIDIN... POWERFUL HEART DITURGENTS! YOU SHOULD HAVE BEEN DEAD WEEKS AGO!
WHAT!

And since the Green Turtle's costume doesn't include a shirt, we also get an eyeful of his skin. The publisher had him colored an unnatural pink, as if to emphasize just how Caucasian this hero is supposed to be.

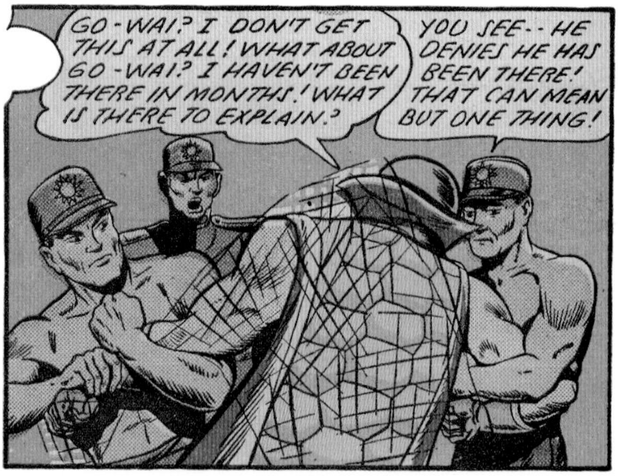
GO-WAI? I DON'T GET THIS AT ALL! WHAT ABOUT GO-WAI? I HAVEN'T BEEN THERE IN MONTHS! WHAT IS THERE TO EXPLAIN?
YOU SEE--HE DENIES HE HAS BEEN THERE! THAT CAN MEAN BUT ONE THING!

The Green Turtle's face isn't all that Hing keeps from us. Over and over, the Green Turtle's young Chinese sidekick, Burma Boy, asks him how he came to be the Green Turtle. Every time, an emergency interrupts before the Green Turtle can give his answer.

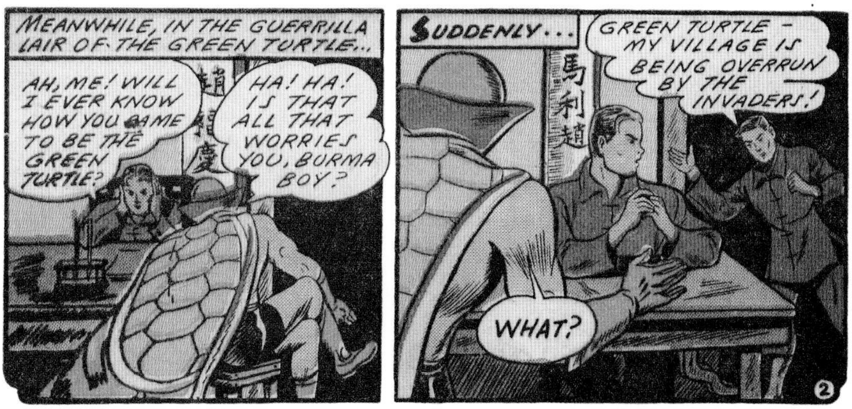
MEANWHILE, IN THE GUERRILLA LAIR OF THE GREEN TURTLE..
AH, ME! WILL I EVER KNOW HOW YOU CAME TO BE THE GREEN TURTLE?
HA! HA! IS THAT ALL THAT WORRIES YOU, BURMA BOY?
SUDDENLY...
GREEN TURTLE — MY VILLAGE IS BEING OVERRUN BY THE INVADERS!
WHAT?

Did Hing hide the Green Turtle's face and origin so that he could imagine his character the way he wanted, as a Chinese superhero? The comics read like Hing and his publisher are wrestling within the art itself, through the compositions and colors and hidden details.

The most off-putting aspect of the original Green Turtle comics, for modern readers at least, is Hing's use of racial stereotypes in his depictions of the Japanese. Before America and China formed a wartime alliance, Chinese immigrants were the targets of the same stereotypes: the impossibly slanted eyes, the buckteeth, the menacing Fu Manchu grins, the inexplicably pointed ears.

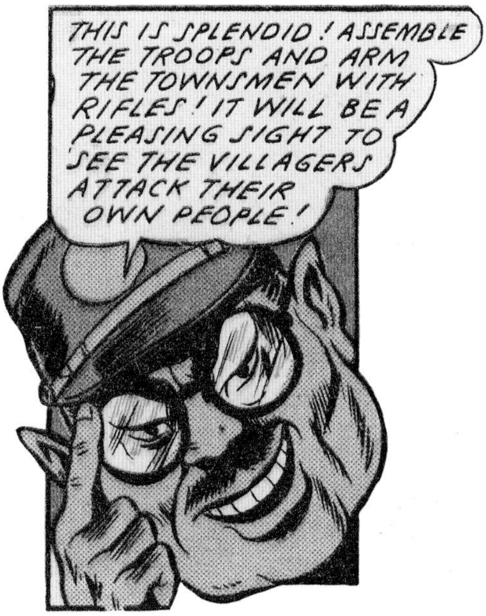
THIS IS SPLENDID! ASSEMBLE THE TROOPS AND ARM THE TOWNSMEN WITH RIFLES! IT WILL BE A PLEASING SIGHT TO SEE THE VILLAGERS ATTACK THEIR OWN PEOPLE!

Perhaps Hing was expressing the anger that Chinese immigrants felt when they read about the Japanese military's atrocities in their homeland. Or perhaps Hing hoped that by directing the surrounding culture's stereotypes toward someone other than his own community, he could help the Green Turtle gain acceptance.

That yearning for acceptance pervades Hing's stories. Hing wants to unite East with West. The Green Turtle's costume is typical of American superheroes of the time, yet it incorporates Chinese elements. *Blazing Comics #4* begins with a phrase in Chinese: 美國及中華民國 (the United States united with the Chinese Republic). In that same issue, an American general fights along side the Green Turtle's team of Chinese guerrillas. In *Blazing Comics #3*, Hing presents us with an old proverb that expresses humanity's connectedness: 四海一家 (four oceans, one family).

The Green Turtle never did find an audience. His adventures came to an abrupt end after just five issues, leaving Burma Boy's question unanswered. We never learn how the Green Turtle became the Green Turtle.

That's where Sonny Liew and I step in.

The Shadow Hero is our answer to Burma Boy's question, our imagining of the Green Turtle's origin story. We firmly establish him as an Asian American superhero, perhaps even the first Asian American superhero. Our Green Turtle is a shadow hero. Not only is his identity secret, so is his race.

I've never been able to confirm those rumors about Chu Hing and his publisher. I've read. I've researched. I've talked with collectors of Golden Age comics. No one really knows for sure. I guess that's just the nature of rumors.

In the pages that follow, we present the Green Turtle's very first adventure, ugly stereotypes and all, straight from the pages of *Blazing Comics #1*. Read it and decide for yourself whether those rumors are true.

But let me end on a fact: Studying Chu Hing's comics, imagining what might have been going through his head, and then writing this book in response were a lot of fun—a crazy, Golden Age sort of fun. I hope reading it is, too.

—Gene Luen Yang

158

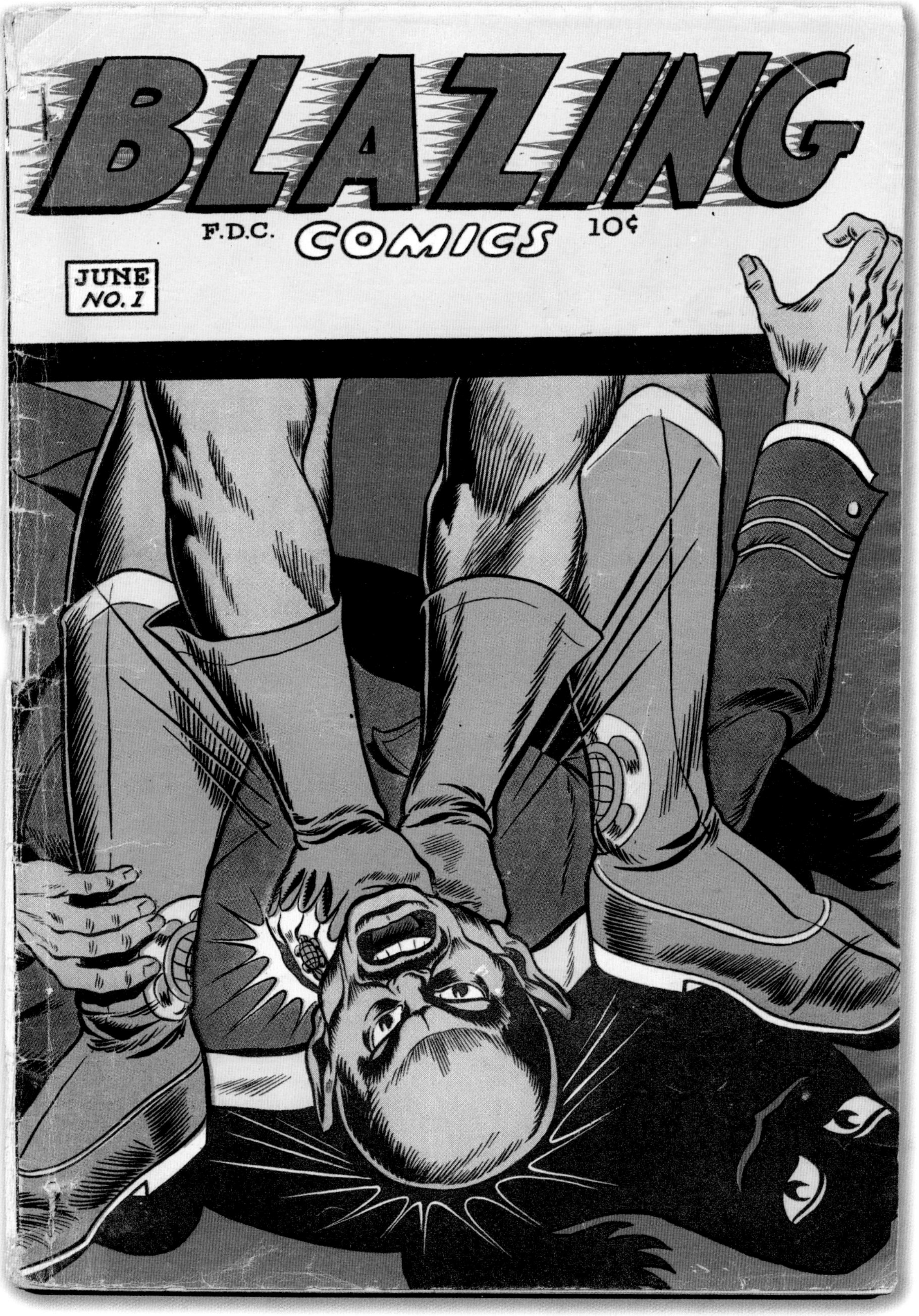
BLAZING
F.D.C.
COMICS
10¢
JUNE
NO. 1

BLAZING COMICS published monthly by REWL PUBLICATIONS INC., No. 500 Fifth Avenue, New York City, N. Y., U. S. A. Place of publication Wilkes-Barre, Pa., U. S. A. Subscription price $1.20 yearly in U. S. Single Copy 10c. Application for Second Class entry pending in Wilkes-Barre, Pa. Copyright 1944 by Rewl Publications. No actual person is named or delineated in this magazine except historical personages. Printed in U. S. A. Vol. 1, No. 1, June 1944.

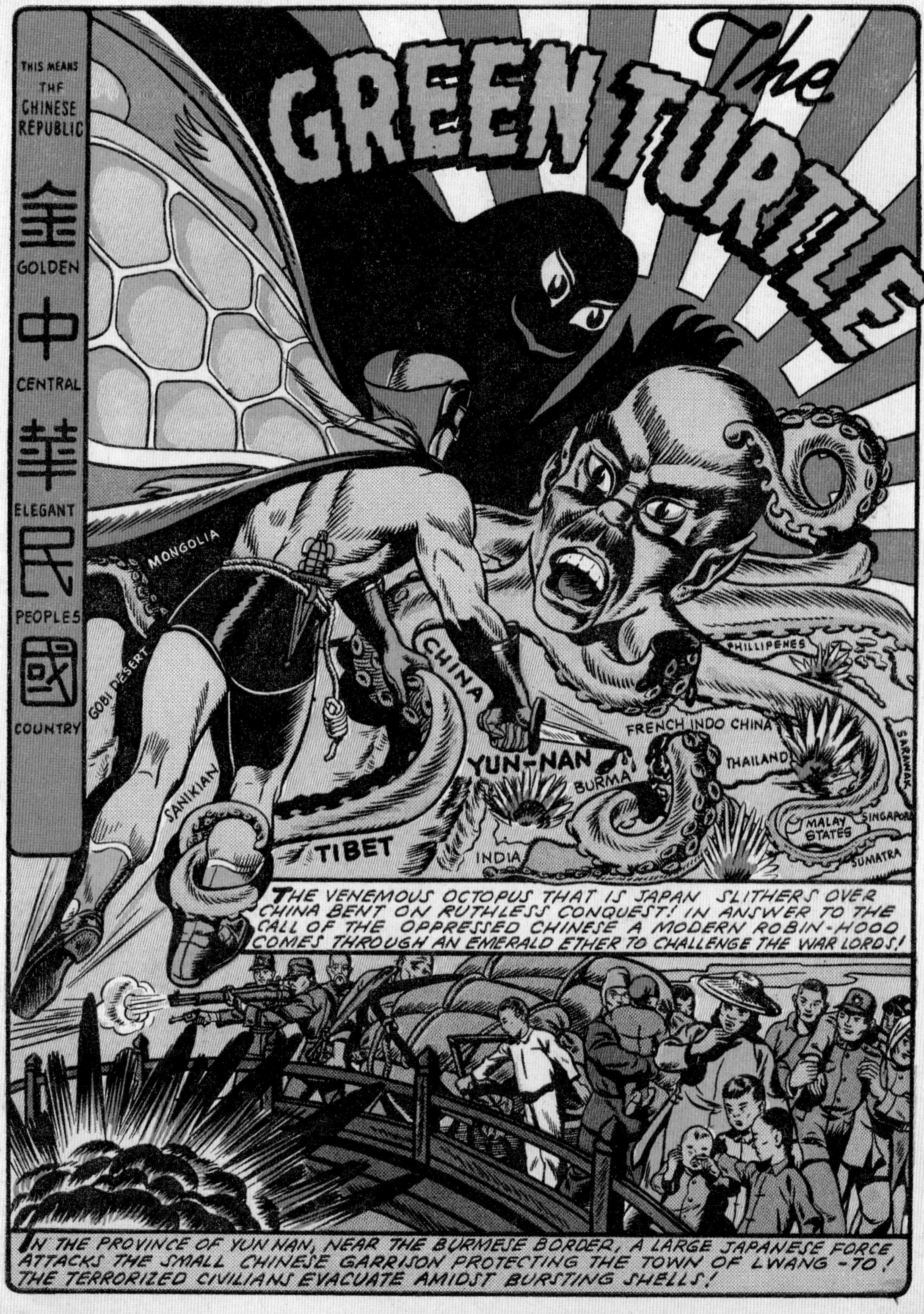
THIS MEANS THE CHINESE REPUBLIC
金
GOLDEN
中
CENTRAL
華
ELEGANT
民
PEOPLES
國
COUNTRY
The GREEN TURTLE
MONGOLIA
GOBI DESERT
CHINA
SANIKIAN
YUN-NAN
TIBET
INDIA
BURMA
FRENCH INDO CHINA
THAILAND
PHILLIPENES
SARAWAK
MALAY STATES
SINGAPORE
SUMATRA
THE VENEMOUS OCTOPUS THAT IS JAPAN SLITHERS OVER CHINA BENT ON RUTHLESS CONQUEST! IN ANSWER TO THE CALL OF THE OPPRESSED CHINESE A MODERN ROBIN-HOOD COMES THROUGH AN EMERALD ETHER TO CHALLENGE THE WAR LORDS!
IN THE PROVINCE OF YUN NAN, NEAR THE BURMESE BORDER, A LARGE JAPANESE FORCE ATTACKS THE SMALL CHINESE GARRISON PROTECTING THE TOWN OF LWANG-TO! THE TERRORIZED CIVILIANS EVACUATE AMIDST BURSTING SHELLS!

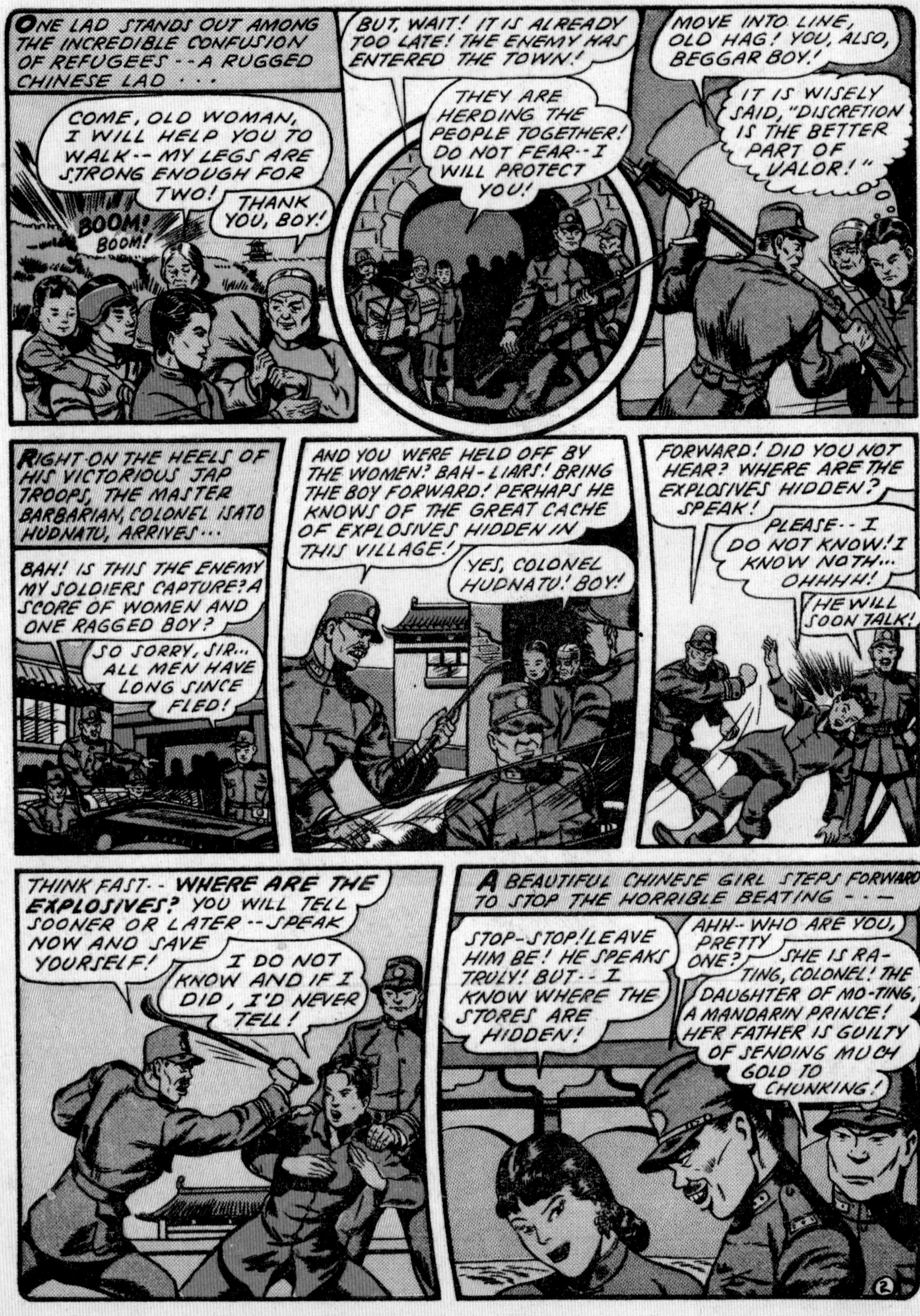
ONE LAD STANDS OUT AMONG THE INCREDIBLE CONFUSION OF REFUGEES -- A RUGGED CHINESE LAD . . .
COME, OLD WOMAN, I WILL HELP YOU TO WALK -- MY LEGS ARE STRONG ENOUGH FOR TWO!
THANK YOU, BOY!
BOOM! BOOM!
BUT, WAIT! IT IS ALREADY TOO LATE! THE ENEMY HAS ENTERED THE TOWN!
THEY ARE HERDING THE PEOPLE TOGETHER! DO NOT FEAR -- I WILL PROTECT YOU!
MOVE INTO LINE, OLD HAG! YOU, ALSO, BEGGAR BOY!
IT IS WISELY SAID, "DISCRETION IS THE BETTER PART OF VALOR!"
RIGHT ON THE HEELS OF HIS VICTORIOUS JAP TROOPS, THE MASTER BARBARIAN, COLONEL ISATO HUDNATU, ARRIVES...
BAH! IS THIS THE ENEMY MY SOLDIERS CAPTURE? A SCORE OF WOMEN AND ONE RAGGED BOY?
SO SORRY, SIR... ALL MEN HAVE LONG SINCE FLED!
AND YOU WERE HELD OFF BY THE WOMEN? BAH - LIARS! BRING THE BOY FORWARD! PERHAPS HE KNOWS OF THE GREAT CACHE OF EXPLOSIVES HIDDEN IN THIS VILLAGE!
YES, COLONEL HUDNATU! BOY!
FORWARD! DID YOU NOT HEAR? WHERE ARE THE EXPLOSIVES HIDDEN? SPEAK!
PLEASE -- I DO NOT KNOW! I KNOW NOTH... OHHHH!
HE WILL SOON TALK!
THINK FAST -- WHERE ARE THE EXPLOSIVES? YOU WILL TELL SOONER OR LATER -- SPEAK NOW AND SAVE YOURSELF!
I DO NOT KNOW AND IF I DID, I'D NEVER TELL!
A BEAUTIFUL CHINESE GIRL STEPS FORWARD TO STOP THE HORRIBLE BEATING --
STOP-STOP! LEAVE HIM BE! HE SPEAKS TRULY! BUT -- I KNOW WHERE THE STORES ARE HIDDEN!
AHH -- WHO ARE YOU, PRETTY ONE?
SHE IS RA-TING, COLONEL! THE DAUGHTER OF MO-TING, A MANDARIN PRINCE! HER FATHER IS GUILTY OF SENDING MUCH GOLD TO CHUNKING!
2

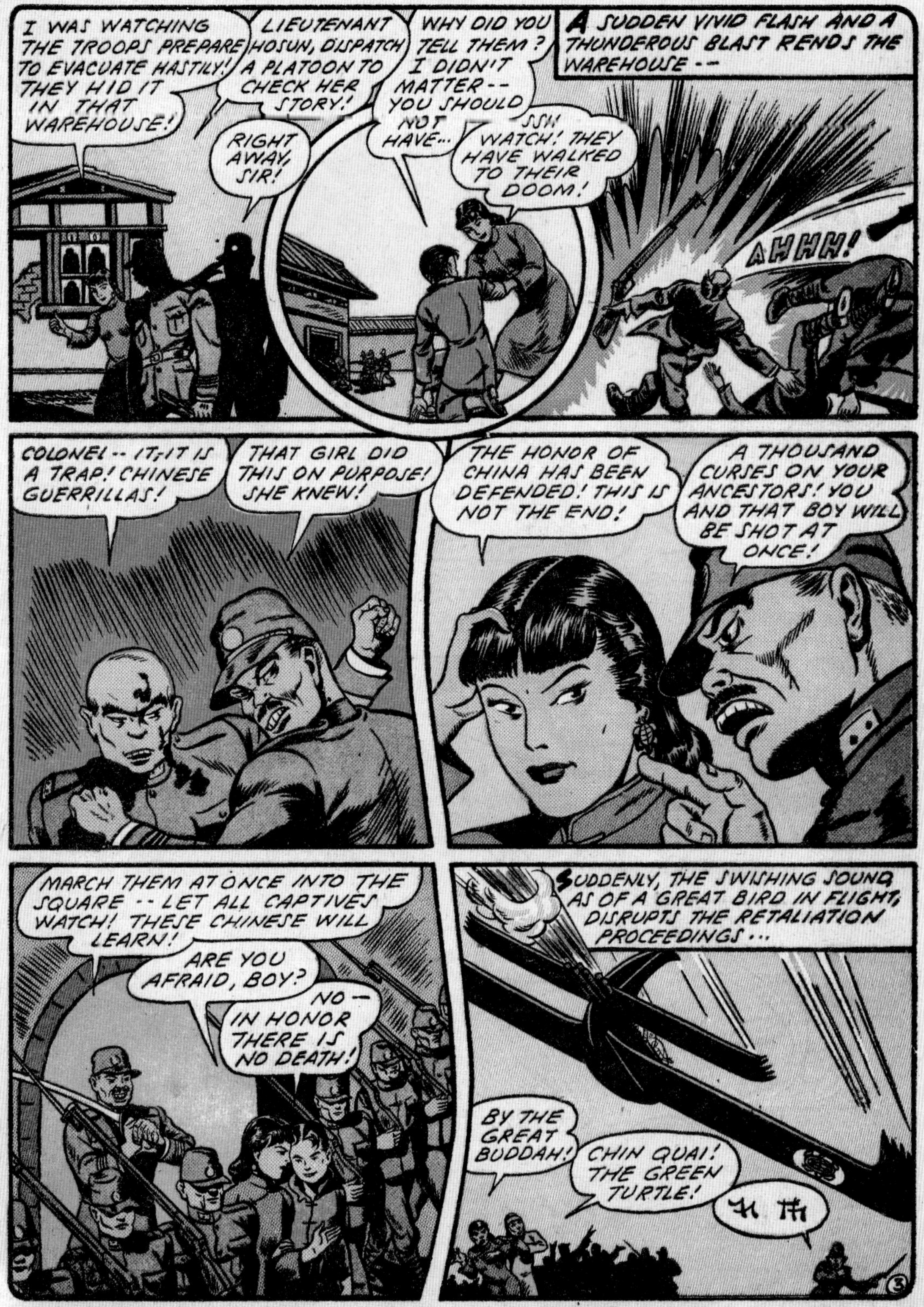
I WAS WATCHING THE TROOPS PREPARE TO EVACUATE HASTILY! THEY HID IT IN THAT WAREHOUSE!
LIEUTENANT HOSUN, DISPATCH A PLATOON TO CHECK HER STORY!
RIGHT AWAY, SIR!
WHY DID YOU TELL THEM? I DIDN'T MATTER -- YOU SHOULD NOT HAVE...
SSH! WATCH! THEY HAVE WALKED TO THEIR DOOM!
A SUDDEN VIVID FLASH AND A THUNDEROUS BLAST RENDS THE WAREHOUSE --
AHHH!
COLONEL -- IT,-IT IS A TRAP! CHINESE GUERRILLAS!
THAT GIRL DID THIS ON PURPOSE! SHE KNEW!
THE HONOR OF CHINA HAS BEEN DEFENDED! THIS IS NOT THE END!
A THOUSAND CURSES ON YOUR ANCESTORS! YOU AND THAT BOY WILL BE SHOT AT ONCE!
MARCH THEM AT ONCE INTO THE SQUARE -- LET ALL CAPTIVES WATCH! THESE CHINESE WILL LEARN!
ARE YOU AFRAID, BOY?
NO — IN HONOR THERE IS NO DEATH!
SUDDENLY, THE SWISHING SOUND, AS OF A GREAT BIRD IN FLIGHT, DISRUPTS THE RETALIATION PROCEEDINGS...
BY THE GREAT BUDDAH!
CHIN QUAI! THE GREEN TURTLE!
3

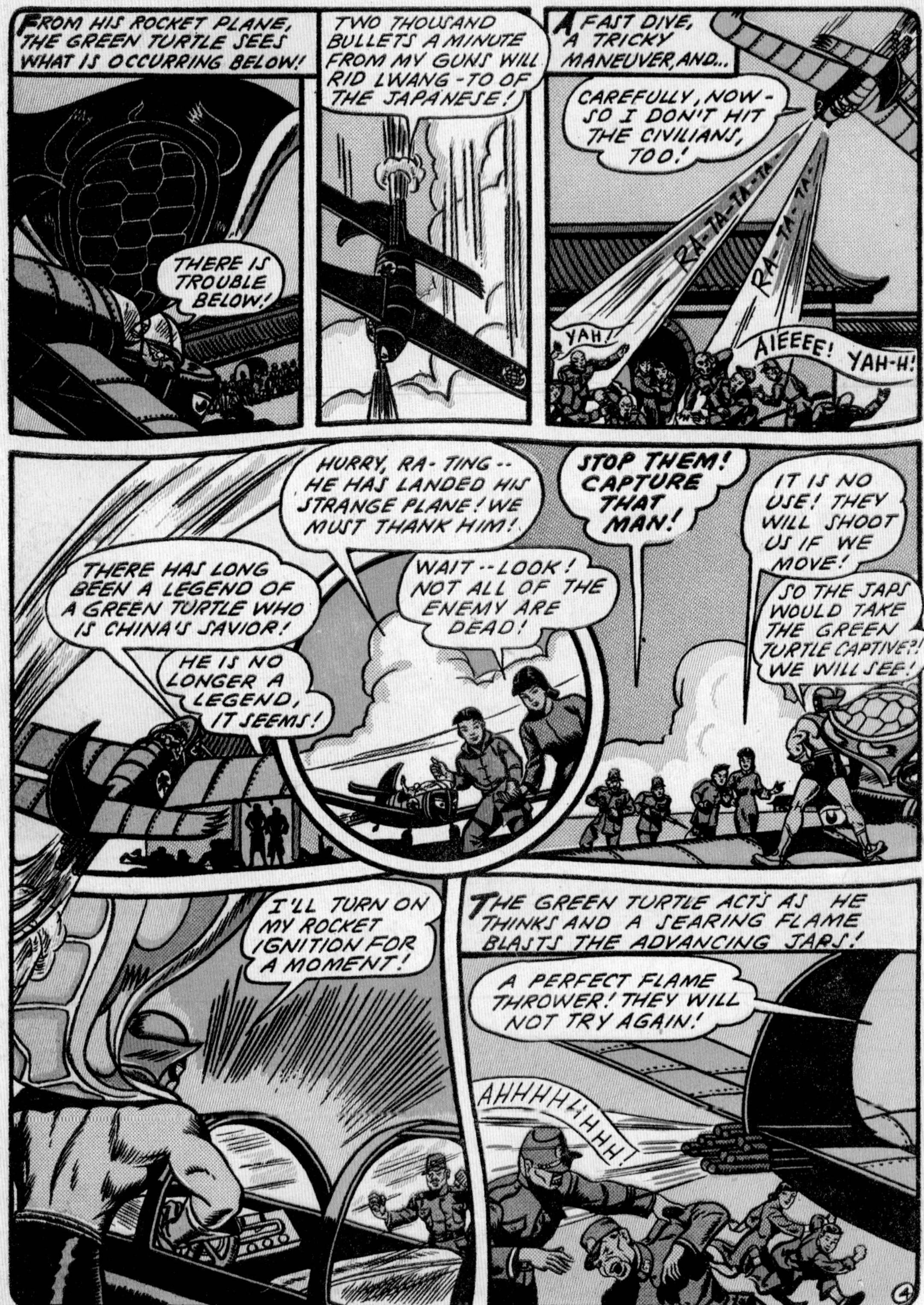
FROM HIS ROCKET PLANE, THE GREEN TURTLE SEES WHAT IS OCCURRING BELOW!
THERE IS TROUBLE BELOW!
TWO THOUSAND BULLETS A MINUTE FROM MY GUNS WILL RID LWANG-TO OF THE JAPANESE!
A FAST DIVE, A TRICKY MANEUVER, AND...
CAREFULLY, NOW - SO I DON'T HIT THE CIVILIANS, TOO!
RA-TA-TA-TA-
RA-TA-TA-
YAH!
AIEEEE! YAH-H!
THERE HAS LONG BEEN A LEGEND OF A GREEN TURTLE WHO IS CHINA'S SAVIOR!
HE IS NO LONGER A LEGEND, IT SEEMS!
HURRY, RA-TING -- HE HAS LANDED HIS STRANGE PLANE! WE MUST THANK HIM!
WAIT -- LOOK! NOT ALL OF THE ENEMY ARE DEAD!
STOP THEM! CAPTURE THAT MAN!
IT IS NO USE! THEY WILL SHOOT US IF WE MOVE!
SO THE JAPS WOULD TAKE THE GREEN TURTLE CAPTIVE?! WE WILL SEE!
I'LL TURN ON MY ROCKET IGNITION FOR A MOMENT!
THE GREEN TURTLE ACTS AS HE THINKS AND A SEARING FLAME BLASTS THE ADVANCING JAPS!
A PERFECT FLAME THROWER! THEY WILL NOT TRY AGAIN!
AHHHHHHHH!
4

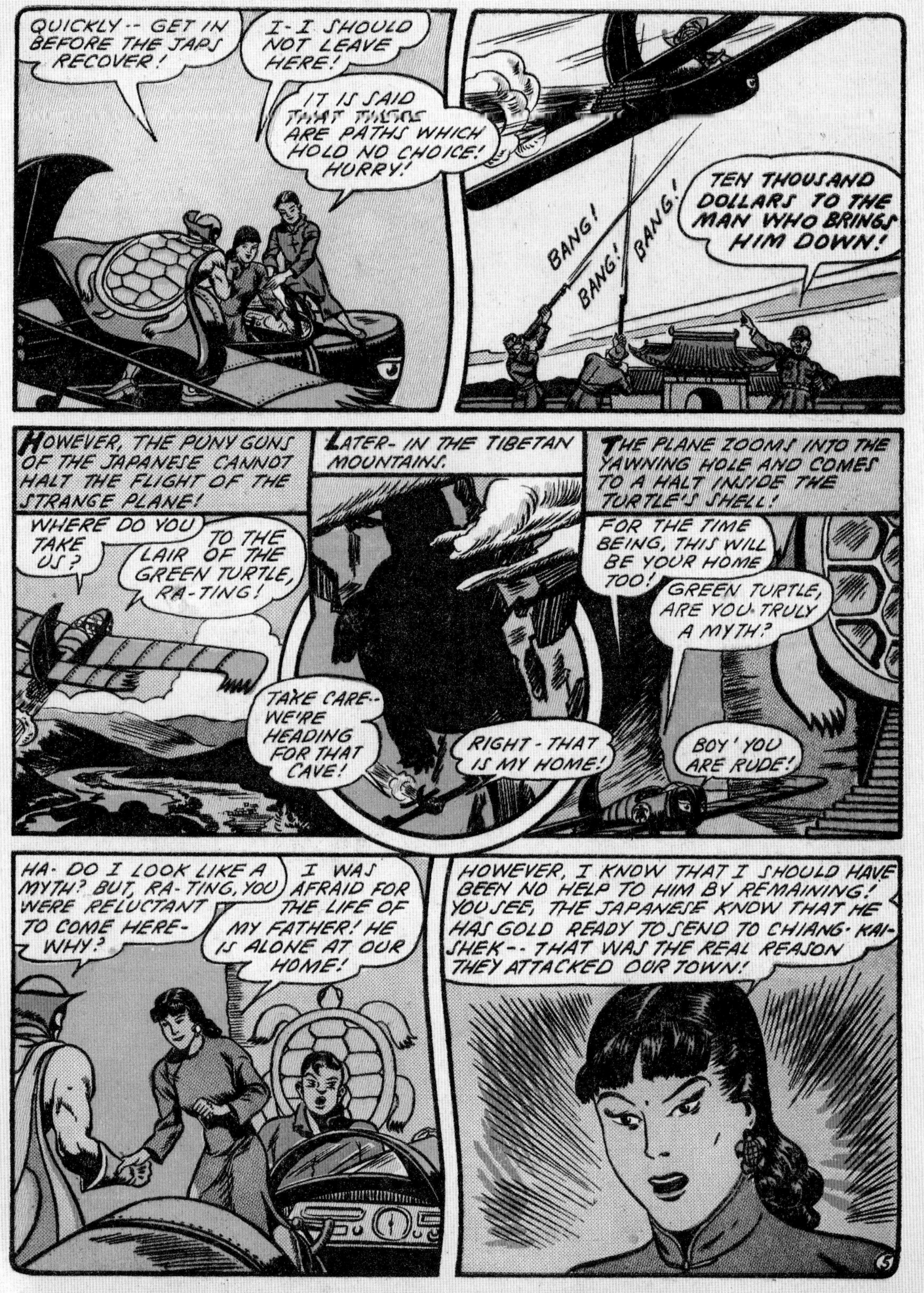
QUICKLY -- GET IN BEFORE THE JAPS RECOVER!
I-I SHOULD NOT LEAVE HERE!
IT IS SAID THAT THERE ARE PATHS WHICH HOLD NO CHOICE! HURRY!
TEN THOUSAND DOLLARS TO THE MAN WHO BRINGS HIM DOWN!
BANG!
BANG!
BANG!
HOWEVER, THE PUNY GUNS OF THE JAPANESE CANNOT HALT THE FLIGHT OF THE STRANGE PLANE!
WHERE DO YOU TAKE US?
TO THE LAIR OF THE GREEN TURTLE, RA-TING!
LATER- IN THE TIBETAN MOUNTAINS.
TAKE CARE-- WE'RE HEADING FOR THAT CAVE!
RIGHT - THAT IS MY HOME!
THE PLANE ZOOMS INTO THE YAWNING HOLE AND COMES TO A HALT INSIDE THE TURTLE'S SHELL!
FOR THE TIME BEING, THIS WILL BE YOUR HOME TOO!
GREEN TURTLE, ARE YOU TRULY A MYTH?
BOY! YOU ARE RUDE!
HA- DO I LOOK LIKE A MYTH? BUT, RA-TING, YOU WERE RELUCTANT TO COME HERE- WHY?
I WAS AFRAID FOR THE LIFE OF MY FATHER! HE IS ALONE AT OUR HOME!
HOWEVER, I KNOW THAT I SHOULD HAVE BEEN NO HELP TO HIM BY REMAINING! YOU SEE, THE JAPANESE KNOW THAT HE HAS GOLD READY TO SEND TO CHIANG-KAI-SHEK-- THAT WAS THE REAL REASON THEY ATTACKED OUR TOWN!
5

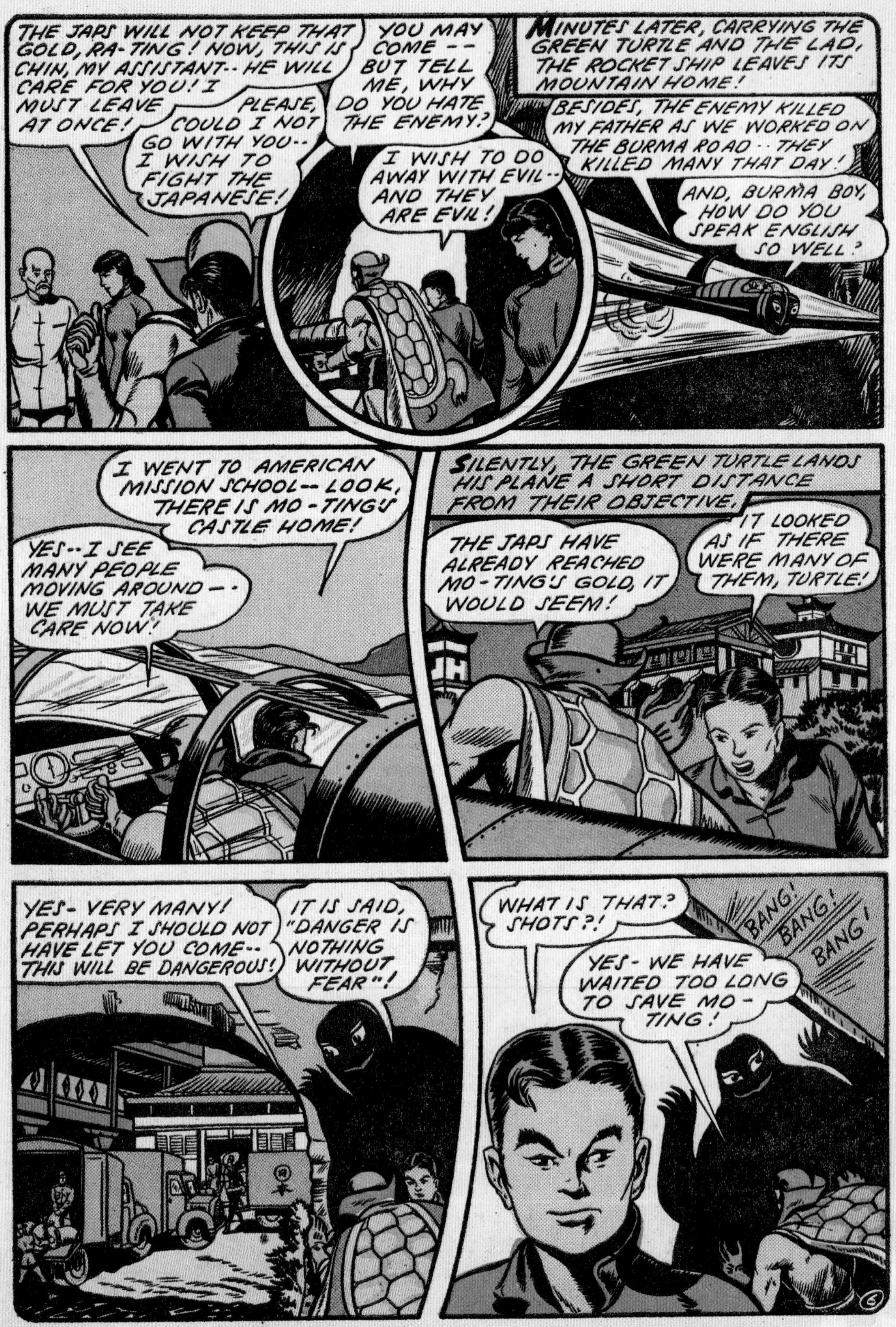
THE JAPS WILL NOT KEEP THAT GOLD, RA-TING! NOW, THIS IS CHIN, MY ASSISTANT-- HE WILL CARE FOR YOU! I MUST LEAVE AT ONCE!
PLEASE, COULD I NOT GO WITH YOU-- I WISH TO FIGHT THE JAPANESE!
YOU MAY COME -- BUT TELL ME, WHY DO YOU HATE THE ENEMY?
I WISH TO DO AWAY WITH EVIL-- AND THEY ARE EVIL!
MINUTES LATER, CARRYING THE GREEN TURTLE AND THE LAD, THE ROCKET SHIP LEAVES ITS MOUNTAIN HOME!
BESIDES, THE ENEMY KILLED MY FATHER AS WE WORKED ON THE BURMA ROAD-- THEY KILLED MANY THAT DAY!
AND, BURMA BOY, HOW DO YOU SPEAK ENGLISH SO WELL?
I WENT TO AMERICAN MISSION SCHOOL-- LOOK, THERE IS MO-TING'S CASTLE HOME!
YES--I SEE MANY PEOPLE MOVING AROUND-- WE MUST TAKE CARE NOW!
SILENTLY, THE GREEN TURTLE LANDS HIS PLANE A SHORT DISTANCE FROM THEIR OBJECTIVE.
THE JAPS HAVE ALREADY REACHED MO-TING'S GOLD, IT WOULD SEEM!
IT LOOKED AS IF THERE WERE MANY OF THEM, TURTLE!
YES- VERY MANY! PERHAPS I SHOULD NOT HAVE LET YOU COME-- THIS WILL BE DANGEROUS!
IT IS SAID, "DANGER IS NOTHING WITHOUT FEAR"!
WHAT IS THAT? SHOTS?!
BANG! BANG! BANG!
YES- WE HAVE WAITED TOO LONG TO SAVE MO-TING!
6

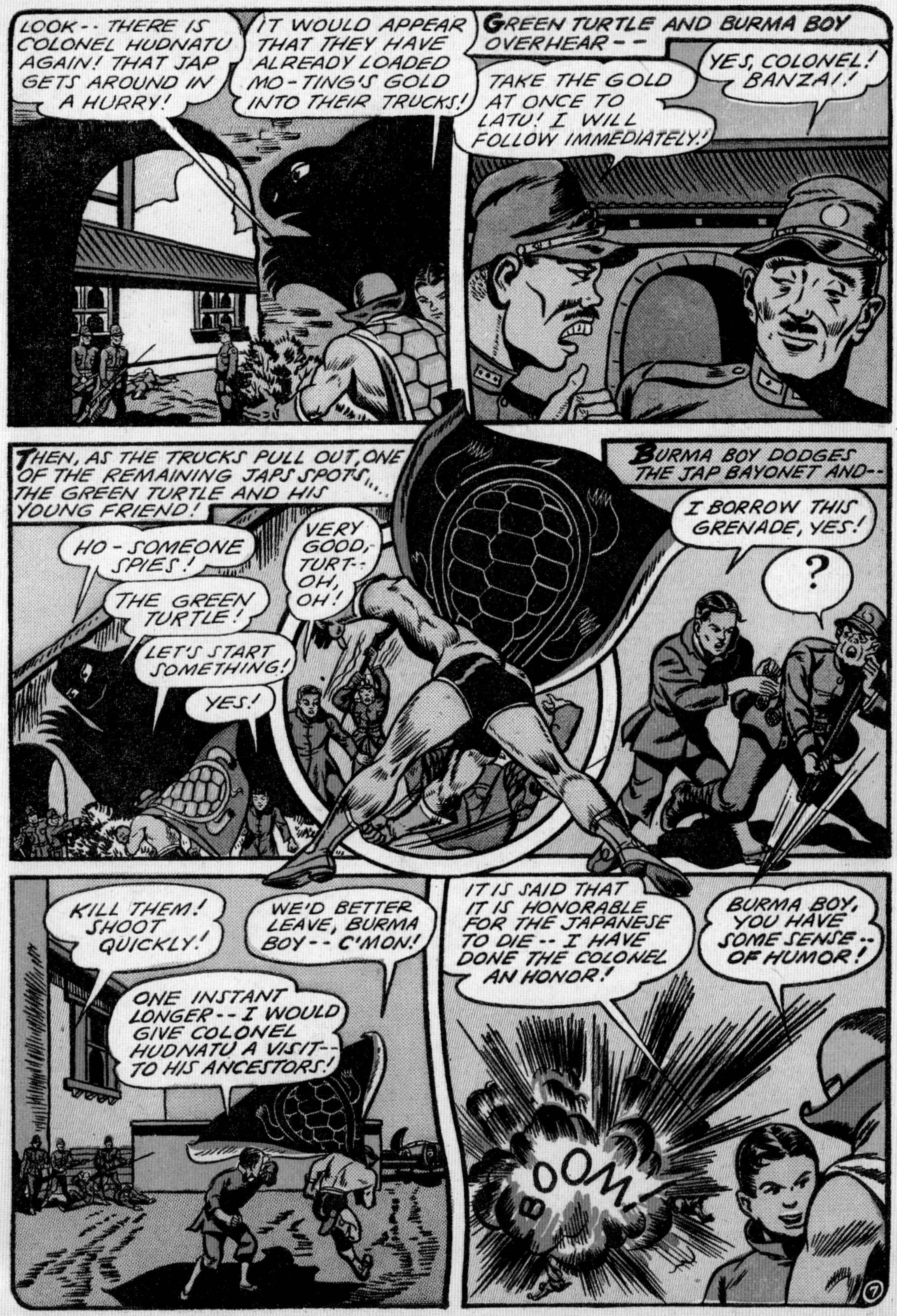
LOOK-- THERE IS COLONEL HUDNATU AGAIN! THAT JAP GETS AROUND IN A HURRY!
IT WOULD APPEAR THAT THEY HAVE ALREADY LOADED MO-TING'S GOLD INTO THEIR TRUCKS!
GREEN TURTLE AND BURMA BOY OVERHEAR--
TAKE THE GOLD AT ONCE TO LATU! I WILL FOLLOW IMMEDIATELY!
YES, COLONEL! BANZAI!
THEN, AS THE TRUCKS PULL OUT, ONE OF THE REMAINING JAPS SPOTS... THE GREEN TURTLE AND HIS YOUNG FRIEND!
HO-SOMEONE SPIES!
THE GREEN TURTLE!
LET'S START SOMETHING!
YES!
VERY GOOD, TURT-- OH, OH!
BURMA BOY DODGES THE JAP BAYONET AND--
I BORROW THIS GRENADE, YES!
?
KILL THEM! SHOOT QUICKLY!
WE'D BETTER LEAVE, BURMA BOY-- C'MON!
ONE INSTANT LONGER-- I WOULD GIVE COLONEL HUDNATU A VISIT-- TO HIS ANCESTORS!
IT IS SAID THAT IT IS HONORABLE FOR THE JAPANESE TO DIE-- I HAVE DONE THE COLONEL AN HONOR!
BURMA BOY, YOU HAVE SOME SENSE-- OF HUMOR!
BOOM!
7

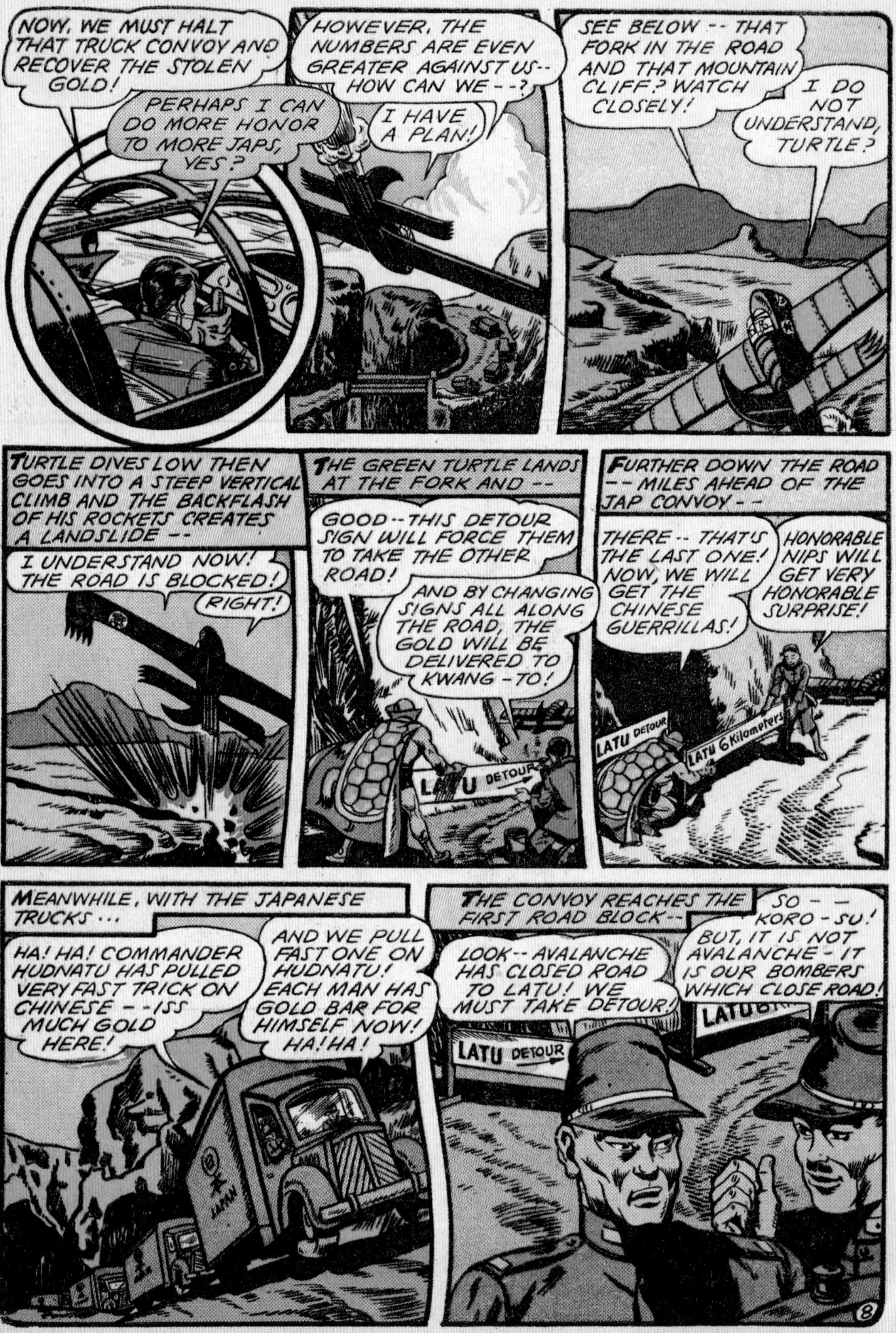
NOW, WE MUST HALT THAT TRUCK CONVOY AND RECOVER THE STOLEN GOLD!
PERHAPS I CAN DO MORE HONOR TO MORE JAPS, YES?
HOWEVER, THE NUMBERS ARE EVEN GREATER AGAINST US-- HOW CAN WE --?
I HAVE A PLAN!
SEE BELOW -- THAT FORK IN THE ROAD AND THAT MOUNTAIN CLIFF? WATCH CLOSELY!
I DO NOT UNDERSTAND, TURTLE?
TURTLE DIVES LOW THEN GOES INTO A STEEP VERTICAL CLIMB AND THE BACKFLASH OF HIS ROCKETS CREATES A LANDSLIDE --
I UNDERSTAND NOW! THE ROAD IS BLOCKED!
RIGHT!
THE GREEN TURTLE LANDS AT THE FORK AND --
GOOD--THIS DETOUR SIGN WILL FORCE THEM TO TAKE THE OTHER ROAD!
AND BY CHANGING SIGNS ALL ALONG THE ROAD, THE GOLD WILL BE DELIVERED TO KWANG-TO!
LATU DETOUR
FURTHER DOWN THE ROAD -- MILES AHEAD OF THE JAP CONVOY --
THERE -- THAT'S THE LAST ONE! NOW, WE WILL GET THE CHINESE GUERRILLAS!
HONORABLE NIPS WILL GET VERY HONORABLE SURPRISE!
LATU DETOUR
LATU 6 Kilometers
MEANWHILE, WITH THE JAPANESE TRUCKS...
HA! HA! COMMANDER HUDNATU HAS PULLED VERY FAST TRICK ON CHINESE --ISS MUCH GOLD HERE!
AND WE PULL FAST ONE ON HUDNATU! EACH MAN HAS GOLD BAR FOR HIMSELF NOW! HA! HA!
JAPAN
THE CONVOY REACHES THE FIRST ROAD BLOCK--
LOOK-- AVALANCHE HAS CLOSED ROAD TO LATU! WE MUST TAKE DETOUR!
SO -- KORO-SU! BUT, IT IS NOT AVALANCHE -- IT IS OUR BOMBERS WHICH CLOSE ROAD!
LATU DETOUR
8

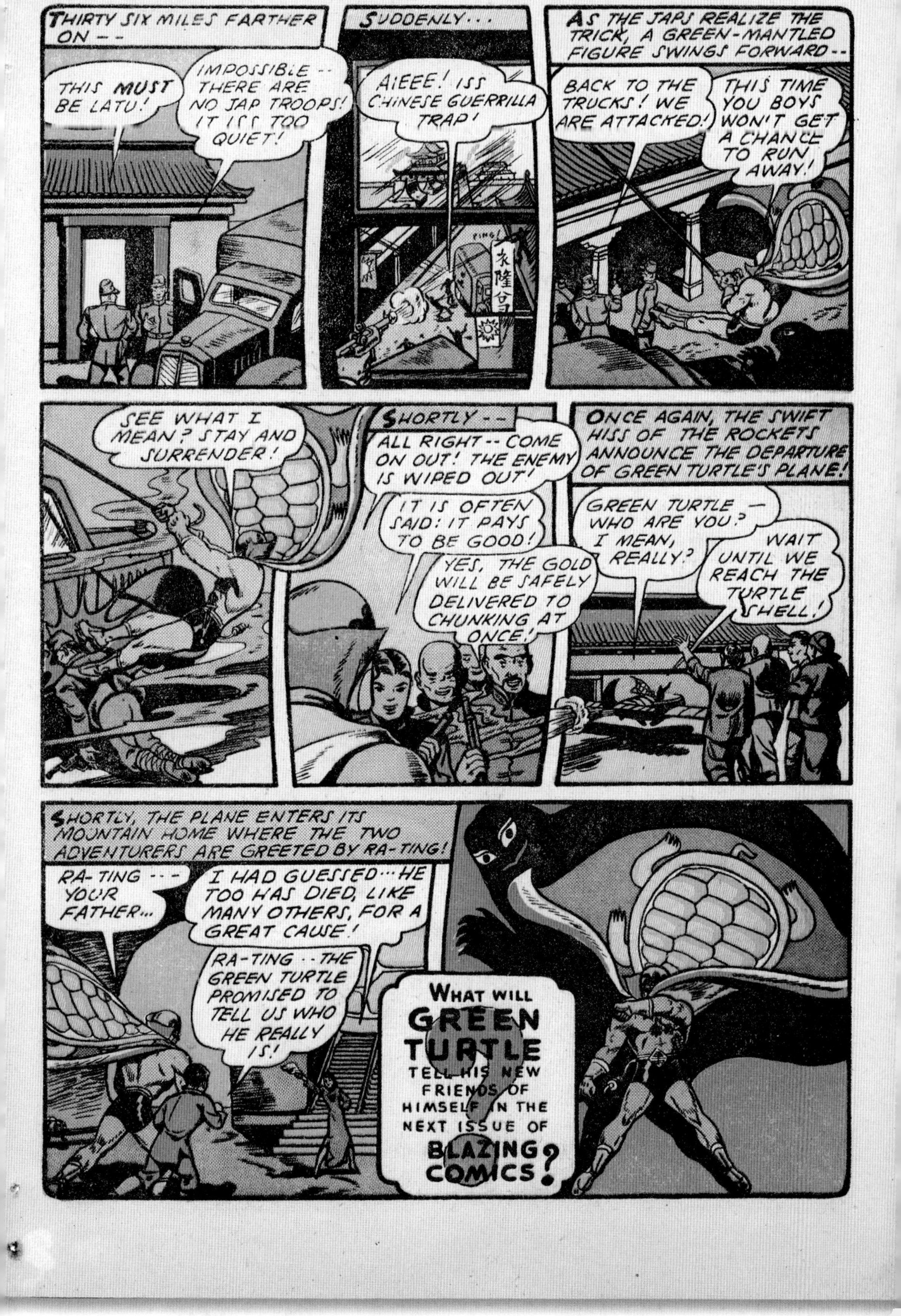

THIRTY SIX MILES FARTHER ON --
THIS MUST BE LATU!
IMPOSSIBLE -- THERE ARE NO JAP TROOPS! IT ISS TOO QUIET!
SUDDENLY . . .
AIEEE! ISS CHINESE GUERRILLA TRAP!
PING!
AS THE JAPS REALIZE THE TRICK, A GREEN-MANTLED FIGURE SWINGS FORWARD --
BACK TO THE TRUCKS! WE ARE ATTACKED!
THIS TIME YOU BOYS WON'T GET A CHANCE TO RUN AWAY!
SEE WHAT I MEAN? STAY AND SURRENDER!
SHORTLY --
ALL RIGHT -- COME ON OUT! THE ENEMY IS WIPED OUT!
IT IS OFTEN SAID: IT PAYS TO BE GOOD!
YES, THE GOLD WILL BE SAFELY DELIVERED TO CHUNKING AT ONCE!
ONCE AGAIN, THE SWIFT HISS OF THE ROCKETS ANNOUNCE THE DEPARTURE OF GREEN TURTLE'S PLANE!
GREEN TURTLE -- WHO ARE YOU? I MEAN, REALLY?
WAIT UNTIL WE REACH THE TURTLE SHELL!
SHORTLY, THE PLANE ENTERS ITS MOUNTAIN HOME WHERE THE TWO ADVENTURERS ARE GREETED BY RA-TING!
RA-TING --- YOUR FATHER...
I HAD GUESSED... HE TOO HAS DIED, LIKE MANY OTHERS, FOR A GREAT CAUSE!
RA-TING -- THE GREEN TURTLE PROMISED TO TELL US WHO HE REALLY IS!
WHAT WILL GREEN TURTLE TELL HIS NEW FRIENDS OF HIMSELF IN THE NEXT ISSUE OF BLAZING COMICS?